FÉLICIEN CHAMPSAUR

THE LATIN ORGY

Translated and with an Introduction by

BRIAN STABLEFORD

THE LATIN ORGY

FÉLICIEN CHAMPSAUR (1858-1934) was a prolific French novelist and journalist. A core member of Émile Goudeau's literary club, the Hydropathes, he later became, through his own periodical, Le Panurge, loosely aligned with key figures of the Decadent Movement, such as Jean Lorrain and Rachilde. Though writing novels in a number of different veins, and attempting to establish himself as a "serious novelist" he was never able to shake off his reputation as a composer of risqué romances and erotic fantasies, a reputation that was not at odds with his public image.

BRIAN STABLEFORD has been publishing fiction and non-fiction for fifty years. His fiction includes a series of "tales of the biotech revolution" and a series of metaphysical fantasies featuring Edgar Poe's Auguste Dupin. He is presently researching a history of French *roman scientifique* from 1700-1939 for Black Coat Press, translating much of the relevant material into English for the first time, and also translates material from the Decadent and Symbolist Movements. He has previously translated for Snuggly Books a number of titles, including *The Soul-Drinker and Other Decadent Fantasies* by Jean Lorrain, and *The Unknown Collaborator and Other Legendary Tales* by Victor Joly.

SNUGGLY BOOKS

CONTENTS

INTRODUCTION / *xi*

BOOK ONE: THE DANCER FROM TANAGRA

  I. The Egyptian Encampment / *5*
  II. The Prediction: Karysta Will Only Dance Three More
    Times /*7*
  III. The Dancer from Tanagra / *14*
  IV. Futile Plaints / *19*
  V. The Via Appia, at the Sixth Hour / *22*
  VI. Karysta Dances for the First Time / *28*
  VII. The Pity of a Passer-by / *32*
  VIII. A Fête on the Palatine / *34*
  IX. Karysta dances for the Second Time / *39*
  X. The Deceptive Appearance / *46*
  XI. Karysta Dances for the Third Time / *54*
  XII. The Prediction is Accomplished / *62*

BOOK TWO: ANCILLA DOMINI

  I. The Salute of the Doomed / *65*
  II. Vanquish for Vengeance / *66*
  III. In the Wings of the Circus / *71*
  IV. An Artless Hecatomb / *73*
  V. Masters and Debutant / *76*
  VI. Sepeos Victorious / *79*
  VII. An Encounter of Hatred and Love / *80*
  VIII. The King of the Sword / *89*

IX.   An Evening of Spring and Feasting / *92*
X.   The Gladiators' Lair / *95*
XI.   Lodgings in a Tavern / *102*
XII.   Drunkards in the Street / *106*
XIII.   The Apparition of Filiola / *108*
XIV.   The Caresses of Speech / *110*
XV.   The Elect of an Evening / *116*
XVI.   The Gladiators' School / *118*
XVII.   On the Ramparts / *125*

BOOK THREE: THE NAKED EMPRESS

I.   Messalina at Liberty / *137*
II.   The Empress in the Brothel / *147*
III.   A Suburban Idyll / *152*
IV.   In the Catacombs, Toward the Light / *156*
V.   Voices of Heaven on Earth / *162*
VI.   The Forgiveness of Offenses / *167*
VII.   A Drunken Conversation Between Gladiators / *169*
VIII.   Before the Games / *172*
IX.   The Imperial Box / *175*
X.   The Archon Melkios / *177*
XI.   Salute to the Beloved / *179*
XII.   The Commencement of the Games / *182*
XIII.   Posthumous Roses / *184*
XIV.   The Triumph of Sepeos / *189*
XV.   Further Hecatombs / *192*
XVI.   At the Artistes' Exit / *193*
XVII.   Incarceration / *195*
XVIII.   Luxuria's Ultimatum / *200*
XIX.   Virtuous Spittle / *205*

BOOK FOUR: THE MARTYRS

I.   Verses of the Lily / *209*
II.   At the Foot of the Cross / *211*
III.   An Amorous Bear / *214*

<table>
<tr><td>IV.</td><td>Pasture for the Dogs / 217</td></tr>
<tr><td>V.</td><td>The Gratitude of a Beast / 219</td></tr>
<tr><td>VI.</td><td>The Miracle / 222</td></tr>
<tr><td>VII.</td><td>The Strength that Faith Gives / 224</td></tr>
<tr><td>VIII.</td><td>Mater Dolorosa / 229</td></tr>
<tr><td>IX.</td><td>The Descent from the Cross / 232</td></tr>
<tr><td>X.</td><td>Christian Dawn / 236</td></tr>
</table>

INTERLUDE

Interlude / *243*
Seneca and Messalina / *244*
April And Winter (Diptych)
    I.   The Echo of the Faun / *245*
    II.   The Frozen Nymph / *247*
Mortal Error / *249*
Aphrodite's Dove (Diptych)
    I.   Phallos / *252*
    II.   Chrysis / *253*
Stupidity and Wisdom / *255*

THE DEATH OF MESSALINA: A TRAGIC FARCE IN TEN TABLEAUX, WITH A NUPTIAL BALLET

<table>
<tr><td>I.</td><td>The Sovereign Lovers / 259</td></tr>
<tr><td>II.</td><td>The Evil Omen / 266</td></tr>
<tr><td>III.</td><td>The Marriage of Messalina and Silius / 277</td></tr>
<tr><td>IV.</td><td>The Freedmen / 281</td></tr>
<tr><td>V.</td><td>Claudius at Ostia / 287</td></tr>
<tr><td>VI.</td><td>The Road to Ostia / 292</td></tr>
<tr><td>VII.</td><td>The House of Silius / 297</td></tr>
<tr><td>VIII.</td><td>The Praetorian Camp / 299</td></tr>
<tr><td>IX.</td><td>Dust of Desire / 304</td></tr>
<tr><td>X.</td><td>The Last Spasm / 306</td></tr>
<tr><td>XI.</td><td>Apparition on the Threshold: Nero / 311</td></tr>
</table>

APPENDIX: LUST IN LIFE, LETTERS AND THE ARTS / *317*

INTRODUCTION

L'ORGIE LATINE by Félicien Champsaur, here translated as *The Latin Orgy*, was first published in 1904 by Eugène Fasquelle. It was the author's most successful book, overtaking the two titles that had first made him a best-selling author, *L'Amant des danseuses, roman moderniste* [The Man Who Loved Dancing Girls: A Modernist Novel] (1888) and *Lulu, roman clownesque* [Lulu: A Clownish Novel] (1900; based on an 1888 one-act play), steadily racking up sales for the next twenty years, with a brief hiatus during the Great War. It contributed greatly to a reputation that was already slightly scandalous by virtue of the author's preoccupation with erotic matters, although Champsaur might conceivably have seen the project as a bid for greater respectability, which would place that preoccupation in a more appropriate context, justified by historical necessity as well as affiliating it to an auspicious tradition in French Romantic literature and also permitting extravagant praise of early Christianity.

Since the era when the Romantic Movement first began to produce prose fiction in abundance, there had been a flamboyant core within fiction embracing the Romantic philosophy most wholeheartedly that consisted of extraordinarily lush historical fictions attempting to reconstruct and celebrate the glorious barbarity of remote eras, paying particular attention to epochs of excess and decadence. The first foundation stone of the subgenre had been laid by Victor Hugo's *Notre Dame de Paris—1482* (1831; tr. as *The Hunchback of Notre Dame*), but an equally significant precedent was set by Théophile Gautier's novella "Une Nuit de Cléopâtre" (1838; tr. as "One of Cleopatra's Nights"), which focuses on one of the great *femmes fatales* of legend, employing the glamour of that central character as an archetypal symbol of splendor, decadence and erotic obsession, summarizing and encapsulating the Romantic attitude to the sumptuousness of the pagan past. That example was followed by several of the classic novels that continued the tradition, most notably by Gustave Flaubert in *Salammbô* (1862), Anatole France in *Thaïs* (1890) and Pierre Louÿs in *Aphrodite* (1896). The fervent eroticism of the last-named, in particular, is one of the key models that Félicien Champsaur would have had in mind when deciding to make his own contribution to the tradition.

Champsaur was not the first writer to select the Roman Empress Messalina as the central figure for such a study. Alfred Jarry—like Pierre Louÿs, an old acquaintance of Champsaur's from the days when they were all habitués of Le Chat Noir—had published his *Messaline* (1901) three years before. Jarry's novel, however, was an obvious sidestep from the Romantic tradition, not merely into the Symbolist *avant garde* but into the uniquely quirky sector that Jarry subsequently called "pataphysical fiction," a significant precursor of Surrealism. Although it follows the recorded legend fairly closely, with numerous pseudo-scholarly references, Jarry's novelization treats its erotic element playfully and ironically, and Champsaur might well have felt that Jarry had not made the most of his topic.

In addition to Jarry's novel there was also a recent opera, *Messaline: tragédie lyrique en quatre actes et cinq tableaux* (premièred in Monte Carlo 1899; published 1903) with music by Isidore de Lara and a libretto by Armand Silvestre and Eugène Morand, and if—as seems not unlikely—the concluding section of Champsaur's book was written before the main narrative, its composition is more likely to have been prompted by the success of the opera than Jarry's offbeat novel. The printed version of the opera was issued—in the same year as its first performance in Paris—by Charpentier et Fasquelle, and Eugène Fasquelle, who was the dedicatee of *L'Orgie Latine* as well as its publisher, and might well have suggested to Champsaur that more could be done with the character.

L'Orgie Latine probably had other recent influences as well as Jarry's novel and de Lara's opera, the most significant of which is surely Henryk Sienkiewicz's hugely successful novel *Quo Vadis?* (1895 in Polish; French translation 1900), similarly set in Rome, albeit in the later period of Nero's rule, which features a love affair between a Roman patrician and a young Christian woman. The theme of the persecution of Christians—unmentioned by Jarry, there being no historical evidence for any such persecution during the reign of Claudius—had been foregrounded and luridly dramatized in Sienkiewicz's novel, in a fashion that might well have seemed to Champsaur to provide excellent fuel for his own exercise in melodramatization, as a useful counterpart to Messalina's lubricious excesses, even though it required an anachronistic invention.

Félicien-François-Louis Champsaur (1858-1934) was born in Turriers in the Basses-Alpes, the son of a gendarme. He completed his early education in the nearby town of Dignes before going to Paris in the late 1870s, ostensibly to complete his studies, although he quickly lapsed into the underworld of literary "Bohemia." He published a number of items in *Les Écoles: Journal des Étudiants* in 1877, and wrote the text for a series of pamphlets on *Les Hommes d'aujourd'hui* [People of Today], which featured portraits by André Gill, issued in the same year. He rapidly moved on to publishing articles in such popular periodicals as *Paris-Plaisir* in 1878. In the meantime, he involved himself enthusiastically in the literary life of Montmartre brasseries, becoming a core member of Émile Goudeau's literary club, the Hydropathes, in which he was sufficiently prominent that when the society's journal,

L'Hydropathe made its debut in 1879, he was the fourth member to be individually profiled in its pages, after Goudeau, Gill and Paul Vivien, and ahead of Alphonse Allais and Charles Cros.

Champsaur first reached a wide audience via critical essays written for the newspaper *Le Figaro*, the cream of which were reprinted in four collections, including *Le Cerveau de Paris, esquisses de la vie littéraire et artistique* [The Brain of Paris: Sketches of Literary and Artistic Life] (1886). He became a significant champion of Naturalism, lavishing praise on the work of Émile Zola, but his primary literary allegiance was to Victor Hugo, the one-time doyen of Romanticism; his memorial to Hugo, reprinted in *Le Cerveau de Paris*, imagines God welcoming the great writer to Heaven as a peer. His own periodical, *Le Panurge*—which published some thirty issues in 1882-83—conspicuously favored writers who subsequently became core contributors to the Decadent Movement, featuring early work by Jean Lorrain, Rachilde and Jean Richepin and late work by Villiers de l'Isle Adam, among others, even though the articles in *Le Cerveau de Paris* suggest a certain disapproval of decadent style in literature—though certainly not in visual art.

Champsaur might well have been adapting his stance to the expectations of the readership of *Le Figaro* in his disapproving pieces, and a similar policy decision might have been responsible for the ostentatious disapproval of excessively decadent lifestyles in many of his novels, even though he became moderately notorious for the allegedly decadent aspects of his own lifestyle, which he presumably considered moderate. His reputation for debauchery might have been exaggerated as a feature of his public image, but it is suggestive of some turbulence in his private life that he married in 1886, was divorced in 1894, and then married again in 1909, and was divorced again in 1912.

Champsaur's swift success as a popular journalist did not entirely endear him to his fellow Hydropathes, some of whom regarded such endeavors as what would now be termed "selling out." Like any prolific critic—especially one inclined to casual irreverence—Champsaur soon began to raise hackles, fighting the first of numerous duels with rival journalist René Stoll in February 1879, over a piece in *Le Figaro*. Unlike most literary duels, which were conscientiously artificial and bloodless, that one only ended when Stoll was wounded. Champsaur's subsequent opponents included the painter Jean-Louis Forain, another victim of a bad review, and Maurice Bernhardt, with whom he had quarreled publicly in a theater foyer, but the only fatal damage he did was indirect; after the novelist Robert Caze refused to fight Champsaur when challenged in 1886 he was accused of cowardice by Charles Vignier and had to fight him instead, suffering a fatal wound in consequence.

The early resentments Champsaur stirred up were considerably exaggerated when he published his first novel, *Dinah Samuel* (1882), a *roman à clef* whose eponymous central character is based on Sarah Bernhardt, and in which several Hydropathes are recognizable in minor characters—Émile Goudeau appears in caricature as Kardac. Champsaur was sufficiently disliked in some quarters for the American periodical *The Forum* to describe him in 1889 as a "detestable journalist," but he seems to have maintained many of his friendships in spite of his antics, and appears to have thoroughly enjoyed his reputation as an *enfant terrible*. Although Goudeau, passing judgment on Champsaur in *Dix ans de bohème* [Ten Years in Bohemia] (1888), sadly regretted the fact that "the journalist killed the poet at a stroke," he dutifully recognized that a novelist of note had "emerged from the ashes" thereafter.

Although he continued to publish prolifically in newspapers and other periodicals throughout the 1880s, Champsaur appears to have found his true vocation during that decade as a novelist, although he also dabbled extensively in the theater and had various theatrical pieces staged, including the one-act "pantomime" *Lulu* (1888), which attained even greater success when he novelized the plot in 1900. By far the most prestigious work for the stage to which he contributed was, however, based on *L'Orgie Latin*: the "lyrical drama" *La Danseuse de Tanagra* [The Dancing Girl from Tanagra] (1911), for which Paul Ferrier assisted with the libretto and Henri Hirschmann wrote the music.

From the outset, Champsaur's novels were sufficiently various that literary critics and historians were never able to pigeon-hole him, although his second novel, *Miss America* (1885) developed features that eventually came to be seen as most characteristic of his work: an ostensibly disapproving but avidly fascinated depiction of the opulence and decadence of fashionable Parisian society, and a fervent analysis of the enormous difficulty of finding, pursuing and maintaining true love in such a hostile cultural environment. He wrote several others in the same vein, although he was very careful not to settle into a rut by repeating himself too obviously.

Strive as he might to vary the characterization of his output with such venturesome subtitles as *roman moderniste*, and eventually to seek a reputation for seriousness with such critical social studies as the three-volume *L'Arriviste* [The Social Climber] (1911) and the four-volume *L'Empereur des pauvres* [The Emperor of the Poor] (1920-22), Champsaur never shook off the reputation he had acquired as a writer of risqué romances—and in all fairness, he never managed to set aside his own preoccupation with such matters for long, no matter how exotic the subject matter was that he decided to tackle—and it became very exotic indeed in the afterlife fantasy *Pierrot et sa conscience* [Pierrot and His Conscience] (1896; expanded 1902 as *Nuit de fête* [Carnival Night]). His ventures into Orientalia, *Poupée japonaise* [The Japanese Doll] (1900) and *Le Semeur d'amour, roman hindou* [The Sower of Amour, a Hindu novel] (1902), like *L'Orgie Latine*, look suspiciously like attempts to justify his erotic obsessions by moving them into ostensibly-appropriate ethnic contexts.

Following the interruption of his career by the Great War, Champsaur had some difficulty maintaining his popularity, and responded, in part by increasing the variety of his work even further, producing a number of experimental texts that met with a very mixed reception at the time, although several of them can now be seen in retrospect to be ground-breaking. One of the most earnest of his extravagant love stories, the near-futuristic fantasy *Les Ailes de l'homme, De Paris à New York en avion* (1917; tr. as *The Human Arrow*) was written in early 1914 but torpedoed by the war, and had to be awkwardly fixed up with a supplement that turned it into a propaganda-piece. He ventured into *roman scientifique* again in *Homo-Deus, le satyre invisible* (1924; tr. as "The Invisible Satyr" in the omnibus *Homo Deus*), to which he later added a sequel, *Nora, la guenon devenue femme* (1929; tr. as *Nora, the Ape-Woman*)—which is also a sequel to the remarkable fantasy *Ouha, roi des singes* (1923; tr. as *Ouha, King of the Apes*)—after giving its lead character a small part in *Tuer les vieux, jouir! roman vache* (1925; tr. as "Kill the Old, Enjoy!" in *Homo Deus*).

In other late novels Champsaur gave his erotic fantasies freer rein, notably in *Le Baiser du soleil* [The Sun's Kiss] (1926); the trilogy consisting of *Le Chemin du désir* [The Path of Desire] (1926), *Le Combat des sexes* [The War of the Sexes] (1927) and *Les Ordures ménagères* [Household Filth] (1927); the mock-Arabian Nights fantasy *La Princesse émeraude* [The Emerald Princess] (1928); and an omnibus of two sequels to *Poupée japonaise, Impératrice d'ivoire* [The Ivory Empress] (1931), although such concerns are much less obvious in the peculiar comedy *La Pharaonne, roman occulte* (1929; tr. as *Pharaoh's Wife*) and are played down dramatically in *Le Crucifiée* [The Crucified] (1930), an ostensible reconstruction of the life of Jesus, devoid of miracles. The last-named, another attempt to move into more serious literary territory, has obvious links with the subplot of *L'Orgie Latine* dealing with the early history of Christianity, in which the author evidently retained an earnest interest.

Although *L'Orgie Latine* remained the author's only venture into ancient history—or, to be more accurate, ancient legend—it is by no means unconnected with his other fiction, clearly reflecting a perennial fascination with *femmes fatales* and female dancers. Perhaps it is surprising, given the story's enormous success, as an opera as well as a novel, that he did not attempt to follow it up with another work more obviously similar in setting, but perhaps he felt rightly, that having put Messalina center-stage, there was no other figure that could possibly compete—including Cleopatra, who had in any case already been brilliantly depicted by Gautier—and that there was, in consequence, little scope for addition. On the other hand, the evidence of the text suggests that he found it a difficult novel to write; some of the later chapters seem distinctly synoptic, and it is significant that the book is filled out with supplementary texts, some of which are utterly irrelevant to the main story; it might simply have been the difficulty of the task that deterred him. Nevertheless, the legend of Messalina was surely a theme worth attempting, and a challenge worth meeting.

✳

In the context of introduction, it is also worth making some observations about the historical background of the novel. It is most probably set in the year 48 A.D., the year of the death of its eponymous anti-heroine, about whom almost nothing else is reliably known, even her birth-date being uncertain. We can, however, be reasonably sure that she married the 48-year-old Claudius in 38 A.D., perhaps while still in her teens, and she bore him two children—Claudia Octavia and Britannicus—before Claudius was suddenly and unexpectedly proclaimed emperor by the Praetorian Guard during the chaos following the murder of Caligula in 41. She was probably executed for treason, but the calculus of probability suggests that the charge in question was trumped-up, as most such charges always have been.

The bases of Messalina's legend were provided by Tacitus (56-117), although the section of his *Annals* dealing with the reign of Claudius was lost, and Suetonius (69-122), in his scurrilous *De Vita Caesarum* [The Lives of the Caesars]. Both were writing long after her death, with no authentic documentary sources on which to draw, and both with a definite political agenda that required them to blacken the entire dynasty to which she belonged, by blood as well as marriage, leaving no accusatory stone unthrown. They made Claudius out to be a stammering imbecile, although his reign was one of the most successful and progressive in the period, achieving far more than the ones that preceded and succeeded it—although Caligula and Nero might also have been considerably less mad and evil in fact than they were painted by "history."

xviii

Whether the scandals that Tacitus and Suetonius related in respect of Messalina's loose morals have any real biographical basis is impossible to tell, but they certainly made for first-rate yellow journalism, and their scanty accounts became the basis for further scabrous inventions by Pliny the Elder and Juvenal, whose lurid accounts of Messalina's sex-competition with a prostitute and secret pseudonymous employment in a brothel were pure inventions, but naturally attracted the attention and repetition of later scandal-lovers like a powerful magnet, thus becoming core elements of the myth that made her an unparalleled archetype of sexual voracity.

Artists and litterateurs in search of themes and comparisons, of course, have always been unconcerned with the question of whether Roman "historians" might have been lying in their teeth and have gratefully accepted the garish legacy bequeathed to them, just as they have accepted Christian propaganda regarding the violence and extent of persecution at face value, even while rejecting many of the tales of spectacular miracles with such accounts were routinely embellished by their tellers. Even Christian propaganda, however, reserved its ire for Nero and leveled no accusations against his predecessors that might have provided some license for that element of Champsaur's plot.

In both of the major respects of his invention, however, Champsaur dutifully aims for moderation, obviously being aware that accounts of the mass slaughter of Christians in the arena by lions and tigers are difficult to square with the known facts of natural history, and carefully leaving scope for a possible naturalistic interpretation of the one miracle he allows into his plot, but his concern with natural accuracy is tokenistic, and he is perfectly willing to accommodate ludicrous implausibilities when they serve the purposes of his plot and his theme, as all writers are. In that, he probably has much more in common with the likes of Suetonius and Pliny than the latter would have cared to admit, and it can certainly be said in Champsaur's favor that he would never have dreamed of pretending that he was telling the story as it really happened, as his mendacious predecessors had.

It has often been observed that the art of storytelling and sex have a lot in common, not just because they both consist, in essence, of fiddly foreplay and a certain amount of mechanical grinding, accompanied by deliberate fantasizing, eventually leading to a climax, but also because both are immensely conducive to promiscuity, deception, criticism and hypocritical censure, and because both are perennially vulnerable to unplanned and unwanted impotence—and, even when successful, prone to a deflationary aftermath. Even readers sometimes feel the effects of those similarities, let alone writers, who have to work at all the various aspects of the process much harder. As fantasies nurtured in the process of guidance toward a literary climax go, the legend of Messalina must certainly be reckoned intriguing raw material, but whether that raw material could ever have lived up to its legendary promise in practice is a different matter. Perhaps not—but that's literature, and life, and at the very least, *L'Orgie Latine* is a lusty effort.

This translation was made from the copy of the 1904 Fasquelle edition reproduced on the Blbliothèque Nationale's *gallica* website. In the original version the justificatory essay is placed first, as a preface, but I have moved it to the end, feeling that its justificatory role is no longer necessary and that its initial position would function more as an obstacle to be surmounted than a useful foundation for what follows, although its arguments are certainly not without interest. In the original, too, the "interlude" is labeled "Book Five" and the concluding drama "Book Six," although they are very obviously separate works, unconnected with the main narrative; I have abandoned that pretense by leaving out those headings.

—Brian Stableford

THE LATIN ORGY

BOOK ONE

THE DANCER FROM TANAGRA

I

The Egyptian Encampment

THE odorous brazier crackles. All around, the Wanderers sing, or, crouching down, dream in the dwindling dusk. The children and the elderly have gleaned, in the woods and the fields, the dead branches of laburnums, acacias, eucalyptus, olives and vine-stocks for the evening fire, which is rising in the commencing night.

From carts, arranged in a semicircle, the breath of animals is exhaled. Dark-haired little girls play with knucklebones, or sketch the steps of gracious turns on flowery Oriental carpets. Little boys, almost naked—one might think them diminutive bronze statues come to life—chase one another, squealing, while the recently-born slumber. Couples escape into the nearby wood, and their silhouettes sometimes appear in the luminous zone of the blaze, which causes reflections to dance on the bark of the trees on the edge of the clearing, illuminating the gold of coppery torsos, causing sparks to play in the glass beads and metal of necklaces, or the barbaric settings of amulets suspended over the young breasts, exposed here and there, fresh and firm, of the daughters of Egypt.[1]

They are thirty pilgrims of the roads and towns, preluding nocturnal repose with games and conversation. In the sky, the stars are born, one by one, seeming to play at appearing and

____

1 I have transcribed the original text's references to "Egyptiens" directly rather than substituting the more commonplace English abbreviation "gypsies."

disappearing amid the fleecy clouds, or, suddenly, illuminating in pleiades, as on the somber backcloth of an infinite peddler's tray from which an invisible jeweler has taken away the veil. Around the clearing where the Oriental strolling players are camped, the trees, pines and firs, cut out their fantastic shadows, protective or menacing, projecting their branches like weapons or placidly advancing them, as if to welcome those who have called a halt in their shade.

The chief of the band is counting the money brought to him by the acrobats, the dancing girls, the snake-charmers, the musicians and the fortune-tellers. Harsh voices scold the young who are as yet insufficiently supple or indocile to the lessons of elders who are instructing them in fire-eating, handling reptiles gracefully, juggling with sharp blades, dancing to entrancing rhythms while agitating sparkling fabrics, seductive steps in which the beauty of draped forms can be divined at every gesture.

Suddenly, a dog barks at the rising moon, whose face, pale and slyly cheerful, appears between the crowns of three poplars, black steeples pricking the azure of the calm sky.

II

The Prediction:
Karysta Will Only Dance Three More Times

A N EXCEEDINGLY handsome adolescent with bold features advances toward a young woman sitting some way
apart from the group, who seems anxious about some secret
concern, in order to surprise her in her reverie. Bushy hair frames
his narrow forehead with ebony curls, and his crimson lips draw
apart over nacreous teeth in a happy smile at seeing her alone and
pensive, without any involvement in the others' games.

"How serious you are, Karysta!" he says, in a quiet voice,
placing his right hand on the round and slender shoulder of the
dreamer, who starts.

"Oh, it's you, Sepeos. You frightened me. I was meditating on
the stories of the wise old mother, and I thought a demon had
come to take me to the fêtes that the infernal spirits hold while
the earth sleeps."

Karysta bursts out laughing, and throws the florets she has
been holding in her hand at the young man's face. "That's to punish you, miscreant! There's sage there, which puts you to sleep
and gives you dreams of insatiable desire; mistletoe, which makes
everlasting bonds out of ephemeral affections; two sprigs of mimosa to attract gold, and bindweed, symbols of amorous chains.
If you escape me after such a charm, it's because the gods, destiny
and magic are liars. You're caught!"

Piously, while she was speaking, Sepeos bent down to pick up
the florets; then, getting up again, he takes Karysta's shoulders

and envelops her with the seductive gaze of his long, dark and wild eyes, beneath long silky brown lashes, which bring out the Orient in his irises.

"You know full well that other charms—yours, Karysta!—are sufficient to bind me. Your cheeks are as flavorsome as the grapes of Hellas, the fatherland, and your mouth is a marvelous cherry, which troubles me. Your bulbous forehead is as smooth and soft as the petals of an iris. Your eyes, little grace, have more brightness than mimosas; they are gold and amethyst in your delicate face of a precious idol, and your eyelids are like captive butterflies, unable to quit the exquisite abode of your eyes, two profound flowers."

Karysta, proud in spite of a hint of gentle mockery in her great friend's dithyramb, contemplates Sepeos ardently.

"You love me? Yes . . . but I have an inexplicable apprehension of destiny . . . fatality breaks hearts, and also lives, for the pleasure of the contrary gods."

Without making any reply, Sepeos draws the slender dancing girl away, whose fragility contrasts with his strength, a masculine energy betrayed in more than the broad shoulders and bulging torso, the curved nose and square chin of Aryan races, remained unalloyed.

Karysta has the pure profile, the thin and narrow nose and the arched mouth of Hellenic girls; slim-waisted, her hips protrude superbly beneath her light tunic of blue silk, embroidered with silver, that is fraying; her breasts, as round as cups, appear half-outside the garment that they seem to be retaining; and her neck rises up like a frail column, a stem on which the corolla of the face blooms.

Now, sitting on a stone, Geo, the oldest woman of the tribe, is muttering while consulting the tarot cards displayed on her knees, whose signs glimmer in the uneven light of the fire. No one is as skillful as the old prophetess in deciphering the future of individuals; she has lived for more than sixty years, and her prophecies are never vain.

Sepeos, her son, is proud of that material science; he knows that Geo releases the secrets of fatality. Since the last moon, he has been betrothed to Karysta, the pretty dancer from Tanagra. Geo had read their love in certain signs; she had foreseen the moment when he would dedicate his life to the existence of the nimble ballerina, the pride of the troop, which is to celebrate their wedding at the next ides.

Innumerable times, Geo has reliably predicted fortune and misfortune; nothing is done in the camp and no journey is undertaken without the chiefs and the elders having consulted her. The sons of Egypt venerate Geo for her wisdom, and foreigners fear her, for she can cast evil spells upon them and somber spirits.

Karysta is sitting beside her fiancé, under an acacia, a few clusters of whose white flowers constellate the grass; Sepeos, whispering, is soon intoxicated by the folly of their caresses, and she leaves her hands in his, murmuring her exaltation in being loved. But Sepeos reproaches her for her frequent bouts of sadness.

"Who can have caused you chagrin? Are you not the most beautiful and the most fêted of the dancers of the tribe, and also the most glorious? Famous patricians applaud you and vainly desire to possess your body of Aphrodite. All of our people cherish you, Karysta; even the women are not jealous of you, so conscious are they of your generosity. You love and are loved. Are you not blessed among the young Egyptian women?"

"Certainly; I must seem ungrateful. But it's precisely because I'm so fortunate that I tremble for my happiness. Do you not know that all the divinities are jealous of lovers and those who are content? I love you too much, Sepeos, and your heart is too full of me; too much felicity is around us, like the ripe harvests of a beautiful summer. I fear the storm that might rot the fruits and massacre the golden wheat, devastating the ears. Shall we bring in our crop? That doubt spoils my hopes."

"How silly you are, object of my adoration!"

Sepeos laughed to hide the dolor awakened in him by Karysta's presentiments. At that moment, Geo sang more loudly some invocation of the spirits. Sepeos indicated his mother.

"Listen. Will you believe her, if she promises you a future of joy? She has never made the tarot lie, and the gods inhabit her soul, dictating her oracles. Ask her what your destiny is. Would you like to?"

They approach Geo, and consider her momentarily. Then, as the mysterious sexagenarian, emerging from the meditation in which she is plunged, raises her eyes to the two children:

"Mother, mother! Tell us Karysta's fate; she wants to lead her life in accordance with your advice and presages."

The old sphinx stares at the young dancer, and says in a slow voice:

"If, truly, you want to know, it's necessary that you believe. Don't curse the gods, but listen to their signs, and live in accordance with the oracles. The true wisdom, you see, child, is to be able to remain ignorant. If the future is sad, one hopes nevertheless for unexpected felicities; if it is full of radiant days, knowing them in advance takes away the joy of successive surprises, when tomorrows remain bright and blue. . . . Tanagran, you who are beautiful and beloved, can you not enjoy, insouciantly, the present moment, inasmuch as it is as beautiful as you, and loves you?"

The breath of thyme, sharp and a trifle rude, mingled with the heavy odor of flowering elders, and the voluptuous reek of syringas and jasmines, in the warm night of the Roman spring. A woman, who had taken a few brands from the fire in order to deposit a bowl full of milk thereon, squatted on the ground beside it, waiting for it to boil, and sang a ballad;

> The flower that the dew
> No longer vivifies, dies.
> Must I, then, die
> Since my lips are withering
> Of no longer being kissed?

At the summons of the mothers, the last children playing, hiding in the grass or chasing one another, squealing, like flocks of martins against the azure of the summer sky, had gone back into the tents or the carts; only a few shadows were vacillating near the fire; the young woman picked up the hot milk; with her foot she pushed the hot brands into the fire; sparks caused the spangles in her dress, and the metal pins in her curled hair, to scintillate.

Geo, having shuffled and laid out the cards, hesitated. "Seriously, do you want it? You demand it?"

This reticence exasperated Karysta's impatient slenderness; she struck the ground with her heel, crying:

"If what is boasted of your science is not mistaken, Mother, tell all. The worst of oracles is better than uncertainty."

Geo, in the process of turning over the tarot cards in accordance with the rituals, chants a prayer to the gods of secret wisdom. Shivering, Karysta looks at the figures and fugitive symbols in the wrinkled hands of the aged cartomancer. Geo raises a long, thin index-finger, and then shakes her head.

"My dear, here is much happiness suddenly broken; you dance, you are applauded; hearts flutter round you, and invisible birds—the desires of men. You dance; and suddenly, there is no more harmony; the interrupted gestures suddenly stop. Yes, that's it, you have a red star . . . one of those of the adornment of Cassiopeia. . . .

"Mother," Sepeos asks, anxiously, "can you read the life of the star in the firmament?"

The old woman interrupts him. Standing up, she designates, between the cumulus and the nimbus, a vacillating gleam, like a night-light in the darkness of a sanctuary, obscured by the smoke of incense. Three times a brief cloud eclipses the star, and three times, the flickering light vanishes.

"Karysta the Tanagran, you shall dance three times . . . and will please everyone with your mimes. But the cloud is swallowing your star, as a griffin swallows a little bird. You shall dance three times more, and you will die. Thus speaks Destiny through my mouth."

In the silence that followed, there was a wild cry from Sepeos, a cry of anger and passion, as dolorous as a sob.

Sepeos has seized Karysta by the shoulders and the waist in order to carry her away, he knows not where—far from that mysterious and terrible menace. Geo has sat down again on the stone, and, her chin in her hand, seems to have fallen back into her dream.

The pretty dancer from Tanagra resists the efforts of her lover, and laughs.

"Let me be; I'm not of your credulous race."

"Karysta, Karysta," says the sphinx, raising her head, with piercing and saddened eyes, "children are reckless. I repeat to you, don't gamble with destiny."

Geo chants again, while she moves away, tottering.

"No one is able to thwart fate. Those who laugh or those who lament, the believers and the incredulous, each in turn is caught in the future's nets. The future is a monster that lies in wait for humans at the bend in every road. There are reptiles in the most florid hedges. Pick flowers, don't awaken the spirit; he will have wounded you before you have seen his blue neck charged with venom, ornamented with living gems. No one, I tell you, has been able to avoid the ambushes of the future depicted in the pages of the Book. Karysta will only dance three times more."

Sepeos hugs the Tanagran and begs:

"Come Karysta, let's go into the mountains, just the two of us. My arms are strong and can carry you, to spare your feet the stones of the road. No one must know our retreat; neither the chief of the tribe nor the richest of the patricians of Rome will be able to request your prestigious veils. I no longer want you to dance, because, my adored one, I don't want you to die."

"My fortune and my glory are in the grace of my gestures. Is it living, my friend, to renounce one's art?"

Sepeos, the magnificent Egyptian, rocks her, and implores her, and then he orders her; finally, weakening, the frail Tanagran dancer murmurs in a kiss, after he has scolded her like a child and seduced her by turns, in order to convince her:

"Since I belong to you, I cannot take myself back. I love you, Sepeos, so I shall obey you; my love is dearer to me that the art of beautiful gestures, voluptuous dances and mimes. No, it's not the time to die, when the dawn of love is rising. Except, listen; I want, in exchange for my submission, to make you a plea. Before quitting the encampment, let this night pass, and tomorrow too, until dusk. I want to embrace my friend Lerya, and to carry away my veils, my rings and my loops, in order that the Tanagran, if she dances no more, can at least adorn herself for you . . . in order that, in these supreme hours among our people, who admired me, I can fill my eyes and my memory permanently with those I shall no longer see . . . and with the artiste that I shall no longer be. There are two women within me, of whom one, the slighter, is expiring today, since that is your wish. . . ."

III

The Dancer from Tanagra

ALONE among the tribe of Egyptians incessantly wandering over the whole world, Karysta, the dainty dancer, was not of the nomadic race. They were accustomed to call her by the name of her natal town, the Tanagran, to distinguish her from the daughters of the pure Roma caste, as the "People of the Iron Ring" disseminated over the globe designate themselves. In any case, she was differentiated from the daughters of Egypt by the mat whiteness of her complexion beneath the light golden patina with which the sun and the winds colored her cheeks. Her lips did not project in a glutinous *moue*, but, fugitive at the dimpled corners, resembled the fine blades of curved oriental daggers.

Karysta knew nothing, or hardly anything, of her childhood years except that she had been tempted one day, many years ago, by the pearls and glass beads that old Geo showed her—for she could not remember having seen the soothsayer any less decrepit and wrinkled than she was now; it would have astonished the dancer greatly to hear talk of a Geo who was young and beautiful and who was yet to be the mother of Sepeos, and her adoptive mother.

Every day, in the time when she had lived in Tanagra, the child had gone to play on the spangle-strewn golden sand of the beach of the Asopus with other children, while her father modeled amphorae and statuettes of dancing girls and goddesses,[1] in

---

1 The Greek town of Tanagra was famous for its typical figurines, mostly in terracotta, large quantities of which were discovered in excavations carried out

14

accordance with the rhythmic forms transmitted by the potters, his ancestors. He lived poorly but happily, for foreigners often stopped before his display, merchants from Athens and the islands, and it pleased him to hear them say: "That's very good, that!" The artist, his orphan daughter—for her mother, Mavia, had died bringing her into the world—and the unique slave charged with cultivating the garden and their interior care of the hearth, lived on the sales of pottery and statuettes.

From what chagrin was her father suffering? He sometimes murmured phrases of melancholy remembrance while modeling the moist clay, or while he was enlivening with crimson the nipples of breasts or the curve of lips, or fixed with the tip of his brush in hollow orbits the antimony of which eyes were made, or lacquered eyebrows and eyelashes lowered over the artificial gazes of figurines; he cursed the child as soon as her awkward fingers wanted to play with the terracotta dolls. Sometimes, however, he set her naked before him, in the sunlight, and forbade her to play noisily, telling her that she was pretty and that he would make an infant nymph, a thin goddess or a minuscule ballerina in her resemblance.

Karysta did not understand everything that the potter muttered; she obeyed him in order not to be beaten, and also because of a vanity of hearing herself called beautiful in her slenderness of a paltry living thing. Later, her father's phrases resounded unexplained in her memory, without her knowing precisely where she had heard them, and it was for her like a distant prophecy, the oracle of her adolescent prettiness:

"Everyone says that my statuettes all resemble Mavia; Mavia isn't dead, then. Karysta, our daughter, is as troubling as a little nymph, and infant fauness. . . . By selling Mavias and Karystas and sculpted amphorae, one earns drachmas. . . . One exchanges them for smooth amphorae and goat-skins that are not beautiful. . . . But the sculpted amphorae are empty, and I sell them; the others contain retsina wine, the elixir of Samos and Chios, and that's forgetfulness . . . that's joy!"

---

in the 1870s, after which they became popular collector's items—to the extent that they were faked in great abundance.

At other times, Karysta heard her father cursing during the night, when he came home late, and from her bed she heard heavy sandals falling on the floor.

Of all that the young woman only retained confused memories, as from an ancient dream, of a time unknown, infinite years ago. Only a few pictures remained inscribed in her memory: the garden from which she stole white figs and red figs from the low branches; the beach where she went to play; a man with a gray beard who dirtied his hands stirring colored clay or showing passers-by statuettes and vases ornamented with figurines.

One day, she had lingered on the beach, and neither the slave not her father had come to collect her; a Roma encampment had seduced the child, careless of the hour and the dusk. The women were dressed in blue, green, orange and red garments; beautiful necklaces clinked on the gilded bronze of their throats and semi-naked breasts. Little girls were playing, others making tours with supple young men, burglars like the monkeys she had seen on the Agora when sailors and strolling players showed animals on the days of public fairs.

The Egyptians had surrounded her; women gave her cakes made of maize and perfumed rice, and honeyed milk. Karysta did not understand, and accepted, with happy smiles, the caresses and the treats. And as they had heaped up their clothing and personal possessions in covered carts, they dispersed their fire, and whipped the horses with cries. Then the little girl, fearful of being left alone in the fallen night, heartbroken at seeing the tinsel and the voices of her new friends draw away, had started to weep.

"Hey! Hey there!" And she had extended her thin arms, bare outside her tunic, toward the departing caravan.

An old woman, getting down from a cart, had taken her on to her shoulder. The child ate sugared broth, drank an aromatic liquid, and went to sleep, rolled up in a piece of multicolored carpet, in the corner of the cart, which slowly progressed through the olive groves and vines, while the old woman, with a face like a dried-up grape, intoned a mysterious song.

Among the Egyptians, Karysta grew up, leading their life; happy, she had no regrets; she was not ordered to do any fatiguing work, and she had ornaments and shiny clothing. She was taught to dance while shaking a tambourine with little bells, her hair undone, and to drape herself with scarves of gauze and silk, to make her hips and small breasts stand out, to strike the poses of idols, under the sharp gazes of spectators.

Through the African provinces of Rome, in the various counties of Hellas, and on the forums of Latin towns, she danced, guided by the seeress Geo. More often, it was at crossroads, where numerous carts and pedestrians were passing by. People stopped to watch her, sesterces rained down around her—and her name flew from mouth to mouth because, for a long time, the Egyptian troupe traveled through Italy and Sicily, where people love dancing and the performances of strolling players. Karysta smiled, very proudly, when people said as they stopped: "That's the Tanagran who dances!" and added to the spectators.

At fifteen, the frail ballerina felt desires growing within her that were unfamiliar; languid, she wept for no reason by night as soon as she was alone, or under the trees, away from the encampment; she sought the caresses of old Geo, who treated her like a precious doll, not without a certain affection, which she did not show her too frequently, for fear of rendering her caprices demanding.

One evening when she was sobbing, doubtless at being so alone with thoughts that the others would not understand, Sepeos, the son of Geo, the wrinkled sphinx, surprised her. She had not heard his footsteps on the green velvet of the moss. Before she had perceived the young man, two hands had closed gently over her eyes.

"You're weeping? Has someone been nasty to Karysta, or doesn't she possess enough finery?"

"It's not that. I'm hurting, Sepeos, without knowing why."

Sepeos had been the girl's playmate, and he had remained her great friend, the one from whom she most willingly received lessons in dancing and dexterity, who taught her songs and the art of plying the cithara and the harp, and shaking little bells harmoniously. He had always treated her very tenderly. More ardently than all the others, he knew how to depict her nimble slenderness in soothing words, and she sensed that he spoke the truth in eulogies that were sometimes slightly troubled.

Karysta had acquired the habit of confiding her slightest secrets to Sepeos; the young man explained the mystery of his youthful anxieties to her, and how he would suffer an atrocious torment if she did not love him. And Sepeos then told Geo about his love for the Tanagran. Karysta made no difficulty about confessing her tenderness. Then the marriage of the young couple was decided by the Roma tribe for the following April, in accordance with the Egyptian rites.

IV

Futile Plaints

"YOU must remember, my son, that it is forbidden for the men of Egypt to live alone with their spouses without any companion," Geo quavered, for her voice was feeble and broken except when the prophetic breath came to strength and sustain the inspiration of her words. "Yes, woe betide those who neglect their duty and their tribe, to pursue temporary amour. Then again, I've told you, no one escapes their destiny. Karysta can go—she isn't retained by any blood tie."

The Egyptian had just informed his mother definitely of the resolution that he had made, as firm the next day as it had been the previous evening, to take his fiancée, whose waist his arm was presently around, away from the danger of death. He had declared his fear, as profound as his love was immense, of seeing Karysta dance for the sake of some sudden obligation—or out of pride, so much was the ballerina intoxicated by frantic saltation, her own grace and the applause of men, enraptured by desire before her.

"Yes," the mother continued, "the Greek is not of our race, she can leave without the spirits pursuing her. She's an ingrate. She will forget you, my son, and you will forget her. . . ."

At these words, the adored foreigner almost wept, but her plaint turned into angry exclamations protesting her true love; the dancer from Tanagra stood up on tiptoe as the famous fighting cocks of her homeland do on their spurs. Then, the mother begged her with tender phrases, and the sibyl in her was silenced, in order only to leave in play the dolor of being in her final days, deprived of the fruit of her loins. But Sepeos remained inflexible, so much was he dominated by his passion; his eyes burning with feverish ardor, he repeated his determination boldly, and punctuated his farewells, by way of excuse and prayer, by repeating several times: "She's too young to die!" while pointing at Karysta, already enveloped in her veils.

The fiancé now listed, respectfully but decidedly, the militant reasons for their voluntary exile from his nomadic family:

"Karysta cannot dance any more, and she knows no other Egyptian work. What use would she be to the tribe? The other women would look at her askance, because of the idleness in which she would live, for, being so pretty, so slender, so delicate and patrician, she ought not to participate in labor and cannot serve as a domestic slave."

"But you, are you not to be the next chief? Who will guide our people then, if you interrupt the filiation of actions? You ought to command us one day."

Sepeos shrugged his shoulders. Power interested him less than his amour and Karysta's salvation.

The Sphinx persisted: "You don't care, then, about abandoning me for this prancer who will deceive you?"

"Don't irritate me, Mother! I respect your white hair, don't act in such a way that I shall banish the memory of your face when I'm far away with the one I love, and who loves me."

The Egyptians had made a halt beside the Via Appia in order to prepare the evening meal. They were going to traverse Rome before nightfall and camp on the other side of the Janiculum, in a wood, because a decree by the Aediles forbade wanderers and strolling players, who did not belong to a house, to remain in the city after nightfall. The Egyptians were accustomed, during that season, to travel around the Latin cities; messengers had warned Sepeos' comrades of the approach of a troupe of their brethren who had come from Cisalpine Gaul. They had orders to join them.

The women had begun preparing the meat and peeling the vegetables, sitting cross-legged in the grass, still warmed by the ardors of the spring sunlight. The children were heading cheerfully toward the rare clumps of trees to gather dead branches. Young women, carrying amphorae of clay and bronze pitchers, were going to the springs in search of water for cooking in the open air.

In the meantime, men of the tribe lay down nonchalantly to dream, while others practiced juggling. Acrobats between twelve and sixteen years of age devoted themselves to extraordinary leaps on Oriental carpets, with shrill cries and guttural syllables, by way of calls and signals. They bounded on to one another's shoulders, pirouetting in mid-air, and their perilous leaps caused the thousand spangles of their picturesque rags to sparkle in the antepenultimate gleams of daylight.

Presently, old Geo, grumbling, consulted her tarot cards again, her eyes burning with a passionate curiosity. She called to Sepeos, who, still delaying his departure, was prowling around.

"Son," she said, "don't leave us, at least before the light of day has died away. The chief will oppose your flight if he foresees it, and you know that it's necessary not to defy destiny by breaking its bonds in the sunlight. Then again, perhaps the Master of the Roma will send me a better presage. Who can tell?

"Ah . . . I see it, my son; you will quit your mother without regret, and those of Egypt, for that daughter of Hellas, for your love for her speaks more forcefully than the vagabond and independent blood of our race. . . ."

V

The Via Appia, at the Sixth Hour

NOW, because, in that epoch, it pleased Messalina to go, almost every evening, to the imperial villa of Ormizari, situated in the environs of the capital of the world, not far from the Via Appia, and because a number of patricians also possessed summer residences, little palaces and hot baths on that side of the outskirts of Rome, the most magnificent of the Roman roads was always furrowed between the fifth and the sixth hour—the movement taking place then—by a multitude of vehicles, horsemen and pedestrian.

It had become a fashion, an elegance, to make excursions, in chariots, on horseback or in lecticas, along the Via Appia. From the Forum all the way to the far side of the tomb of Caecilia Metella, to the gracious temple formed by a double portico, erected in open country to Venus Physica, the favorite goddess of the Pompeiians, idlers and courtiers, senators and magistrates, after finishing their day's work—everyone in Rome who had the leisure and wanted, while strolling, to see or be seen, was there. Proconsuls were encountered there, neglecting their distant governments in order to come to the city to solicit the most elevated magistrates; the commanders of legions and military tribunes who had distinguished themselves in the recent wars could be saluted there with a flattering murmur. Navigators with sun-tanned faces and profound bright eyes, mirrors of the immensities they sounded; Numidian or Syrian princes, the former

22

coiffed in ostrich plumes, the latter in the Oriental mitra, Kirghiz and Celts, Dacians and Persians, Greeks and Assyrians, rich bankers, former slaves uplifted by treason and villainy, patricians of good family and popular tribunes, all mingled and crossed one another's paths. Among them, the great courtiers and immodest matrons looked one another up and down, and calculated the value of their adornments; the Via Appia was the battlefield of their coquetries.

The Egyptians paid no heed to the hubbub that was beginning on the road. Troops of citizens, parasites with anxious and questing eyes, began their promenade in search of their evening meal. Philosophers held forth, and poets, perched like rhetors on tombstones, recited their verses before audiences of idlers who paused to listen to them. The poems and the speeches almost always treated the adventures of gods or goddesses; or else they were dithyrambs to the glory of Augustus Claudius and Messalina, the magnificent Empress.

But now the chariots are rolling more rapidly along the busy road, raising clouds of dust, ardently colored by the dying hues of the sun; the Star appears, between the western hills, like an enormous lamp, the laughing face of a drunkard, on which vague luminous features are designed; that this hour, Phoebus takes on the face of Bacchus, haloed in crimson and gold.

The Campanian villas, with their marble, are reminiscent of white birds in the clumps of trees. Apple trees, almond trees and cherry trees in flower shed snow on the slopes of the hills, pink and white with that litter, in which scarlet corollas are sometimes rutilant, like the nipples of breasts, dots of living flesh on the bodies of young women.

From lilacs and sunflowers, flowering orange trees, roses and mimosas, all the budding cassolettes of renewal, perfumes escape into the lukewarm air of the vernal dusk. Around the tombs, the resting-places of renowned ancestors, multicolored flower-beds festoon both sides of the road. Little bells around the necks of horses tinkle; mounted centurions, after their service, prance under the gaze of bands of strollers, and laughing suburban courtesans lie in wait for the fortunes of the evening. In litters, on crimson, sapphire blue, celestial azure or hyacinth cushions, patrician couples, honored old men and priestesses of amour pass by, under the fire of adoring, admiring or envious gazes.

A proconsul and senators, preceded by lictors armed with fascicles, go past one another, saluting. Elegant men, more nonchalant than the women, allow creamy hands sparkling with gems to dangle from their gilded litters. African chiefs, a king of Armenia and subjects of Rome file past, some drawn by zebras, one mounted on a two-humped camel whose slender head, flanked by supple tufts, sways like the neck of a swan, above vague plebeians, in curious eddies around luxurious vehicles. A troop of cavaliers passes by, acclaimed by the people, and beauties lean out of chariots in order to unleash smiles at the mounted soldiers helmed in bronze, on whose breastplates sculpted golden eagles gleam.

Women guiding their own chariots with two, three or five horses, become impatient at being retained in the files that climb and descend toward Rome or toward the pleasure palaces. In the distance, to the North, in the luminous dust, the domes of palaces and colonnades loom up, glowing red with silver streaks; the summits of temples and obelisks are drowned in mists the color of amethyst, orange-tinted; above innumerable mosaics and roofs of stone or carmine tiles, beyond the porticos and the statues that seem to be floating above Rome, the sky, like an immense volcano, stirs, and its ephemeral riches sink into the invasive grayness of the twilight.

A rumor rises, compounded from the cries of water-carriers, merchants, the voices of actors, singers and women—the respiration and voice of the city—dominating the sound of wheels, of bells, of criers and coachmen; all of that blots out to some extent the song of the foliage, the shrill chirping of sparrows, the hymn of nature, the rut of saps, of the spring that vivifies things and shines in the eyes of men and women.

Already the courtesans with powdered cheeks, their eyelids heightened with antimony, are hastening toward the glimmer of the city, and, further away, emboldened by the decline of the light, laughing, parting the flaps of multicolored robes to leave tempting corners of flesh visible.

Suddenly, a great stir, a tidal bore in the crowd, is produced; criers launch themselves forth, and guards partially armored over the silk of tunics with plumed helmets form a hedge.

"Make way! Make way, for the Empress Messalina!"

And the people and the chariots mass at the sides of the road, in order to let the Augusta pass.

It is for her that so many men, athirst for her splendid beauty, are waiting feverishly. It is for her that the gazes of ardent faces shine, male and female pupils avid for that divine flesh, hoping that hazard might serve them, panting with their desire to be the voluptuous guests of the debauchery with which public rumor incessantly maintains all the desires extended toward the Queen of the world, the lustful Majesty that so many subjects in Rome know so fundamentally that a satirical poet, in a presently-celebrated song, had nicknamed her "the naked Empress."

First, a squadron of praetorians on horseback, armored in silver, with golden eagles on their breasts, through a cloud of dust in which the imperial standard floats, and then a maniple of foot-soldiers, similarly armored in silver, march at the head of the Augustan cortege.

Domitius Ahenobarbus, the husband of Agrippina and father of Nero, arrives in the first rank; Decius and Miso, consuls, preceded by lictors on horseback; Vernax, a Gaulish traitor who exchanged for the title of knight and a fortune his city and his tribe; the Archon Melkios, sent to Rome to represent the interests of oppressed Greece, who, senile and decrepit, is forgetful of his task in the incessant erotic and Bacchic revels of the court; Veracchius, a military tribune devoid of glory, whose finest title is to have given Claudius his two daughters; others, less infamous, perhaps by laxity, or wearing the masks of obsequious courtiers in order to conceal a fear mingled with disgust for the cruelties and ignominies of sovereigns—such are the principal members of the cortege preceding the imperial litter; Camillus is on horseback and Senio, the praetor, is guiding a chariot harnessed to two brown chargers, whose long tails brush the ground. All are wearing the entirely crimson[1] toga of the Augusta's friends, and, in the whirlwind, they seem like passing flames.

On great gilded chariots are dancing girls, whose naked bodies are garlanded with roses and rare corollas, gem-studded and bejeweled at the vagina and around the breast, forming harmonious ensembles of attitudes and gestures, in perfect rhythmic lines, with coachmen from the circus and singing actors, accompanied by players of lyres, flutes and citharas. Finally, amid the whinnying of the horses of a squadron of gladiators, twenty tame lions, in pairs, are guided by animal-keepers by means of golden and silver chains, drawing ten sumptuous chariots, in which Messalina's dearest friends are standing.

Among the people, various rumors salute the cortege. Whistles greet Pallas and Narcissus, the favorites of Claudius,[2] while cheers salute that perversity Messalina, splendid and sculptural, in a network of golden mail, quasi-naked, shining with nard and cinnamon, diademed with three circles of gold in her ebon hair. The Empress almost offers her radiant body, worse than naked, exquisite and white on crimson damask cushions fringed with white, to the gazes avid for her glorious immodest beauty. Her face is partly protected by a transparent gauze, on which the features are stamped in a vague shadow, and her aquamarine and jet irises shine beneath an exceedingly white marmoreal forehead. Two black giants are waving fans of the feathers of white swans and pink ibises around her lustful head.

---

1 The original has *pourpre* here, as in the phrase "imperial purple," but the color in question was actually a kind of red, not purple as currently understood, and that is what the French word signifies. I have therefore translated references to the color as "crimson," except for a number of instances where it is used in the same figurative sense that is still used in English to speak of "imperial purple."

2 The freedmen Narcissus and Pallas are credited by Roman historians with significant conspiratorial roles in the courts of Claudius and Nero. The former was Claudius' secretary and principal confidant, providing the basis for the significant part played by the former in Jarry's *Messaline* and the play by Champsaur employed as an appendix to the present text.

Nonchalant, clad in a toga of fine white and red damask, his blond hair secured by an elegant head-band, his pink face carefully depilated, his dark eyes, ardent and troubled, ringed with bistre, Senator Silius is lying next to the Empress, in a post full of morbidity, leading his elbow on a scarlet cushion that contrasts with the whiteness of the body of the man resting upon it.

In the face of amused Rome, the lovers, careless of the sovereign debilitated by debauchery, display their mutual passion like a challenge and an example to the sensuality of all around them. Messalina is, truly by her beauty, the idol of the people and the soldiers, the supreme mistress, LUXURIA,[1] the Dominatrix of Rome and the Empire, for she governs Claudius, the Emperor, Silius, twice consul,[2] and the praetorians and the legions via their leaders.

An immense acclamation runs along the Via Appia as she passes. Hands are raised, bristling in the groups. Liberated beauties, in quest of amour and the gold of wealth, cry: "Ave, Venus Messalina!" They lean forward and blow kisses, gluttonously extending their painted faces and their white hands with fingernails painted red and with antimony, in the hope of being distinguished.

---

1 Luxuria is Latin for lust, so the attribution of the epithet to Messalina implies her personification of what was not yet reckoned as one of the seven deadly sins of Christian dogma.

2 In fact, the Gaius Silius who was reportedly Messalina's lover was only a nominee for the consulate when he was executed in 48 A.D., although his similarly-named father had been a consul before being stitched up on a charge of treason and forced to commit suicide in 24, eleven years after the younger Silius was born.

VI

Karysta Dances for the First Time

AT A SIGN from the Empress, the cortege halts momentarily. Messalina has perceived the carts of the Egyptians not far from the road, and Sepeos standing up, holding Karysta's hand, both ready to quit the tribe.

In her simultaneously indolent and sovereign voice, she says:

"Bring those adolescents here, and those people of Egypt; they know pleasant tricks and dances. I also want my future to be told—mine and that of Silius. I'm sure that we shall learn bizarre things. . . . Isn't that true, my slave of amour?" Luxuria shrills, with a malevolent laugh, at the indifferent Silius, one of whose hands in mechanically rotating the rings on the other.

To obey the Divine One, the Egyptians run to the chariots. Carpets in Oriental hues decorate the causeway and the grass between the tombs; young women wave rattles and sing ardent and passionate songs in an unknown tongue, in which prayers are mingled with melodies and phrases of joy; the rhythm of their heads and entire upper bodies accompanies their strophes.

Geo squats down, legs crossed, beside the imperial litter, solemnly silent, laying out tarot cards on a carpet, or lodix, on which are embroidered reptiles and scorpion, salamanders and symbolic chimeras, and astral figures. Luxuria, leaning over, has removed the gauze veil, allowing the incarnadine of her lips to shine resplendently in the nacreous whiteness of her face.

The old woman raises her hands in horror.

28

"I see atrocious things in your life; you are beautiful, dazzling Empress, you are cruel and voluptuous, and from all of that emerges your physical and sentimental amusement, which is as much a need for Your Divinity as breathable air, but also your misfortune in the future. . . ."

"What do you man, sorceress?"

"Don't interrogate me, troubling Majesty, or promise that, if I tell the truth, your anger will not weigh upon your servant!"

With a gesture of impatience, Messalina, laughing, orders the wizened sphinx to continue.

"Say whatever you want, sorceress. What does tomorrow matter to me if this evening, new kisses will rejoice my lips, and my flesh quivers in an unprecedented frisson. Speak!"

"In a garden veiled with shadow, armed men are advancing toward the secret retreat where you are frolicking in the arms of a freedman who was still a slave yesterday. They lie in wait for brutal words to spur the bodies in rut: the sighs of your lasciviousness, Empress. They launch themselves forward, and one of them, an officer, tears away your robe while another strikes you. In the gardens, not far away, citharas are playing, the hymn of harps and lutes is dying away; and you croak, and your palpitating beauty is dragged over the gravel of the pathways. It is the conclusion of your destiny, but you have, before then, stupors without number. . . ."

A silvery burst of Imperial laughter rings out.

"To enjoy! To die! You hear, Silius? Throw talents, she has spoken as no poet ever will. What greater pleasure than such death throes? Kisses, and then the warm crimson of blood. . . ."

During the prediction, the eyes of Silius have not quit the dainty body of Karysta, the Tanagran, standing with her back to a stele on the edge of the road. He has made a sign to the dancer, who has come forward. He asks her name, and strokes her cheek with his hand, while Sepeos' eyes sparkle with anger and dread.

"You're exquisite. No statue in my palace equals your supple and lovely callipygian slenderness, Karysta. I suppose, from your tunic slit over the hips, that you must be a ballerina. . . ."

"Indeed, Lord," replied the fragile dancer, her attitude frigid and fearful before those two perverse lovers, monstrously complicit, before the two masters and the Roman she-wolf.

"What fire burns in those adolescent eyes!" whispers Messalina to Sepeos, for her part. "You're handsome; I like male beauty. Your ardent eyes have another flame than Latin eyes, and do not have the insipid softness of Gaulish irises, nor the stupid fixity of Numidian gazes. You will follow my cortege, man; I want to find you at the imperial palace."

"I cannot and must not; I have buckled my belt for a long journey."

"Eh! What does it matter to me?" she said, irritated and calm by turns. "You will follow me." Then, turning to Silius, she smiles on seeing that he has put his arm round Karysta, circling that living flower of amour. "Dance, child, to please my friend, and you shall have a beautiful new aureus, with the effigy of the Emperor Claudius.

Sepeos leaps forward. Defying the Empress and Silius, the Official Lover, he shouts with a combative attitude: "She shall not dance! I am her fiancé . . . I do not want her to dance."

Silius sniggers, and with a weary finger points at the Egyptian.

"Lictors, bind him to that stele"—as he speaks he designates a truncated column next to a tomb, "and whip him, so long as he opposes the Augusta's desire."

The soldiers run forward, and bind Sepeos' limbs with cords. He twists his arms in vain, all his denuded upper body taut in a great effort of impotent wrath. Two lictors brandish willow rods, and already the blood is trickling over the bronzed shoulders; red streaks burst forth on the torso of the mute adolescent. Karysta, kneeling down, extends her pleading hands toward Silius, content with that facile triumph.

"I'll dance," she says, "provided that he is freed."

"You love that wanderer?" sniggers the Empress.

"With all my wanderer's soul. To pay for your clemency, I'll dance. . . ."

Then, on the carpet florid with colored corollas, Karysta sketches light steps, embroidering capricious leaps with her pink sandaled feet. For the sake of her amour, in spite of the sinister prophecy, without any other care than preventing Sepeos from suffering, under the cruel eyes of Messalina, Silius and the courtiers, Karysta dances, while her unbound lover is brought to the Empress.

"Follow me, handsome adolescent; at the palace, surprises unknown to the senses with recompense you for docility to my orders. My lips will tell you more, during nights without words, than all the verses of poets."

Silius takes Karysta's two hands and proposes that she share his bed that evening. Karysta shakes her head.

"I am his fiancée," she says.

Meanwhile, Sepeos refuses the horse brought by a soldier on Messalina's order.

Furious with the Egyptian's disdain, the Empress gives the order to take Karysta away, and lets herself fall back on to her crimson cushion, after having indicated the road to Rome, all white in the vermilion-, sinople- and orange-tinted blue of the horizon. Among the cheers and the salutes, the cortege moves off, and in the distance, in the rising violet shadow of the dusk, the white form of the dainty ballerina struggles between the silver reflections of armor.

VII

The Pity of a Passer-by

SEPEOS, clamoring his despair and his maledictions, has precipitated himself among the soldiers. He is seized and gagged; at a sign from the centurion, praetorians strip him again, beat him with the flat of their swords, while spitting in his face, bruising all his quivering body, laughing at the insults and threats on his lips.

They attach him to a tree: an acacia, a cluster of whose flowers falls on his naked body. The strollers curious to watch his torture have become rarer, all having rushed off behind the cortege, in the gilded dust, toward the City.

Now Geo, kneeling down, tries to undo his bonds, despairing over his bloody wounds. Indifferent to the pain, he watches the soldiers and the chariots draw away, and the fans of lotus-leaves and peacock feathers above the moving imperial couch. All his soul escapes from his impotent and wounded being; Karysta is being taken away, a prisoner, the Tanagran whom they will force to dance, for their sensual pleasure . . . until death.

Geo laments, murmuring that she had said as much: the revolt of her son against Roman law would bring misfortune. With her trembling hands, too old and too debilitated, she cannot untie the hard cords and leather thongs that are making sinister grooves in her son's flesh, dripping blood. How can she succeed in freeing him, then? The others, the people of their tribe, being frightened, have run away, and now the night is rising toward the summits of the hills. She can already scarcely see in daylight; her eyes are worn out, by dint of reading the past and the future.

A voice beside her extracts her from her despair.

"Stand aside, woman; I'll cut the bonds that are holding the brave fellow. He's your son, I think? In any case, he's as bold as he's handsome; I was witness to his courage, even in the face of Her, the terrible divinity."

While speaking, the unknown man, whose breastplate, doublet of laced leather, cnemides and sword testified to the profession of gladiator, had already cut the ropes with his dagger.

Sepeos tore away the gag that closed his mouth; he took the hands of the passer-by and clasped them forcefully within his own.

The man said to him: "I followed Messalina, with an enjoyment she knew, the filthy and vain woman, looking at Her as if I held Her . . . and yet again, I have witnessed another futile cruelty."

Drawing away from the effusion of the mother and Sepeos' thanks, he disappeared in the direction of the cortege, toward Rome.

Idlers had witnessed the entire scene without daring to intervene. Sepeos, no longer finding his liberator, asked: "Who is that sword-bearer who freed me? Do you know him?"

"That's true," someone said, "they're not from Rome. You don't know, then, Egyptian, the celebrated Manechus, gladiator of the troop of imperial fiscals, whom the City pays to entertain the Divine Augusta?"

"He's the one who killed Merax."

"He mortally wounded the famous Greek Seinex," said someone else.

"Yes, he's been victorious in more than twenty combats, and he'd already be rich if he cared about gold and didn't squander it in artistic prodigality."

The crowd in the distance was flowing toward Rome. Dejected, Sepeos meditated, sitting by the roadside with his head in his hands.

Squatting not far away, Geos dared not speak.

VIII

A Fête on the Palatine

IN the opaline night, Silius' gardens stand out on the flanks of the Palatine in long sinuous streaks of light. Chandeliers and iridescent lanterns color the plants and flowers with improbable fiery hues. From flower-beds rise heady odors of roses and sunflowers, lilies and tuberoses, verbenas and syringas and flowers of the Orient, brought back in former days by the proconsul.

A portico looms up, the roof of which reposes on marble columns; in the nave beneath the arch, around a table ornamented by the rarest corollas of roses of all colors and forms, patricians and women are lying three by three on each crimson bed, all crowned with jasmine, orange-blossom, myrtle and more roses, leaning on their elbows, feasting, chatting merrily and laughing.

In the center of the joy, Silius and Messalina are alone, extended on the same cushion, made of soft swansdown. The lovers do not seem to be paying any heed to the presence of their guests; their faces brush one another and, from time to time, their limbs enlace and their mouths come together. On the couches of the triclinium, the others imitate the imperial example; hands stray, voluptuous and caressant, into the folds of tunics sometimes meshed with metal.

All the most depraved celebrities in Rome are there: Carvilus Marbo, the beardless ephebe, and his inseparable friend Sollius, both clad in similar soft silk mantles over white robes embroidered with golden flowers: Marcus Pollio, the old senator, between two courtesans, busy with minute and grotesque attentions with which he strives to veil his decrepitude, groomed, perfumed and painted in the fashion of aged courtiers; Avia, the daughter of a former consul, fluttering between Tullia Virginia and the aedile Mucius, a brown-haired adolescent with an Oriental gaze.

Impassive behind each of the guests, a slave moves a fan; one might think them huge flowers whose stems are human, agitated by the wind. Valerius, one of the officers of the praetorian guard and Polina, the sister of a consul, a daughter of Lejean, the prefect of the late emperor's guard, are there, pell-mell with beautiful girls unknown the day before and unknown young men that Messalina's caprice has made—for their beauty, which is an aristocracy—equal to the nobles. Slaves—bread-carriers, cup-bearers, porters of trays of silver, gold, antimony and silver-plate—come and go around the table, under the supervision of solemn freedmen, giving orders by discreet signs.

From bowls of precious metal, haloed by flowers, in which multicolored petals float, naked Africans, and statuesquely beautiful women fill the cups in the form of chalices or sculpted horns, precious crystals from Egypt or Asia, and the guests of the imperial orgy drink . . . and drink.

Words buzz like obscene and libertine moths, born of gaping lips. Sollius, in a feminine voice, relates the recent scandal of a candidate for the quaestura, who solicited votes by bribery and obtained them.

"To each one he said: 'I'll make you a present of a beautiful slave-girl, for I'm a little short of money and I no longer have time to sell her before the votes. You can give me the votes of your clients and I'll sign the bargain if you lack confidence. . . .'

"He's a honest man—he kept his promise to the three most powerful."

"Bah! Didn't he offer you exquisite carp, and the day before yesterday's debauch? The sauce was perfumed with cumin and amber. Livia had no complaint that evening of the spices born of verbena. When the wine is good, why malign the life?"

"Claudius," said Messalina, "has a right to complain about it. He stammers at the beginning of the second amphora and staggers after three. In bed, his limbs are like the tentacles of a headless squid. I wait for him to get drunk and then I send Mikalia to him; he calls her Messalina."

"Perhaps he's happier," moans Pollio. "He embraces all of his dreams, in his imagination."

Messalina parodies the gestures of the aged emperor, mimes his inertia, his whims of impotent debauchery. She explains his bizarre tastes, analyzes the ridiculousness of the old husband, his quarters of virility, his pouts, and everyone bursts out in noisy, staccato laughter. Tullia Virginia groans, saying that Avia is weighing upon her numb hand. She starts to weep because her fingers are inert. Mucius rubs the young woman's hand, soothing her with consolatory phrases. Then Avia sneezes, because of the curry powder that has been thrown into the Falernian, weeps again, and everyone laughs until they shed tears. Sollius quarrels in a low voice with Marbo, and then stares at Messalina with a drunken insistence.

But the Empress has consulted her lover, and makes a sign.

In alternate processions of white, pink, orange, sapphirine or sinople tunics, clad in transparent gauzes and golden nets dotted with rubies, with strange flowers in their hands, the beautiful girls advance, the dancing girls, with the acrobatic ephebes and the mimes. Distantly, but drawing closer every second, the chords and pizzicati of lutes, harps and citharas are audible.

Barbaric soldiers surge forth first, to the right and left of the table of the feast, drawing loud sounds from brass and silver tubae,[1] and then fade away, disappearing into the darkness of the bushes. From the awning of blue silk extended in a fan over the guests, an odorous dew rains down.

Processionally, in white robes slit along the body, letting show through the pink of flesh, young ballerinas, bearers of fragile lutes, whirl, miming the appeals of amour and tender coquetries. Together, two by two, they dance enlaced, their supple bodies and their small breasts advanced toward the guests, their lips scarlet in the cream of faces, mouths tautly arched, the mouths of temptresses.

---

1 *Tuba* is Latin for trumpet, so the "tubae" featured in the story are trumpets of a sort, not tubas of the modern kind, although Champsaur seems to distinguish them from the instruments he identifies as *trompettes*, for which I have retained the translation "trumpets."

Slowly, they sketch hieratic steps, hands raised, seeming to beg for mercy; then the rhythm accelerates, and a new dancer appears in the midst of the groups, clad in strings of pearls, which rattle and part over the graceful nudity of a body adorably tightened at the waist by a golden girdle studded with turquoises, rubies, emeralds and white pearls. The dancing girl translates, in harmonious gestures the fête of caresses that she does not know, and appeals, imploringly, to Aphrodite, of whom she appears to be hallucinating an imaginary vision; and her mouth quivers with an amorous thirst.

Squatting in a circle outside the portico, the flute-players double their efforts and the singing slaves give voice to seductive pleas; finally, an annunciatory bursts forth and all eyes are fixed on the pathway by which Karysta, the dancer from Tanagra, ought to appear, whom Messalina of whom has exalted the supreme delicacy. The ardent Silius, his eyes ablaze, watches the darkness in which the Apparition will shine.

Plaintively, at a languid pace, she approaches.

The Tanagran is naked beneath a hyacinth gauze, her brown hair scattered over shoulders brightened by gold, her long fingers ornamented with rings, a metal serpent with amethyst eyes around her neck.

Messalina encourages her, and Silius solicits from her the dances, unknown in Rome, that she must know. With a pleading gesture, Karysta begs for mercy; an invincible lassitude weighs her down.

"I will dance tomorrow . . . another day," she says, rounding her arms delightfully, "but this evening, I have I know not what softness in my wings."

The dancers have stopped, in beautiful poses. Messalina smiles, indulgently, at the last words of the Tanagran's plea, idle and picturesque, and Karysta lies down beside the Empress while the dancers leave.

Then come the gladiatresses; there are three pairs.

Two wrestle, trained for athletic games. Their bodies muscular, like supple marble, enlace, and the men, semi-excited by the attitudes, throws, and the parting of legs in mid-air during leaps, acclaim the phases of the combat, intoxicated by the odor of the women, in the reek of the orgy and the perfume of roses.

Armed uniquely with a sword and buckler, two others fight; they are robust Campanian girls, slightly masculine, whose hard rumps and breasts protrude. They make their weapons scintillate in the lamplight, as well as the faces sculpted at the summit of their bronze and silver helmets; their swords clash until one of them falls, her right breast pierced. "Like a pear," says Marcus Pollio, "in which one plants a knife." Blood flows, striping the belly of the wounded woman; she is carried away.

Two others fight with spears, and both, simultaneously spitted, are also carried away by the slaves, in agony, on a stretcher of flowers, watered by their mingled blood. Applause bursts out, and cries of pleasure.

Now, a juggler strives in vain to capture the attention of the guests, entirely devoted to discussing the circus games and the merits of celebrated gladiators. Silius' ardent eyes caress the gracile forms of the languid Tanagran at Messalina's feet. Sometimes, with her lustful hand, the Empress strokes the curls of hair on the nape of the dancer's neck, perfumed with myrrh, evocative of that youthful spring.

Branches in which the nocturnal breeze is sighing rustle softly. The sounds of the flutes are distant, and the lyres are weeping and laughing in the shadows where the musicians are hidden, when a hymn bursts forth to the glory of the Empress, sung by an invisible choir:

"You are so beautiful, with an august beauty . . . that all eyes light up at your approach. . . Imperial Venus able to guide toward you . . . universal desire.

"To swoon with ecstasy in your arms . . . enraptured with delight by the marvels of your body . . . Messalina! . . . there is no warrior, barbarian king, or secular patrician . . . who would not give all his tomorrows to have for an hour . . . your sacred embrace."

"Oh, yes, by Hercules! A sacred embrace!" says a young Gaulish soldier, a tuba player, to his companions, in the depths of the gardens. And he recounts details.

IX

Karysta dances for the Second Time

GUIDED by the intensity of the illumination, Sepeos has been able to penetrate Silius' gardens. He is hidden in the trembling foliage of a clump of myrtles.

From the encampment, where his mother Geo dressed his wounds, moaning, he has escaped through the darkness while everyone was asleep in the carts around the extinct fire. People who had stopped around the Egyptians to watch their dances and their acrobatics were chatting that afternoon; he chanced to hear them. He knew that Silius was hosting a fête in his gardens that same evening, in honor of Messalina. The words overheard filtered through his fever: "Gollio told me there would be a novelty, a dancer from Tanagra—very pretty, it appears."

For three days that he was in bed, bruised by the blows and the rods of the soldiers, and the flats of sword-blades, Sepeos lay in wait for the return of his strength, obsessed by the idea of going to Rome, of finding Karysta there, even at the price of death. "She must not dance again!" Those prophetic words harassed him. In a tormented slumber, he woke with a start, launching himself forth to prevent his beloved from whirling, in accordance with the rhythms of a light, quasi-aerial art, for the distraction of Augustans and courtesans, for Luxuria, the naked Empress.

The adolescent devours Karysta with his eyes, jealousy biting him at seeing her sumptuously dressed next to Messalina, amid the desires of Silius and others. At other times, indifferently, he has watched her dance almost devoid of clothing, and it did not wound him, but there is now an ardent burning in his breast as he contemplates her, prey to that bisexual concupiscence. Before, she was the anonymous and graceful dancing girl, admired by passers-by solely for the suppleness of her gestures, and that was all. This evening, Karysta is a slave of pleasure, the objective of ennui and lust, a captive virgin at the mercy of those voices.

Not for an instant do Sepeos' eyes abandon the motionless Karysta, lying next to Messalina, who, fatigued with being horizontal, stands up, laughing, drawing up over her breasts the loosened tunic that molds them, and quits the triclinium.

As soon as he has seen the imperial shadow disappear around a bend in a path, Silius takes the fearful hands of Karysta, who dares not flee. The other guests continue drinking; slaves renew the crowns; they put into golden and silver bowls the frothy wines of Sicily and the thick Falerinian, the fizzing foam of Campanian vines and the golden nectar of Attica.

"Karysta, the goddesses and nymphs of your homeland do not surpass your seduction, little Tanagran! Listen to me: I'm not a hard master, and I love you. As soon as I saw you, slender dancer, by the side of the road, your amethyst eyes captured my heart. Would you like to adorn my bed this evening? Around the marmoreal colonnette of your neck, like an ex-voto of amour, I want to suspend precious stones. You shall be more ornamented than the goddesses of temples, by the gratitude of a master of the world for his mistress. . . ."

Karysta makes a slight negative movement of her head; energetic and timid at the same time, she draws her quivering body away, frightened by the male's approach, striving to extract her hand from the hands of Silius, who is leaning over her, his eyes and his lips gleaming, enlivened by desire for her young flesh.

"What dread is making you shiver?" Silius continues, laughing. "Karysta, don't be harsh toward me, who adores you and is imploring you. You will be mine, and I will make you rich, richer than Livia, who is so proud of her necklaces and bracelets, more powerful than a matron, for I shall give you numerous slaves.

Tonight, when the lamps flicker and they will all be gone"—he indicates the guests—"I will carry you away in my arms and cover your pink and white flesh with kisses . . . and your corolla, O Flower."

With rapid hands, Silius tries to vanquish Karysta, but she moves away swiftly, and with an effort, tears herself away from the gripping gestures. She flees along the pathways of the garden, terrified, like a hunted hind; she bounds away, disappearing behind the trees; between the black trunks, at intervals, her robe flutters, like the wings of a dragonfly in which reflections play.

Sepeos has followed the scene. He is about to launch himself forth, to catch up with Karysta in the meandering pathways, to reconquer his promised bride, the Tanagran, when two perfumed hands are knotted about his neck; a body molds itself against his breast, and lips close his mouth with a firebrand of flesh.

Tottering at first, he exclaims, after a cry; "Messalina!"

"Yes, me . . . the Empress. I recognized you, Egyptian. I know your name: Sepeos. I like to know the names of handsome men with fiery eyes. I left the feast to be alone for a while; I was yawning at the stupid things that those drunken pigs, my guests, were saying. And suddenly, I saw you! You did well to come, handsome boy. I noticed you immediately, the other day, and since then, I have thought several times about your brown adolescent beauty . . . . I'm glad! Come . . . you must be a good lover! I have a great desire for you . . . yes, a great desire. . . ."

Coldly, Sepeos looks into Messalina's eyes. He sketches a recoil, and a gesture.

"Don't say anything to forbid yourself my love. What does your rank matter to me? Whoever you are, you're beautiful, your eyes are amber and jet, your lips crimson coral . . . your body is a palpitating bronze Apollo. You're strong! I want to swoon in your arms, Sepeos, gasp in your embrace. . . . I'll give you a palace—or, rather, no . . . you'll remain with me, and charm the idle hours of my existence. . . . One sometimes gets tired of being the sovereign of everyone and everything, often devoid of desire. . . . And now I desire you, my dear, because . . . I'm intoxicated merely by repeating it . . . you must be a very good lover. . . ."

Stammering and imperious by turns, Messalina rubs her nipples on Sepeos breast; she holds him by the neck, and seeks his mouth.

"I'll be yours, this evening! Are you not glad? Thank your gods, Egyptian, for sending you such good fortune. Have you ever dreamed of its like, during the nights of wandering?"

Seductively, the Empress strokes him, envelops him with caresses; but he slowly draws away.

"I only came to fetch my fiancée, Karysta."

"Imbecile!" sniggers Messalina. "She's in love with another!"

Grimly, Sepeos says: "Don't lie, Empress; don't try to torture me by slandering my fiancée. I'm as sure of Karysta as I am of myself."

Without replying, Messalina tempts him with the effluvia of her lascivious eyes; she makes him a necklace of her white arms, on which the glitter of bracelets illuminated by rubies and turquoises, chalcedonies and topazes, emeralds, amethysts sapphires and diamonds. And again, the Imperial mouth seeks the lips of the insensible Egyptian, who pushes her back, and takes his face away, freeing himself from the lustful hands.

Fury at the scorn of a man of vile race suddenly fills Messalina's heart; no one has ever dared to refuse himself to her caprice; the greatest swell with pride at the slightest favor from her. Suffocated, she examines the man audacious enough to want to escape her desire.

"The animals in the circus will feast on your flesh, or I'll have you crucified like a slave! Lashes first, and rods, will lacerate the bronze of your body! Brute! You refuse my kisses! Would you prefer tortures, then? I have Asiatic slaves who know how to extract a thousand screams of pain before permitting someone to die."

Mutely, she watches Sepeos' face for the effect of her threats—but the Egyptian's eyes, his ears and his entire being are attentive to the sounds and gleams of the feast; he is afraid of seeing Karysta brought back to Silius, dreads hearing the beloved voice reciting the songs of the nomadic Roma for the erotic senator.

Wrathful, Messalina continues breathlessly, with a malevolent laugh: "Listen—it would be too much happiness for you, vile wanderer, to perish with faith in your love in your heart, and it would be stupid. Karysta the Tanagran is your fiancée? You love her, you say? And she loves you? Well, this evening, she'll be lying in the arms of another; I'll give her to Silius—I'll give her to him, you hear! She'll belong to him this evening, because that is my will, my vengeance."

She stands still momentarily, palpitating, facing Sepeos, whose eyes are rutilant in the night. The sound of flutes proclaims the rut of fauns and the fear of nymphs; lutes incite amour and harps implore, not far away; in the illuminated portico, the invisible flowers embalm the air, and Luxuria continues:

"Reflect. . . . When the feast ends, come back to hide here, where I begged for your kiss. From this flower-bed, among the flowers, you shall see them . . . Karysta enlaced by Silius. And you'll no longer doubt, and you'll be mine, beautiful boy. . . ."

"I'll kill her!" mutters Sepeos.

"No," exclaims Messalina, radiant at the idea of her victory, "you won't kill! My kisses are magical philters that can cure the worst wounds of amour. You'll inundate me with voluptuousness, and I'll be enraptured by your ecstasy. I like people to be happy, and this everything, everyone around me should be beautiful. Oh, how I desire you! Long live beauty!"

Messalina goes toward the portico, from which the voices of the guests are escaping in joyful rumor.

Sepeos plunges back into the foliage with heavy tread, crushed by the weight of doubt, entered into his heart like an invisible thorn into the finger of a child picking roses.

Cries and applause welcome Luxuria on her return. Silius, standing up, has come back a few minutes before her, laughing, and holding Karysta by the hand, whom he had been able to overtake and bring back. He takes his place again beside the Empress, and flowers fly from the hands of young men and beautiful girls toward the sovereign lovers. Messalina orders new wines to be poured into cups of onyx and marble. Insensate wagers are laid. Pollio invites the golden blonde Avia to follies. She dips the strawberries of her breasts, in turn, into a bowl of Chios wine, from which the liquid gold drips; the senator empties the bowl and then, drunk, remains immobile, mute, widens his eyes and babbles.

Again, dancers come forth, They are dressed in tunics like flowers; multicolored, they whirls around mimes with the bodies of statues, who make the gestures of picking them and kissing them, while the lutes whisper and the viols implore, and suddenly accelerate in a crescendo of sensuality.

The naked dancers have wings of gauze and iridescent silk; butterflies, they come to chase and plunder the red, white and saffron-tinted roses, roses of flesh and crimson-fringed white carnation, on to which droplets of the blood of doves have rained down. Bacchantes then surge forth, spinning, pursued by fauns who carry them away, laughing, and lay them down in the flowers.

But everyone is bored by these banal customary dances, and desires the gracile flexibility of the Tanagran, the pepper and pimento of dances that they do not know as yet.

"Karysta . . . ! Karysta . . . ! Karysta . . . ! Augusta Messalina, tell her that we want to applaud her. . . ."

Instead of giving orders, Messalina begs the frail dancer with flattering politeness. She says to her: "It's to offend the gods to remain sad during the libations, and Venus will punish you, Tanagran, for carelessness of her worship. Dance for the enchantment of our eyes, for our distraction, and we'll adorn you with the most dazzling jewels, for you are henceforth the most cherished of our ballerinas. Dance as the gods of your homeland danced in the valleys of Hellas."

Now, while the other dancers, living flowers, come to a halt, exhausted, Karysta smiles a melancholy smile. She has remained a heartbroken spectator of the feast. Will she ever see Sepeos, her fiancé, again? Old Geo, in spite of her fatal prediction? And her Egyptian comrades? Why not dance, then, in order to die sooner, among the splendors that imprison her and weigh upon her?

All those thoughts darken her nostalgic gaze, and the gaiety round her aggravates her sadness.

Karysta dances . . . madly.

Madly, she has launched herself forward, raising her robe of violet gauze, spangled with gold, silver and precious stones, with both hands. One might think her a dragonfly with the body of a woman. She leaps, and it seems that she takes flight, so light is the saltation of her frail white limbs, scarcely gilded with the gold of grapes brightened by sunlight.

Beneath the light of torches and lamps, she flutters and whirls, a flower of flesh, of light, of gemstones . . . and of youth.

More slowly, she garlands rhythmic steps in which her entire body offers itself, an artistic callipygian liana, only to escape, with a modest gesture, a sudden imaginary embrace, in a game alternately provocative and chaste. Sometimes, the slender and marvelously modeled body of the dainty ballerina half-retreats beneath the transparency of the robe, and then blossoms again, vertiginously beating wings iridescent with reflections.

Karysta the Tanagran—flower, woman, flame, joy, dolor, amour, gem, butterfly, enchantress—dances madly, bewildered by the sad intoxication of her soul.

X

The Deceptive Appearance

THIN and ragged, old Geo's sinister silhouette looms up in the midst of the slender and richly-ornamented dancers. In her pauper's garments, with her brown hands and crooked fingers, with her wrinkled face like desiccated apples, beneath the pitiful tangle of her sparse, dirty white hair, the Egyptian woman resembles, momentarily, a blind bat fallen in broad daylight into the midst of a flock of little birds.

"Oh! Karysta, don't dance any more! It's death that's lying in ambush for you. The oracle has said that you will dance three times, and sleep forever. . . ."

The chords of the flutes, viols and lyres are broken; cries of stupor have greeted the ill omen of the apparition. Abruptly, all the dances are interrupted.

Karysta remains motionless, breathless from the precipitation of her steps, when she was whirling to stun her chagrin, amid the flowers and the harmony of the music, in the glare of the orgy.

Geo had watched over Sepeos during the dolorous nights, and that evening, when he was calmer, she had fallen asleep, sure that her beloved son, wounded by his love, the soldier's rods and the flat of heavy swords, would recover.

But her slumber, tormented by dreams, had been disturbed by footfalls; in the moonlight, she had recognized Sepeos fleeing the camp. She had followed him, taking infinite precautions not to give herself away.

He had hastened toward the City, signaled in the darkness by its gleam. She saw him penetrate into Silius' gardens, staged on the slopes of the Palatine Hill. Trembling, she had spotted the silhouette of the future chief of the Roma through the shadows of the bushes, but she had lost sight of him momentarily, and had collapsed, exhausted by the long journey and the rude climb.

When she had reached the location of the feast, Karysta was dancing, and one sole sentiment had gripped her: the unspeakable fear that her son might die if, for having danced and pleased three times, the little dancer from Tanagra died.

The guests, at first, are a little frightened by that apparition of a sorceress—some demon, they think, in their drunkenness. Several of them make the sign of the cornuta, and laugh, Messalina more loudly than anyone; Pollio blows a mocking kiss to Geo; Sollius and his friend, disdainful of the incident, stare at one another tenderly, without saying a word.

Meanwhile, the decrepit Egyptian woman has placed her hands, like the claws of a night-bird, on Karysta's shoulders.

"Come! Come quickly, child, if you don't want to die. Not one more time, you know it . . . the gods have spoken. Come!"

But the impetuous sovereign leaps from the crimson bed where her arrogant beauty is displayed; standing before the sorceress and the dancer, after a mocking burst of laughter, she says: "What, old woman! You want to take away my favorite, the ballerina I have chosen, among all the Greek, Roman and Oriental dancers? Are you insane, then? Go! No one will do you any harm, but Karysta belongs to me; she pleases me, and I shall keep her. No one leaves without my permission."

A murmur of approval salutes the words of the Empress, and remarks spring from groups of guests.

"You are as beautiful as merciful, divine Augusta Messalina."

"The old crone is obviously a madwoman, whom the guards did not see coming in."

"The soldiers must be drunk."

"What will become of the Empire?" moans the austere Pollio, whose tongue is thick, "if such misdeeds remain unpunished?"

Sepeos has launched himself forth from the bushes where he was hiding. He throws himself at the knees of the Empress, extending supplicant hands toward her. At the sound of raised voices, guards have come running, a praetorian centurion at their head.

"Throw this fanatic out of the gardens," Messalina orders. "She's howling—quickly, drag her away by force. As for this Egyptian, tie his wrists securely behind his back, and let him wander as he will through the pathways."

While the soldiers gather around Sepeos, hastening to bind his arms of bronze, an ardor, stimulated by the man's refusal, troubles the sovereign. When the soldiers have finished, Messalina advances toward the handsome captive and whispers in his ear: "This very spot, within an hour—wait and watch. . . ."

Then everyone, amphitryons and guests alike, return to the beds; under the illuminated portico, the feast resumes, more licentiously. A thousand exuberant speeches overlap; even philosophy is prostituted in the mouths of the drinkers.

Messalina extols the art of pleasure.

"I like to be loved and I like everyone around me to love one another. I seek Beauty everywhere, always, and I wish, for my friends and myself, to gather together, palpable and enjoyable, all the beauties of the universe. Gourmand lips and flavorsome fruits, splendid corollas, rigid stems, flesh and gems, flamboyant eyes—they are feasts, bouquets of pleasures. The task of wisdom is to collect, for their own sake, in an ideal sheaf, the most frequently renewed of sensualities, of delicate leisures, of ardors . . . in sum, of all the unexpected adornments that the worst of realities might have."

"Neither the most intoxicated nor the most sober of rhetors could not have put it better," Silius applauds, negligently. "See, Karysta is looking at us and seems not to understand your counsel of intense life. Delightfully youthful and pretty, however, she comes from the homeland of the blonde and immortal Helen, with whom men, since she caused the ruin of Troy, have always been somewhat infatuated."

"You hear, child? Thank the senator for the compliment. Oh," she says, laughing, "there's only one fashion of thanking a man when one is a pretty girl. Have no fear, I'm not jealous; offer him your lips, which are like ripe strawberries."

Luxuria makes the child lie down between herself and her lover, pushes her gently toward him, and looks at them with indulgent eyes. But as heavy tears form in Karysta's eyes, which fall on to the white roses that are passed through the clasps of Silius' robe, Messalina, furious, drives her away.

"Go away! Go up to the room in the palace that has been designated for you. I don't want to see sadness here. It's because of you, and in order not to cause anyone chagrin"—she points at Silius, whose eyes are pleading for mercy for her—"that I disdain to have you punished."

At a signal, the patricians launch themselves toward the musiciennes and the dancing girls, who are twirling again, living flowers, as if buoyed up by the singing wind. All of them, with the laughter of pursued faunesses, run away nimbly, and through the pathways and the flower-beds their tunics of silk and gauze fly, with the sparkle of precious stones.

Soon, however, the reflections of necklaces and the deployment of silken wings sink down beneath the branches. Enlaced couples, beneath the trees, scarcely patch the darkness. Sighs rise up in the mystery in which the lutes and viols have fallen silent. Dancers, mimes and musiciennes are flowers fallen in the flower-beds, picked by the invited fauns. Messalina, finally excited by all the scattered spectacles of that gallant enchantment, presses herself against Silius; tenderly, she has knotted her arms around his neck, then, seductively, settles the crimson butterfly of her mouth on his eyes and on his lips.

"Oh, my dear love, never, I think, has my flesh desired yours as it does this evening. Never has such a thirst made me desire its caresses. Silius, in the fever of this man spring, and entire renewal of love is reflowering in me."

"My divine Messalina, we love one another; we have many beautiful hours to live in one another. But like you, I am transported tonight; kisses sing within me, rising toward you, and I dream that you are infinitely mine beneath these trees in flower . . . . Immediately, you desire?"

Silius embraces Messalina, but the Empress slips away, laughing, from his disappointed arms.

"Wait for me, my love, for a few minutes, and you'll be even happier than you dream. . . . A surprise . . ."

Luxuria moves away, running, through the arbors where artificial gems of light tremble on the branches. Breathless with stupor, deliciously tormented by divining the promise of his perverse lover, Silius stretches himself out on the crimson cushions where detached petals and crushed corollas are strewn.

Silius meditates. By turns, and then confounded, Karysta and Messalina whirl before his eyes—his crazed, drunken eyes— both troubling, and so different. The Empress is a perfume that always reawakens him, and attraction of the skin, the memory of unforgettable hours of contact, fantasy and lust. The dancer from Tanagra is the feverish appeal and exquisite approach of a supreme and unknown caress, ardently summoned.

Now the lyres of the invisible musiciennes begin to sing again, the harps, the viols, the citharas and the flutes; the instruments play in a distant harmony; a choir of fresh voices celebrates youth and pleasure. Slaves come to extinguish the lamps, and over the orgy, now silent, in the nacreous night, at the zenith, among the nymphean troops of stars, the diadem shines of Diana, Astarte, vesperal Venus and blonde Helen, haloed with silver.

Sepeos, whose feet are sliding rather than walking, silently approaches the bed where Silius remains plunged in the voluptuousness of his dream. He hides behind one of the pillars of the portico, then, immobile, breathless with anger and expectation, he watches for the coming of the other—who? Messalina? Karysta?—calculating his imminent dolor, ruminating impossible vengeance.

The chorus expires on a languid strophe of amour. The musiciennes' melodies fall silent. From the palace, whose monumental silhouette is blurred in the darkness, a woman emerges, dressed like Karysta, the Tanagran ballerina. It is Messalina who comes forward, matching her steps to the rhythm of the prelude of the golden lyre she is holding.

Within the soft pleats of a violet gauze, constellated with gilded gems, a young and splendid body, marmoreal in the twinkling starlight, appears, sometimes raising up, at the whim of the rhythm, the flaps of the tunic split over the hips.

Now she sings, softly, in a voice like Karysta's, a passionate introit:

"Among the golden vines with green leaves . . . there are flavorsome grapes that the sun has ripened . . . beneath my veils, fruits await loving lips . . . even more tempting, more delicate, more perfumed . . . than the grapes of Crete, or the golden fruits of Hellas.

"Who shall cut the fruits and make the supreme vintage . . . ? You, is it not? You, the strong and handsome vintner whose blade I await amorously. . . . The grape-gatherer blesses the vine . . . but soon scarred over, in a new season . . . she has other grapes, heavy and ripe, for new mouths.

"Extend your lips to my lips . . . your fingers imprison my breasts . . . see, my beloved, they are also similar to doves. . . . raising their crimson beaks for kisses . . . in the bright mornings . . . the blue dawns, of silver, crimson and gold . . . the aurorae that drink the dew.

"Kisses, fluttering butterflies . . . you make me hungry for more profound embraces . . . tear away my veils to hasten sooner . . . and when I am naked, clothe me with caresses. . . ! Let me be no longer cold at heart . . . in my arms, my mouth, and everywhere . . . where I am brown and I am beautiful."

Messalina has come all the way to Silius—and her lover, mad for her, seizes her. Enlaced, they intoxicate themselves with one another, in a frenzy, in which the illusory genius of the false dancer seems to exalt.

Oh, the impetus, the bound of the captive Sepeos toward them! He has surged forth from the shadow of the portico and stands facing the enraptured lovers, amid the emotion of dying roses.

Frantically, he twists his impotent bound hands, and the veins of his half-naked body swell with the futile and supreme effort that he makes to break his bonds. Silius has scarcely turned round, flagellating him with mockery, and he embraces Karysta ardently, careless of the wrathful writhing of the bound barbarian.

Then Sepeos, standing facing them, burning with wrath, no longer capable of reflection, no longer observing, duped by the darkness of that adventure and that night, scourges the lovers with insults.

"Karysta! Prostitute! Viler than the sluts of Suburra! Liar! You promised me the flower of your spring, and you know the art of a common whore. . . . You will fall tomorrow, with slaves, into the ordure of the lowest complaisances that a Roman consul, today, is paying you. Oh, the man that is buying you, powerful, who knows nothing but the orgy, I shall emasculate with my own hands! In this city of filth, Rome, that it is necessary to burn, the patricians are the opprobrium of the world, sacrilegious pimps and thieves. Oh, gluttons of every feast, the day will come when the others, the petty will want to be invited in their turn. They will cast your whores from their beds, including the greatest of all, the naked Empress; they will lacerate your shoulders, breast and face; they will mark your forehead, Silius! And I, be certain of it, will castrate you! As for you, apes and pigs will feed on your flesh, soiled Tangran!"

His anger pouring out, the Egyptian rushes the obscene group. "I'll separate you, at least, with my kicks, like dogs!"

Messalina, in the dancing girl's slit tunic, and coiffed like Karysta, ornamented by her jewels, runs away at that threat, hiding her face with one hand, for the sake of prudence, while sketching a mocking gesture with the other addressed to the shackled Bohemian. Anxiously, Sepeos follows that flight with his eyes, until the slender silhouette disappears at the threshold of the palace.

Silius bangs a gong to summon his lictors and the praetorians of his guard. Sitting up on the bed, while the torches of soldiers are already shining in the depths of a path, draped in his toga embroidered with a crimson stripe, he points at Sepeos, who, with the intelligence of a deceived bull, is vomiting drool.

"Take that man away, and have him whipped with rods. Then, shut him up in the ergastule. I want him delivered to the beasts in the circus games, offered by me to the people of Rome, for the kalends of August, in honor of Messalina. I have spoken."

XI

Karysta Dances for the Third Time

CRIES and appeals overlap in the hubbub of the Roman crowd, amassed along the steps of the immense amphitheater, along with greetings and wishes of good omen. From the Forum, the multitude plunges incessantly beneath the arches of the Circus; the knights and the plebeians swarming and noisy on the holiday, surge from the vomitoria and spread out on the steps. Men and women, pell-mell, bump into one another and jostle one another in order to reach the most sought-after ranks of stone, facing the entrance to the arena, though which the wild beasts and gladiators will come to do battle. Quarrels break out; citizens, arrived the day before or during the night from neighboring towns, have taken possession of the first steps as soon as the doors opened, from which the newcomers want to dislodge them. The supervisors charged by the aediles to maintain good order intervene, indicating to the spectators the places they have to occupy, without paying any heed to the gibes raining down on them from the upper galleries where the slaves are crowded.

The sunlight pierces the blue awning suspended above the steps and the arena. Its rays play over faces illuminated by the morning's libations, over-excited by the expectation of the grandiose and bloody spectacle. The sand of the arena, speckled with minuscule stars, is pink in the filtered light; and the podium, where the sovereigns, the vestals, the senators and the priests are coming to sit down on the crimson of cushions, is a mixture of violet, gold and red: a bloody violet, in which the gleam of braid lights up in metallic reflections.

A rumor still rises from the plebeian masses in the Forum, held back by the soldiers; acclamations salute the popular patricians as they pass by. Merchants of beverages and fruits hawk their goods. The circus is full from top to bottom; in the gigantic enclosure there is a swell of shaven or exaggeratedly hairy heads, and flashes glitter in impatient eyes.

The noisy crowd relates the splendor of previous combats offered for the advent of Claudius; the glory of gladiators is discussed; people criticize or praise the fashion of striking of men of various lands; names take on an emphasis of admiration as they pass from mouth to mouth, the beloved names of those who have never been defeated. Young women make themselves more gracious and smiling in order to obtain better places; lovers squeeze against one another, and children astride the shoulders of men laugh. Little girls nibble fruits, and the juice of oranges and watermelons stripes their puerile faces. All eyes seek to distinguish the podium, as well as the silhouettes of the fighters between the bars of the gates. Sometimes the roaring of lions or tigers mingles with the tumult of human voices—the raucous voices of wild beasts, imprisoned and starved.

A formidable clamor suddenly fills the circus; Messalina, among fan-bearers raising screens of plumes, and Silius appear. Claudius, the Emperor cuckolded twenty thousand times—for Messalina's lovers, it is said, would fill a seventh of the circus— feeling ill, has remained in the imperial palace.

"Long live Augusta Messalina!" cry the crowd.

"Long live Silius, *Consul Amatucus!*"

Thus Rome applauds the patrician lovers, in transports of joy for the games that are offered to them.

The precious cushions and sumptuous harmonies of the podium are disappearing now under the white of togas, stolae and carbasi, and the robes of the vestals. The people salute each new arrival, the magistrates, the courtiers and the patriciennes. Sometimes, strident whistles ring out at the entrance of some tyrannical aedile, or a quaestor, for example, suspected of enriching himself on the wheat destined for the plebeian, or a patrician detested for his arrogance in former or current functions.

White silhouettes are strung out between the colonnades of the first step; they are the dancers and musiciennes of the Empress, among them Karysta, crowned with myrtle. They throw flowers in homage to Messalina, extended on her bright crimson pulvinar, whose parted silk palla allows the perception of the figure circled with gold, a necklace of emerald and rubies streaming over her breasts, with a mesh of gold in which diamonds scintillate. Around Messalina and her lover, the musciennes are squatting; the Empress keeps Karysta, the Tanagran, at her feet, occasionally stroking the forehead and hair of the slender dancer with a familiar hand.

Silius is convinced that he possessed the young woman the other evening, after the feast in his gardens; Messalina has not undeceived him; he found an imaginary savor of novelty on the lips and in the caresses of his imperial mistress, to which his mind alone gave birth. Now, the consul is blasé from the first; a corolla looted no longer tempts him. However, the gratitude of his flesh dictates a merciful thought to him.

The fanfares of the buccinas have finished celebrating the entrance of the Empress and the consul. In the arena, a black bull is at odds with a Numidian panther, but the contest, a mere prelude to moving slaughter, scarcely amuses the public impatient for the imminent emotion. Distracted, Messalina pays no heed to the acclamations that resound from everywhere to her glory and her beauty. She listens to Silius, remaining, while smiling, the Enigma, divine and superhuman in power and sensuality.

"You're too beautiful not to be accessible to what I want to say to you, divine Messalina, my adored mistress. . . ."

"What do you want, Silius?"

"Just now, before the games, I went to see those who are going to fight. Sepeos is one of them; he knows how to handle a sword like the best of our centurions, and throws a javelin into the dead center of a target. Would it not be amusing to make love—pardon me, to enable love—by returning to Karysta her magnificent and stupid fiancé?"

Roars rise up from the arena; ten mountain bears are at grips with ten lions. Projectiles fall from the steps—fruit-stones and peels, little stones, apples and oranges, whose rain inflames the anger of the beasts. And the people laugh, applauding the phases of the battle. An orchestra of tubae, trumpets and shrill flutes accompanies the rumor of a hundred thousand exultant voices.

Without making any reply to Silius, Messalina leans toward Karysta and says to her: "Tanagran, I want you and your people to bless my name. Do you know what happiness is going to be given to them, little grace?" Laughing ironically at the false delight she is causing, Luxuria continues: "You're weeping for Sepeos, your future husband. You're going to see him again. You'll be set free, both of you, and no obstacle will any longer separate your united mouths and exquisitely joined hands. It's me, Messalina, who wants to put you in one another's arms. And it's him"—she indicates Silius—"whose solicits it for both of you, in memory of the kisses he collected from your lips. . . ."

"Without listening to the conclusion, the Tanagran throws herself at the feet of the Empress, kisses her tapering fingers effusively, expressing her infinite gratitude in a precipitate flood of words.

"I knew, goddess, that you were as good as you are beautiful. If you had suffered Karysta's suffering . . . she would be dead without your clemency, O Messalina!"

"If you were ugly and the sight of you had not delighted my eyes, I would have cared little about making you cry," says Luxuria, nonchalantly, and then, pointing at the consul again: "It's the recompense for the caresses you lavished on my lover."

The dancer, who does not understand the allusion and is unaware of the other night's comedy, turns to Silius and bows, with words of gratitude.

"Exquisite ballerina, this morning, in memory of the honey of the Greek tongue, I had the generous idea of setting free the savage who pleases you. Oh, little Tanagran dancer, I shall not soon forget your minuscule mouth."

"What do you mean, Lord?"

"I would have thought you as inexpert and maladroit as the vestals of old, ignorant of the art of the kiss, raised in the temple . . . but the sun of Hellas pours science into the heart of its nymphs. You were troubling, child, and you were naked under a light veil, and every one of your gestures excited desire in me. And you were better than naked under the violet gauze, and as if the touch of a mist of amour prowled in each of the folds of your split tunic."

Karysta does not grasp the meaning of those words. *Perhaps,* the young virgin says to herself, *Silius emptied too many cups during the sacrifices of the kalends . . . or it's a game in which he wants to catch me.* And she smiles innocently, with the indulgent amused mockery in her eyes, like that of children who see some joyful staggering drunkard pass by, singing out of key and laughing like a faun on the day of the grape-harvest.

An indescribable joy swells in her breast. She is going to see Sepeos again, her adored lover; nothing else in the world will be important to her, from the moment they have found one another again. He will doubtless take her away to the Campanian mountains; they will live there, careless of everything except their love. They will live the life of shepherds. Kisses and words of which they will never weary will fill the charm of the hours.

Carried away by her idyllic dream, Karysta does not retain any rancor for her suffering. She does not hear the roaring of the ferocious beasts, nor the rolling of chariots, nor the cries of the drivers, nor the sound of the impacts as the vehicles break, nor the sonorous crack of whips, nor the bells that give the signals, nor the proclamations of the heralds. Confusedly, the enormous rumor of the crowd orchestrates the joy that is singing within her.

"Will he come soon, my beloved?" she asks, with a sudden audacity, raising her dainty hands, two pink lotuses, toward Messalina in an offering, such as her priestesses present to Venus.

"In a moment," says Silius—and he orders a centurion to go in quest of Sepeos in the subterrain where he is waiting among the condemned.

After the races, an interval is announced for the preparation of the human combats. Then, between the praetorians, whose weapons and shields are shining, upright and proud in front of Messalina and the consul, Sepeos climbs the steps of the podium.

He is naked save for a short red campestre, held around his loins by a metallic belt, sandals and a helmet, with iron bracelets on his wrists. While he marches between the soldiers—his hands bound, as is done to the condemned before they are given weapons—he pretends not to see Karysta. She, her eyes ardent, her body leaning forward, her face illuminated by the joy of seeing her lover again, watches him come, and her heart leaps in her breast, uplifted by a jerky movement of her small, firm breasts beneath her white tunic.

She launches herself toward him—but Sepeos shoves her away scornfully, and, indicating Silius, says: "Am I a slave, to take the residue of his caresses?" And he hurls an insult at her: the vulgar name of courtesans whose concha is fodder for slaves and low freedmen in the crapulous hovels of Suburra.

What crime has she committed, Karysta wonders, anxiously, ignorant of the calumny that has soiled her, of the pretence that has deceived the jealous lover. What is his grievance? She fills him with horror; he hates her. All of her ingenuous being declares astonishment.

"Oh, Sepeos, what demon has taken possession of your heart, to render your soul insensate?" demands the slender Tanagran. "What have I done?"

And tears pearl at the corners of her eyelids, blue-tinted with antimony, rolling down her cheeks and into the furrow of her breasts, over which the loose tunic has slipped.

Sepeos points at Silius. "Ask this ruffian for further kisses, for the evening of my death—this evening."

"Oh, but you're mad, my beloved; never has a single one of my thoughts been of anyone but you."

The Tanagran lets her chagrin melt into an explosion of sobs. Sepeos has seen on the lips of the mute consul, twisted in an ironic smile, the confirmation—unnecessary in any case, after the testimony of his eyes—of his ineluctable and dolorous bitterness.

"You are unworthy, Karysta, and I am glad to die."

"Die?" questions Karysta, stupefied and terrified. "But why, Sepeos? Why? What misfortune unknown to me has struck us? Oh, my lover, my husband, why die?"

Silius straightens up. "Because he is still affronting me," he growls. "The beasts will tear him apart."

"O Messalina! O goddess!" cries Karysta, precipitating herself at the knees of the Empress, immutable in her smiling beauty. "Is he culpable toward you, toward your lover, to such an extent that I cannot merit his mercy? Goddesses are powerful, but even less than the adored, and you are a sovereign, a woman and a lover. Be clement, august Empress, to love, by virtue of which you reign!"

Weeping, all the lines of her delicate and supple body extended toward Messalina, Karysta the Tanagran implores with all her youthful grace, as beautiful as a nymph of Hellas. The Magnificent seems to allow herself to yield, and, kissing the forehead of the dancer, whom she draws toward her, says:

"I don't want, little beauty, such an exquisite child to weep. I want to spare her tears—but Sepeos has insulted Silius, a consul and my lover. Would you like to redeem his failure, to pay his debt?"

"Oh! All my will, all the blood in my veins are yours—for him."

"Well, then, dance, Karysta, dance the steps of Egypt and twirl, in the fashion of the Orient, the Hellenic fashion. Dance, and you shall both be free, free to go wherever you please, free to love one another in life, until death . . . and death, henceforth, is far from your adolescence!"

"Oh, with all my heart, yes, I will dance! But have his bruised hands untied, O divine Messalina, in order that the dolor of seeing him suffer will not prevent my dance being light and sweet."

Messalina gives the order to the soldiers, with a sign, to untie Sepeos' hands. Impassive, the Egyptian allows the praetorians to undo the metal-tressed cords.

Then Karysta, for the third time, dances.

On the carpet, between the crimson cushions where the players of flutes and golden lyres, at first to a slow melody, the rhythm of which is gradually enlivened, emboldened an impassioned, she dances.

The Tanagran lifts up her veils, envelops herself with them and draws them apart, seeming a marvelously white butterfly, circled, in the middle of her body, by a ring of gem-studded gold; then, a dragonfly with long wings, she seems to flutter over flowers.

Karysta whirls and delights. Her lips, flamboyant with carmine in the mat pallor of her face, and her breasts surge forth from the whiteness of her transparent veils, rosy with the reflection of her delicately-outlined body.

A murmur of pleasure runs through the crowd, in spite of the impatience for the gladiatorial combats expected as soon as the second part of the spectacle begins. Everyone acclaims Karysta; thousands of eyes caress her. Some have recognized her, and soon a nickname runs from step to step, repeated with admiration: the Tanagran.

XII

The Prediction is Accomplished

SEPEOS, astonished at first, has raised his arms of bronze and stretched his wounded fingers, his hands weary of being captive.

With a gesture as prompt as lightning, however, the Egyptian seizes a soldier's sword, and strikes Karysta, who, her arms raised for a second, causes her beasts to undulate like flowers on the motionless stem of her body. A slight cry, and she collapses, in a white heap, from which a crimson poppy erupts, palpitating with the struggle of life, amour and death.

In a supreme effort, toward Sepeos, who has dropped the sword, the amorous child extends her arms again, borne, in spite of the suffering, and the imminent eternal night, to her beloved. Sepeos contemplates her, hesitantly, still with a somewhat grim expression, but moved nevertheless by a pity that rises to his throat and which he can no longer suppress.

Messalina leans over, then, toward the stupefied Egyptian, led astray by all these aristocratic games, and, pointing at the thin body, quivering like a butterfly broken by childish hands, says, with her immutable smiling irony: "You can love her, Sepeos. Kiss her forehead, kiss her lips. Hurry, beautiful boy . . . before she expires. It was me you, great fool, that you saw in Silius' arms."

Piously kneeling down, his dry eyes burning with fever, the dolorous and murderous lover kisses the little dead dancer.

"Adieu, Karysta," he said. "Forgive me."

And suddenly, that superb male sobs.

BOOK TWO

Ancilla Domini[1]

---

1 i.e., The Handmaiden of the Lord.

I

The Salute of the Doomed

AT a signal from the gong and the bell, Sepeos is returned to the hands of the soldiers, who escort him, unbound, to the subterrain where the gladiators are preparing for combat.

From the grille, suddenly agape like a profound black maw, the armed men emerge in groups and file forward.

There are Thracians and Macedonians, clad in the hides of bears and oxen, whose muzzles crown their heads; Gauls with bare torsos, with trousers striped with blue, white and red, and long blond, gilded or russet moustaches; then Numidians and Parthians in multicolored costumes, and naked negroes with bodies of bronze and ebony; even saffron Seres armed with lances in the form of flowers. Slaves armed in the Roman fashion strike bucklers of bronze, silver and steel with their angular swords. Latins too, plebeians, old soldiers accustomed to battle, come into the arena.

All of them advance, while fanfares burst forth from buccinas, tubas, raucous serpents and curved horns, to the center of the circus. Upright and splendid, in his demi-cuirasse over his bare torso, Sepeos, his eyes fulgurant, marches at the head of a decade.

A hundred and fifty gladiators, rhythming their footfalls to the cadence of sistrums, cymbals and trumpets, file before the imperial box, and, saluting with their weapons, clamor in a single resounding voice:

"Diva imperia, morituri te salutant."[1]

---

1 According to Suetonius, gladiators saluted the Emperor with the words *"Ave*

II

Vanquish for Vengeance

MESSALINA leaned toward Silius then, and, pointing at Sepeos, said to her lover: "It will be a pity if he is killed the first time. Look at those supple limbs and muscular arms. He might become one of the finest fiscals that the Emperor maintains for our pleasure and that of the people of Rome."

While the buccinas, horns, silver trumpets and long bronze tubae sounded a martial hymn, the combatants, with their faces uncovered, made a tour of the oval arena. The spectators saluted them with a word in passing, especially the women, some of whom knew the names and the performances of each of the gladiators.

"Laberus! Laberus!" clamored a short plump blonde, clapping her hands. "Be victorious! Look! A kiss for you, Laberus!"

And her kiss, blown from her fingertips, traversed the air like an invisible bird. Laberus saluted her with his eyes. He was an Italian giant, clad in a coat of bronze mail with imbricated scales, falling half way down his bare thighs, with the legs protected in front, from the ankle to shortly above the knee, by bronze cnemides encrusted with gold. He was shod in sandals of woven straw, attached by leather thongs starred with silver pearls.

Wagers were made.

---

imperator, morituri te salutant' [Hail, Caeasar, we who are about to die salute you]. Champsaur has modified it in a supposedly feminine version, of which a pedantic Latinist might not approve.

"Twenty denarii against twice as many, that Silon with vanquish Alces.

"I'll take them!" stammered the senator Cornelius Sapir, in the tremulous voice of an old man with drooling lips. "I'll take them, Linus, but on condition that you also bet with me on that newcomer who's marching between the Gaul Kerbrix and the Libyan."

"All right—he might be worth a few sesterces, thin as he is . . . but we don't know who the newcomer will have to fight, nor which trainer has taught him the science of arms."

"Fifty sesterces against double for his adversary."

"No, I'll take fifty against a hundred and fifty—triple."

"You count like a Lombard money-changer, Linus," a young tribune of the people, Salvius, remarked ironically. "It's the proof of a good education."

Linus' father was a freedman who had made his fortune by usury combined with denunciation; his son had gained the laticlavian toga by furnishing Tiberius with precious information on the patricians with whom he frequented the baths and the taverns.

A number of people in the plebeian crowd knew the Egyptian Sepeos. His name, quickly transmitted from mouth to mouth by the chronicle of Rome, ran especially along the high steps where the popular rabble accumulated on days of spectacle.

"Sepeos! They said he was condemned to the beasts!"

"No, he's become a gladiator because he was weary of the nomadic life of performing at crossroads."

"No, he insulted a senator. It's Callia, the Augusta's sewing-maid, who told me that."

"If he crosses swords with Kerbix, he's doomed!"

Interest in Sepeos grew. Young women found him handsome and a few mourned him in advance. "Keep well back, and don't strike like a madman!"

"Hold your sword, friend, without linking blades."

A genteel Campanian blonde blew him a kiss, as the plump brunette had done for Laberus.

"And above all, don't get killed!"

Sepeos, the fiancé and murderer of the dancer from Tanagra, heard none of that rumor. The circus seemed to him an immense morass where creatures were swarming, of which he could distinguish neither the bodies not the mingled voices: a vision and a confused buzz. He marched like a vehicle, unconscious of the means that moved him. In his heavy head, empty of clear thoughts, images succeeded one another torrentially, in a blur. He saw again the gracious and tragic scenes of his brief idyll, heard again the terrible prophecy of Geo: "Karysta will only dance three more times." She had finished dancing, the little Tanagran, before having tasted the exquisite sweetness of amour, and it was him, Sepeos, who had killed her, his mind confused by the games of the masters of the world and the gods.

In groups, after one last salute to the assembled crowd, the gladiators went back into the rooms alternated with the vivaria where the famished beasts were circling, putting their muzzles to the bars and aspiring air, launching their roars from time to time, or sinister and nostalgic mewlings.

The retiarii, armed with net and trident; the gladiators who were to fight wild beasts with a painted cloth, and a lance or sword; the Mirmillons with helmets ornamented with plumes in the form of fish; the Thracians, assassins clad round the waist in animal-hides, brandishing their sharp-pointed national daggers with curved blades; the Parthians with bows and arrows destined to simulate desert hunts; the Gauls wearing sagums of goat's-wool and striped braies; and finally the Italians, the Romans who fought with straight, double-edged blades and bucklers, retired in good order, soon to reappear. A squadron of Numidian cavaliers, Arabs draped in swathes of white wool mounted on fine, muscular little horses, and Latins, armored in the fashion of legionnaires, with bronze strips, circled in a vertiginous fantasia, brandishing spears and shields, which caught the sun's rays, passing between the velaria striped in red and white, extended over the fabulous swarm of thousands and thousands of spectators.

And again, the arena was empty. But before reaching the corridors and rooms where the gladiators were armed, Sepeos had seen once again, lying full length on the crimson cushions, the immodest Messalina, whose palla, with floating draperies, perversely fitted to her erotic body, gaped under the armpits, allowing the perception, at the hazard of a gesture, of the rosy brown nipple of one or the other breast, and sometimes both.

Hatred rendered him conscious of himself. An indescribable anger seethed within him, stronger henceforth than his grief, because of Karysta, the innocent that he had killed with his own hand.

The Egyptian's eyes blazed toward Messalina, while his terrible resentment growled in the depths of his being: "I'll kill you, viper! I shall vanquish in order to be avenged, to kill you in your turn."

He contemplated the space where, on the steps, all the people were agitating: Rome entire, avid for tortures and for blood, well worthy of its Empress, who summarized alone all the passions, all the indecency and cruelty of that rabble. Around those patricians exhausted by debauchery, those knights uniquely preoccupied with lucre and avid for the favors of a libidinous Caesar devoid of grandeur, those citizens ready to sell anything for enjoyment and gold, the plebeian swarm of freedmen, barbarians and slaves crowded like the dogs of a pack behind the bloodhounds guiding them and drawing them along in the hunt.

Then, Sepeos understood that Rome, the city of light, the center of the civilized world, was gasping in an agony like an old libertine surprised by death in the arms of his prostitutes, at the moment when he was wallowing, writhing in a supreme spasm, on an infamous couch. He cursed the City and Messalina, the two murderers of Karysta, the pure Tanagran, the symbol of Beauty, grace and Amour. He dreamed of extinguishing all those creatures at a stroke, simultaneously, with a single terrible gesture: all those atrocious voices and those gazes, which burned with the attraction of blood and ignominies.

Vanquish! He no longer thought about anything but the fact that the men he had to fight were the most experienced and the strongest, the most expert in killing. A new energy, indomitable, carried Sepeos away. It appeared to him that his heavy sword weighed no more than a wisp of straw in his muscular hand. Agile and swift, accustomed to manipulating halters and weights, juggling with all kinds of objects, knowing how to leap and twist his hips at the exact requisite moment to avoid a blow or a fall, trained since childhood in unusual gymnastics, he could wield his weapons, in spite of his ignorance, with a skill that, although inexperienced, would aid in his defense, and perhaps his victory.

III

In the Wings of the Circus

THE LANISTA, the master of the gladiators hired for the day, examined his men. A tall Roman, an old soldier of Caesar, now a gladiator, Saper, questioned Sepeos mockingly.

"Who's got the job of delivering you to Pluto, then, my lad?"

Sepeos raised his head.

"That man might well be disappointed, mercenary," said the adolescent, raising his arm and making the muscles stand out.

"By Pollux!" cried Kerbrix, the Gaul. "Is he trying to teach us a lesson, the greenhorn?"

And he laughed loudly, the worthy blond giant, disdainful, forceful and gentle. The Macedonian Chylaides clapped Kerbrix on the shoulder and grimaced, with his nose, which was very long and mobile, as well as his thick, twisted lips, toward Sepeos.

"Perhaps that's him, the phenomenon that the rhetor Sapeius promised us, and whom none of us will escape?"

Without replying, Sepeos looked them up and down.

Callixtus, a former maniple leader degraded for inveterate drunkenness, challenged Kerbrix:

"Semio, the quaestor, hadn't seen him, Gaul, before wagering on your carcass. Have you prepared the as that you'll give to Charon this evening to pass over the Styx?"

Chylaides made a gesture of dusting the shoulders of the braggart.

"You glorify yourself, Callixtus and you already have the dust of the spoliarium on your shoulders, where I can see you, stripped of arms and campestre, lying stark naked."

In a corner, a few young patricians examined their preferred combatants. They discussed their merits in loud voices.

"Simias is a better horseman than Arizanus; he's been a victor four times already this year. You have no chance, Camillus; I can hear the sound of the denarii leaving your purse."

"Arizanus has never looked like much, but wait and see him in action, and don't order the feast you intend to give your mistress with my money yet; it will increase your debt at the poulterer and the fruit-merchant inconveniently."

"Septimus Gelion, is it true that you'll buy Saper if he beats the Libyan?"

"Yes, I want muscles I can trust to accompany me to Egypt."

But the lanista Casper had the ordinator proclaim the prohibition issued by the praetors against occupying the wings of the circus. Respectfully, the centurions of the praetorian guard, under the orders of Claudius Severo, called the laggards to order.

The instructors employed by the lanistas distributed and checked the weapons, Sepeos lent an ear to the murmur of a group of men, disciples of Christos, the new Nazarene god—pushed pell-mell into the arena, which he could see strewn with blue and saffron powder, in intersecting stripes.

"You'll be fighting, charlatan, in Cornelio's decade. Do your best, and you'll touch the seven quadrigati . . . unless you only cost the price of your funeral. . . ."

From the next room came the cries of rage of the wild beasts that the valets of the bestiarium were chasing from their cages by beating iron bars on the walls, making a din that mingled with the formidable mewling of the tigers and leopards, and the roaring of the lions.

IV

An Artless Hecatomb

IN the arena, a crowd of men and women, some of whom were clad, derisively, in the skins of animals—sheep, calves and goats—had been pushed out of the vomitoria by valets. Women were holding babies in their arms; other children, slightly older, clung to their relatives, trembling with fear, their eyes riveted to the gaping openings of the vivaria, from which the beasts, released from their cages, were about to emerge. Women and virgins, naked because the guards had taken away their robes and the pallae that covered their shoulders, hid their breasts modestly with their crossed arms. They were Christians—illuminates, it was said, who did not recognize any power, against whom the people were furious, because they had been accused of numerous murders of patricians and rich citizens, whose cadavers the Tiber carried away every morning. They were also an object of hateful mockery because the rumor was going around that they worshiped the head of a donkey and a fish, which they called by the name of Christos. Several public misfortunes were attributed to them: the defeats suffered in Venetia, and that inflicted by Mithridates,[1] because it

---

1 The intended reference is presumably to Mithridates of Armenia, restored to his throne by Claudius after the death of Caligula; the historian Cassius Deo relates an unlikely confrontation between Mithridates and Claudius, but there was no battle between their forces. There does not appear to be any record, either, of contemporary conflicts with "Venetia"—the Breton land of the seafaring Veneti, after whom Venice was later named—although Claudius had campaigned there successfully some years earlier.

was them, it was believed, who offended the gods, indisposing them against the city. The anger of the crowd was exasperated.

Lions, ten superb beasts captured in the Numidian desert, on the thresholds of cages suddenly opened, blinded by the daylight on emerging from subterrains full of shadows, hesitated, beating their flanks with their tails. Then they bounded forward. No tremor agitated the victims. Their ecstatic eyes seemed to be fixed on a sign invisible to the spectators, on high, in the sky.

"Cowards! Cowards! Arrows! Let the lions be slain like the useless Christians!"

One lion, hungrier or more ardent than the nonchalant monsters that were stretching themselves, their four braced limbs driven into the sand, lifted one of its clawed paws over a woman whose horrified swiveling eyes suddenly closed in a faint. And blood, in droplets, shone like rubies in snow, beading the whiteness of her breast.

Then the beasts charged.

Breasts were lacerated, limbs torn away, bodies suddenly collapsed in a red sea, quivering. Coldly, the patricians discussed the beauty of the adolescent girls and ephebes, their grace in the supreme spasm, with an enthusiasm from which pity was banished, but sometimes regretting the behavior of those splendors of voluptuous flesh, whose attractiveness was ardently enlivened in the terror of death, the tears and the ecstatic attitudes of beautiful bodies in agony.

The martyrs made no gesture of defense or dread. They only traced, from the forehead to the breast and the shoulders, a mysterious sign in the form of a cross. Two children held in the arms of a man, doubtless their father, were snatched away by two formidable sweeps of a huge lion's paws.

Sepeos had never seen these terrible spectacles. He stood still, his eyes riveted on the arena striped for him by the iron bars of the grille closing the subterrains, where the gladiators were waiting for their turn to die.

But the sated beasts, nonchalantly extending their limbs, were yawning. They had appeased their hunger, and snorted at the excessively numerous prey. Then the crowd, irritated by their laxity, drunk on the odors of humanity and death that were rising from the arena and the whole circus, howled filthy insults, threw fruit and innumerable debris at the giants of the desert, splashing the disdainful tigers, supple panthers and the formidable majesty of the ions with mud.

Silius, the director of the games, commanded that a troop of gladiators be unleashed on the condemned still standing. And there was, for ten minutes, an atrocious massacre.

The tribune Claudius Severo said to the senator Praemius, with a shake of the head: "The art is dying; they would never have dared, in the old days, to show the people a slaughter of sheep instead of a battle."

The condemned were all dead. Two hundred sectarians had been butchered by the beasts or exterminated by swords and short spears. Valets led horses as black as Erebus from beneath the circus, drawing small wicker hurdles without wheels in a sinister fashion.

The servants dragged the inert cadavers over the sand with ropes, and piled them up. With two curt sweeps of a rake especially designed for that funereal purpose they had assembled the dangling legs and brought arms back to the bodies, without bothering to check whether any retained a breath of life. And rapidly, the sleds carried the mass of human flesh away into the darkness of the spoliarium.

Immediately, the valets of the arena, naked slaves, spread new sand, which they sprinkled with a profusion of borax and cinnabar, to the enthusiastic applause of the crowd, satisfied with that luxurious prodigality.

V

Masters and Debutant

TWO decades of gladiators, armed in the Roman fashion, then appeared—finally. They were hardened men, former soldiers for the most part, too debauched to remain in the legions, or weary of the discipline. Some were former slaves whose courage, athletic strength or the science they had acquired in fighting with all kinds of weapons had permitted them to buy their freedom. The people cheered them. In spite of their lowered visors, the habitués of the games recognized them by certain signs they attached to their armor, or by their stature, their rotundity or thinness, or their familiar silhouette.

Abusive remarks and wagers filled the circus with a great rumor. Young women leaned closer to their friends in order to confide an impression of one or another, or their preference. Young voices saluted the combatants.

"Strike well, Callixtus, and don't let yourself get hurt!"

The leader of the first decade replied with a gesture of his naked blade.

"Kerbrix, I tell you, will defeat Callixtus and many others!"

"You're mad, Pigion. He's a Gaulish barbarian who can't be as skillful as a citizen wounded ten times in war."

"Twenty-five sesterces that you're wrong, Maglorius?"

"I'll take them, but I assure you that you'll ruin yourself."

The young patrician to whom that mocking reply was addressed shrugged his shoulders. "Thirty denarii to one that the Egyptian marching between Chylaides and Saper will be killed."

"Taken! Perhaps he's better instructed than you think."

Sepeos marched with an assured tread, holding his sword firm in a hand clenched with hateful anger.

At a signal from the lanista Casper, who was watching the combat, the decades hurled themselves man against man. Ten blades landed, making the bronze of shields resonate. Sparks flashed.

Sepeos found himself fighting against Simias, a former Greek slave renowned for the clever feints of his swordplay. However, either because the impetuosity of Sepeos, falling upon him brandishing his sword at the end of an extended arm, had put him off, or some temporary awkwardness, only a backward leap saved Simias from a formidable impact, of which his buckler bore the visible trace; clamors and stamping feet greeted the debutant's blow. The supporters of Simias were not anxious, certain of their man against a novice on whom very few men, if not very few women, had had the audacity to wager. A few voices, however, exchanged numbers on the two names.

In the meantime, Callixtus against Kerbrix, Cylaides against Saper, Arizanus against Manechus, the negro Sapion against old Verilis, and all the rest, battled with leaps, the sound of bucklers struck and blades that grated as they clashed.

A great cry greeted the sudden fall of Simias, whose body collapsed in a red flood. He was shedding blood from the throat, which Sepeos' blade had partly severed.

Having raised his visor, Sepeos saluted the crowd with his sword, after a glance at the cadaver of his dead adversary, who was not even his enemy. Then, turning toward Messalina, Silius and the vestals, he awaited the verdict of the people, the king with a thousand heads, and of the smiling Empress, who applauded him.

Messalina leaned toward her lover. "He's really very good, for a debutant—that was a masterly blow."

"Yes," said Silius, "it's necessary to enlist him in the imperial fiscals—he has a future, and, by Jupiter, I know men!"

"Me too," replied Messalina. "But truly, that Simias was very stupid to let himself be defeated like that. I lost a thousand sesterces on him."

"And me, five aureus. So much the worse for him. He doesn't merit mercy."

In any case, before the great vestal Calpurnia, the Empress and the consuls had decided to cut short, by their sentence, the opinion of the crowd, whose extended thumbs were inverted, thumb down or raised as a sign of mercy, a great spasm ran through the recumbent body of the wounded gladiator, whose loins, legs and back arched, and then fell back, no longer giving the slightest evidence of life.

At that moment, Callixtus, touched in the shoulder, let his sword fall from his right hand. The whole circus applauded the blow struck by Kerbrix, the victorious Gaul. Immediately, however, the raised hands unanimously pardoned Callixtus for his defeat, perhaps the first, because of the numerous medals fixed to his bronze armor, which attested to his former military valor and glory of old.

Sadly, the old soldier stood apart from the group of combatants.

VI

Sepeos Victorious

THE EGYPTIAN now found himself in line with the Gaul Kerbrix, who had mocked him in the subterrain where they were waiting their entrance to the arena. Supple, when in confrontation with the blond giant, he covered his shoulder and side with his buckler, while keeping his adversary at bay with feints toward the face, rapid deceptive thrusts that caused his triangular blade to flash, in a whirl in which the design of his swift swordplay vanished at times, with a lightning promptitude. Four combatants of the compact platoon of the others were weakening almost simultaneously.

Kerbrix, harassed, suddenly launched himself forward like a bull. Sepeos extended his arm violently in the direction of the belly, and with a violent blow of his buckler against that of Kerbrix, deflected that defense of the Gaul's body. Run completely through, the blond giant, thrown backwards by his adversary, who withdrew his bloody blade from the human sheath—collapsed on his back; his sword lay beside him on the sand. And the Egyptian, as magnificent as a statue of animate bronze, placed his right foot on the pale, russet and crimson cadaver, leaving his visor lowered, and raised his buckler, this time, as a cockerel raises his crest, in triumph and homage toward the crowd.

Sinister forms armed with short swords and helmed with an iron crow finished off the wounded by slitting the artery in the neck. Hooks and hurdles dragged the cadavers away, seven out of twenty combatants, and perfumes suddenly fell like dew from the friezes, while Messalina shouted to Sepeos:

"You fully deserve to live. You shall be an imperial gladiator."

VII

An Encounter of Hatred and Love

DAZZLED on emergence from the gladiators' vomitorium after the darkness of the subterranean rooms, Sepeos went forth at random. Rome, set alight by the sun that was about to set, was ablaze. From the frontons of temples, gold and silver rays radiated in trophies. Chariots with two or four horses, curricula harnessed to dwarfish horses from Sicily or Liguria and litters borne by black slaves like living caryatids in motion, crowded the Via Sacra and the Via Appia, accompanied by cries and the crack of whips.

On the Forum, a crowd of idlers was coming and going; parasites competed for the ears of the rich, congratulating the knights and the merchants in the hope of obtaining a meal. And everywhere, on both sides of the great highways and across the Forum, passing ostentatiously before the Thermes where, under the colonnades, men were idling after bathing, courtesans were strolling, clad in pallae clasped on the shoulder that allowed their depilated armpits, thighs and legs to be glimpsed in flashes of flesh. Slaves escorted the most luxurious, carrying their silver or gold mirrors. The humblest provoked men brazenly by winking their promising, painted eyes. Others passed by lying on multicolored cushions in lectica drawn by horses or surrounded by slaves who worked in relays as porters every hundred paces. Groups of lictors and squadrons of soldiers cleared a path through the crowd for some magistrate clad in a laticlave with a broad crimson band, or some military leader going to Caesar's palace on the Palatine.

There was also a number of affranchised Orientals coiffed in the mitra, their cheeks and lips enlivened by carmine and their eyes ringed with kohl, causing their prominent rumps to undulate, equivocal perverse tempters whose loose robes spread perfumes around them.

Sepeos traversed the crowd, indifferent to the hubbub and all the rumors of the city. The image of the horrible scene in Silius' gardens, and the dead face of Karysta the Tanagran, with her dear closed eyes, haunted him, pell-mell with the atrocities of the games, the combat and the beasts.

Like a malevolent goddess, however, Messalina dominated all those things. Her superb figure, her arrogant and voluptuous silhouette and her blue-green eyes, cruel and soft, sparkling with ferocious sensuality, pursued Sepeos, stimulating his hatred. He walked through Rome, which he scarcely knew, without knowing where his mechanical legs were taking him. Empty and enervated, the Egyptian wandered, muttering between his teeth three phrases endlessly repeated:

"I'll kill her! Filthy bitch! I'll kill her!"

Then he no longer whispered anything; he increased his pace, weary of the collisions and contacts of the crowded Forum. The city and the joyful people seemed hostile to his dolor and exasperated him. All ideas quit him. He was something in pain, marching by instinct, without objective and thoughtlessly. He was no longer thinking about anything, no longer seeing the crowd, the people, the faces or the smiles.

In that fashion Sepeos reached almost deserted streets where women of the people were chatting on doorsteps. Finally, feeling weary, he sat down on a boundary-marker at the intersection of the Via Appia and the Via Nomentana, on top of a hill, and remained there, his chin in his hand and his elbows on his knees, gazing at swarming Rome, which he did not see.

Suddenly, Sepeos felt a heavy hand fall upon his shoulder, at the same time as a cordial voice greeted him.

"Bear up, comrade—you're a brave man!"

The Egyptian raised his head. Behind him stood a tall, broad-shouldered man clad in an ornate toga; memorial medals on his breast were evidence of his past exploits.

"Do you know me, then?" asked Sepeos, astonished. "Oh, that's right—you were in the decade of Kerbrix the Gaul; I saw you in the circus."

"A fine blow. Truly, for someone who isn't of the métier, it's a fine blow that sent Kerbrix to the realm of Pluto. All the same, by Pollux, the Gaul's shade will be ashamed of being on the bank of the Styx by virtue of the hand of a novice. Oh, well! Poor Kerbrix."

The old gladiator sat down on the other boundary-marker facing the Egyptian, whom he studied attentively, as if Sepeos' face evoked some vague memory in him that his mind was striving to recall more precisely.

"My name's Manechus Bombyx. You?"

"Sepeos. But it seems to me that I've seen you before somewhere." He passed his hand over his forehead, searching his buzzing head, fatigued by too many unforeseen events. "I don't know where it was, though. . . ."

"But yes, Sepeos—remember, out there on the Via Appia; you were with a troop of Egyptians—their chief, even, I think. Messalina took away a little dancing girl, a Greek. The soldiers had tied you to a tree and beaten you. They made the child dance to buy your release. I was the one who cut the cords binding your limbs, remember?"

"Oh, yes! That was you! You told me that they'd give her back, that Silius doesn't maintain his caprices for long."

"That's right. You see, we're already old acquaintances. I like men who aren't afraid, and you conducted yourself very well at the Circus; you're worthy of being a gladiator. Obviously, you don't have all the finesse of the métier, but if you work hard, you'll get somewhere, I'm sure of it."

Manechus seemed to Sepeos to be sincere and good. He was not a stranger. Once, already, he had rendered him a great service; and he sensed a nascent amity in the frank gaze of the gray eyes shining between the wrinkled eyelids of the old swordsman.

Manechus was ugly, with an energetic ugliness; his big red nose sat between crimson cheeks tanned and bronzed by the sun. A scar cut diagonally across his forehead, from one temple to the other. The rounded chin receded beneath a mouth with thin and glabrous lips, which parted to offer a glimpse of his fine teeth. Strips on his forearms revealed other blows received in continual combats. But that rude face was imprinted, with regard to Sepeos, with an expression of profound and veritable sympathy.

"You're free, then? They haven't retained you?"

"The lanista Casper had me given seven silver denarii at the end of the combat. He told me to present myself at his school, in Suburra. I'm to enter Caesar's college of fiscals. It's by order of the Augusta."

"Eh! Right away you're taking a fine rank among us, by Jupiter! There are some who would envy you, perhaps envy you already. But you've already worked—you know how to fence, at least in the fashion of Barbarians?"

"Not at all, but we vagabond gymnasts, accustomed to all games of skill and strength, are somewhat prepared for combats in the arena."

"Well, my lad, I'll teach you our métier myself. And no one can say that I know less about it than any lanista. No one will mock the friend of Manechus, I can answer for that, because I'll teach you thrusts that only I know. But forgive my curiosity—perhaps you think I'm as talkative and indiscreet as a Greek rhetor or a poet in the public square. Did they return the little dancer to you? Your sister? Or your mistress?"

"Karysta! She was neither. I loved her!"

"They've taken her from you? Poor fellow! They'll return her to you. *She* wearies quickly of her favorites, and she'd never permit Silius to love anyone but her for long."

Sepeos shook his head vigorously in a sign of negation, and replied, dully: "She can't be returned to me any longer. Karysta's dead. Messalina . . ."

"Her! Always her!"

"So she's made you suffer too? She's tortured me in my love and in my life. She could have had me killed by her soldiers or crucified like a slave, or beaten with rods until my bloody body drank the dust of the Via Appia, and she'd have done me less harm. Oh, I hate her! I'll kill her! I'll kill her! No one shall have her skin but me . . . her life, I mean. I want to delight in hearing her throat, caressed by so many hands and lips, gasp her death-rattle!

"You don't know, Manechus . . . listen . . . this is how she caught me. It's her that made her dance three times, and my mother Geo had predicted it: according to the signs, she had to die, the third time she danced. That's not all. In Silius' gardens, on the night when the trees were florid with a thousand lamps with several beaks and wicks bathed in fine oil, lychni suspended from the branches, shining in the somber foliage in fiery clusters and garlands. During the feast, the slut had my hands bound behind my back, and on the bed where her infamous lover was . . . Messalina had taken Krysta's gauze robe and gilded belt; the Tanagran's gems were glittering in her hair . . . she lavished Silius with the caresses of a filthy courtesan.

"And I, in the gloom, I believed, insensate that I was . . . I believed that it was Karysta, my beloved. And when, today, in the Coliseum,[1] hoping to save me, the Tanagran danced for the third time, I killed Karysta, thinking her unfaithful, culpable! She expired while the Augusta told me the atrocious trick that had deceived me . . . but I'll avenge myself; I'll follow her everywhere, and the hour will come when I'll avenge myself. I hate her! I hate her! I hate her!"

Manechus had listened attentively to Sepeos' confidences. He shivered every time the Egyptian mentioned the Empress. He shook his head sadly. A sudden tenderness, rude and frank, passed through his eyes.

"But at present, comrade, what are you going to do?"

"I don't know. To resume my old life as a traveler of the roads, going through towns and questing for my living there with my own people, no longer pleases me now that Karysta is lost to me. Old Geo, my mother, and my former companions have been

---

1 Champsaur does not mean the edifice currently known as the Coliseum, which was only inaugurated in 80 A.D., but the Circus Maximus, now vanished, to which he is attaching the label as a kind of honorific.

obliged to join the bands that the Master of the Ring has commanded to go to Iberia. In any case, Messalina has given orders; she wants me to be a gladiator. Everywhere, no matter what corner of the world I might try to go to, I'd be caught and delivered to the praetors before I reached my destination."

"Oh, if she wants it, that's certain. But you've started well, Castor and Pollux! You'll be one of us. Where do you live?"

"Nowhere yet, Manechus. Yesterday I was a prisoner. Today, after the combat, the lanista Casper gave me seven silver denarii. Here they are: two with the head of Jupiter; two with the effigy of the twin brothers Castor and Pollux; these three with the profile of your helmeted goddess Roma; on the other side, the four horses of her victory chariot, and the quadrigarius standing up, brandishing a triple whip. That's all I possess. As he gave them to me, he ordered me to come, every day, to his lodgings, in order to train me in the handling of weapons. He lives not far from the Via Suburra, at the foot of the Aventine. So I'll go!"

"And you'll be a famous gladiator—it's me who tells you so. But it's late. Have you had supper?"

Sepeos made a gesture of indifference and shook his head.

"Eh! None of that, my lad. You need strength; courage isn't everything. Go on, come with me, Sepeos. I'll take you to a lodging-house, and I'll introduce you to my comrades."

Mechanically, Sepeos got up, and followed Manechus.

Presently, the sky, marvelously illuminated by the setting sun, seemed to be trailing a sheet of its blue robe constellated with fulgurant gems, pennants of cloud hanging like multicolored flames on the summits of the seven hills.

"You'll find friends among us," Menechus went on, clapping Sepeos on the shoulder amicably. Where I'm taking you there are solid, brave men. Some of them saw you fight this afternoon.

The Egyptian was scarcely listening to Manechus' affectionate words. From their present elevation, half way up Monte Celio, the entirety of Rome was visible. To the right, on the flanks of Monte Palatino, the palace of the Caesars stood out magnificently; around it, superb gardens flourished. The Forum raised up its temples and obelisks of gray or pink travertine between the seven hills. A gigantic cloud, the color of blood, now unfurled above the imperial palace, draping the Palatine with an immense crimson mantle, which advanced, swallowing the azure of the sky, while nebulous hints of amethyst, the hue of the garments of deified sovereigns, floated above the temple of Vesta. The great red veil gained ground, devouring everything, effacing the gold and the silver, the enormous petals, as if plucked by the sun, whose reflections were trailing.

Sepeos indicated the sky to his companion with a sweeping gesture.

"Look, Manechus—blood, blood everywhere! It really is the royal mantle of cruel and sluggish Caesars, and ferocious Empresses. Blood and flames: it's the sign of the calamities that they'll unleash on Rome, by dint of injustice. And it also signifies the death of the Empire, in the conflagration that will overturn the world. Those of my race know how to read these things. Yes, there are flames and blood over the city."

As the shadows thickened, the roads and the squares, almost empty at supper time, began to fill up with crowds again. Lovers hastened toward the houses of their beloved. Chariots recommenced rolling along the highways, and litters, preceded by runners and torch-bearers, cleaved through the floods of people, amid the glimmer of little lamps of clay or bronze, tremulous fireflies, or candles of pitch or wax, if not tallow, which, in the streets or in the houses, almost everywhere, were already dotting the darkness, growing denser by the minute.

The ephemeral gems of the sky were extinct; only a few dying red glimmers subsisted in the west. And as if to justify Sepeos' prophecy, the giant statue of the City—the statue of the founders suckled by the maternal and ferocious she-wolf—disappeared into the shadows along with the triumphal arches, the columns, the memorial porticos, the rostra resounding with the inflamed words of the tribunes of the people, temples to forgotten gods and trophies.

"Yes," said Manechus, "the beneficent night will come to efface all ignominies and sadness. In the meantime, Sepeos, it's necessary to live."

The two gladiators, the veteran and the novice, marched for a while in silence through the rumor of the people.

They reached the Aventine, and then the part of the Suburra quarter, which lodged poor parasites, gladiators, actors and low prostitutes in leprous houses or false luxury.

Suddenly, Sepeos put his hand on his new friend's shoulder.

"After all, Manechus, what thought pushed you to show affection to me . . . an obscure nomad, whom you've scarcely known for a few hours—you who have vanquished your adversaries so many times, and whose name all of Rome knows?"

"It's because of *Her*."

He turned toward the Palatine, toward Messalina, the invisible presence of whom a single word evoked all the Power and the Beauty.

"Oh! I hate her," said Sepeos. "I hate her!"

"Me," said Manechos, "I love her."

"I'll kill her! Filthy bitch!"

The gladiator raised his hand, and looked straight into Sepeos's eyes. "Yes, but me first. Not before I've possessed her, and my arms have made her loins crack under my embrace and my kisses. I want that! Afterwards, she'll be yours."

"She's rendered you unhappy too," said Sepeos, "the deadly goddess?"

"For months, for years, she's tortured me. I love her, I love her like a madman. Hundreds of others—comrades of the Circus, boatmen on the Tiber, street-porters, freedmen and slaves—have possessed her. One day, at the exit from a combat, she complimented me. She crowned my head with golden laurels; I'd killed two men, after a lion. And I said to her: 'What do you want me to do with your eulogies and recompenses? It's not words, or medals, or crowns that I want from you, divine Augusta, it's you and you alone, your lips.'

"Oh, the memory of that day of disaster obsesses me. It's because she sensed the immense desire that was burning me, because she understood that I was—from my brain to my testicles, passing through the marrow of my bones and my loins, as in all my sinews and all my blood—conquered by her beauty forever,

that I belonged to her, because she was certain of having vanquished the victor, of her emprise over my amour until death,
that she refused, that she refused herself. To me alone! What
was the point of giving herself to me, since she possessed me so
completely. Do you understand, Sepeos, do you understand what
attraction binds us together?"

Sepeos shook his head, and, his eyes staring obstinately, proffered: "She must perish by my hand. I'll kill her!"

"I'll hold her in my arms, Sepeos. I'll crush her lips under
mine. I want to feel, under the burn of her mouth, the coolness
of her teeth, the softness of her tongue. I shall caress her body;
I shall bruise her breasts; her rump will quiver and her waist flex
between my muscles. She'll gasp with erotic excitement, her body
pressed to my flesh."

"I want to see her expire like a vanquished monster. I want to
see her eyes glaze over, revulsed. Her blood will flow, and it will
be me—me, Sepeos, a vagabond Egyptian—who will have killed
her: her, the Empress, the goddess of Rome!"

"Oh, to feel her palpitate beneath my breast, under my desire,
finally entering into her entirely, like a dagger plunging to the hilt.
But do you know, Sepeos, that it's very imprudent to proclaim
your dream of killing the Augusta? Informers might hear you . . .
and in any case, *me first*, Sepeos. Afterwards, she's yours! Do you
want that? We'll be friends and accomplices."

"So be it! I don't want to aggravate your pain; you love her, I
hate her; we'll be allies."

Calmer, because of the numerous idlers and women who surrounded them, swarming obscurely on the thresholds and in the
street, the two men, having concluded their pact, said nothing
more, absorbed by their obsession and the contemplation of its
goal.

One was dreaming of Death, the other of Amour—Sepeos
haunted by the idea of his vengeance, Manechus carried away
by his incessant dream of Messalina, hypnotized by a mysterious
triangle, all his mind extended toward the female animal in the
milieu of the Empress, toward her vagina, as plants instinctively
turn, as a necessity of their existence, toward the Sun.

VIII

The King of the Sword

THE GLADIATOR MANECHUS, since he had vanquished the Numidian Golias, had attained the highest renown that can illustrate a man of his sort. He was certainly more famous than many a military tribune, vanquisher of the enemies of Rome. Bathyllus, the mime, the yellow coachman Salvecion, the uncontested chief of the Greens, Lormius, and the actor Casper, who had no equal in the plays of Menander, had every right to be jealous of the marks of popularity that the plebs lavished upon him at every opportunity, and the innumerable gifts that the great heaped on him. Even Claudius Caesar had given him, after a combat in which he had killed a white bear from the Caucasus, a necklace of gold plates in which opals and amethysts were alternately embedded.

So, there were scarcely any games held in the Circus in which Manechus did not appear. He had begun by learning his métier in the band of the famous Janex, the Gaulish lanista. Since the age of puberty, when little Romans have scarcely quit the juvenile robe, Manechus, like a young lion, had killed four out of ten of the men armed with swords opposed to his maniple.

In combat he had the fury of youth, robust and supple, with unexpected and disconcerting feints that had immediately signaled him to the connoisseurs. A former consul, senator Rufus Vero, acquired him from his chief. A refined lover of the bloody games of the arena, his new master demanded that he remain for two years without being produced in public. He sent him to Sicily, where there was then a famous school, in order that he might perfect himself in every branch of his art, that he would become both a retiarius and a mirmillon, that he could handle the scythe as well as the ax and the swords of all lands, that he excelled in the use of the spear and the Balearic sling.

In Africa, Manechus had to take lessons from black Libyans who measured themselves against lions, leopards and tigers, to which their skill, combined with Herculean muscles, strength and cunning, sometimes put an end. He had to confront them with the simple weapons of those barbarians, the wood-and-iron pike, the spears of hard wood, the barbed arrows that stuck in the wounds or the hide of the irritated monsters, if they were not hit full in the heart at the first shot—or in the orbit of the eye, which allowed the point to penetrate the brain.

Passionate for his métier, Manechus became, perhaps, the strongest of Romans and their slaves. He was glorious in his bodily form and his superb arms. At that time, Rufus Vero kept him in reserve, in order to make him appear again in the circus games that were offered to the people at the ides of Autumn. Manechus was to fight a lion, with no other weapon than an iron-tipped pike, and then two other celebrated gladiators, the Gaul Pensilis and the undefeated Thracian Rigor, who had challenged him, measured their swords against his.

Rufus Vero had promised his slave liberty, with a mocking smile, if he was victorious, at the request of Claudius Caesar, who marveled at the unparalleled audacity, and the courage of carrying out such a boast.

On the third day of the ides the games commenced. The lion, confronted by the agile and robust man, fell dead, struck in the heart. Pensilis was the second to fall, his head cleaved by an admirable blow from Manechus. After a long duel in which the clashing swords gave birth to showers of fugitive sparks, Rigor fell, his breast pierced, raising a disarmed hand to beg for mercy. And from that day on, Manechus was the lion of the Nemean wood, the recognized chief of the men of blood. He was known as the King of the Sword.

What madness, one day, gripped his brutal and rudimentary soul? What aberration had drawn his imprudent gaze and gesture of oblation toward the divine Messalina? How had he dared, with stupor in his eyes, on the day of victory when the Empress crowned him, to address audacious words to her? But always the freedman seemed to be sacrificing, as if to a troubling and sanguinary goddess, splendid and maleficent, the victims that fell quivering beneath his ax, his inevitable spear, or his terrible and infallible sword.

IX

An Evening of Spring and Feasting

THE CITY, at present, was entirely dressed in shadow, punctuated by the flames and lanterns of torch-bearers running from all directions, before litters in which patricians, matrons or young women were lying. There was a fête at Caesar's palace. Augustans clad in crimson passed by on horseback, or guiding their own chariots, following the course of slaves whose loud cries parted the crowd of plebeians curious to contemplate at close range the friends of the divine Caesar. Often, they struck the densely gathered idlers with their supples canes of osier or vine-stems: "Make way! Make way for the illustrious tribune Cormilon!"

Claudius Severo passed in front of Manechus and Sepeos as they were traversing the Forum heading for the foot of the Aventine. The people cheered him; he had become popular by virtue of his victory over the Parthians, and even though he corrected the severity of Roman costume with innovations in the Oriental style, like colored sashes over his toga or long loose robes of precious fabric, his masculine beauty, his reputation for courage and his proverbial generosity pleased the old Romans, at the same time as his grace and the elegance of his lifestyle won him the affectionate admiration of all the women and the amity of the young men. It was also said that he hated informers and disapproved strongly of the promiscuity of the baneful freedmen, the flatterers of Claudius, the counselors of his cruelties and his courtiers in debauchery.

Other Augustans, favorites of Claudius, disliked by the plebeians, were greeted with prudent jeers. From between the colonnades of the temples bloody insults departed, recalling crimes, concussions and misdeeds that remained unpunished but the resentment of which brooded.

It was the hour when, the estival heat of the spring day having passed, after the intoxication of their emotions in the Coliseum, the Romans enjoyed the mildness of the atmosphere. Even more numerous than before the sixth hour, which was that of the evening meal, the effeminates paraded their languid stride and their equivocal rumps, and the courtesans, bolder, provoked idlers and passers-by of all ages with their eyes, libertine words and sometimes gestures. At the doors of the thermes, carillons of bells announced that the hot water for the baths was ready.

A thin poet in a ragged toga had climbed on to a boundary-marker at the corner of the Via Appia; a slave had stuck a torch into the ground, while a flute-player played a prelude and accompanied with monotonous notes the chant intoned by the Orpheus of the crossroads, who, leaning on the long staff habitual to rhetors and philosophers, celebrated the grandeur of Augustus Claudius Ahenobarbus, vanquisher of the Scythians, Parthians, Dacians and Gauls, as well as the generosity of the senators and patricians who doubtless granted him a meal from time to time or—more elegant than the old little round wicker basket full of provisions—a silver sportule.

Manechus, blasé with regard to the spectacle, and Sepeos, too ardently preoccupied by his mourning and possessed by his desire for vengeance, passed by quickly. They nearly collided with the lectica of Medianus Babion, consul, and zealots of the "familia" who were escorting it, were already raising their fists to strike the insolent plebeians who were hindering the progress of a litter in which such a considerable person was relaxing, but Manechus grabbed two of them, waved them violently in the air, and then put them down again. He was recognized; the crowd shouted his name in noisy acclamations.

Presently, they reached the Via Suburra. Sepeos was not paying attention, and saw nothing—neither the transparent phalluses serving as signs in places of ill repute, nor the signals of prostitutes of all ages, whose loose pallae allowed glimpses of depilated flesh and wrinkled, sagging breasts, or at intervals, firm and smooth ones.

"We've arrived," said Manechus. "You'll meet this afternoon's brothers in combat again here, and several of the adversaries from the Circus."

X

The Gladiators' Lair

A GOAT-SKIN GOURD beneath a bouquet of tamarisk and hay served the *popina* as a sign. In the window of the tavern, which was both a wine-shop and restaurant, in order to show off what there was to drink and eat, a piece of meat surrounded by vegetables was displayed, as was customary, in a bottle full of water, in order to magnify the foodstuffs in the eyes of passers-by and attract them. In front of the entrance, like that of a subterranean cellar, a table bore empty bottles and amphorae, pell-mell. A hubbub of coarse voices, the heavy laughter of men and the bright tones coming from feminine mouths, escaped from the lair, which a trellised door separated from the street, full of footfalls cries and calls, a murmur of speech and prattle, the sounds of clinking blades and armor, at an hour when soldiers were thronging to the low quarters, taverns and houses of pleasure.

"Salve, Manechus! You had the purse at the amphitheater; your duty is to regale your comrades and the vanquished."

"Well said, Cadmio! Poor Kerbrix couldn't have put it better."

"I've brought you his vanquisher, Sepeos the Egyptian, who is my friend and is going to be my pupil."

The gladiators—there were six of them—muttered a vague assent. Some Tiber boatmen, leaning over a table of chance and calculation, impassioned by the game of twelve lines,[1] stopped

---

1 *Ludum duodecimo scriptorum* [the game of twelve lines] was a board game similar to backgammon. Champsaur uses a version of the Latin name from now on,

95

in order to look more closely at the man who, without having received any lesson from the lanistas, had felled the giant Gaul and wounded other no less famous performers with the sword.

Arizanus and Chylaides threw their dice.

"You've lost, my Athenian," said Arizanus. "That makes enough sesterces to pay for the slippers embroidered by Mauritanian women for my beloved Mycelia."

Saper, having risen to his feet, said to Sepeos: "Comrade, you still have a great deal to study before being the equal of those who are drinking here."

Simias pulled a face.[1] "Certainly, I'll drink a hundred more cups of Falernian before he makes the smallest buttonhole in my skin, through which the stem of a rose of Paestum might pass. So, young man, you want to handle the iron? Personally, I'd advise you to begin in the provinces."

"He killed Kerbrix," Manechus replied.

"Pooh! The Gaul must have emptied too many cups before the games," said Arizanus.

"Fortune has inexplicable caprices. A stroke of luck, yes, a real stroke of luck for an amateur. Destiny must have been on his side."

Sepeos did not like what he heard. He understood that these vain men, avid for applause, proud of their exceptional strength, were mocking him. He sensed, beneath the vague courtesy of patronizing remarks, a muted hostility against the newcomer whose victory over a meritorious gladiator offended their professional self-respect.

He replied: "It's in Rome that I won my first victory, in Rome that I'll edify my renown."

"Good!" exclaimed Manechus. "There's one who speaks like a man!"

Striking the wine-moistened table with an empty iron tankard that lay among the dice and knucklebones, the veteran cried "Hey, respectable Gueranus, what are you doing, then, instead of bring-

---

albeit one of which pedantic Latinists might not approve.

1 The author has apparently forgotten that Sepeos killed Simias in the arena.

ing us an amphora of the Umbrian wine I like to drink, to the exclusion of any other? Take care not to give me the bitter juice of the grapes of Latium! By Pluto, your body would be emptied sooner than your soul . . . than a jug of our wine when divided into four!"

A judas-hole opened at the back of the shop, in the center of the wall painted with frescoes, which represented naked gladiators exercising with wooden swords or throwing the discus. Ornamental phalluses rose up among the symbolic flowers framing the Circus scenes, while, on the ceiling, lubricious images representing enlaced couples in all the sexual positions seemed to promise the combatants on the walls similar recompenses.

"My husband is yours, Lord Manechus; just give him time to stopper a wineskin whose cord has cut the neck and let the wine leak out."

"By Castor, let him not bother," shouted Simias. "Come and serve these fellows yourself, Lenia, if you're a brave woman."

"I'm not dressed, Lord. I was asleep, being ill."

"All the more reason for showing us your charms. Casper, the lanista, affirmed yesterday that you have all the attributes of the stronger sex."

"You have only to ask Simo Barbax," replied Arizanus, joyfully.

Everyone burst out laughing.

"Gueranus wanted an heir," said Arizanus. "One has these weaknesses—and then, Barbax is very rich. He made a fortune selling wild beasts bought on disembarkation at Ostia, Neapolis and Palermo to the organizers of the games and patrician amateurs."

Lenia appeared; she was an Illyrian from a rural family, strong, with a bulging rump, exuberant and firm under the dirty white woolen garment with sleeves and a hood, a bardocucullus, lightly slit at the bottom on the right side, which covered her solid, angular, fleshy body all the way to the feet. The emphatic features of the face, a suspicion of poorly depilated hair at the corners of her thick straight lips, a strong hooked nose born between eyebrows that were forbidding in their bushiness, black hair whose tangled tresses were going gray, and hands with thick scaly fingers and massive palms, made the innkeeper's wife a rather redoubtable individual, capable of holding her own in a brawl, even between the gladiators who made up, with the Tiber boatmen and the street-porters of the Trastevere, the popina's usual clientele.

"Manechus, I'm bringing you a jug of Umbrian wine, but I won't serve any more to these drunkards. No thanks! They'll only break everything and attract the watchmen, as they did the night before last."

While speaking she indicated the gladiators sitting around the tables on hard wooden stools with feet crudely sculpted into the heads of ferocious animals. They grumbled, but none of them challenged the Megaera's words.

Chylaides inspected the newcomer.

Saper asked: "What's your companion's name, Manechus? He doesn't have very stout limbs to risk himself in our company."

"Sepeos. He'll overtake more than one of you. He already has a quick hand and a sure thrust. Wait a while, my masters; Casper and I will make a man of him."

"Young debutant," said Saper, "do you know how to handle a cestus, like Chylaides?"

"Well enough not to fear him."

"I have no equal at Greek wrestling," said the Ionian gladiator. "The Romans don't like that game, in which I won six crowns in six years. Yes, your limbs are too thin, handsome acrobat, and I have no fear of you at boxing . . . the leather straps of the cestus gloving your hands and wrists arm them with lead or nails all the way to the elbow . . . which you put in the eye."

With smiles, Claudius Saper, Simias, Arizanus and Callixtus hastened around the newcomers' table. Their tankards were empty and they did not want to confront Lenia's wrath for the moment.

"Chylaides," said Sepeos slowly, looking him up and down, "You're a brave man; I believe you worthy of measuring up to me with the cestus, or the celtiberian blade with the straight cutting edge, long and straight, or, if you prefer, the curved sword with the fragile tip."

Claudius Saper sniggered. Sepeos went on: "As for you, Saper—for I've remembered the names of heroes during the summons in the vivaria . . ."

That last word drew protests "Insolence! Are we animals?"

"Peace!" said Manechus. "Are we, as free citizens, going to quarrel among ourselves, when we're the flower of robust men, the glory of Rome and the kings of the sword?"

Saper muttered dully: "Vivaria! Vivaria! Let him take back the word. They're beasts that are caged in the vivaria, not men. . . ."

"He's a foreigner," said Manechus, "and doesn't know the finesse of our tongue."

Gueranus suddenly showed his broad-shouldered silhouette in the embrasure of the door that led from the shop to the cubiculum where the redoubtable proportional couple slept. The popinarius had scarcely more surface than Lenia, except that his belly formed a remarkable rotundity between his enormous thighs and bulbous thorax, from which an ox-like neck emerged, supporting the head of a bird, small in proportion to his body.

"Ah, by Pluto!" cried Saper. "Here's Gueranus, who knows the ins and outs of the arena. He'll tell us whether it's possible to put this scrawny individual in line with our Chylaides."

"I've seen thinner who have hooked fellows stronger than you with the funereal fang. Kerbrix was big, and a new man who resembled this fellow had him dragged to the dust of the spoliarium."

While speaking, the tavern-keeper shook his head with the air of an expert who knows the question thoroughly and who has found a good example to justify his words.

"Well," exclaimed Manechus, "*ecce homo!*"

He pushed Sepeos by the shoulder, who frowned, apprehensive of a storm.

Then Gueranus said: "You're the one who vanquished the giant Gaul? Lenia, you can bring something to drink, so that they can all clink glasses with this valiant fellow."

At that moment, a gladiator in laced armor came in, helmeted in bronze, his cnemides sparkling and his thighs superb, holding in his arms a very young woman dressed in a robe the color of yellow iris, with a violet palla hanging like a flag before the group they formed.

"Salut, Cornelio!" exclaimed Manechus. "But you're not coming from a combat?"

"Yes, at Caesar's place, tonight, my decade was commanded to show the Asiatic ambassadors what Roman gladiators can do. Blood and wine were abundantly mingled under he tables of the feast. Giulus and Ramo are dead, Verbex wounded in the neck. Caesar, Augustus Claudius, rewarded the victors richly. Hey, Lenia, wine! Here's the sesterces, Gueranus!"

A rain of small coins fell on the table nearest to the popina's entrance.

"Good!" said Lenia, "If you serve them, Gueranus, at least make sure they don't frighten the passers-by in the street with their shouting. Medulla and Carissa haven't come back yet. They're miming the androgyne mystery at the house of the senator Camillus. They'll run into the door, but it's better to close it than risk another fine."

Arizanus and Simias were discussing the method of Chylaides, who, instead of trying to strike in the face during fights to the death, affected low feints.

Lenia, who had picked up Cornelio's money, scolded her husband: "Since you're too heavy to fight again in the arena, be good for something, Gueranus—go down to the cellar and don't hang about there drinking alone, or else . . ."

Without paying any attention, the popinarius, taking part in the discussion of the three gladiators, criticized Chylaides. He argued for the old style and cited the authority of Casper, the reputed lanista, who had been chief of a decade at the same time as him. Lenia began to move the shutters outside, before fixing them to the shop-front with iron pegs.

Just as she was lifting them up noisily, however, three young women invaded the lair. Linela, Cornelio's mistress, leaned on the gladiator's shoulder and assumed a dignified expression.

"Salve! Good evening, all! This little fool Baltrix has trailed that old impotent Ilius Gasper so far, from the brothel to the thermopolium and the caupona to the popina, that he no longer has an atom of reason left, or a single sesterce. . . ."

"And he hasn't had *that* from me, my adored Saper, not that, and without furnishing a single kiss, I've earned at least two aureus."

With an affectionate gesture, she slipped the two gold coins into the gladiator's hand—who kissed her on the lips for a long time.

Between Arizanus, Saper, Simias and Chylaides, the other two girls sat down. All three of them were wearing pallae without a tunic underneath, which molded their very young bodies at the slightest gesture.

"Lenio adores me," said Sabina, "but I don't want to let go of my ox-merchant before being sure that he won't leave me as soon as he's had me. . . ."

Candilia leaned toward Chylaides. "When you've won the purse in the amphitheater, we'll rent the house of the money-changer Carmius, who's killed himself, and live happily with our savings, without my having to hire out my four lips by the course and by the hour. . . ."

"And the brown eyelet you sit on," said one of the girls, laughing.

Manechus was explaining a point-thrust to Sepeos and Cornelio, but an indescribable sadness weighed upon the new gladiator—who was sitting under the carnarium suspended from the tavern roof, the rails fitted with hooks to which salted provisions, dried legumes, herbs, sausages and a smoked ham were attached—amid the cordial intimacy of those brave men and the whores.

<h1 style="text-align:center">XI</h1>

Lodgings in a Tavern

"OH," cried Candilia, suddenly, putting her arms around Chylaides' neck, "it's surely him who'll win the hundred aureus. He'll see my eyes facing his; between two flashes of the blade, he'll be able to glimpse the rose of my mouth. If he isn't the victor, it's because he isn't worthy of my beauty."

Baltrix, pinching her lips, struck the broad shoulder of her lover of the heart, Caius Saper. "It's him who'll win the golden cup, even against Chylaides, so you're wrong to praise your lover with such exaggeration."

The two rivals, Chylaides and Saper, stood up, and as they hurled abuse at one another, Manechus called to the tavern-keeper. "Hey, Gueranus, are you going to let them quarrel over their muscles, you who could best any gladiator in Rome not so long ago?"

"Bah! They're mewling, but they won't get carried away. I'm sure they'll wait for the games to cut the question to the quick."

Proudly, Simias, disdainful of words, stood up in order to have his comrades contemplate his arms and his powerful torso, where the sinews made a network of nodules and projecting cords.

"Look, then! Saper beat me in my second combat. Do you remember, Caius? Your blade sliced my shoulder to the bone; you struck me on the forehead . . . and here." He made his bulging chest resound with a blow of his fist.

"Yes, I remember; it's from that day that our friendship dates—at least," he added, with a coarse laugh, "from a couple of weeks afterwards, for I really believed that the mercy would be futile."

"And since then, I've acquired a strength and skill redoubtable even for you, Caius."

"That's true. You won the consular cup against me at the last autumn games."

Cornelio and Linela, isolated in a corner, made an amorous group worthy of the chisel of a Praxiteles: she slender and dainty, her stola loose, with no subucula underneath, crossed under her palla, which two sculpted silver lion-claws retained upon the right shoulder, leaving the rosy nest of the armpit visible, and sometimes the delightfully-curved flanks, and one breast, a fraction of that pretty statuette of flesh, Linela.

"Barbax! Ah, this time it's him! Salve and Lucre, Simo!"—be well and earn money.

A small and knotty bearded man appeared, reminiscent of the trunk of one of the enormous pollarded elms, invaded by mosses and lichens, that border old roads. His little gimlet eyes gleamed with malice; his nose was like a vegetable-stalk, flowering at the end with red and violet buds, beneath a narrow and low forehead invaded by the tangled brown curls of a black and gray shock of thick hair. His mouth gaped, minuscule in the faunesque nest of his chin. He wore heavy rings on all the fingers of his thickset and strong hands; golden ear-rings hung from his lobes. He waddled over the threshold like a bear.

Lenia, hearing the door open, bounded out of the cubiculum wearing nothing but her night-gown. "Ah! What is it now? The door isn't shut, then? And what a racket, by Pollux and Vesta! We'll have to pay another fine, Gueranus, I tell you!"

Rudely, the Megaera repelled the ironic caresses with which the gladiators tried to placate her. Arizanus kissed Candilia under cover of the tumult; furious, Chylaides fell upon him and grabbed him by the waist and neck.

"You're a thief of kisses! Pig! Andabata!" The latter insult was the more serious; it was the name of comic gladiators who, to amuse the Roman people, after the grim games, fought with blindfolds over their eyes in a sealed helmet without an opening in the visor. The incidents of these random combats were the source of laughter and jeers.

The two men rolled on the tiles whose mosaics represented a multitude of erect penises. Cold and smiling, the stout Barbax watched the scene, shaking his head, like a man taking pleasure in contemplating superb animals.

"They're almost as beautiful," he muttered, "as the two lions I've just sold to the consul Avicius Miso."

Lenia managed to reach the threshold in order to close the popina herself. "Oh, if my idler supported me," she threatened, spitting out the words like a bad-tempered dog, "the two of us would throw you all out! And to think that I'm ill! Ill, by Pollux!"

Manechus grabbed her by the hem of her night-gown as she came back, after closing the shop-front securely.

"You can go out by the door behind the atrium, as my maid, that little hussy Filiola, won't open up for you this evening." She laughed malevolently. "That I promise you."

"I was just waiting for her or you, Lenia, because I wanted to ask you whether you'd consent to lodge this young man, a new gladiator, in your house. You can see that he's already collected the price of his first combat, and he won't cause you any trouble; he's not a noisy fellow . . . in fact he has a rather doleful character."

The Megaera looked at Sepeos; she doubtless took a certain pleasure in his face and his appearance, for her dark eyes, which had once been very beautiful, brightened with a covetous, perhaps lustful, gleam.

Sepeos showed his seven quadrigati.

"I'll be glad to take you in, and you can also eat in the popina if you like. I'll give you a nice little cubicle over there at the back of the atrium, with a bearskin. It'll only cost you twelve sesterces a week, handsome lad."

She took an advance of three silver denarii from Sepeos' hands as he acquiesced, in spite of Manechus protesting against the dearness of the lodging and the table.

"But he'll be very well lodged, Manechus. I'll give him Gueranus' and my old room, not far from the redoubt where the maidservant Filiola, the wretched Christian, sleeps."

"What have you done to the child, that she isn't serving us this evening?"

"I've punished her; she disobeys me . . . and then, you know . . . just think! A girl I bought when she was nine years old, for whom I paid, out of pity, four aureus . . . didn't she take it into her head to weep in the common room, as if I'd martyrized her—me, her adoptive mother! I ought to punish her, though, as schoolmasters do their pupils, with an eelskin whip. To make people think I maltreat her! As if anyone could say that! But since the tribune Cassius' law in favor of young slaves, all the children are dreaming of having cause for complaint, in order to be redeemed. Well, thanks for that! Where are we headed? Where are we headed?"

"She's your maidservant?" asked Sepeos, emerging from his long mutism.

"These last seven years. And thanks to us, a pretty girl. Just like the form of the little Tanagran who came to sing and dance on the Via Appia and the Forum recently—the one whose lover killed her. He was condemned to serve in the games for that, and I'm told he was victorious. You were there, Manechus? And you too, doubtless, adolescent?"

Sepeos' eyes blazed.

"Oh, it is you—I was sure of it! She made you suffer, undoubtedly? And she left you to go partying with Messalina and Silius? All the same, you took a hard revenge!"

"Peace, woman!" said Manechus. "Leave Sepeos alone and go set Filiola free."

"Oh no! Not that!"

"Who, then, will install my friend, since you're ill?"

"Eh! Gueranus, if he's not too drunk, for they're drinking like the whole land of Italy on a stormy day in summer."

<h1 style="text-align:center">XII</h1>

<h1 style="text-align:center">Drunkards in the Street</h1>

IN the tavern the voices of the gladiators rose more violently as the number of empty bottles and pitchers increased. The Tiber boatmen got up to leave, but one of them thought he saw a mocking expression on the ugly face of Simo Barbax.

"Are you laughing at me, old mirmillon?"

"Was I even looking at you, son of Charon?"

An impetuous movement of the boatman's two companions threw the drunkard on to Simias. But Lenia made a sign to Gueranus, who opened the door to the street; the Megaera took hold of the man and deposited him, sitting, in the gutter. Simias and Arizanus shoved the other two after him. Bewildered, cursing, and lashing out at one another clumsily, they completely lost their heads in the nocturnal fresh air after emerging from the dense and overheated atmosphere of the popina. Everyone started laughing.

There was no longer anyone in the street, save for a few passers-by in dark cloaks emerging from houses of ill-repute where, guided by the luminous phallus and the red triangle, the symbol of the female sexual parts, they hastened toward their lodgings, their amours or their debauches. In rare windows, lamps were still burning; through the trellis-work doors of steam-baths, artificial female laughter flowed, with sounds of clinking metal. In the distance, the moonlight designed fragments of facades, col-

106

umns and sections of porticos, against the tapestry background of an ardent dark blue, pricked with the tremulous glimmers of stars.

However, from the depths of the precipice of shadow in which the black and solid mass of the Circus could be divined, like a crouching monster, before the enormous, twisted silver serpent that the Tiber made in the night, an enormous roaring filled the air, rising into the atmosphere to fill it with a long, raucous terrible clamor. And other roars immediately rose up, like echoes, nostalgically—voices of menace and, at the same time, of distress: wild beasts imprisoned in the vivaria, perhaps sniffing, on the sea-breeze, the effluvia of the distant homelands from which Rome, the mistress of the world, had snatched them.

XIII

The Apparition of Filiola

THE GLADIATORS inside the popina were quarreling again. The women—save for Linela, swooning in the muscular arms of Cornelio, who had unlaced and taken off his bronze armor—were discussing the sums that their charms brought them and the quality of their rich lovers, the lovers of the heart siding with one or other of them. Already, blades were clinking in the furious hands that were drawing them from scabbards with trefoil points.

Manechus and Sepeos had remained in the doorway, seeking the cool air of the street, now peaceful. They turned round just as Arizanus had got to grips with Chylaides, while Gueranus, interposing himself between Saper and Simias, forced the Greek back into a corner, where he bumped into empty tankards. And Lenia, the tavern-keeper's wife, going in search of help, slipped out through the door of the atrium that gave access to the stairway leading to the cubicles.

Manechus and Sepeos each took hold of the bodies of Simias and Saper. Simias was bleeding from the thigh. The doyen, Gueranus and Sepeos called them to order vehemently.

"Come on, warriors, are you not noblemen of the sword and the lance? Challenge one another, and the city, Rome, will decide which of you merits her love."

"Casper the lanista," Gueranus proposed, "will tell you tomorrow how gladiators settle their quarrels honestly."

Without wanting to listen, the gladiators struggled; the most cultivated, Chylaides, growled imprecations and obscenities in the Homeric fashion.

Suddenly, however, on the threshold of the atrium, where the light of the full moon struck with its silver darts the basin between the flagstones of the ruddy travertine, a young woman appeared, clad in a white palla over a sky-blue subucula secured at the waist by a girdle.

She raised two thin and very pale hands and, tilting back her head, aureoled by a flood of amber gold in order to avoid the sweep of a blade, said: "Lord, lords! Don't shed your blood for love of yourselves. Regrets will gnaw your souls tomorrow, and more than one will weep over his actions of a bad hour. Don't you know that there's a God who doesn't like bloodshed, and don't you fear his wrath? He has said, of murderers, that those who live by the sword shall perish by the sword! And it's not only the death that you dread that he means, but the death of your good deeds, the forgetfulness and loss of love. Love your neighbor, warriors, and kill no more, if you dream of the joy beyond the present life."

And all of them, having heard the melodious voice of the frail virgin, lowered their blades, and, not really understanding the meaning of all those words, bowed before her, as if she were a sacred and inviolable messenger bringing the caduceus of peace between belligerents, murmuring in a tone of respectful softness:

"Ave, Filiola!"

XIV

The Caresses of Speech

"SALVE to you all!" she replied.

And, smiling now that the gladiators, having calmed down, were standing there, not really knowing what fury had precipitated them against one another a little while before, Filiola went to Simias, who had a bad cut on his hand, from the middle finger to the wrist, and whose pierced thigh was letting droplets of blood rain down on the flagstones. Swiftly, she opened the hidden door of a cupboard, on which a lewd scene was painted, of two matrons bringing a virgin to a faun with goat's feet and a hairy and monstrous virility: Pan, Priapus and Satyr, whose torso was cuirassed with overlapping plates, and who had a helmet like that of a velite on his head, behind his horns.

Filiola took out some delicate fabric, and a bottle, with which she impregnated the cloth. Without false modesty, she unlaced the buffalo-leather thigh-guard to expose the wound, the edges of which she washed carefully with olive-oil, and, in spite of the resistance of the mercenary, who affected to find those cares unnecessary for an insignificant wound, she insisted on being allowed to apply unguent and bandage the limb.

"It's better, Simias, not to put the cnemides back on. The bronze is too heavy, and will make you suffer a fever.

"Yes," insisted Lenia, obsequiously, "you can collect them tomorrow before going to Casper's place—for you'll be healed tomorrow."

Fortunately," said Simias, "it's my left hand that's wounded."

"Caius Saper," said Gueranus, brining a bottle with a narrow neck and a belly rounded like a melon, "I offer you this *ampulla*, which I recommend to you, of true Falernian, if you give your right hand to Simias."

"So be it—we aren't enemies. Your hand, comrade."

"It's the maid who'll clasp yours," said Simias, laughing. "She has no rancor against you." As he spoke his eyes encountered the mauve irises of Filiola.

Thus, all those turbulent, uncouth men, accustomed to shedding blood as a métier and a game, uniquely preoccupied with violence, contemplated the delicate virgin, charmed, and listened to the soft and persuasive voice, as musical as that of the women of Campania, but with a very personal nuance in its melody. Thus, as if her spirit impregnated the atmosphere of the popina with a sudden fluid of amour, all terror and all evil thought had been dissipated merely by her presence, by the charm of her gracious youth and the seduction of her new beauty.

Manechus clapped Sepeos on the shoulder, who was looking at Filiola pensively. She had taken refuge behind the massive table that served as a counter. Seated on a high, capacious oak-wood chair, where Lenia was habitually enthroned, the slender silhouette of the young woman stood out against the brown background of the chair-back, sculpted with lion-heads by some ingenuous artist. The darting tongues of the wild beasts had been painted red; in the carved wood of their tangled manes, the unsteady glow of the smoky three-beaked lamp, whose copper chainettes were greasy, illuminated golden reflections, lending the profiles and gaping maws an artificial life of hieratic and immobile creatures, as if tamed.

Her hands leaning on the table and her golden hair floating, Filiola seemed a figure of dream strayed into the brutalities of the décor among the grim characters that populated it, filling the fetid popina with raucous voices, already replete with winy fumes and a strong male odor of hair and skin, mingled with the reek of the fried fish and roasted meat that Lenia sold from the fifth to the seventh hour for people who ate in the establishment, not having the leisure to cook their own meal.

White, with the carnal whiteness of spring roses, Filiola's complexion had the transparency of azalea petals or white irises. Her face seemed to Sepeos a pearl encased in the golden setting of an item of jewelry: her hair. Her mauve eyes, beneath arched light brunette eyebrows with reflections of ardent blonde, had the melancholy color of autumnal anemones, below a slightly low forehead, broad between the temples; the straight nose with palpitating nostrils, rosy with a nacreous pink, surmounted the delicate arc of the mouth, which one might have thought modeled with two parted leaves of the corolla of a crimson fuchsia. And her oval face seemed, in its ensemble, a magnolia flower in which the frozen auroral dew had formed the gems of her eyes, along with two droplets of the blood of doves forming her lips. And her white palla rendered her in her entirety a great lily that might have grown in that sewer.

The new gladiator saw her smile at him. And more than anyone, he submitted, at that moment of poignant sadness, remorse and rage, to the indescribable charm of Filiola—more than any of his rude companions, whose primitive and ferocious wrath her mere presence had calmed.

"You find her beautiful," Manechus said to the Egyptian. "She's Gueranus' maidservant. She's very sweet, but a little crazy."

He summoned her, not roughly, but in the manner in which one talks to an inn slave. "That's not all, child. You have to show this boy to the room where he'll lodge, tonight and many other nights.

"Come, if you want to, gladiator," she said. "Your room is ready; I took care of it, on my mistress Lenia's order, as soon as she released me—for it appears that I was at fault."

"No," said Sepeos, "not yet. Would you care to sit down with us, Filiola? To sad hearts the perfume of such a flower as you is sweet and consoling."

"You're suffering?" asked the virgin. "Are you not going to confide your pain to the One who is able to collect its tears, in order to water the corollas in the depths of souls that dolors sow with rude hands, like those of laborers? They ripen nevertheless, the fruits and the wheat that slake the thirst and nourish the bodies of human beings."

Manechus interrogated her: "You said, little slave, that you've been punished?"

"The mistress had attached me, in her cubicle, to the marble and oak sideboard. She thinks she is torturing me thus, but during that time, I dream; I have time to think of the ideas that render me happy, and I see exquisite things, people who neither swear not quarrel, nor insult me, during those hours."

"At least she hasn't beaten you, the old woman?"

Filiola blushed and said nothing. She did not want to lie, nor to tell the truth, to accuse Lenia. But Sepeos showed his friend the violet and red streaks that marked the delicate pinkness of the girl's thin wrists.

"Oho!" cried Manechus. "By Pollux! You see that Megaera, Sepeos? See to it, yourself, in the house, that they dare not torment that child any more. It's because of Simo Barbax, who wants to hire her in order to take her to his villa in Neapolis once a week. She's afraid of him, and weeps every time it's a matter of going to his house." He turned back to Filiola. "Barbax is rich, though; he might free you, if you knew how to capture him, as one captures that kind of bear."

And Manechus burst into coarse laughter, which, in his view, ought to complete his thought sufficiently.

Filiola looked at the doyen of the gladiators pityingly. "Yes," she said, "I'm afraid of that man. There are sentiments that you can't comprehend. Christos wants us to be chaste, that one should keep for the beloved the flower of one's flesh and the kisses that a great love inspires toward one alone, the elect of the heart who is everything to you. You don't know Christos, you can't understand."

"Who, then," asked Sepeos, "is this Christos that you're mentioning to us for the second time."

"The one who died to redeem men from the sin that engendered the suffering of the human race. He's God, and yet he wanted to incarnate himself, to be among us and to be a dolorous victim for us. He taught truth, tenderness and scorn of violence. He said to people: 'Love one another!' He's the Apostle of the entire love that will one day embrace the whole world, with no more distinction of sex, nation or rank. To those who suffer he said: 'Your pain is sowing inexpressible joys for the future, for my Father, who is in Heaven, loves those whom life has rolled as a river does cadavers that are thrown into it.' And those who believe in Him are happy, for they hope, they love others and seek goodness."

"Then it's because you hope that you're beautiful and good?" said Sepeos.

"I'm still an abysm of sin," she replied. Then, fixing him with her gaze, she said: "You're the one who vanquished Kerbrix? You killed the poor Gaul? His wife is one of us; she has three children as blond as summer wheat. You didn't know him?"

"No," Sepeos stammered. "He had three children as blond as ripe wheat . . . and I killed him!"

"Did you know him, Kerbrix?"

"No, I saw him in the vomitorium for the first time, as well as Callixtus, and Manechus, who was fighting against my decade but who wants to be my friend, as I am and always will be his."

A large sigh inflated Filiola's breast. "I knew it; you're not wicked men, but all the soul of soldiers and gladiators passes into their swords; they kill without hatred. Christos abhors blood and wounds."

"You know," said Manechus, while Filiola was serving other clients, "don't be impressed; the child is a Christian and, like all those of the new sect, a little crazy. Those people adore a donkey's head, or a fish. They gather together to sing bizarre hymns and profess love in the fashion of Oriental freedmen and Asiatic slaves. As for the child, she's a virgin. Not for much longer, though. I think Lenia will soon sell her to Barbax."

"To the merchant of ferocious beasts? Oh, the poor thing! A strange impression took possession of me while she was speaking, Manechus. It seemed to me that a warm caress enveloped my head and all my flesh, which was burning with an intense fever. My dejection was attenuated into a tender melancholy."

As he spoke the words *dejection* and *melancholy* Filiola was coming back toward Sepeos; she soothed him with one of those strange phrases that came to her from who knows where.

"Your heart is like the withered roses that retain a little of the perfume they had in former days, in the dew of the dawn, in the glory of dusk. Be tranquil; for you, happiness will flower again."

XV

The Elect of an Evening

AN immense tumult suddenly filled the Via Suburra, of furiously rolling chariots, coming from the heart of the city, which stopped not far from the popina. Joyful vociferations, squeals like those of abducted faunesses and laughter overlapped.

Lenia had already gone back to her cubicle. Gueranus, Barbax and Manechus, in advance of the others, ran outside. Emerging from an infamous house, the phallus of whose sculpted façade was glowing with the reflections of Phoenican fire, crimson and amethyst, a woman veiled in silver tulle, superb and arrogant in her tread, passed over a platform of bucklers formed by gladiators. A gigantic Dacian, on an oblong lectica, was carried beside her by Mauritanian slaves clad in orange yellow; Augustans followed, dragging prostitutes whose ripped garments allowed the sight of bare flesh and sexual foam.

The crazed cortege was howling "Ave, Stella mundi!"—hail, star of the world—"Salve, Venus!" and "Ave, Luxuria!" amid the bloody glare of torches and the odor of perfumes of Araby that the thurifer-bearers, men and women admirable in beauty, were burning in cassolettes and incense-burners, as if around a divinity.

Quivering, Manechus gripped Sepeos' shoulders with both hands. "It's Her!" he grated, in a low voice. "Messalina! She's having herself brought to the steam-baths of Suburra with the elect of an evening, the decade leader Lucion, a barbarian! All, I tell you, all those who have not shown her love . . . all except me!"

"You're trembling, Manechus!"

"It's with rage. . . ."

The other gladiators and Barbax, after a rapid "Salve," joined the cortege.

"Ave Diva!"

"Juno!"

"Venus!"

"Salve!"

"Luxuria!"

They knew they would find more wine and lust behind Messalina, whose triumphant magnificence caused the eyes, blades and desire of all the males in Rome to be raised in her honor around her.

While Gueranus bolted the door again after Manechus' departure, however, Filiola picked up a wax candle and led Sepeos to the threshold of a cubicle where a marble bed awaited him, covered with brightly-colored carpet and a bear-skin. Women representing the hours were painted on the wall.

"I hope Christos, in response to my prayer, will give you pleasant dreams."

With that wish, like a dream vision, she disappeared.

XVI

The Gladiators' School

THE slave gladiators, arranged under the arcades of an immense atrium, emerged under the conduct of decade leaders through rather low bronze doors, which obliged some Gauls, Celts, Dacians and colossal Lithuanians to duck their heads. Several were dragging chains that shackled their legs; others retained at their ankles heavy dentellate plates which the lanista's valets unfastened on one side only, without removing them, in order that the chiefs could see immediately which ones had been punished. When they were all lined up, the decade leaders inspected them. The monitors of each chamber came to read and hand to the masters of gymnastics, palestra, etcetera, the list of men who were ill, killed in brawls, put in the cells or who had broken a limb during the previous day's exercises.

Salvaz, Birus, Lacero and Cornelio—who doubled his combat salary as an instructor in fighting with the sword, the ax and the spear, because of the debauches that ruined him incessantly, and gambling, of which he was a passionate victim—allowed their discontentment to burst forth. Seven gladiators from their maniples were dead, nineteen wounded.

The previous day, during the night, in a moment of excited nostalgia, those men who were prisoners of war brought back from Asia to serve in the triumph of the consul Avicius Miso, or Gauls expedited by Appius from Gaul and Venetia, had taken advantage of a lack of surveillance on the part of those monitors— doubtless occupied in playing *duodecima scripta,* throwing dice or

118

counting the number of knucklebones—to attack one another with all the daggers and short spears that they had been able to steal, not to mention unbolting the iron fittings of their prison doors to make deadly weapons of them. In order to quell the riot it had been necessary to summon other gladiators from nearby dormitories to apprehend them one by one, separate them and tie them up.

"Camillus, my patron, is going to bear a terrible grudge," said Salvaz, "when he finds out what a wretched state they've reduced our Lanion to."

The gladiator in question had been celebrated for his skill and legendary strength before even having combated once. It was known that, in defense, almost alone by the side of his chief, Birlix, he had routed a band of the consul Vernes Aro's most robust cavaliers; ten ordinary men could have been held in check by the giant, whose agility ceded nothing to his Herculean strength. The young patrician Camillus had offered a Lithuanian bear, acquired from Barbax at the enormous price of four hundred sesterces, and an aurochs, to do battle with the captive giant successively.

"It appears," said Cornelio, "That enormous bets have been laid, and that the consul himself . . ."

"Himself! Avicius Miso thinks more about gambling than occupying himself with the affairs of the Empire. And perhaps he's right; in truth, it's more prudent.

"Yes," growled Lacero, "putting large sums on charioteers, gladiators or lions, he's not risking his head, whereas public affairs resemble the wood of Cacus:[1] there's a fanatic of the god Caesar at every turning."

"Shh!" said Salvaz. "Risk your own life if you want to talk like that, but don't compromise your friends."

As he spoke those words in a whisper, the decade leader indicated his colleague, the somber Birus, with a wink. "Messalina has distinguished him. Claudius sent him a golden crown at the games last ides. He frequently stands guard in the Augusta's apartments.

---

1 Cacus was a giant said to have lived on the Aventine hill before Rome was founded; Ovid depicted him in particularly lurid terms; he was killed by Hercules.

A slave physician by the name of Mirzan, who wore the Oriental mitra, approached the group of leader. "The wounded man can be cured; I won't answer for his life as yet, but it's not as serious as it might have appeared."

"By Jupiter! Camillus might well be capable, if you save him, of giving you more gold than you need to liberate your paltry person," Salvaz replied. "If I were you, I'd reach an understanding with him in advance on that subject. You hold your fortune or your ruination in your hands."

Mirzan sniggered, showing teeth like a wolf's, and bowed obsequiously. "Thank you noble warrior, for your advice; I'll take it as soon as I know whether he'll be able to live and fight."

The free gladiators—mostly former slaves freed in consequence of victories in their first combats in the circus or enemy soldiers captured in war and then liberated for their bravery in the arena—were beginning to flow into the establishment, *ludus gladiatorius*, where, under the direction of the lanista Casper, they formed pupils in the practice of their art.

Each of them had to take a section, under his orders, and instruct them, while the decade leaders lent their troops, already trained, and regulated fights—simulated only, in the sense that the weapons were curtailed: wooden swords that affected the form of a blade, spears that were staffs fitted with wadding at the tip, and axes of fir-wood, with which one fought after being coiffed with old discarded helmets with lowered visors to protect the face.

Thus, Manechus, Cornelio, Birus, Lacero, Salvaz and twenty other accomplished gladiators made their men maneuver in the immense stadium, their arms rising and falling heavily, or briskly parrying blows launched by their adversaries. Archers were firing at targets from one end of arcades to the other, challenging one another to hit distant and imperceptible objectives. Other warriors, at the chiefs' command, were learning to handle a spear—or the shorter pilum of the Roman infantry—which they brandished and hurled at wooden mannequins.

These exercises normally lasted several hours, punctuated by rest periods, during which the men drank their ration of wine from earthenware cups, or hydromel, which the Celts, Germans, Dacians, Kimris and Saxons preferred.

Into small adjacent courtyards floored with white black and gray marble, the monitors and instructors, recognizable by their belts of white or yellow leather, took each pupil one by one in order to teach him the principles of combat. An awning made of sailcloth filtered the sunlight falling on the Corinthian atrium and the vast courtyards that slaves sprinkled with water from time to time.

In the center, amid the cries and groans of gymnasts and wrestlers, the jets of fountains murmured, in a monotonous twitter, the interminable and gentle song of water. The great courtyard, thickly sanded, shone as if strewn with myriads of tiny gems, which the fall of agile human bodies and the violent gestures of muscular feet displaced, sometimes causing them to fly with scintillations tinted with all the colors of light.

To begin with, the apprentice gladiators had to make their oiled bodies supple, by movements in unison, which made a hundred arms extend like threats toward the sky, or twenty swords and twenty axes fall simultaneously, while wooden blades or padded lances clashed rhythmically, one decade against another. Two by two, others attacked one another; they were the most skillful, the ones who had made their debut in the arena and had been judged worthy of measuring themselves against famous rivals in the presence of the superb Messalina or the Roman people, under the aegis and the menace of the divine Emperor Augustus Claudius.

Casper, the lanista, usually supervised the second hour of exercises. On the most remarkable he lavished encouragement and advice, demonstrating the thrusts that he preferred, scolding those whose laxity irritated his sanguine vigor. Sometimes he wrenched the weapon from a monitor's hand, and manipulated it with unparalleled dexterity, or stopped in front of a decade, and mocked a clumsily delivered thrust or a maladroit parry.

"Faster, by Jupiter! Faster! Your arms are made of wool, Milito. What were you doing last night for your limbs to be so sluggish? Good, Simias! Watch your head, there! Bring the spear across in a single gesture, Saphis! If you hesitate, Lacero will cut your throat well before having encountered wood or iron!"

That day, Casper became very angry when he learned about the night's tumults and its results. Luc Sapercion, the guardian of the slave gladiators, was summoned. The man, a Herculean Greek from the mountains of Macedonia, trembled as he approached the big boss.

"How many dead are there?" Casper roared.

Silently, the Greek lifted nine fingers, for two Syrians had died of their wounds in the morning.

"Which are they? Reply, or I'll . . ."

"Master, it's not my fault. Yesterday, about the ninth hour, I made my round; I put irons myself, with the aid of three slaves, on Boris and Machani, whom I surprised in their cubicle *in flagrante delicto* wasting strength. I had the Gauls' guard beaten with rods, and two others who are dragging chains on their left leg over there, near the third pillar on the left. They were all playing *duocedima scripta*."

"Which are the dead?"

"Balthis, Cormo, Virgex, Salpestros, Larminus, Formicola . . ."

"Oh, Lord Mars! Formicola, the only one who really knew how to kill the finest black lions gracefully. . . ."

"Moreas. . . ."

The lanista seemed to explode like an overripe grenadine. His dark brown eyes flashed; his nose turned crimson, dotted with rubies; his frowning eyebrows punctuated his forehead, marked from one temple to the other by a red scar, with a grim accolade. His entire person, of medium height, rigid and wiry, seemed to clench and contract, as big cats do before pouncing.

Luc Sapercion, terrified, stood their mouth agape in the face of that anger, as if some monster had fascinated him.

"That one alone was worth more than your life!"

With a sweep of his terrible hand, the lanista grabbed the back of the guardian's neck, the bones of which cracked horribly, and then, turning the unconscious man round like a parcel of rags or some boneless mannequin, as actors do in tragicomic parades, he threw him with all his might into the fountain in the center of the sanded courtyard. The slave's head split as it struck the white marble rim, suddenly splashed with bloody brain tissue, while the body, too large to be completely immersed, was agitated with tiny spasms, under the play of the water, glinting in the concentric cascade.

Sepeos saw the faces of the lanistas clouded by distress before the wrath of their chief; even a slave who was three times a murderer, the gladiator Barcomus, visibly feared such a death, devoid of glory.

But Casper, satisfied, his muscles relaxing, suddenly spoke affably, asking for news, and giving his own of Ostia, to which he frequently went to make purchases of men, horses or ferocious beasts for the public games and the sanguinary amusements of the patricians. Then he wanted to see Sepeos, had him stripped naked, commanded him to stretch his limbs one after the other, admired his bulging muscles, wiry arms and the suppleness of is precociously athletic body.

"Poor Kerbrix! His manes must be sad, on the banks of the Acheron, for having been beaten by an ephebe. But if it's any consolation to him, at least it was a handsome rival."

Meekly, Sepeos rehearsed, under the orders of Manechus—who had made the master lanista party to his intentions and special benevolence toward the new gladiator—the rudimentary movements by which pupils were prepared in the manipulation of the sword. After the hours that he devoted himself to those violent gymnastics, Sepeos felt a certain lassitude in all his limbs, but the vanity of his strength, the self-respect of the métier in which he had made his debut with a success already famous in Rome, made him vanquish the fatigue and excited him to the extent of inspiring unexpected leaps. Casper questioned him; he did not want to believe that the Egyptian had never studied under one of the classic fighting instructors of the cestus and the sword. He was obstinate, curious to know the past of the lover of Karysta, the Tanagran acrobat.

"You say that you haven't been taught anything, except for how to throw a discus, wrestle in the Hellenic fashion and to fight with fists gloved with the cestus?"

"Yes. I'd never held a sword before the games given by Silius."

"Amazing! Mars himself, by Pollux!" the foremost lanista of the epoch muttered between his teeth, like a dog gnawing a much appreciated bone. "You have, at least, cultivated the wooden sword, brandished the club?"

"No, but I'm one of the Roma of Egypt, who are the descendants of the athletes and acrobats of Persia, Arabia, Syria and the mysterious isles of the Levant. Since childhood, my body's been accustomed to all flexibilities."

Sepeos spoke proudly, in the face of men who were reputed to be the strongest and most adroit in the Empire. Their gaze and Casper's exclamations fortified his increasing hope of being admitted, in accordance with the Augusta's desire, to the number of the hundred gladiators, *Divae imperiales*, the favorite guards of the sumptuous Messalina, the sanguinary, sadistic and superb Aphrodite. Thus, easily, he would be able to realize his ambition, and attain the atrocious and delicious objective of his present existence: to avenge the extinct graces of the Tanagran dancer. He would get close to the filthy Messalina—in order to kill her.

Finally, the slave gladiators, with the blissful laughter of vegetative individuals devoid of thought finally delivered from quotidian labor, went in long files past the eyes of the decade leaders, who made them return the weapons, counting them carefully for fear that even more of them might have been stolen.

The sun declined, tinting the canvas panels of the awning hung over the courtyard pink and gold. Sepeos followed Manechus and Casper, at a sign from his master and friend, into an oblong arena open to the sky. A horse was brought by a slave and, on the affirmation of Sepeos that he had been riding since birth, the chief of the lanistas put him through his paces without a saddle stirrups or bridle. Finally, behind Manechus, among a troop of equestrian gladiators who were ordered to separate into two distinct platoons, Sepeos, exhausted, but his soul empty and joyful, his taut nerves relieved by action of the heavy burden of his thoughts and memories, turned and spun, leapt and charged in a glad fury, in which, harassed by movement and the blissful lassitude of living brutally, his sadness faded away.

XVII

On the Ramparts

ON that ardent summer's day, Rome seemed prostrate in the intense heat of a leaden sun. In the Forum, the temples and the porticos were like monsters irradiated by light, which filled the square with ardor and reflections. Under its colonnades, the money-changers and usurers were half-asleep, with their elbows on their counters, simple benches where coins from all the lands of the Empire glittered in wooden bowls.

In Suburra, during these heavy hours, Filiola remained free to come and go as she pleased, under the slightest pretext. Clients hardly ever came into the popina in broad daylight, where Master Gueranus went to sleep between the second and third hours, heavily, while Lenia slumped, her limbs soft and her elbows on the massive table that served as a counter, among the empty vessels of earthenware or wood.

The young woman escaped from the shop then, and followed the lines of shadow that the walls provided from the burning sun. She went to visit one of her coreligioinists, a slave like her or a humble servant, unless there was a gathering for a sermon or some office in the home of Villia Samelina or Apia Coroddina, two patriciennes who, one in the center of the Trastevere and the other in her villa at the Porta Capena, gave hospitality to the apostles and priests of Christos, and welcomed the disciples of the Galilean god to their homes.

As often as not, though, when no gathering solicited her,

Filiola liked to wander through the suburban streets of Rome, sometimes cut by fields where market gardens had been established, and where trees allowed a little of their green and russet tresses to overhang walls or fences.

Today, Filiola was wandering thus, pensively, in the direction of the Via Nomentana, when a man emerged from the house of the lanista Casper, in front of the gladiators' barracks, to whom the janitor and the porter, who were stroking the guard-dog, addressed a respectful and cordial salutation. Filiola did not recognize Sepeos because of the bright sunlight that was blinding her, and she was internally astonished that her footsteps, guided by an unconscious thought, had taken her to a place where the Egyptian might be, since he was not taking a siesta that afternoon in his cubicle, near her own room.

"*Ave dulcis puella!*"—hail, sweet adolescent.

"You, Sepeos? You're not taking a siesta either, since you're coming from Casper's house?"

"Too many thoughts are buzzing in my brain, obsessing me. I prefer to idle, wandering no matter where, rather than deliver myself to nightmares and the demons that trouble sleep. But you, little Filiola, where are you going at such an hour through deserted Rome, under the ardor of the sun? If you like, I'll accompany you. By Pollux, that would be a great joy to me in the solitude where I become sad."

"I'd like that!" she replied, swiftly, very simply, letting out her pleasure at not being alone in dreaming and listening to the whining of the cicadas on the hot branches of the garden trees.

"Where shall we go? I'd like to give you an enjoyment; if any place pleases you by preference, I'll gladly take you there."

"Wherever you wish, Sepeos; it doesn't matter to me, since . . ."

She did not finish, and blushed. She had very nearly said, ingenuously, what she was thinking: . . . *since you're with me.* So they walked on through the streets, slowly, Sepeos allowing himself nevertheless to be guided by Filiola, and following her.

"Do Gueranus and Lenia know that you've left?"

"Oh, of course. I told them that I'd be back before the fourth hour. They didn't make any objection. They're too afraid that my friends, the disciples of Christos, might want to buy me out, and that I'll escape them. They've fixed the price of my liberty at two hundred sesterces. It's much more than I'm worth, but they fear that even at that price, and in spite of their poverty, the faithful of the Lamb might deliver me from my servitude."

"It's very little for so much beauty," Sepeos complimented her.

"Christos has said that a beautiful face is often like a fine robe that masks ugliness."

She pronounced the final words while smiling, with a hint of naïve coquetry and mischief. Without replying, Sepeos gave her the lie with a gaze that expressed all his gratitude for the flowery spring with which she brightened the mourning of his present life.

They had arrived at one of the gates of Rome, and were now going along the ramparts that make a girdle of burned emerald, made of calcined grass, for the city. Bare, like the brown and russet backs of old lions, the fortifications of the capital of the Empire formed a circle of banks of jaundiced earth, raised on foundations of hard marble that almost disappeared in the ground. Rare and thin, stunted plants made a meager fleece for those elevation, similar in their desolate monotony, under the sun, to a motionless flock of sheep. Here and there a tree bristled, some gray olive-tree, pine or eucalyptus with sickle-shaped leaves.

Beneath one of those precarious shelters, Sepeos and Filiola sat down. He was holding a branch torn from a bush, on which a few leaves still remained. She let her head incline forward slightly over her breast. Both remained silent for a time, each following the thread of their reverie. Sepeos, tall and strong, in his white tunic tightened at the waist by a leather belt, scratched the ground mechanically with the end of his stock. Filiola was only wearing a long subucula, without a palla, knotted at the waist by a cord of woven wool that two tapering tassels terminated over her right thigh. She seemed thus almost a little girl who had precociously acquired a woman's eyes, and the first fruits of a virgin at the age of puberty.

A cry went up from the Tullianum. It was a heart-rending and terrible human wail that seemed to be several voices. Filiola shuddered, from head to toe.

Sepeos asked her: "You know that the captives in the Mamertine prison are to die at the next games? They're all chiefs."

"Yes," she said, "and I weep sometimes in secret, thinking about it. I've been assured, at the assembly, that there are several of our brethren among the Gauls and the Germans. One of ours, who is a priest, was able by some subterfuge or other to get into the Tullianum. He told us about the suffering of those prisoners, and the tortures of hunger and thirst that have made them thin, with the pale faces of invalids. They're treated like the wild beasts destined for the games; they're starved in the hope that it will make them more ferocious and fight harder. But none of ours will defend themselves, because it's forbidden for the disciples of Christos to kill."

"Must they allow themselves to be devoured, then, without making any effort? They must be devoid of courage, and I don't understand such a renunciation."

"You don't understand, Sepeos! That's true. You can't understand. You don't know that they die like that in order to confess their faith by martyrdom. They prefer to be massacred than to soil their hands with blood, even that of their executioners. Christos, sitting by his Father's side, orders his angels to prepare crowns for them. For the martyrs, the celestial choirs tune their citharas, and Paradise is full of a rumor of celebration, when their souls are exhaled, blissfully from the poor bruised bodies that the beasts and the weapons have torn apart."

Sepeos stared at the young Christian, with an astonishment that frightened him. The enthusiasm of Filiola, who was transfigured as she spoke, moved him with an inexpressible, indescribable sensation. He did not understand the strange impression the gripped his soul as he listened to those bizarre statements, astonishing words that expressed sentiments so different from those he experienced. So these people did not experience any hatred against those who tortured them? Death appeared to them as the great liberator from human misery. An immense hope attracted them. All those ideas, sown in him by the young woman, collided obscurely in his primitive mind with the seeds and first shoots of a new love.

In that epoch, when the doctrines of paganism were no longer a refuge for an infinity of skeptical souls, belief in the gods, in another life, the Elysian fields, seemed to the sons of a worn-out world coming to an end to be very uncertain and problematic. A question mark hung over death and the future existence. Many hoped for final annihilation, the abyss into which body and soul would sink, without any further consciousness of being or having been, in the joy of no longer suffering, of no longer experiencing with apprehension the painful tomorrows and misfortunes incessantly suspended over human beings, like eagles with inevitable beaks and claws.

Filiola emanated a charm that Sepeos could not explain. It was not the sensual attraction of youth that had rendered him the slave of Karysta, the Tanagran dancing girl; but an authority, perhaps unconscious, gave Filiola a power over those who listened to her: a mysterious power to which Sepeos, more than anyone else, had to submit, by reason of his melancholy—which is always a depression. When she spoke, her golden hair formed a nimbus around the delicate oval of her face, and her violet eyes were starry with bright reflections, like stars illuminating in a bright sky.

Again, they remained silent for a long moment. Then, as the Egyptian sighed, she said: "You've been very unhappy?"

Sepeos lowered his head; his eyes filled with tears.

"You loved Karysta a great deal?"

"Yes. She's dead, but my dolor is more alive than ever. The thought of vengeance consoles me and sustains me."

"Avenging yourself? On whom will you avenge yourself?"

With a terrible gesture, Sepeos pointed at Monte Palatino, where the palace of the Augusta loomed up in the midst of gardens. "*Her!*"

"Messalina! She's omnipotent—but the gesture of God threatens the princes of Rome."

"Filiola, your God isn't as strong as the armed hand of a man moved by the idea of vengeance."

"He disposes of everything and everyone, including you, Sepeos; you serve his designs, although you think you are acting of your own will."

"He wanted Karysta dead, then? In that case, your God is as infamous as theirs, whose hands are soiled with blood and whose eyes smile at the ignominies of this atrocious world."

"Don't blaspheme. Are you the only one suffering, then? And by Christos, many others have been consoled."

"I was in love. Messalina has pillaged my heart. I was living insouciant of everything, at the whim of the weather and the hours, content with the fruits of my labor. Karysta danced, and I, the strolling player, among the crowd on every forum, in the midst of the fêtes where she had so much success, saw nothing but her, the Tanagran, in whom all grace and all beauty shone then, for me. But you, Filiola, you often seem sad. Does your life also conceal troubles?"

She formed an ineffable smile of resignation. "Oh, me . . ."

Sepeos made a gesture of soothing protection toward Filiola: a hand on one shoulder, while the other held both of hers. And she did not experience any fear, quite naturally, and did not make any modest gesture, as when, among the gladiators, she folded herself up, like a brushed mimosa, in the middle of the tumultuous popina. At present, the cloud that veiled the face and tarnished the eyes of Sepeos had dissipated. He questioned the virgin quietly.

The city was now beginning to emerge clearly from the sheet of dense blinding light that almost prevented its contemplation. Immaculate marble frontons were beginning to outline their caryatides. Pink bands of travertine on the facades of edifices seemed to be smiles on immense stone faces. The Tiber rolled its foamy wavelets, which came to die against the flanks of the heavy moored galleys variegating the banks with the bright colors with which they were painted.

Gradually the daylight paled, while the rumor of a crowd breathing contentedly rose, from the Forum and the streets, a noise of awakening, after the torpor of heavy days.

"You want to know about my life?" said Filiola. "I only remember a little of my early childhood, incidents that make me think that I was born free. My father was absent for months on end. He guided one of the ships that go to the blue islands of the Ionian Sea. My mother was beautiful, always draped in long white veils with rhythmic pleats. Sometimes, she wept, waiting beside the stormy sea for the crimson sail that she recognized among all the rest. It was, I think, on the coast of Sicyone, for I can still hear that name pronounced, in a very soft and musical tone, which I remember—my father's voice.

"One day, mad with joy, he said to my mother: 'Florina, we're rich. A merchant who has already made several thousand aureus in that traffic, has offered to associate me with his business. It's a matter of taking products from the peninsula to the African coast and bringing back to Ostia, Syracuse or Athens, to exchange for gold, the skins of beasts—lions, tigers, hippopotamuses—elephants' tusks, gum Arabic and fine swords that can be sold for their weight in gold. I'll take both of you on my first voyage.'

"Alas, on the return journey we were boarded by black pirates, who appeared on the deck of the ship. I can still see one of them laughing, with an enormous rictus, while striking my mother with a blow of an ax, and then carrying me away, in tears, on to the other ship."

"You mother was dead?"

"She fell with her throat split, bathing in a pool of blood. And I also saw, at the foot of a mast, the face and staring eyes of my father, whose tunic and pallium were stained with large red patches."

"Poor, poor Filiola! But how did you come to Rome?"

"I don't really know. We sailed for a long, long time. Often, the pirates went ashore in the evening, with the ship moored in some port. And at night, nothing could be heard but the shouting of the sailors and the monotonous creaking of the yard-arms, sometimes punctuated by plaints: the captives, in the hold of the vessel, lamenting. On clear mornings I saw the unfortunates, their feet shackled with heavy chains, crowded on the deck, where the chief mariner counted them. Several of them died, whom the black sailors threw overboard, with a sinister grunt when they lifted the cadaver to send it to the sharks, a band of which always followed our stern. Finally, all of us were disembarked in a little port near Neapolis. Rough men who all looked like Simo Barbax marched us to Suburra."

"How old were you, Filiola?"

"Ten years."

"And since then, you've been a servant in the Gueranus' popina?"

"No—first I was bought by the majordomo of an old knight, Caius Simianus Vero. My master was good to his female slaves and didn't allow anyone to mistreat the pretty ones. I learned there how to weave silk and wool. I was taught the art of draping togas with graceful pleats and dressing the hair of elegant women, for my master loved Arnicia and wanted to keep her with him incessantly. She didn't like me."

"She was afraid of your eyes," said Sepeos, "of your youth. You might have been redoubtable for her, a virgin and so pleasing. . . ."

"Perhaps that was her thinking. Once, she wanted me to arrange a section of her palla that had come undone, and as I wasn't going fast enough for her liking, she hit me so hard with one side of her silver mirror that my head bled and I fainted. The next day Caius Simianus gave the master of the ergastule the order to sell me right away. That's when Lenia bought me."

She's often harsh, the tavern-keeper's wife?"

Filliola hesitated to reply; she did not want to accuse her mistress, and her mouth was reluctant to lie, especially to Sepeos, whose simple, very pure affection caressed her to the depths of her young, new and delicate soul.

"Oh," said the gladiator, misunderstanding her thought, "you know that it isn't me that will betray you, Filiola. I thought I divined that you were suffering, and your suffering seemed to me to be sister to mine. Lenia isn't patient."

"She rarely hits me. Only there's Barbax, who would give her a lot of money if . . ."

"Barbax! Oh, the vile creature. He resembles the bears he sells to the animal-keepers. So it's for that reason that Lenia locked you up in the cubicle the first night I lodged in Guerianus' house?"

"Because I was weeping and had said that I would never go to that man's house."

They chatted about their present life. But suddenly, at a word from Sepeos, Filiola's face was transfigured. Her eyes were radiant. She was telling him how she had met, in an ergastule to which Lenia sent her to spin wool with other slaves, who paid the masters for the daily work, a man of great indulgence and a fleecy white beard, framing a calm and venerable face.

"During the spinning, he told us about the work of the redemption of the human race by the Hebrew, Christos, who died on the cross for having announced to the unfortunate their imminent participation in happiness and justice. And many have listened to him, who are slaves and who believe, like me, that their soul is still free, and who hope for the distant and magnificent recompense of the poor, who are the elect of God."

Sepeos listened, finding nothing to respond to those unaccustomed words, and without taking account of it, was subject to that mental influence, slowly welcoming in his barbaric mind a mysterious leaven.

They chatted thus for a long time.

Then, as it was getting late, glad of their mutual amity, linked by their secrets and their common suffering, they went back along the ramparts, the bare melancholy of which was intensified in the redness of the evening.

BOOK THREE
The Naked Empress

I

Messalina at Liberty

MUCIUS SAPHIS, a handsome brown-haired ephebe, muscular but slim, with a delicate wiriness, his hair carefully curled by tongs, was lying softly on cushions that he had had Lenia bring from the cubicles, dreaming. At least, if he was not dreaming, he was not doing anything, except examining his fingernails from time to time; they were pink and scrupulously polished, and he rubbed them with a soft brush that he took from a case suspended over his breast.

A former slave employed in the baths—a water-carrier notorious for his licentious habits—he brought water, poured it over the bather, filled the large basin, the labrum, with the wide round brim curled externally like a human lip, and was obliging. He was affranchised by a senator; then, a famous lanista into whose affection he had entered, and reciprocally, had taught him his art, and now Mucius Saphis had his special celebrity. Disdainful, he seemed not to be taking any notice of the coarse and noisy conversation of a group of valets from the Circus; they filled the room with their raucous voices and impregnated the atmosphere with an odor of male sweat mingled with the reek of horses and wild beasts.

But he suddenly frowned and lent an ear to the voices of women who were chatting cheerfully and volubly.

"Saphis resembles us so much, my dear, that I'm assured that Simo Barbax took him instead of a woman one evening when he had drunk too much at Gueranus' and opposite at the caupona of the Nubian Lion."

Others guffawed with laughter. "Oh, really, really? Ha ha! It's too funny. Candilia! Candilia, come over here!" And to the others: "We need to tease her. She has an infatuation for Mucius Saphis."

"You don't say, Linela. That proves she has the same tastes as Sabina."

"I'm not speaking ill of him; he has the best tongue in Rome."

"After the divine Messalina, my dear."

"A goddess must excel in everything, including the cubicle. Ah! here comes Candilia."

"Don't say anything that'll give her pain."

"It's just to laugh. I won't irritate her, your darling."

"Balseth assured me that he'd give a lot of money to measure himself with Birus and Fortex, if the first drawn by lot doesn't kill him. Now, you know that I've bet on him thus far. If I want to marry Cardo, the spice-merchant, I don't have much time to amass the dowry he'll need to install our commerce more handsomely in the Via Nomentana."

"Ambitious! He'll be defeated!"

"Shut up, Sabina, you'll bring me bad luck. I'm going to make a pilgrimage to Pompeii, to make an offering of flowers and two golden phalluses to Venus Physica."

Mucius Sapis shivered, irritated because the amphitheater valets, drunk on strong Campanian wine, were launching themselves into the street shouting formidable *Evohés*, as initiates do at the festivals of Eleusis and Bacchus. He did not get up, too haughty to want to seem interested, more keenly than was appropriate, in petty courtesans. Lenia, having gone to the threshold, laughed like a madwoman—gross epileptic laughter that caused her breasts to quiver gelatinously, along with her swollen belly beneath her Illyrian bardocucullus.

But the valets from the bestiarium shoved her aside as they came back in. The first three picked up Linela, Baltrix and Sabina. The latter two struggled, uttering squeals. Candilia appeared on the threshold, with the bewildered expression of a woman pursued; cries from outside reached the ears of the customers in the popina and the hostess.

"God!" said Lenia. "They're going to pick a quarrel, those brutes, with the lovers of the women who lodge with that riff-raff Isponius."

Gladiators, the regulars of the tavern, came in at the moment when Mucius Saphis was beginning to abuse the valets of the amphitheater, masking with his body the frail Candilia, who was weeping with fear and rage, begging her lover not to involve himself—him, a swordsman—with that rabble.

Caius Saper, Manechus and Simias, followed by Sepeos, came in then. Quickly, they had weighed up the situation and sided with Mucius Saphis. As soon as the amphitheater valets had been expelled however, the latter became the target of joking remarks.

Filiola brought jugs of gilded wine of Vesuvius for each new group. Without paying any heed to the mockery, Mucius Saphis had escaped with Candilia to a cubicle that Lenia rented to couples on a temporary basis.

There was a sudden invasion of laughter and joyful painted faces: Linela, Baltrix and Sabina. A string of prostitutes less familiar in the steam-baths and Suburra—Carosia, who was not yet thirteen and who was naked beneath her loose subucula; Clycera, a haughty blonde adolescent whom the military tribune Marcius Quinalis had affranchised for three kisses; Balsis, Antilla, little birds in red, violet or yellow stolas—came in to see the gladiators.

For Filiola they all had a kind and slightly pitying word. "She's pretty," Candilia said of her," but a little crazy. These Christians don't know how to profit from their youth or their charms."

It was partly because of that, and because they did not fear any rivalry on her part that they pampered her, knowing that she was good and gentle, and consoled the petty chagrins of the fragile scatterbrains.

Dice clattered on the tables. The blows of heavy fists, thumping the wood, underlined good and bad luck. Artisans not far from the popina were working on the hasty fabrication of a new kind of barbed spear for the Scythian expedition that imperator

Marcus Miso was to command, and the resonances of hammers on metal could be heard in the smithy, mingled with the rhythm of their monotonous songs and the cheerful rumors of the street, the exuberant din of Suburra, the ardent quarter.

Everyone was soon taking part in an ardent discussion on the subject of Mormix, the Arverne that Lacero, the decade leader, affirmed to be capable of killing ten men in the same combat with nothing but his formidable hands gloved with an iron cestus that could break spears as a flail crushes ears of wheat. Cornelio declared that he would challenge him the following day. Then the girls stopped laughing in order to look at him admiringly. Linela took his hands, climbed on to his knees and kissed him on the mouth. She had not finished when the echoes of a great joyful racket reached the popina. Sistra rattled and cymbals rang. Nubian runners appeared, their only vestment a panther-skin attached at the shoulders by a tiny gold chain, from which torchlight was reflected. They were carrying naked negresses, illuminated by fulgurances. Chariots rolled in the midst of a sudden glare, laden with Augustan women, intimates of Messalina—and men in Oriental robes or draped in laticlavian togas with wide scarlet bands.

Superb, sometimes obscene, in transparent subuculae of gauze lined with gold and silver lamé, which allowed their breasts and flanks to be seen—patriciennes enlaced with freedmen advanced at the pace of caparisoned horses harnessed to chariots by tethers of precious metal. Other women, lying among the cushions of their lecticas borne by black slaves, who changed relays every hundred paces, raised acclamations or jeers as they passed, which left them disdainful, a fixed smile on their painted lip, their eyes shiny with lustful desire, a desire for amour and blood.

Street-porters, Tiber boatmen, arenarii, all those who fought on the sand of the arena, whether against men or wild beasts, animal-keepers, gladiators, and even bakers, who emerged with bare torsos from the kitchens where they were kneading the bread that was to nourish Rome, appeared on the thresholds. In processions, common prostitutes that the madams tried in vain to retain in the brothels, escaped therefrom with the screeches of drunken bacchantes, brandishing flowers and throwing rose-petals at the passing nobles.

But a maniple of praetorians with golden breastplates, striking their similar bucklers with sparkling javelins, cut a path through the crowd, which scattered, uttering screams, cheers and sexual implorations, as if toward an indecent and venerated divinity. From the corners of streets and behind the boundary markers, through the interstices of shutters, muffled abuse, like handfuls of bran, was launched from nearby houses by hateful mouths—those of mothers whose sons or daughters had disappeared, or whom Claudius, Messalina, Silius and their favorites had soiled. Or the voices of men spat out their rancor or their unslaked desire, at the scorn of their lives, toward the Idol, the Spermatic, the Magnificent, on whom the crowd lavished epithets.

"Ave! Salve! Diva Messalina!"

"Our hearts, we launch them toward you like flowers before Venus or at the foot of altars!"

"Our desires burn before you like cassolettes."

"Ave! Diva! Luxuria!"

The gladiators and soldiers in debauchery, raised their blades symbolically, like erect phalluses, in honor of the mistress of the Roman people, the Naked Empress, the divine slut.

"Ave Augusta Diva Messalina! Ave Venus!"

In the center of a near-naked group of Augustan women, on a sumptuous litter, with a crimson pulvinar that the light of pink horn lanterns caused to blaze like a furnace, Messalina, draped in a mauve palla with scarlet embroidery that allowed the sight of a magnificent stola of golden cloth, brandished a thyrsus encrusted with marvelous gems. And among the rabble of clamoring courtesans, the head of the unkempt Augustans of both sexes, Luxuria, the Empress of Rome and the world, steered toward Gueranus' popina.

Belated honest citizens, knights and merchants scampered fearfully away along the walls. Everyone knew that the Augusta was sometimes seized by strange caprices, such as delivering honest women to the praetorians and her favorites, or constraining peaceable men to abnormal lusts of which, to stimulate her senses, she wanted to be a mocking spectator, in an orgy that often ended bloodily. Then the odor of blood, males and females in rut, mingled with the ardent effluvia of cassolettes, and the perfumes of crushed lilies, jasmines and roses.

As the cortege passed by, the shops closed their doors precipitately. On the contrary, the steam-baths, taverns and brothels illuminated their facades with lamps with several beaks and long round lanterns, also made of transparent pink horn, affecting the form of enormous penises.

The lowest plebeians loved the Empress for the splendor of her body and the windfalls she was worth to paupers—everyone could hope to be the Emperor for an evening, to enjoy himself like Caesar Augustus, and swoon in the same embraces—and even pretty pauperesses, for her caprices, which sometimes led her to throw gold to the most pitiful, at the slightest opportunity for pleasure. So the protests and indignant clamors were soon silenced.

Messalina had the torches extinguished. The rumor of her troop of familiars, however, caused a bizarre society of effeminates and whores to emerge from inns, thermes and shady lodgings, which a platoon of gladiators held back.

Almost alone, having commanded the cortege, the porters, the soldiers and the friends of the feast to wait for her in the steam-baths of Suburra, situated very close to the ramparts of Rome, Messalina appeared, splendid and radiantly beautiful, in the frame of the doorway of Gueranus' popina.

None of the gladiators even made a gesture of deference toward her. Only Gueranus and his wife Lenia bowed, with Filiola, whose delicate white-clad silhouette was blurred by the shadows of the interior, immaterial, like a celestial vision that should have floated in all its purity above the ignorance of the place.

"Ave, Diva!" said the inclined innkeepers.

"Ave, Imperial!" murmured the virgin, who did not want to recognize the divinity of Messalina, the wife of the infamous Caesar.

Smiling, the Empress marched toward Sepeos and Manechus, seated facing one another. The familiars and the Augustan women took their places at the tables while, in the clear and nacreous night of the street, the rich shadows of a maniple of six praetorians could still be seen, left there even so under the orders of a centurion, striped with gold and comparable to statues.

"Good day, Sepeos! I've come to drink to your imminent victories."

"Don't mock, Majesty. Death, also a Majesty, is here, watchful and prowling around us. She is the one who will make our blades ring as they collide, and will light the fires in the night of the world."

"Yes, but Amour is also here, who jeers at Death. Tell me, gladiator, am I not in your opinion, Beauty, Amour, Joy and Life?"

Without responding, Sepeos pushed the stool on which he was sitting back into a corner in order to avoid the contact of the Omnipotent, who had sat down beside him.

"Wine! I want to drink from your cup, Sepeos."

Admiring the marvelously sculpted rings in which Oriental gems sparkled, the pendant ear-rings with aquamarines set between diamonds, and the diadem of pearls that ornamented her hands, ears and head, the customers, weary around the half-empty jugs and pitchers, whispered. Eyes sparkled, envious of the good fortune of Sepeos. Was it not known in Suburra and in all the infamous places in Rome or Campania that the Augusta, in recompense for male lust, permitted the lover of an hour or a night to pillage something of her jewelry, glad of the violence that left her still panting with desire and ardent lassitude.

Messalina inclined her delicate head toward Manechus, who was containing his disdained passion with difficulty, and indicating Sepeos, whose neck and face she fondled with the polished nails of her perverse hand, like cornelians

"He's very handsome, your friend! And he pleases me! Above all, he's magnificent in the arena . . . but I also like to see lions in repose."

Flirtatiously, she put her arm around Sepeos' neck; then, boldly, furious because he did not obey that caress and did not flex his neck to allow his lips to be plundered, Messalina got up, greedily, slid on to the gladiator's knees and gripped his lips violently with hers.

He turned away with an abrupt gesture.

Without becoming angry, Messalina slid her right hand into the gap in the tight-fitting leather garment that Sepeos had unlaced because of the torpid heat, and with the other, she picked up the shallow and circular earthenware cup decorated with black varnish, a shining chalice in which wine was stagnated, drained it completely, and then let the last drops fall on to the table, fixing Sepeos with her gaze.

"To Eros, gladiator, I offer that libation—and to you, my lover of the night."

"No," said Sepeos, in a loud voice. "Never."

His hand had clenched on the hilt of his sword. All his hatred had risen to his lips in that single word. He felt an indomitable desire invade him to kill the slut, since he had her there, full against his body, which she was penetrating with her warm and perfumed skin: Messalina the murderous, Messalina the voluptuous, who sowed dolor and watered the orchids of her filthy stupors with blood. Why not kill her immediately, at this moment—perhaps unique in his life—when she delivered herself, when, superb and indecent, she had penetrated into the lion's den to madden them with her sexual power?

Suddenly, the Empress spotted the frail white silhouette of Filiola at the back of the popina, fearful of the gestures of the Augustans and the patriciennes, who were drinking wine from vulgar cups and desire from the lips of brutal men.

"Come here!" she said. "Come here, child—and drink."

Filiola did not dare refuse to brush the proffered cup with her lips.

"How you look at Sepeos, child! Do you love him?"

"She loves another," said the Egyptian, "who is higher and greater than us."

"She's a virgin?" An infernal thought suddenly lit up in the green and gold irises of the Omnipotent.

"Perhaps," mocked Manechus, with a coarse laugh. "Who can be sure that a girl has as remained as closed as a flower whose pistil the sun has not yet seen?"

The Empress pressed herself against Sepeos; her ardent hands moved along his thighs, brazenly seeking the male in the man, a sign of desire. But the gladiator half rose to his feet, his expression sickened, to avoid the contact. Manechus, who was following them with his eyes, stopped Sepeos' hand from drawing his sword, gripping his wrist.

"Me first—that's agreed."

"What are you saying, Manechus Victor?" Messalina interrogated. "What are you to have first, then, before this handsome lad?"

"You, Empress. You, slut!"

She burst out laughing. Then, after a kiss stolen from Sepeos: "Me! Your turn isn't ready to come. . . ."

"And yet," said Manechus, "we shall both have you . . . but him in a fashion that you don't expect."

"He has, then," Messalina said, "a particular fashion?"

"Yes, of which you have no suspicion . . . a supreme embrace in which you'll gasp. . . ."

Sepeos went on: "Another sovereign, more powerful than you, passed close to us, invisibly, just now. That one will possess us all, men and women alike. She is the definitive mistress of both. She is a goddess for all the earth. She holds the world and all must submit to her—even You. Even You!"

Camillus, the son of a consular personage, thought to seize an opportunity to pay his court.

"That, Omnipotent, is the philosophy of the gladiator. But let him beware of the net—that of your charms, lovely retiarius, has captured bigger fish."

Turning back to Sepeos, the Empress, taking both his hands, looked him directly in the eyes, her lips attempting to approach his mouth, and said: "You're rambling, my dear! Come. I, a goddess, want to make you a god, and I mock the one of whom you speak. Come with me, for that supreme embrace in which one gasps as Manechus puts it . . . I have a mortal desire for you."

"Not yet!" growled Sepeos, looking at the gladiator, his master and friend.

Then Luxuria, irritated by that delay imposed by an infimal and stubborn soldier, gestured to summon the centurion who, standing in the frame of the gaping doorway, was nonchalantly swinging the vine-cep that he used to correct his soldiers, a badge of his rank, in front of the gold-armored praetorians.

"Have him taken away. The beasts . . ."

The officer made a sign—but when the soldiers came in, Messalina sent them back with a gesture. Involuntarily, she had scanned Sepeos' magnificent stature with her gaze; she was already regretting his death, which, in a fit of pride, she had scarcely commanded before having repented of it. In condemning him, she would kill his kiss without killing her exasperated desire.

The praetorians went out.

"I won't say adieu, Sepeos—nor to you, Filiola, nor to you, my brave fellows!" So saying, she made a sign to each and all of them.

Clamors burst forth outside. "Fête! It's a fête in Suburra! Venus has descended among us."

The black porters lifted up the lectica in which, trying not to think any longer of her desire for the man rebellious to her caprice, Luxuria had extended herself, in a nervous, aggravated, titillating morbidity.

She departed with a retinue of intimate friends, patriciennes, naked or draped purely in transparent fabrics. Attracted by the odor of her imperial flesh, the reek of her lust, bands of men followed her as dogs follow a bitch in heat; all the plebs of Rome, from the slopes of the Aventine and the Celio to the Transtevere and all the way to Suburra, were maddened by her passage. Negresses whose sculpted shoulder-pads blazed in the night, girdled with gem-studded gold, agitated immaculate fans made of the plumes of ostriches and pink flamingos around the Imperia, surrounding the crimson lectica with luminous globes that were still spreading ruddy light.

II

The Empress in the Brothel

BEFORE the Suburran steam-baths, men, and women—prostitutes—were agitating. At the head of the Augustan women, Messalina charged into the atrium of the brothel.

In the center of the immense tiled room, the matron, a woman of about forty, weary and faded, who might once have been beautiful, smiled at the arriving women, and even more amiably at the men. The Augustan women surrounded the massive wooden counter where Priapuses bestrode nymphs while a recumbent Bacchus struggled, raising his natural thyrsus in the midst of bacchantes and faunesses who were violating the entirety of his pot-bellied body with mad kisses.

Around Messalina there were Livia Callina, the wife of a senator, whose devouring ardor for men had not been wearied by twenty years of frenzied amour; Soevilla Loris, a wife twice divorced, who, at twenty-two, had finished wearing out Mucius Caro, a tribune of soldiers, after Lomerus Gamo, an aedile and quaestor, who was ardently seeking the proconsulate, as well as her first husband, Vaninus, whose divorce had sent him to Numidia, where he had died at the head of his legion on the day of Scipio's victory;[1] and also Blanca Saponina, Tullia Chirones, Salvia Vero and Tullia Corvidis. That whole swarm of aristocratic butterflies assailed the merchant of amours at the same time.

---

1 This reference seems to be grossly anachronistic, apparently referring to an event more than two centuries before.

The infamous courtesans of the brothel came out one by one, and pushing forward with laughter and cries, abused them.

"Why, Iris herself isn't more obliging than you, Blanca. You've arrived just as I was getting tired."

Another clapped her hands. "After the bath I'll run off to find Mucius Saphis, my handsome gladiator. And if he wins the crown and the purse at the imminent games, that'll be the last we'll see in the steam-baths of little Candilia."

Faces with painted eyes showed themselves, politely startled at gaps in doorways and mingled at the entrances of corridors. More timid, the lovers appeared behind the women, or the hoarse and furious voices of abandoned males, left in the lurch inside the cubicles, called out to them.

Each of the Augustan women, after Messalina, threw a gold denier on the counter in front of the proprietress for permission to occupy for the night, until dawn if it pleased them, the chambers and beds in which amour is sold in Subirra. Banded centurions and half-drunk soldiers surrounded them.

"Me, I want the daintiest," cried one, a giant helmed in bronze who was a head taller than anyone else. "The one with hair as black as night and powdered with carmined mica."

"And me the one who puts her hair in a golden net and who has such beautiful rings on her fingers."

Mocking her, without suspecting her veritable rank, a mercenary said to Morinela: "If there were true gems of the Orient, my beauty, you wouldn't be so young. It requires a lot of lovers for such results after so few years of amour. Are you coming?"

His arms lifted up the frail body of the nervous patricienne, who uttered squeals that the searching kisses of the soldier changed into mad laughter, while her slender body wriggled like a worm, quivering, and then became enraptured.

Messalina took time making her selection, allowing a tessera—a metal disk attached by a string—to hang down over her breasts, whose firm mat roundness was left visible by her low-slung sub-ucula, on which the number of her public chamber of amour was engraved. But she soon set forth, on the arm of a street-porter from Ostia, recognizable by his red bonnet, his heavily swaying gait and his arched back. She confirmed the location of her room by showing the tablet hanging around her neck to a black Hercules, one of the guardians of the steam-baths, charged with keeping good order in the brothel and monitoring the entrances and exits of the women.

Through long corridors illuminated by candles with phallic forms she went, guiding the man, the random lover whose bulging muscles had tempted the unhealthy desire, the folly of her exasperated senses. Triangular lamps in the form of the female sexual parts were suspended from the vaults by three gilded chains. Sealed in the walls, arms holding up human members from which the light fell fuliginously and murkily, fouled the atmosphere with the reek of burnt oil, mingled with the crapulous perfumes of low prostitutes. Obscene frescoes ornamented each side of the long corridors radiating around the atrium, where the brothel-keeper stood, immutable, her hands making as and denarii clink and distributing tessera.

The street-porter and the Augusta thus saw file past the amours of Jupiter and Leda, the abduction of Io, with the god, formidably armed, erect. Elsewhere, bodies were entangled in a pell-mell of rumps, bare breasts gripped by hands, and clasped mouths, of males and females, crazed by lust, bitter and delicious mouths, taut smiles on lips twisted with the exquisite dolors of orgasm.

Here, on a golden bed covered by the hides of panthers, a blonde woman was surrendering herself to three men, and the eyes of the voluptuous woman, wide open and staring, expressed a supreme bliss. Elsewhere, bacchantes harassed a Silenus like bees falling in whirling swarm on a flower coveted by each, or on a streak of honey. There was not one dimple of the demigod, not one furrow of white and pink flesh from which ardent hands and avid lips were not plundering joys while they all panted in completing the sexual act. Couples frolicked around the principal group; fauns sylvans and Pans, chasing nymphs and women whose nudities were florid in heat. Lesbians were caressing one another tenderly in front of furious men, linked in embraces where the sexes remained separated. Animals—stags, wild boar, leopards, tigers, lions, monstrous bears and aurochs—coupled in bestial fury. There were strange kisses; quarrels, sometimes bloody; scenes of feasting and orgy; dances and Oriental rituals in which men violated stones in the form of female organs and women pleasured themselves with phalluses of bronze, ivory, marble or wood.

The vestibules resonated with the footsteps of couples of hazard, sighs, the odors of enamored flesh, the sound of kisses and frictions, cries of passion, voices arguing over payment for kisses that the courtesans ransomed; insults overlapped with the outbursts of echoing voices. Sometimes the guardians had to intervene, and the blows of their wooden laths on fleeing backs or the legs of men who did not want to leave punctuated the infamous house's perpetual rumor of dolorous lust. Doors opened to let sated men out, and closed on couples shutting themselves away in the cells.

There were cubicles of various kinds: uniformly, to the right, a bed of stone or bricks, a smoky lamp with three beaks hanging from the ceiling; and, hollowed out in a flagstone, a bowl in which water gushed from a conduit; always, on a pedestal, a phallic divinity, A Venus Physica or Venus Impudica, smiling sardonically, making the gesture of life. Roses, lilies and crowns of jasmine decorated them, as offerings.

According to the price of the tessera, the beds were covered with buffalo hides, or beautiful animal fleeces. A clepsydra, in the richest chambers, let droplets of perfumed water fall slowly and monotonously.

The poorest cells were strewn with reeds or straw. On the floor paved with a mosaic of little cubes of a composite imitating stone—abaculi—there were, once again, depicted by that polychromatic marquetry, orchids with erect pistils or phalluses, the open lips of women, seductive fingers, sensual symbols or erotic mottoes.

Already, in the arms of the porter, both proffering grateful words pell-mell with intimate crudeness and filth, Messalina was gasping. And soon, as if gripped by a sudden professional fury, she pushed him outside, with vulgar insults delivered with verve, because he had only given her a poor silver denarius or two as a velite passed by, whom she summoned.

Then, in a room in the middle of which was a piscine full of warm water, Messalina surrendered to Libyan masseurs. When, after the kisses of three successive lovers, and multiple caresses from which all of her nerves had vibrated, the Augusta, still thinking about Sepeos, the Egyptian who had rejected her, reappeared in the midst of her familiars, impatient and weary, under the colonnade of the house of debauchery, her eyes circled with bistre, curbed by the fatigue of stupors. The black porters laid her down on the litter, limp and utterly exhausted, but still unsatisfied.

III

A Suburban Idyll

IN front of the door of the popina, Filiola was weaving a basket with reeds. In the inn, empty of clients at that hour. Lenia was coming and going, wiping tankards of pewter and baked clay on which cocks were crudely painted, quarreling or crowing to suns whose faces, toward the neck or rim of the vessel, were smiling broadly. Gueranus had gone to buy wines in Neapolis, where the vintages put the sulfurous and fertile country in joy, perpetually menaced by Vesuvius, its crater smoking by day and fulgurant by night, amid the stars.

Filiola was dreaming while weaving the reeds, in the softness of the evening that was beginning to decrease. A firm tread on the uneven pavement drew her out of her reverie. She recognized it now among all others, that tread, as she recognized the sonorous and musical voice of Sepeos among all others. And she shivered with a great joy.

Thus, almost every evening, nowadays, on emerging from the School of Gladiators, instead of going with his comrades to the taverns of the Aventine and Suburra, or the places of pleasure that flourished in all the low quarters, as soon as he was out of the bath he headed for Gueranus' house, at an hour when he knew that he would find the young woman free and often alone, since Lenia was beginning at that time to prepare the food for the evening meal.

He greeted her, leaning toward her as she raised amethyst eyes that the light flecked with silver gleams.

"Ave, Sepeos," she said, smiling. "You're free again . . . you must have walked very quickly to be here already. The sun is scarcely approaching the sixth hour on the frames dotted with a triangle."

"Yes, I was sad and I've come. You often say things to me that I don't really understand, but which soothe me like caresses. And then, coming entirely from you, a fluid envelops me, which puts my dolors to sleep. You're so good and so pretty."

He took her hands; she left them in his, but as he leaned over to brush her lips, Filiola stood up, detaching herself from the gladiator's grip.

"Are you annoyed, Filiola?" he asked, slightly ashamed of his abruptness.

"No, but my lips belong to my husband. I've vowed my person entirely to him."

"Who is he, then, that fortunate man?"

"He'll be the one that Christos wishes, or Christos himself, beyond terrestrial existence."

"I don't understand. How can Christos posses you, if you're no longer the living Filiola, if your body and your flesh are inert and your soul is released?"

"You'll know that, if you wish, from the one who teaches me the true belief. I didn't understand either, in the beginning. But Christos, through him, has taken the scales away from the eyes of my spirit. I've seen, and I'm happy."

Yes, a strange charm emanated from Filiola's eyes, from her entire person, and something akin to an exquisite perfume of mystery, especially when she talked about Christos and the new ideas that his apostles were sowing throughout the world—seeds that, in spite of the persecutions, were yielding a hundredfold.

"However, Lenia beats you; Gueranus is brutal and coarse; they sometimes make you work until your strength is exhausted; they oblige you to remain in the midst of orgies that sicken you. You should have been born a patricienne, Filiola . . . but then, I wouldn't have known you."

"Perhaps I wouldn't have had the same joys. Christos prefers the poor and the humble."

The crimson, green and orange horizon was paling. The triumphal arches, obelisks and colonnades were drowning in the diffuse light of an atmosphere gradually invaded by shadows, denser by the minute. Instinctively, as the night advanced, the voices of the lovers—lovers without being aware of it—became lower and softer.

Filiola had let the finished basket fall from her frail fingers. She blushed, because her subucula was slightly undone, allowing the perception of a corner of her shoulder and the roundness of her young breast.

Meanwhile, artisans whose labor had finished, courtesans commencing theirs, lanistas and gladiators and amphitheater valets gradually flowed into the quarter of stupor. From the Via Appia, the Forum and the Palatine, a rumor rose. Suburra was beginning to swarm with people in quest of base pleasures and nocturnal lucre. Already, here and there, soldiers were vociferating coarsely in response to the appeals of sellers of amour, and strangers were prowling, recognizable by their hesitant and curious expressions.

Interrupting the crepuscular conversation on the threshold of the popina, regulars—Saper, Lacero, Birus, Mucius Saphis and Candilia came into Gueranus' establishment. Filiola served them swiftly, and then she rejoined Sepeos—who was not yet hungry, he said—on the threshold, glad of the open air, paying no heed to the renascent racket and reek of the tavern.

The young woman sighed. "They're content, and they make a noise. There will be great games for the kalends, and blood will flow in the arena. They'll have gold, those whom the blades haven't killed. The malediction of the times blinds them."

"I'm designated to fight in those games."

"You! You too are a man of blood!" She had almost shouted those words—then, suddenly, she dissolved in tears.

"Is bravery, then, a crime in your eyes, Filiola? What does death or life matter to me? My heart is dead. However, it still quivers in your presence, and I believe, by your charm, it might live again."

"Your heart can and must live, if you're still capable of love, Sepeos."

"Don't you know that—don't you sense it, Filiola? I dream, sometimes, of taking you in my arms and carrying you far away from here, of commencing a new existence with you. . . ."

Lenia called to the little maidservant in a hoarse voice, scolding her: "Would you care to occupy yourself with the clients, damnable idler!"

Quickly, escaping and withdrawing her hands, which he had taken, she said: "Then wait for me tonight, if you want, at the tenth hour, at the corner of the Via and the street of the bakers. I'll have a rose pinned to my white cuculla, and well go together into the catacombs."

"Where to?"

"Toward the Truth, toward the Light."

IV

In the Catacombs, Toward the Light

SEPEOS, waiting, was sitting on a boundary-marker at the corner of the Via Suburra and a tortuous street that led to the Trastevere. The tenth hour was approaching. In Suburra, the tumultuous quarter that remained the last awake in Rome, people were passing by calmly and furtively, all heading in the same direction. Although silent, their lips sometimes moved, as if they were talking to themselves or reciting prayers. Young women in high-necked subuculae, from which their faces emerged like the pistils of great lilies, went by. The street, on the edge of which Sepeos was waiting impatiently, led through a maze of small house and lodging-houses with innumerable cubicles that the proprietors rented to the poor, all the way to the Transtevere. Numerous groups of hooded men and women of grave demeanor were emerging therefrom.

Like everyone in Rome, Sepeos knew that the Transtevere was an ill-reputed quarter, where freedmen, people exercising vile métiers, street-porters and Tiber mariners lived crowded together.

Christos counted his disciples mostly among the poor, and even among slaves. The former, the suffering and the humble, had been informed of the existence of a God, clement to misfortune, who required neither offerings nor material sacrifices of his devotees. Because of that rapid progress in a society that seemed despicable to their pride, aristocrats, whose philosophy and doctrines were nevertheless closely related to the soul of Christianity,

156

were reluctant to discover any more about the new religion than slanderous rumor recounted.

As he had heard it rumored, Sepeos genuinely believed that the Christians worshiped a donkey's head, and that frightful mysteries bloodied their secret ceremonies. It was also said that they preached the intercourse of the same sex, in accordance with the Asiatic rites extolling androgyny: a bizarre regeneration of humankind in which each sex would be self-sufficient, without having any need of the other for amour or procreation. Sepeos found those theories revolting, in spite of being familiar with the promiscuities of the Circus and adolescents, and having no disgust for them, by force of habit, and because the Oriental vice, very widespread in Greece and Rome, did not appear to him to be anything but an aberration similar to intoxication, or other passions not involving, in his eyes, the slightest degeneracy.

Filiola kept him waiting for a long time. Lenia, alone in the popina with the maidservant, closed up early during the absence of her husband Gueranus; evidently, the young woman had been counting on that circumstance to escape by night from the ignoble tavern and meet him. Perhaps, though, Lenia had been woken up by the noise of sandals on the mosaics of the atrium, or even the creak of a door.

However, he had heard whispering coming from the innkeeper's cubicle on the previous two nights. The sound of an argument had woken him up the previous night, fearful for Filiola, but he had quickly recognized Lenia's hoarse voice mingled with coarse words, expectant implorations and muttered invectives in a barbaric accent—that of Simo Barbax, the merchant of wild beasts.

Toward the Porta Capena the silent procession of strangers flowed. They were coming from everywhere. Emboldened by the calm of the streets or by their number, groups were arriving in the night, singing very softly with a suave serenity, although, from the words that Sereos could grasp, they did not seem to be sinister conspirators, nor people in the process of meditating black deeds and criminal practices.

A young woman's voice said: "Mother, it seems that it's certain. Septimus Vilio will come this evening . . . but you're tired, and the journey is long for your old legs."

"My child, I want to hear the man who has seen the divine Master and brings us, on his behalf, words of consolation. Help me, and I'll get there. And if, when we return, my legs are too weak, you can ask our brethren to help you bring me back to our dwelling."

Sepeos could see some of the faces of the pilgrims and women who were traveling thus, mostly by the tremulous light of their little round bronze lanterns, with perimeters of transparent horn, under lids in the form of a cupola, linked to the wrist by a small chain and holed in order to let air in and smoke emerge, with minuscule stars. Impressed by the mildness expressed by the gazes of the noctambulants, he saw their shadows gushing forth form all directions, all heading for a location unknown to him, and he could not help being astonished by their multitude.

"What joy he gives his faithful followers, this man who died of an infamous method of execution, for culpable slaves and thieves!"

But a slender white silhouette, well known to Sepeos, came along the Via Suburra. Sepeos could not mistake it for an instant; he went to meet her, and saw her amethyst eyes smiling beneath a white hood, with a pink rose pinned to the side.

"Salve! Be happy, my brother and my friend. I've made you wait a long time. Lenia isn't asleep yet and there was someone in her room, someone scolding and threatening her, who frightened me."

Sarcastically, the Egyptian replied: "Oh, you know very well that when the male is away, females lament in the moonlight—and your mistress isn't a woman to renounce her god of amour for long. Was it Barbax?"

"I don't know," said Filiola. "It's not my concern, and no one has the right to judge anyone else."

Women who were passing by saluted Filiola, who replied to them: "*Ave, sorores*"—greetings, sisters

"You know these people, then, Filiola. They go by incessantly in troops."

"They're my brothers and sisters in Christ. Come with me, Sepeos, among them. You'll thank me later, for having brought you, for you'll see and hear things you don't suspect. And perhaps . . ."

She stopped talking for a moment, hesitant, fearful of wounding Sepeos by supposing him versatile and capable—him, a swordsman—of being too easily impressed.

"You're going to a meeting, then, Filiola? And you want the man who loves you to go with you?"

"Yes. I know that you're too good and honest to betray the place of our gatherings, and I hope to procure you a happiness."

"If it comes from you, what sensuality could equal it? It's already a delight for me to feel my hand brushing yours, to contemplate your eyes and hear your voice. For everything is good and beautiful that comes from you, whose kindness soothes my lassitude and my distaste for life."

They walked side by side through the sleeping city. From the Tullianum, the subterranean vaulted prison where captives of war were held, a respiration compounded of hundreds of slumbering breaths rose up, with plaints; and from the Tiber, over which the vivaria looked, the raucous voices of imprisoned wild beasts roared.

Filiola, to his right, made a sign in the form of a cross on her forehead, breast and shoulders.

"You hear them? And you too, Sepeos, you'll confront weapons and beasts! Alas, alas! If, at least, you believe in Him, your soul will survive your body, blissfully."

"To suffer further, after the life of this world! I prefer, a hundred times, the oblivion for which, besides, I wish for as a unique benefit."

"Don't blaspheme. And in a little while, listen," said Filiola, emotionally. "You'll hear stories of Christos and his holy apostles. You'll finally begin to know Him, and perhaps your eyes will see the divine light in the infinity of the heavens."

Suddenly, a melody became audible, attenuated, as if veiled—and yet the Roman countryside, infertile and bare, devoid of trees capable of hiding the singers from view, seemed empty, with the consequence that it was hard to tell whether the canticle was descending from the sky or rising from the ground, carpeted by spare and meager grass.

"What are those voices?"

"They're our sisters and brothers singing the praises of Christos and his Father, who is ours."

And they fell silent, as did the groups who were arriving, gathering increasingly as the sound of voices came closer,

A light was shining in a dip in the terrain. It was a flickering lantern that a great shadow was waving in the darkness, like a signal.

"Let's hurry," said Filiola. "He's about to speak."

"Who is?"

"An apostle who has come from the depths of Gaul to confess the new faith in Rome, in the city where the most Gentiles are in league against Christos and his disciples. He was one of the companions of Peter the Fisherman, and yet, he had been our enemy to begin with, like Paul of Tarsus."

They now found themselves at the entrance to a long corridor, hollowed out in the plaster, which it was easy to recognize as the opening of an old abandoned quarry, of which there were many in the vicinity of Rome. Filiola took a small earthenware lamp from beneath the white paenula to which she had attached her hood. When she had lit it at a lychnus suspended from the vault, low enough for that usage, the little flame gave the light of an enormous glow-worm in the catacombs.

Filiola walked ahead of Sepeos. He was able to perceive mortuary inscriptions along the walls, painted in raw colors on the stone itself. Crosses, and also fish, recurred at frequent intervals. Filiola showed him square panels on which names had been painted above dates.

"Here we put in the ground, after having buried them, all of our brothers that it is possible to preserve from the aediles, who burn them."

Doves, carrying a crown of roses, surmounted the words: *Kiligo, virgo, requiescat in pace Domini. Vigesimo aetatis anno, defuncta.* Further on, a lamb, naively designed, carried a cross that its right foot retained; and underneath: *Sapicus Veridis, amicus afflictorum, bestiis liberatus.*

"That one," she said, "died at thirty, freed by the beasts of the Circus."

The inscriptions, sometimes longer, evoked in a few lapidary words an entire life. But Sepeos who could not read, admired above all the grace of Filiola, whose delicate silhouette guided him through the maze of corridors full of shadows. The voices, more distinct, were singing slow hymns, which suddenly burst forth resoundingly, and expanded, from echo to echo, reverberated by the vaults.

V

Voices of Heaven on Earth

FINALLY, a gleam of light, as if in the depths of an abyss, filling a vast excavation, suddenly appeared at a bend in a lane of tombs. More than a thousand men and women were kneeling before an altar, a square stone covered by a white cloth. In the center of the altar stood a cross, to which the image of a torture victim, in polychromatic clay, had been fixed by enormous nails; a crown of thorns circled his head, from which ruby droplets were dripping; he had long hair; his beard, pointed and gilded, allowed a glimpse of his mouth, the lips taut with suffering, and his side was pierced by a spear-thrust. From that visage, eyes closed in the face slumping, heavy with death, on the blood-stained breast, emanated an immense, ineffable pity; and the long extended arms seemed to be opening up for a gesture of broad embrace.

The singing ceased beneath the vaults. The people were kneeling, squatting on their heels or sitting cross-legged in the oriental manner. An old man, standing up from a niche hollowed out in the rock to the right of the altar, where he had been sitting, with a candle planted in front of him, came to face the faithful, and traced the sign of the cross on his person.

Everyone looked at Macris. The faithful identified him to the neophytes, whispering his name; a quiver of expectation agitated the whole audience. His long snowy beard and silvery hair framed his visionary face. He was tall and thin, and slightly stooped, as if weighed down by the burden of is dolorous past, more than sixty-six years of which weighed upon his shoulders. His face was not handsome. The overly long nose, rooted to an overly vast forehead, surmounted a broadly cleaved mouth, with strong lips, the curve of which nevertheless betrayed tenderness. But the eyes, beneath very long lashes, bore in their irises, of a deep and bright blue, the imprint of ecstatic dreams.

In the midst of the Christians, Sepeos remained standing beside the kneeling Filiola, gazed in amazement. To begin with, he had heard the songs, hymns of reckless hope. The very simple words of those prayers, the monotonous litanies, reminiscent of the song of a spring falling from a height on to pebbles, the harmonious notes of the women's voices, embroidered over the gravity of male accents, had impressed the Egyptian, like an unsuspected grandiose spectacle. Then too, an immense fervor was burning in the eyes of these people, for whom persecutors lay in wait. The muted light of lanterns of horn, little lamps of clay or bronze, the thousand minuscule candles that everyone held or planted in front of them, were like bright butterflies in the penumbra of the grotto, striking sparks on the walls of the vaults, allowing somber fissures between blocks of stone to be glimpsed.

The Christians of Rome had known for some time about the extraordinary odyssey of Macris. Of Druidic lineage at a Son of the Mistletoe—which is to say, destined for the priesthood—he had been one of the most ferocious enemies of the first Gallic sectarians. Out of hatred against the converts, whom he regarded as invaders more dangerous than the Latin conquerors, he had even made an alliance with the Roman proconsul against them. For the Empire, at least, respected and provided safeguards for the religion of conquered peoples, and only imposed its usages and its gods prudently, even admitting barbaric divinities into its temples. One day, however, in the arena in Nîmes, the Gallic priest had sensed grace. In the midst of the sectarians that he was about to examine before the games, he had seen a man standing, already stitched into an animal skin, who was comforting his brethren, exhorting them to submit to martyrdom with joy. And the skeptic had suddenly confessed the Christ in front of the proconsul, who, unable to believe him, had nevertheless had him imprisoned.

Macris' friends had intervened; unshakably, he had declared his new and ardent Faith. His hands had been tormented with hot pincers. "I am a Christian," he replied, obstinately. In the amphitheater of Nîmes he was delivered, with two hundred coreligionists, to the beasts. The savage creatures, sated on more than a hundred cadavers, did not want any more. The survivors were reserved for the next games. Then, Lucius Macerus having been replaced as proconsul of Gaul by Otto Mileius, the Christians were freed. That proconsul obtained a better augury from clemency than the vain persecutions and cruelties that fortified thoughts in progress.

Macris, baptized, became a propagator of the new idea and the leader of a church. His renown of sanctity had spread all the way to the peninsula. Peter, then resident in Rome for nearly six years,[1] but ill, having been unable to preside over this meeting, Macris, standing before the altar, replaced the first pontiff and dominated the assembly with the legend that aureoled his head with the nimbus of martyrs.

He spoke. Men and women, in order to distinguish his features, raised their candles of wax, pitch, tallow or papyrus fibers twisted together like a rope, illuminating their curious and ardent faces, brightening their eyes, reminiscent of gems in the half-light of the vaults, incessantly speckled with fugitive reflections.

From the first words, Sepeos was troubled.

To those people, for whom the claws of death lay in wait, Macris preached the forgiveness of insults and persecutions, gentleness and love. The Apostle, whose silhouette was strangely magnified against the luminous background of the altar, said:

---

1 There is no scriptural evidence for Peter ever having been in Rome, but his presence there is a key aspect of Catholic dogma, which asserts that it was he who founded the papacy there; that item of belief became vitally important during the Reformation, part of the Protestant challenge to Roman authority being the contention that it was based on a myth, the papacy having been an invention of the fourth century. The Catholic version held that Peter was martyred during Nero's persecution, and that is echoed on Sienkiewicz's *Quo Vadis?* Various dates are suggested for Peter's supposed arrival in Rome, but 42 A.D. is the one most widely credited. Diplomacy seems to have prevented Champsaur from actually giving him a role in his plot, substituting the fictitious Macris.

"Be good. Do not hate those who oppress and persecute you. Do they know, those unfortunates, that you bear verity in your hearts? Christos, remember, forgave his torturers from the height of his cross, and yet, at the foot of the fatal tree, his Mother was weeping. Then, several of those who had crucified him said: 'He is true,' and they believed in him. They had caused his body and heart to bleed, and they had been saved, because Love is strong and Faith, even belated, is everything. By Faith, you should vanquish suffering, and it is from Faith that hope is born in souls. Love and believe!

"Love of your neighbor will preserve you from evil thoughts. Do not judge the actions of your brothers, nor those of the Gentiles. Can they see clearly, the people who error blinds and whom the Spirit has not visited, for the love of Christos? Forgive the offenses of those who have offended you. Pray for them to be enlightened. Love, I repeat, even those who do you harm, in order that one day they might conceive the Good. Yes, be good, my brethren, not only in the hope of the Supreme Recompense, but in order to merit the precious joy of the sacrifice. Love is its own reward.

"Tenderness spreads its honey in souls. And it is Happiness to sense oneself practicing Christian virtues, living in beauty and not feeling any villainy. Love, in order to be happy. Love, like the silkworm, in order that the weave of your life should be admirable. Let us not wish our neighbors to suffer harm, even in exchange for sufferings they have imposed on us. The Idea is stronger than blood, and blood shed renders it even more vivid in minds and in hearts. Those who see you will admire the actions you carry out, sustained by Faith and Love. They will be astonished and will seek the reasons for your serenity in the face of death. Thus, death itself will serve life! For the life of souls will be the harvest of the tortures with which your courage will astonish the world. So let it be!"

"Amen! Amen!" replied all the faithful. Above the swell of attentive heads, Macris seemed very tall. The gleam of the prophet's eyes dominated the gems of the gazes raised toward him like sunflowers turning to the sun.

Sepeos, however, could not take full account the intense emotion that moved him to the depths of his soul. He had thought that the Christians were bizarre sectarians; he had expected infamies and abject practices, bloody sacrifices of children and virgins, abominations before a donkey's head, their God. And suddenly, their serenity in the face of tortures whose ignominy glorified them was revealed to him.

Now Macris, dressed by deacons in the chasuble and the stole, held a monstrance over the altar, in his tortured hands, in which there was a host: a loaf of unleavened bread. Humbly prostrating himself before the altar, illuminated by a hundred candles, the apostle, of whom all that could now be seen were the thick silver waves of his hair, prayed, sunk in his mystical contemplation. And the songs awoke echoes again, in the heart of the earth.

Then Macris stood up, facing the crowd of the faithful, and raised the monstrance above his head. His eyes, beneath his luminous forehead, were ecstatic. He blessed the faithful in the name of the Father, Christos and the Spirit; and his voice rose in a supreme prayer:

"Enable us, divine Savior, to remain pure and strong, until in times less hard, which you will regenerate, all those who must die will live, through you, the Life eternal!"

"Amen! Amen!" replied the audience, again.

It was finished. Soon, the Christians left, in calm throngs, through the obscure corridors. As they returned, Filiola took Sepeos' hand in order to indicate the route to him by the pressure of her fingers, and between the rare fugitive gleams on the walls of rock, shadows brushed them. Some retained in their eyes the reflections of the marvelous cerebral communion in which, just now, those wretches had excited one another, drawing one another along, anarchists of the times, gentle revolutionaries against masters and obsolete gods, humble demolishers of Roman society, so formidably organized, and whose pullulation was to transform the pagan world, old and rotten through and through.

VI

The Forgiveness of Offenses

AT the end of a somber corridor that opened on to a section of sky dotted with stars, Sepeos and Filiola came out of the catacombs into the cold of the night. They did not speak, in the bare terrain, until the Porta Capena, which they went through. In the city, where shadows passed by, fearfully hugging the walls, they still walked in silence, both stirred by the apostle's words and their own thoughts.

An unspeakable doubt, mingled with terror, clawed the gladiator's mind. *Have I the right to judge and condemn?* Ought he to realize his ardent and bitter desire for vengeance, at present the unique objective of his life? Would he be serving thus the great human cause? Compared with these people, of whom he had been scornful on the strength of public slanders, was he a sanguinary brute?

For the first time since the death of Karysta the Tanagran, the wandering player turned gladiator thought that there might be more subtle sensualities than exercising his limbs, being proud of the beauty of his body, or his strength or his courage.

The virgin was trotting along beside Sepeos in the darkness paled by starlight. Suddenly, the man stopped.

"Your God, then, doesn't want anyone to take vengeance, or to defend himself against his enemies?"

"What good is vengeance, since blood summons blood and violence death?" She raised her hand toward the firmament full of

167

stars. "Christos has ordered: 'Say to my Father, who is in Heaven: *Forgive us our trespasses, as we forgive those who trespass against us.*'"

"You, Filiola, don't dream of taking revenge on anyone? You've suffered, though."

"Yes, I've suffered, but those who have done me harm suffer too, and for them, as for our brothers, I pray."

Sepeos made no reply. Resuming their march, they soon turned into the street that descends from the Celio to the corner of the Via Suburra. A conflict was agitating the soul of the gladiator: on the one hand, his oath against Messalina; on the other, the vague hope of a mysterious posthumous felicity; which made him hesitant and troubled.

"I will pray for you, brother," said Filiola, on the threshold, "in order that you will be at peace with yourself."

And her smile illuminated Sepeos' heart.

VII

A Drunken Conversation Between Gladiators

CHEERFULLY, toward the fifth hour, Caius Birus and Mucius Lacero installed themselves on stools at a round table in the caupona of the Nubian Lion, a small well-patronized wine-shop, facing Gueranus, a restaurateur and hotelier himself.

"Cauponius! Waiter!"

Men of the people, at the back, were filling their glasses by emptying a bowl, on the rotundity of which were painted pea-plants in flower and two cocks. On the sides of a Pompeiian amphora nearby, processions of women, dancers and flute-players, unfurled, enameled in white and black against the ocher background of earthenware.

Caius had ordered a double bowl of frothy wine of Asti. The hostess, frail and lame, with the tilted head of an injured bird brought it, along with two horn cups, for she had seen that her clients were swordsmen and, for all their lack of distinction, strong men who might perhaps by displeased by clay vases.

In the meantime, on the other side of the street, there was a trio of young Suburran beauties in white tunics that the setting sun tinted with gilt and rose-pink, and Candilia, draped in a brown palla edged with red, a long section of which she had thrown back over her left shoulder, had paused to steal, with youthful laughter, the roses fastened in a garland that decorated Gueranus' popina on that festival day.

"There isn't one of those youngsters worth as much as Her," said Lacero. "And yet, she's approaching her eighth lustrum."

"By Pollux, have you seen her breasts? At the Suburran steam-baths the soldiers want no one but her."

"And the whores are jealous of her."

"I should think so. She made a hundred quadrigati in a single night the other week, and only with men who pleased her."

"Oh, when the Falernian has loosened her thighs, it's sufficient to show broad shoulders and make her feel one's vigor in the right place."

"Have you seen her without any veil? She's Aphrodite with dark hair—very foamy."

"And all perfumed with cinnamon and nard."

"Her belly has a few imperceptible wrinkles," said Birus.

"Carumela has as many, and she's a twenty-year-old merchant of amour."

"Her mouth burns. Her hands are soft, but clawed during orgasm."

"And her eyes, at the voluptuous moment!"

"Emerald carbuncles, flecked with gold."

"Oho!" cried the stout Licus Vivus, a young gladiator of twenty who had just sat down at a table and commenced drinking, with an amiable hearty laugh. "Who is this ripe beauty that renders you so enthusiastic, my masters? For myself, I prefer to all those charms more than thirty years old the firm tits of Irmica the Campanian."

Lacero shrugged his shoulders. "Shut up; your heart is still under your juvenile toga. When you're worthy of a virile toga, in amorous matters, you won't say such stupid things."

"There aren't two women in Rome about whom one can speak in that fashion, naïve adolescent," said Caius Birus, supportively. "And, by Pollux, if you don't know Her, it's because you've never been able to tell the Tiber from the Suburran gutter."

"Anyway," replied Licus Vivus, "that doesn't prevent young and almost new allures from being worth more. Do you know the bloody arc of Candilia's mouth, at the corners of her tapering lips? Do you know that Linela seems virginal after her four days of monthly abstinence? And the three beauty spots Catilla of Ostia has, arranged in a trefoil on the edge of her grotto of amour, force the tongue to dart there for kisses of preliminary adoration."

"Ours is a hundred times more beautiful. Her loins are more often clad in gold than those of your mistress of coarse cloth," said Birus, and punctuated his praise with a mighty blow of his fist, which made the cups shake.

"Damn! Castor crush me! It can't be a patricienne."

"Listen," said Lacero. She crosses her legs over your back during the embrace, or digs her fingernails into your back, and her rump becomes more agile than that of a fawn caught in a trap."

"I can see that she's an ardent woman," the ephebe jeered. "I'll wager it's a matter of Sextilia, the wife of Menorus Caro, the former consul. . . ."

"This ignorant schoolboy doesn't know anything, then?" said Birus

And Lacero completed their common thought: "Who do you think that everyone knows so well, except for the Divine?"

"The Augusta?"

"Herself, La Porca, the most amorous of Roman women."

VIII

Before the Games

FOR the autumn kalends, Marcus Senio, ambitious for the praetura, offered to Caesar Claudius and the divine Messalina, as well as the Roman people, games such as no one could ever boast of having seen since the accession of Claudius, or even under Tiberius. Avicius Miso, the consul, lent him his enlightened collaboration, for no one had such a great authority in the matter of gladiators and combats of beasts now that the illustrious senator Verachus Gravidus, the inventor of combat of men with bound feet, had lost his reason.

Thus, the Senate, the Augustans and the people were in rumor. Foreigners flooded in. In carriages and litters, or heaped in ox-carts, the citizens of the towns and cities of Latium encumbered the Via Appia, Via Celio, Via Suburra and Via Nomentana. It was necessary to set up a cordon of praetorians at the door of the Arena, and soldiers led by decurions were patrolling continuously, to maintain order on the Forum and in the streets, where, too frequently, people from rival villages were engaging in brawls.

Convoys of beasts enclosed in heavy rectangular wooden boxes, closed at the front and back with iron grilles, which mariners and porters were disembarking from rafts brought from Ostia with their cargoes of ferocious animals, attracted a curious crowd to the Tiber in order to admire the preparations for their bloody enjoyments. Gauls and Dacians with fur leggings, Persians with long robes coiffed with gilded miters or astrakhan bonnets,

Syrians clad in striped fabrics, and ebony black Numidians with shining teeth, thronged the banks. Their faces became serene, their nostalgic eyes shining, as they watched the beasts and their conductors pass by, as if those arrivals brought with them a little of their native air.

The effervescence had increased in the city during the last week before the games. Nothing else was any longer heard at the Thermes, on the Forum or in Caesar's gardens but voices exchanging information about the qualities of the animal-handlers, the beauty of ferocious animals and the number of Christians—four hundred at least were to be delivered to the beasts, with previously unseen refinements, the invention of Senio.

Young patricians accosted one another to exchange prognostications. Business and politics were forgotten in favor of the unique discussion of the merits of gladiators. Thus, Camillus engaged his last hopes in the hands of the Hebrew and Lombard money-changers, argentarii and mensarii who sat in the Forum every day behind the wooden benches where their capital was placed, ready for business, under the colonnades of the temple of Mercury.

In the establishment of a barber of patricians and knights:

"Do you think, my dear, that Chylaides will prevail?"

"He's more accustomed to the arena than your Egyptian, Sapor."

"I believe he has too much art and not the impetuosity of the debutant. Casper said so yesterday, after the assault that I saw them make . . . with the young ones, one never knows. But Sepeos might well be victorious."

"Since the death of Kerbrix," said someone else, "I haven't risked a denier. I'll take his vanquisher at five to two."

"Taken, Licis! I'm noting the engagement on my tablets." From a fold of his toga he took out three thin planchettes covered in wax, raised at the edges to protect hat was written thereon from friction. With the broad flat end of an ivory stylet he effaced a few notes from the third leaf, doubtless no longer necessary, unifying the wax; then, turning the stylet around, he engraved the wager worth the point.

"Manechus! Me, I'll take Manechus to be victorious over his ten adversaries."

At the desire of the Empress—an order—Manechus had been engaged to fight against ten of his comrades. It was the great attraction of the imminent games at the Coliseum, that extraordinary challenge to the King of the Sword.

Mucius Saphis, who, at the head of a decade of retiarii, was to fight against mirmillons, nets against swords, also brought together a number of wagers; but he was more the favorite of the effeminates, who pledged their money less on his courage than the grace of his rump, out of snobbery or gratitude.

An arbiter was often chosen to decide which of the two punters had won, and that was, more often than not, some literate parasite or hungry poet, unless it was a critic who offered to debate the beauty of the combatant's moves with a certain expertise.

Mezzanus was cited as the most sought-after among that sort of person; he even accumulated a certain fortune from his métier as a judge of strength, skill and beauty. The mediocre statues that he had once modeled had never permitted him any such luck. Some evil tongues insinuated that he took bribes from the lanistas and rival gladiators to decide in favor of one party or another, but, as Mezzanus was austere and frequented the temples, putting on a show of fervent patriotism and enthusiastic religion, and also because he boasted of the amity of a Cato, people had recourse to his opinion. Even Claudius and Silius had consulted him on that matter.

To cap it all, Avicius Miso, the first consul, having had it announced to the sound of trumpets that a distribution of wheat, oil and wine would be made, gratuitously, by the will of Caesar Claudius, on the eve of the opening of the games, the populace was delirious, giving ovations to the Augustans who passed by in the evenings, lying in their litters or guiding their chariots amid the glare of torch-bearers. As they had bread and could get drunk to the health of the Augusta, the Romans awaited the games patiently but feverishly.

Panem et circenses: what more is there, citizens?

IX

The Imperial Box

THROUGH the vomitoria, moving floods of people spread out on the steps. Argyraspid praetorians—which is to say, armed with a pilum, a sword and a silver buckler—guarded the main entrances. They were commanded by Vigilius Licis, holding a vine branch in his right hand, under the orders of Claudius Severo, a military tribune. It had been decided that the first day of the games would be reserved for citizens living in the city. A tessera—a small brick tablet on which the words *civitalis civis* were inscribed—delivered by the praetors served to check the entrants, in order to avoid deceptions. The designators, employees of the arena, temporary workers of a sort, received the tesserae and showed the public to the places whose number was marked thereon.

Quarrels sometimes broke out: the shoves of excited people jostling those who barred their passage. Then the praetorians intervened, at a sign from the decurions. The entire Trastevere and Suburra populated the higher steps and the side of the arena that faced the setting sun. One immense box was, above all, the meeting-place of young women selling sensuality and the prostitutes of the steam-baths. Amorous celebrities also grouped in front of matrons, as if to provoke a comparison between their advantages and their charms. Thus, a number of patricians and knights escaped in order to go and greet their friends, while the lovers of high-caste women paraded in the company of husbands. But the designators made sure that everyone kept to their rank for the arrival of Caesar and the Augusta, and the tumult, after an announcement by a herald giving the order for the spectacle, calmed down.

Then buccinas resonated at the doors of the Circus, mingling their brazen sonorities with the stridor of sistra and the shrill plaints of flutes, sometimes punctuated by the dull rumble of kettledrums and the thunder of gongs. Then long silver trumpets burst forth, alone, explosively, in a triumphal fanfare. And on the podium among the snowy, pink and crimson flocculations of fans agitated by naked black slaves in golden girdles studded with emeralds, lynx-eyes, rubies and sapphires, Messalina, the Magnificent Empress, recumbent and borne on scarlet cushions, was installed in the front of the sovereign box.

Silius, slightly behind her, remained between Sylvia Carpina and Lorica Salis, two of the lovers' favorites. A crowd of Augustans in crimson tunics, senators in immaculate togas broadly bordered with scarlet and the consuls, took their places around the imperial "family." The people murmured. The Romans were discontented with the lateness of Claudius; the rumor ran round that the Emperor, often ill, would not be watching the games—but Rome could not admit that the god Caesar could not, this time, vanquish the fever in order to render a visit to his people.

Thus, the acclamations that had initially saluted the superb Messalina, hermetically draped in golden cloth and mauve sindon, with a tiara on her head of rubies and diamonds, competed now with violent invectives, departing, along with orange-peel and lady-apples, from the highest steps, where the rabble of slaves was crowded. Praetorians struck with pilums; one skull was fractured, brain-tissue trickling over boxes, from which protests were cried. Other spectators were jostled, shoved into the vomitoria, brutally expelled. Then calm was reestablished. A shiver ran around the circus. A designator repeated, for the Empress, the program of the spectacle.

At that moment, in the midst of further fanfares, Claudius came in and went to take his place between Messalina and Silius. People applauded. But as the spectacle was delayed again, murmurs rose up, less violent than before, mingled with acclamations and frantic invocations addressed to the gods by the friends of Augustus.

X

The Archon Melkios

A SUDDEN diversion changed the grumbling into laughter. That contagious hilarity gained the spectators as they leaned over and perceived its subject.

Staggering among the cushions because he had tripped over a golden stool at the entrance, a bald Augustan at whose temples the last hairs formed two oddly symmetrical silver tufts, stumbled again, this time over the legs of Salvia Caressina, the divorced wife of a senator and a friend of the Empress.

Getting up, the imperturbable clumsy oaf prostrated himself in the Oriental fashion before Messalina.

Gibes rained down upon him in sheaves.

"That Macedonian has a view as low as a skunk."

"*Oia Kephale!*"—Greek for *what a head!*—"Melkios! Sold! Melkios! Sold!" The man was an object of scorn for all those in Rome who knew the role he had played. A former slave, by intrigue and taking advantage of all those he had put forward and served, after having calumniated them and spied on them, he had reached the highest rank of the citizens of Athens, thanks to the riches that secret frauds had brought him. As eponymous Archon—the foremost, and the one who gave his name to the year—he had found the means of further increasing his power or influence and obtaining innumerable advantages therefrom. Even those whom he disgusted, knowing his mysterious ignominy, dared not infringe the frightful power the audacity devoid of courage of a rich corrupt politician had given him.

His abused fellow citizens had delegated him to Rome, to negotiate commercial and political franchises for their city with Claudius. From that moment only his public fall dated. Bought by Caesar, he had sold the rights of his city, and signed disastrous treaties of which the proconsul of Greece, Calpurnius Gallo, had received orders to ensure the execution.

Banished from Athens, declared a traitor, he had donned the Augustan crimson and remained with Caesar, a faithful courtier of the vices of Messalina and an informer against all his compatriots whom he knew to be devoted to the national cause—a denouncer dearly paid by all those who might inconvenience his cowardice, his recantations and his subtle volte-faces. The Archon, as he was always called in Rome, was despised, certainly, but feared nevertheless; his numerous parasites and the companions of his senile pleasures glorified him, sustaining the credit of the man to whom their fortune was attached.

"Melkios," shouted one voice with a Thessalian accent from the heights of the circus, "your feet are impeded by the chain of a former slave!"

That belated insult resonated in the great silence that had just fallen, for the grilles of the vomitoria were opening to the arena, their iron hinges grating.

XI

Salute to the Beloved

THEN, nothing more was heard but a formidable breath, the respiration of a crowd, of fifteen thousand breasts, breathless with an anguished desire for violence and blood.

The first to appear in the initial parade were the giant cavaliers of Libya and Numidia, coiffed in plumes of black and white feathers, mounted on African stallions with long tails that brushed the sand, which their frisky feet scratched and sent flying into the enclosure, where the gravel crepitated. Golden curb-chains retained their golden bits; striped or spotted anther-skins served as saddles.

Then came a unit of Gaulish cavaliers with bulging naked chests that caused women to whisper in admiration. Greek wrestlers followed on foot; the vanquished were to be put to death. After them came Roman cavaliers in decades, gladiators on foot and retiarii who followed by their habitual adversaries the mirmillons with helmets ornamented, by way of a crest, with bronze fish; and then Parthian archers and Dacian animal-handlers, Veneti and Lygians armed with iron pikes and heavy swords that they maneuvered with both hands.

All of them had their visors raised, and their eyes often encountered the sympathetic gazes of women or men in the audience. Soon, for the combat, they would be unrecognizable, save to the habitués and initiates; except that the designator in the arena would shout their names loudly. They arranged themselves in front of the imperial box, in groups with gold, bronze, silver or steel armor encrusted with antimony and sometimes studded with gemstones at the shoulders and the belt-buckle. The Dacian and Thracian barbarians and the Veneti, clad in animal-skins, made a bizarre contrast with those splendors.

And all of them, at a curt command from the lanista Casper, raised their blades in unison toward the august Imperial Majesties, which made a single sound as they emerged from their scabbards. A thousand swords seemed to be naked as a thousand gestures of a thousand men appeared a single gesture. And solemnly, in the silence into which the fanfares had fallen, their thousand voices were only one, just as their fixed gazes on a single objective were only one gaze, which dedicated their death or their victory to the divine Emperor Claudius Ahenobarbus.

"*Ave, Caesar, morituri te salutant!*"

Except that one of the gladiators of the corps belonging to the Empress, one of "Messalina's golden men," raised his eyes higher and further than the imperial box, and his raised sword also saluted other persons than Claudius and Messalina—Luxuria, whose pale painted face, in which only the eyes and mouth seemed alive, like strange flowers on marble, was smiling immutably.

On Sepeos, the first of the decade commanded by Manechus Victor, at the head of the Empress' gladiators, the Augusta's eyes were riveted. But to the magical ascendancy of those Eyes—before the curiosity of which, minuscule only in comparison to Rome, the empire of the world bowed down—the miserable gladiator was not subject. His gaze rose above Her, perhaps seeking another gaze.

Messalina leaned toward Caesar, and her index finger, ringed with gold, where rubies, amethysts and topazes sparkled, pointed at the Egyptian.

"That's the strolling player," she said, "that Silius and I have mentioned to you. He seems contemptuous of our divinities. See, his eyes are not fixed upon us."

"What does it matter?"

"A god does not tolerate such outrages, Claudious . . . unless he is fallen."

"But perhaps it's his lover that is distracting him," said the Emperor, in a mild voice.

Messalina turned round and inspected the steps. "Filiola!" she murmured. Then, to Claudius: "He's saluting an infimal little Christian. She's a maidservant in a tavern, I believe. That, at least, is what one of your familiars tells me, who does not disdain the crude beauties of the suburbs."

"And you think it's her that he's saluting?"

"Yes, I'm sure of it. Filiola is a Christian, and the disciples of Christos are troubling the Empire. You can see that the gladiator has no respect for us."

"But who is the man dressed in a dark blue tunic under a white toga to whom the young woman is talking? Is he a Christian too?"

"I don't know him, O my divine husband, but that doesn't astonish me at all. All the more so as the spectators around him all have a morose expression that is unbecoming, amid the joy of your people, and is an insult to you, who have decreed it."

"That's sufficient," said Claudius. "Both of them will be arrcsted."

XII

The Commencement of the Games

TWO contingents, commanded by Caius Saper and Arizanus, his rival, who had challenged him, appeared as soon as the salute of Caesar had finished. Under Saper's orders were twenty white cavaliers, Celts and Latins, while Arizanus was leading twenty captive blacks who had become slave gladiators, for their bravery had saved their lives temporarily.

The blacks were armored in silver over white leather leotards, the whites in bronze in the Roman fashion; all were armed with lances, with long straight blades at their sides; they carried oval shields that they banged into one another, making a great din. Then they engaged in a terrible melee, while the people vociferated cries of encouragement: *Bene! Age! Evohé!* Blades flew into splinters, while, overturned by the first impact, three cavaliers rolled in the sand. Another, not unsaddled by death, clinging to his horse, his head lolling, his throat half cut, letting out a flood of blood, resembled a marionette with broken strings on the panicked animal, which carried him around the arena.

The blacks were vanquished; six Latins were dead and one wounded, to whom the people granted mercy, while a dozen Africans had bitten the dust.

Retiarii, including Mucius Saphis, came to battle against mirillons armed uniquely with swords. The people took less pleasure in that part of the games; the hecatomb of the debut had given them a taste for blood and they waited, with the growling of a cat at play, for the beasts that would tear apart the Christians, as well as the fights between renowned gladiators that were to precede the great slaughter—and particularly the combat of Manechus, the King of the Sword, against the ten famous rivals that he had to defeat one buy one.

Meanwhile, Messalina had summoned the centurion of the praetorians, Virgilius Licis, and given the order in a low voice or the arrest of Filiola and Sepeos, but only at the end of the games, in order not to provoke a rumor among the people. The young officer bowed, and then moved away in order to resume his service, while awaiting the arrest of the Egyptian—if he were not killed during the games.

XIII

Posthumous Roses

IT was the sensational item: the combat of Manechus, by order of the Empress, against ten successive rivals. The trumpets and buccinas launched three brief chords of a martial fanfare, supported by the clash of cymbals and the shrill stridors of sistra.

That was the signal.

The first who came forward, at a sign from the imperial herald, was a Dacian armed with a short spear and an ax. Their names ran from step to step. Women threw flowers. Finally, Manechus arrived, alone, very straight in his mat steel armor, helmed in silver. Full of confidence in his strength, sure of victory, a voice burst forth in the great silence of the immense circus populated with thousands of men. He indicated the adverse decade and saluted Claudius in the name of his comrades:

"*Ave Caesar, morituri te salutant!*"

Than, at a signal from the herald, he took his place of combat beneath the podium—the platform that supported the boxes of the sovereign, the senators, the two consuls and the vestals. And this time, toward the radiant, splendid and impassive Messalina, to none but Her, he raised his eyes, dedicating to her in a whisper the ten mortal duels that he was about to fight, to please Her, and—while singers proclaimed the glory of combats delivered for sensuality and in honor of the amorous—he contemplated Her, transported, mad, ready for exploits unsuspected by the bravest and the strongest.

To render life more precious to him, to stimulate his energy and oblige him better to surpass his science of shedding the blood of warriors of the circus, did he not have in front of him the most desirable of visions, the adored Empress whose caprice his ten victories would finally vanquish? The King of the Sword admired all that troubling flesh, the divine Augusta, avidly, contemplating her as a wild beast contemplates a coveted prey.

Suddenly, Manechus struck his hexagonal bronze buckler with the flat of his blade, as if to challenge the first of the ten heroes chosen to measure themselves against him.

The Dacian advanced with a measured and confident tread, lifting the spear to his shoulder, fulgurant as a ray of sunlight caught the tip. His left hand maintained the ax in front of him, to protect his breast.

Manechus covered his right flank with his buckler, which seemed united with the iron cnemide, thus protecting the braced thigh, and he waited, blade forward.

The Dacian, having come within two paces of the freedman, bounded sideways, feigning an intention to strike at the left side; with a rapid turn, Manechus swiveled to face him. The ax fell vertically, collided with the sword and, the wooden shaft swept aside, the iron fell, colliding with the bronze shield, which rendered a sound like a cracked bell.

Manechus charged. Avoiding at every step, by means of abrupt jumps, the spear that was too heavy to follow the evolutions of the sword, by default, he struck the leather breastplate garnished with iron plates, in which the Barbarian was clad from head to foot. The man was panting, his movements seemed abrupt, and increasing jerkily. Already, his left arm, broken, was dangling. Blood darkened the brown leather where the shoulder-pad had fallen, detached by a sweep of Manechus' sword.

Finally, the Dacian, lowering his head and shoulders, launched his weapon at Manechus' midriff, and nearly reached it, in spite of the deflection to the right by the terrible blade, immediately raised, which, with a thrust of the angular blade, penetrated his throat. The Dacian fell, gasping, on to the gilded sand, which the sunlight, filtered by a white awning caused to sparkle.

The people and the knights, for the most part, raised their thumbs as a sign of mercy, but Domitia, the vestal, turned her inverted thumb toward the ground. The Emperor ratified that sentence of death.

Seven combatants were unfortunate, successively, including a Parthian who fought armed with a curved scimitar with a florid dentellate point; a blond Gaul with a long moustache, armed with a heavy pike; one of the black Numidians skilled in handling poisoned javelins of hard wood and who made use of a cord furnished with a ball at each extremity to paralyze an adversary and make him fall.

A Libyan with Herculean limbs, clad in a lion-skin and brandishing a club was nailed, his arms cut and his throat opened, in the middle of the enclosure, with a stroke of the sword, whose point, when he tried to withdraw it, was broken. Claudius, curious to see that almost invulnerable man, had another given to him.

The sixth was a Thracian, whose weapons consisted of two balls bristling with iron spikes, linked by chains, and a triangular dagger; the seventh was a Ligurian who attached with a long spear, equipped with a net in the fashion of retiarii.

The eighth, the first of the three survivors to present himself, was an old Roman soldier experienced in swordplay. Furious, his valor multiplied tenfold by the sight of blood, the nervous tension of repeated efforts and the sentiment of imminent victory, of the Empress finally conquered, naked for him too, agape with desire for the hero, the King of the Sword, Manechus felled him with one of the devastating straight thrusts of which he was the master, which annihilate feints and go past the sword at the first pass.

The ninth, haggard at having seen the so many deaths or mortal wounds, advanced. It was a very young gladiator, famous because he had strangled a bear without deigning to make use of his sword, which he had thrown away. Manechus was about to rush again upon him, but then, sensing his mistake, he recovered possession of himself and, knowing that he was tired, almost at the end of his strength, he stayed on the defensive, parrying, watching for the moment when, between sword and shield, there would be space for a murderous lightning thrust.

Manechus felt the glaucous gold-flecked eyes of Messalina, the inciter of these challenges, weighing upon him, cruel and soft.

High on the steps, Filiola, the kindly maidservant of Suburra, in the popina frequented by all the men who came to die, was trembling, in spite of her pity for the others, fearful that Manechus, the master and protector of Sepeos, might suddenly weaken.

She said to the old man sitting next to her: "He's a Gentile, Father, and he's killed eight of his comrades, but he has a good soul."

Manechus had just felled the ninth, whose blood augmented an enormous red pool that the sand was drinking. Sickened, Macris, the apostle, remained very pale in the midst of faces vociferating with savage delight, which he dominated with his bright eyes and his vast forehead with its nimbus of soft silver.

"Let us also pray, Filiola, for those who are to find Christ—for our brethren who are soon going to die."

Manechus was now crossing swords with the tenth and last, Marcus Lacero, a veteran of the arena, loved by the crowd, whose members had often admired his skill and his courage. In front of the imperial box, where the togas of the Augustans and the robes of the vestals formed two broad patches—one white and smaller which the bloody crimson surrounded and seemed, symbolically, to be eroding—the two men, marvelously handsome and strong, caused sparks to fly from their blades, with grim and violent skill.

Messalina, smiling, in order to lose nothing of that supreme encounter, which impassioned the entire breathless circus, had raised herself up on one elbow. Playing with a spray of splendid roses, she fixed Manechus with a caressant, and triumphant gaze, as one gazes at someone who belongs to you, as completely as a flower that a woman can, according to her caprice, savor or shred.

"*Habet Lacero!*" cried a hundred voices. "A hit!"

But Lacero made a sign of negation with his head and, after a splendid salute with his sword, provoked the other blade with its point. Marcus pressed Manechus more ardently; more insistently, his sword pursued the adversary exhausted, one sensed, by his nine victories. Already, people were acclaiming Lacero: "*Age! Gladiator! Bene!*"

The Empress followed the contest with staring eyes in which gleams were ignited. She saw Manechus pressured more closely, precipitately parrying merciless thrusts.

Messalina loosened the gold filigree laces of her embroidered subucula.

"I'm stifling," she murmured.

Mabra, the Egyptian woman, removed the stola and the golden palla. Messalina, with a slow gesture, loosened the last veil over her upper body slightly and, just at the moment when Manechus, as if for a mute invocation offering her his death or his definitive victory, raised his head toward Her—who was looking at him and smiling at him—for him alone, in the amethyst shadow of the garment, she showed her bare breast. At the base of the idol's belly, at the top of the roundness of her joined thighs, under the veils, a mysterious Flower, as if visible for him, hallucinated his desire. For a second, he forgot the enemy weapon, because of the lust bathing those divine eyes, the promise read in that smile.

A sudden formidable clamor: "*Habet! Habet! Eheu!*"

Manechus, struck during that second of distraction, had fallen, like a collapsing pillar. Blood gushed in a red flood from his breast, pierced in spite of the breastplate, which a formidable thrust of the sword had split.

The King of the Sword, finally vanquished, killed by the fatal splendor of the naked empress, the fascinatrix of men, was laid out in the sand, his eyes wide open, the pupils as if fixed on one last image, immutable in the depths of dead mirrors. Leaning over the edge of the box, the vestals raised their thumbs in a sign of mercy. The imperial sentence was awaited.

Messalina, immobile, perfidious and rascally, smiled, her enigmatic smile fixed in her painted face, and respired her roses, when Lacero made a sign with his head that any mercy was futile for his comrade. Then the Empress threw her sheaf of roses over the gladiator killed for love of her.

Imitating the gesture of the generous Augusta, women immediately threw white, pink, red and saffron corollas over the vanquished who had been victorious so many times; and for several minutes there was, during a supreme ovation from the crowd, a rain of roses—which the cadaver bloodied.

XIV

The Triumph of Sepeos

FOUR DECADES of imperial gladiators, armored in gold, succeeded Manechus and Lacero. Sepeos was in command of two, with Caius Birus as his lieutenant; Cornelio and Chylaides were in command of the adverse troop.

Once again, during the salute of swords raised toward the imperial box, Messalina saw Sepeos look toward the upper steps, doubtless addressing to Filiola the supreme invocation before the battle. Taking the Emperor Claudius by the sleeve of his tunic of mauve sindon, embroidered with golden flowers whose hearts, pistils and stamens, she said, precipitately: "Look!"

"They both deserve to die."

"Your thought, divine Caesar, will be executed by my orders. I took measures for those two cadavers, even before you formulated the just sentence."

Meanwhile, in the middle of the gold, red and saffron arena, which the sunlight stained with luminous patches, sixty men were fighting. Sepeos, very handsome in the mat steel of his armor, stationed in front of the imperial box, was fighting Chylaides. Messalina distinguished, beneath his lowered visor, the terrible gleam of his eyes, like a perpetual threat; she was ardent with anger and amour, her hateful admiration exasperated by her insatiable and vain desire.

Beside himself, his heart overflowing with sadness and wrath, Sepeos parried Chylaides' thrusts, pressing his adversary with hasty jabs, with grunts of effort and formidable surges, as if in haste to finish him. All his former rancor and dolor, revived by the death of Manechus, his only friend, assassinated by the coquetry of that slut Luxuria, rose again in the distress of his soul, flooding his seething brain with a terrible hatred.

Chylaides, suddenly, curled up in a fashion so extraordinary that he supported his left hand lightly on the ground, extended his sword with his right and lunged at the Egyptian. With a bound, Sepeos evaded the Greek's attack, and came back at him, with a direct thrust, striking him in the shoulder. The ferociously joyful cry of the habitués of the games resounded in the vaulted arena: *"Habet! Chylaides! Age, Sepeos!"*—Chylaides is hit! Go, Sepeos!

The Athenian tottered. Sepeos aimed a new thrust at him, moving straight at him, head down, covered by his buckler to the knees. Without any restraint, his unleashed fury, which remained skillful, demanded appeasement. This time Chylaides' torso was run clean through. Sepeos, amid the delirious cheers of the abject crowd, withdrew his fuming sword from the body, which fell, warm blood gushing therefrom.

Already Cornelio, having defeated Birus, was facing him. The clash of blades, the grating friction of iron, the impacts of points with armor, filled the silence in which the excited breath of thousands of men and women was palpitating, anguished by expectation and passionate conjectures. Cadavers sprawled, staining the saffroned arena with crimson.

And suddenly, once again, the trumpets burst forth in strident fanfares.

Oh, how Sepeos would have liked to have the Empress in his hands! How he would have liked to snuff her out, to break her, to make her bones crack in his muscular arms, make her blood spurt from a decisive wound. Oh, how he repented of letting her escape him. Henceforth, neither Filiola, with her Christian prayers and reasoning, nor Manechus, his master—had he still been, with his ill-fated and inexorable desire—would be capable of stopping his hand, of preventing him from stabbing or strangling the lustful jade, Messalina.

The flash of a sword that brushed him rendered Sepeos all his presence of mind, in order to make him add his decisive effort to that of his decade. Two men free of adversaries surrounded Cornelio. The valorous chief of the other decade, imploring the people with a rapid gesture of his left hand, from which the buckler had fallen, was still defending himself with his right. The people, clamoring his name with one voice, begged for mercy for him and the seven survivors of his troop.

While the cadavers were taken away, perfumes descended from the arches and the velarium.

XV

Further Hecatombs

THEN, a hundred condemned are the prey of twenty Numidian lions, which, quickly sated, gorged on blood, are reanimated by the sudden invasion of famished tigers and panthers: sectarians delivered to the wild beasts of the arena and the amphitheater, accomplices. The beasts devour them with teeth, and the spectators with their eyes.

In the meantime, standing up in his white tunic on the high steps of the Circus, opposite Messalina and the Emperor, the Gaulish apostle Macris blessed the martyrs.

XVI

At the Artistes' Exit

FINALLY, there is the crush in the vomitoria, the noisy exodus of the crowd toward the doors. Cries and exclamations overlap, amid the plaints of the partisans of Manechus, gamblers who have lost and the exuberant joy of others. Scuffles are produced, which the praetorians break up, even striking the brawlers and the recalcitrant with the hilts of their pilums. Outside, a cordon of argyraspid praetorians surround the western gate, on the side of the Imperial box. Others guard the exit from the rooms where the gladiators equip themselves before combat, where the survivors undress afterwards and make their ablutions.

When Sepeos emerged with Arizanus and Lacero, a number of plebeians, freedmen and slaves—for the people were curious to see at close range the men who risked their lives for their pleasures—cheered them. But the Decurion of the argyraspids, Lucius Famma, put his hand on Sepeos' shoulder.

"Man," he said, "you must come with me."

"Why?" demanded the gladiator.

"I don't know—but it's an order."

Meekly, Sepeos allowed himself to be led away. Citizens who had recognized him booed the soldiers.

"What has he done? Why are they arresting that valiant man?"

The argyraspids pushed back the overly curious without responding. Then the attention of the crowd was distracted because soldiers were bringing other captives from the direction of the western gate. At a distance, Sepeos recognized Filiola and Macris, whom the guards were dragging. The people flocked curiously around the impassive praetorians, whom Virgilius Licis, the centurion, was commanding in a curt voice.

"Who are those people? What is their crime?"

Everyone ignored them. One of the idlers, one of those fellows who know everything and the reason for everything in politics, said: "Let it go—they're worshipers of the donkey's head."

Gradually, the groups dispersed and Rome, draped in crepuscular crimson, continued its ardent life, for those incidents had no greater importance, in the milieu of the immense City in fête, than if the soldiers were picking fruits and breaking a few branches while traversing a forest of Latium, magnificent in golds and reds, all the resplendent rusts of autumn.

XVII

Incarceration

THE PRAETORIANS immediately took Sepeos to a subterranean prison hollowed out under the fortifications surrounding the Porta Capena at the foot of the Aventine.

The games had emptied the immense rooms of a large number of the Christians who had been captive there. A few old men with long beards and hair were dragging irons riveted to their ankles. A woman, on a bed made of garments the others had taken off, was shivering with fever in a dark corner. Sometimes the sick woman's eyes glittered in the gloom of the jail, which daylight only penetrated through ventilation shafts hollowed out in the bedrock and barred with iron spikes. The other prisoners were soldiers of the legion of the Alaude, who had refused to worship the divine Majesties and confessed Christos. There were seven of them, very tall, whose weapons had been taken away as well as their leather jerkins, with the consequence that they shivered in their thin tunics in the cool autumn nights. All of them wore, riveted to their ankles, a bronze chain that clinked at the slightest movement, striking the flagstones in a sinister fashion. The women were unshackled, but their hollow faces revealed the hunger and fever that were eating them away.

Sepeos was thrown among them without any irons being put on him.

At the entrance of their new companion in suffering, who would doubtless share their imminent martyrdom, they got up, and all of them greeted him.

"Greetings, brother; may God sustain your soul and preserve you from weakness."

"So you're a Christian like us?" said one of the soldiers. "And I see from your leather doublet that you're also a soldier."

Sepeos shook his head negatively. "No, brother, all I know of Christos is the stories I've been told. I'm an imperial gladiator; I've killed Simias, Kerbrix and Chylaides, and vanquished Cornelio."

The women could not suppress a gesture of horror and recoil.

"Brothers," said one of the old men, "and you, my sisters, don't repel a man blinded by the errors of the world. This Gentile might be one of the elect of the Lamb."

"Then why were you arrested, brother?"

"I don't know. I came out of the Circus today, where I'd been victorious for the third and fourth time. A decurion ordered me to follow him."

The Egyptian went to squat down in a corner, his head in his hands, in order to be alone and reflect on his new adventure.

Soon, the heavy door swung on its hinges with a dull sound, which reverberated from the vaults. Macris came in, shoved by guards clad in leather tunics, with four men in togas, and Filiola, whose eyes seemed ready to weep. Again the melancholy formula of welcome greeted the new arrivals.

"*Ave fraters! Ave, soror!*"

And immediately, having recognized the apostle, the Christians surrounded him, praising him for having confessed Christ once more.

Conversations began; the four new captives, Mauricius, a former centurion, Leracio, Verus and Sigulleux, knew several of the other prisoners.

"Brothers, death will reunite us in Heaven."

"Faith already unites our hearts on earth. Together we shall climb the path of glory."

Thus proclaimed one of the captives, Milevius. But Macris observed: "It's necessary not to conceive pride, for fear of soiling our pure sacrifice.

Filiola, sighing, replied: "Alas, Macris, if only we had as much sanctity and sagacity as you to redeem our sins! You can envisage death with serenity. Your successive martyrdoms have alerted the angels, and on the orders of Christos, they are finishing weaving your crown."

"How do you know, Fililola, that I am not bearing heavy sins? How can you judge me, if you have not entered my soul? But in truth, Christos favors us and he has been able to recognize his servants; he is extending palms to them and salutary death by taking us away to our supreme happiness."

Why, then," asked one of the legionnaires, "have this young woman and Macris been arrested?"

"Have they overturned gods, then?"

"I don't know; it was at the exit from the Circus."

At that moment, two red-gold sunbeams, the last of the day, passed through the ventilation shafts open to the west. The Egyptian, raising his head at the sound of voices, perceived Gueranus' little maidservant, his beloved.

"*Filiola mea!*"

"You, Sepeos!"

"They want to jail you, you too!"

"But how did they have the idea of taking you, one of the Empress' gladiators?"

"It's *Her!*" replied Sepeos. "Her, Luxuria, who detests me and is avenging herself."

In one another's arms, while he cradled her chastely, the gladiator and Filiola wept soft tears.

"I don't want you to die, my friend."

"It's you that it's necessary to save. You're a lily not yet bloomed; me, I have strewn my heart with chagrins, as leaves strew a flower-bed in autumn."

Macris approached them.

Filiola, suddenly escaping the gladiator's embrace, knelt down before the apostle.

"Oh, Father, pray to God and his Son and the Spirit to forgive me. I'm guilty and I want to cry my sin before my brothers. I'm in love, and I want to uproot that venomous flower from my soul, but . . ." She was breathless with anguish, but went on neverthe-less: ". . . I can't, I can't! Will Christos not reject me from the Kingdom of Heaven, jealous of that terrestrial love?"

"No, Filiola! Christos cannot reject you from his Kingdom, since his entire being is love. He is not jealous of terrestrial love, if that love is pure. The Lamb, who is all tenderness, does not forbid his faithful affection."

"Father, Sepeos is not yet a Christian, but he is brave and very good. His heart is gradually opening, like a flower in the morning dew, to the Truth that is rising over the world."

"In that case, Filiola, be the gardener who enables souls to blossom, and your affection will remain pure and holy."

Night fell. Two guards, illuminated by horn lanterns, brought the captives tin trays, closed with lids, on which lukewarm thin soup was stagnating. Then they lit a four beaked lychnus suspended from the center of the vault.

Until dawn, the Christians slept, except for the ones who, taking turns, maintained vigil over the feverish woman. She was moaning lamentably, like a suffering infant.

Eventually, silence fell and the somber subterrain was full of quietude, only disturbed by rhythmic breathing.

Sepeos, tortured by his hatred, was awake long before daybreak had cast silver and gold darts through the four ventilation shafts that rose from the prison toward the surface of the earth. The lamp was flickering, but he had time to contemplate the bare walls, made of white marble all the way to the sagging vaults, in the center of which four arches served the side walls as ridges. At intervals, iron crampons and rings sealed into the wall, in order to put recalcitrant captives in irons, seemed perpetual menaces. Inscriptions along the walls declared what prisoners had suffered there, what miseries and what ignominies had languished during the days of waiting before the execution.

Three thieves had enunciated their misdeed in iambic verses:

> *"On the banks of the Tiber, it was me, Salvus, who strangled the rich Egyptian Arom. He had two hundred aureus in his belt; it was the means for me to be an honest man for two months."*
>
> *"I, Laurus Ficus, was able to divert two thousand denarii from the treasury of an intelligent quaestor who accused me of having stolen them by breaking into his coffer, disappointed at not being able to enjoy that public gold."*

There were also numerous crosses with, in exergue, invocations, figures crudely sculpted with some point or other, and symbolic fishes. There were infamous inscriptions that unisexual lovers had composed in honor of the beautiful loins of their catamites, or memorial tributes to filthy prostitutes.

To pass the time, Sepeos was examining those mysterious words, which he could not read, when the lamp went out. Soon, the daylight blanching the ventilation shafts allowed him to distinguish, in the dense shadow, the empty tin trays and the varnished flowers of water-jugs. From outside, the regular footfalls of soldiers and their conversations reached Sepeos, as well as the noise of Rome, which was waking up. Anxious female voices asked about the prisoners; one, with a very young timbre, asked the centurion whether it was them who would be delivered to the Asian tigers disembarked from a ship that had come to Ostia from Ancona at the behest of Simo Barbax.

Then he made out the voluble twittering of Candilia, Linela, Baltrix and Sabina, who, while caressing the officer, enquired anxiously about the fate of him, Sepeos, and Filiola, asking whether it was really there that they had been imprisoned. They even offered money to the soldiers, begging them to procure a few favors for their friends, and in order that commands would be given to the guardians not to put them in irons.

And again there was a brutal invasion, through the resonant door suddenly opened, of men clad in leather, with broad belts in which massive keys clinked against the bronze sheaths of steel cutlasses. With ignoble epithets the guardians counted those they had to guard and then brought them pitchers full of water and coarse loaves of bread, which had to last six days.

The Christians, without recriminations or complaints, washed their hands and faces, and then, having gathered round Macris, listened to the apostle's fortifying words. Finally, in a mystical surge of their entire spirit, they praised God, Christos and his mother, in song—morning prayers that appealed ardently for an eternal dawn.

XVIII

Luxuria's Ultimatum

" ARE you the gladiator of the imperial corps named Sepeos?"

"That's me," said the adolescent. "What do you want with me now?"

"Follow me; someone powerful wants to see you. You have very beautiful friends, especially the one who is superior, in truth—yes, divine, by Jupiter! She can save you, pig, better than their crucified donkey's head with the tail of a fish."

The man, one of the jailers, sniggered. He was not overly harsh, and did not exert himself in cruelties against his prisoners, but he took pleasure in showing the scorn of a fervent polytheist for the worshipers of a Galilean thief, a negligible man and a barbarian. And, with the joviality of a good citizen with a placid conscience, he did so joyfully.

Sepeos stood up. He had thought, momentarily, of resisting, of remaining mute and inert, for he suspected what visit was in question. Who could tell? It might also be Candilia or Linela, or some other little fool for Suburra, moved by pity and confident in her prettiness to bend the jailers, who had come to offer him her consolation.

He traversed a somber corridor behind the guardian, whose horn lantern stirred glimmers in the opaque darkness, where shadows seemed to be massed. Two other jailers followed Sepeos, which made him smile because of the respect for his strength to which the precaution testified. Then they traversed immense tiled halls, where truncated columns were mounted, for flagellations. On the walls, the chief jailer's lantern allowed instruments of torture to be glimpsed: pincers of all forms for tearing the flesh of victims; there were some like gigantic lobster-claws, others were like a blacksmith's tongs and others affected the form of flowers of which each petal was a sharp and toothed curve or twisted blade. Sawhorses, boots, levers for dislocating bones—everything that Africa and Asia had bequeathed to Rome for the refinement of tortures was displayed there.

But a broad daylight, immediately after climbing a stairway and the opening of a last bronze door, dazzled Sepeos' eyes, unadapted to raw light. There the jailers bound him, bare-chested, having nothing about his loins but his belt and tunic, to the foot of one of the vast pillars of the atrium, open to the blue sky via an impluvium, a square opening that a white awning, half-extended on the side from which the sun's rays were coming, protected from overly violent ardors the mirror of a basin, florid with lotuses, between which passed the red and gilded gleams of Oriental carp.

A bed of repose, in citrus-wood, covered with multicolored cushions, a little ebony table encrusted with ivory and chairs with curved arms terminated by sculpted lions' heads: all of that sumptuous simplicity seemed to be that of a room in a gynaeceum, in the home of a poor patrician.

There was the sound of a heavy door-curtain being raised and closed again. The Egyptian had time to perceive Thracian slaves commanded by a giant; and Messalina stood before the prisoner, in a pose of smiling and ironic majesty.

"Here you are in my hands, Sepeos! Well, yes, it's me. . . . Is that all that you have so say to a woman, handsome lad—and the most beautiful woman, the most amorous in Rome, so indiscreet people say."

Sepeos' gaze boldly sustained the fire of the Omnipotent's irises. Splendidly draped in an amaranth and violet palla, on whose fabric golden birds with gemstones for eyes spread their wings, the Augusta seemed, with her painted face, a lascivious divinity.

"Your liberty and your life, Sepeos, are well worth the embrace of these imperial arms, don't you think?"

Parting her palla with a slow and gracious gesture, she let slip a white tunic of Cos linen bordered with crimson, so thin as to be transparent. That fall, like the petals of white roses, uncovered the right shoulder, the depilated armpit and a little of her breast, whose nipple was erect.

Sepeos maintained the scorn in his eyes. Then Messalina, having let that little bright cloud, which hardly concealed her, fall to her feet, shrugged off her palla of amaranth and violet sindon—a gesture accompanied by the promise of her eyes, her mouth, her momentarily darting tongue and the entire inventory of her luxurious body. For an instant, the young gladiator half-turned away in order not to see that temptation, but then contemplated it placidly, with the bored expression of a soldier on guard in a public square.

A rush of sarcastic and cruel anger twisted the lips of the vainly naked Empress.

"Are you not a man, then? Only eunuchs remain insensible. Then, have I not made sure of that myself? Has some wound rendered you impotent?"

The Egyptian quivered at the insult. "Are you a woman?" he growled. "No, you're an infernal monster, an impure ghoul, an ignoble female animal with defamed flesh."

Luxuria took a step toward him and tried, with an abrupt movement, to capture his neck with her hand and his lips with her mouth. But Sepeos, unsteady in his recoil because of his chain, nevertheless succeeded in escaping.

Her breast swelling with irritated stupor, clad only in bracelets, precious necklaces and her glittering diadem, she threatened him:

"Choose between amour and death."

"I prefer death."

"On the cross—ignominious torture, you hear?"

"It will be less so than your kiss."

Irritated, she extended an indecent hand toward him, which he repelled.

"I'll have you," she murmured, between clenched teeth. "Whether you like it or not, I'll have you."

Sepeos burst into mocking laughter. "A man can violate a woman; he can take her and penetrate her, in spite of her will, but what woman can possess a man without his consent? Your contact, Empress, would drain the life from my member, as if it had accidentally touched ordure."

"Madman! Insensate wretch! You defy me! Me, the Omnipotent! Do you not know that I can find means of which you have no suspicion to constrain you and have you, my dear? For I want you, and you shall be mine, in spite of you and in spite of everything."

"Try, then, Luxuria, and you'll see whether you can do anything against a man of my sort."

She gazed with an anger mingled with amazement at the petty strolling player—but a handsome fellow—the imprisoned gladiator, with shackles on his feet, attached to the red shaft of an enormous column: somewhat ironic, for Messalina, at that moment.

What could she do?

The naked Empress, panting with desire, irritated, humiliated in her pride as a woman and a divinity before that superb and stupid male, stood there, impotent, seeking a means to bring her adventure to a conclusion regardless.

After a long, erotic and furious silence, she proclaimed, believing that she had found it: "I'll deliver you to whores, prostitutes, on the ground, stark naked. They'll be able, by their caresses, to which you'll be forced to submit, by the expert friction of their hands, the gluttonous kisses of their mouths and the teasing of their tongues, competing for that success, to inflame your flesh, to oblige your desire. Then I, my handsome lad, shall bestride you."

"Perhaps they'll cause my virile strength to seethe, but you'll only have to brush me for all ardor to vanish. Try."

Sepeos, whose entire being signified disgust, challenged the Augusta, suspecting that she would dare more rather than cause his death. Messalina's ringed fingers struck the palm of her other hand twice. The giant Thracian and a decury of Barbarians armed with broad swords came in

"Bind that man more firmly."

To one of the columns sustaining the roof round the impluvium and the basin in which the soft and monotonous murmur of a fountain of water sounded, to the fluted shaft of which he was already attached by his chain, Sepeos was bound more closely, by the feet and the hands tied behind his back. Then, at an imperious sign from Messalina, the soldiers left.

"I want you, Sepeos. I shall take you. I shall play with you, at my caprice. Afterwards . . . afterwards, you can live or die. A tiger, of which you sometimes have the air, or some gladiator stronger than you will reckon with your pride. But before then, I shall have you, my dear."

"No, Empress, against my absolute will, against my inertia in the face of your obscene domination of the world, nothing can prevail."

XIX

Virtuous Spittle

"LOOK! My hand my mouth, my entire body will constrain you!"

Impetuous and avid, like a fauness intoxicated by her sap and the summer who has seen a beautiful coveted fruit amid the foliage, the Empress lifted the tunic of her captive, more beautiful in his rebellion.

Before the anger of the man, in a violent fit of rage, exerting all his strength to break the bonds that were digging into his flesh, to liberate himself, to seize her and break her as one kills a filthy animal, Messalina recoiled.

Calmly, Sepeos mocked the impotence of the lustful Divinity. "You see—I'm still the stronger. Your domination, Luxuria, stops at my refusal. What, then, can you do to infringe it?"

The Empress, kneeling down, took the prisoner in her arms. With an ardent desire of lustful challenge, even more naked, her unfastened necklace having fallen to the ground on top of her tunic of Cos linen, trampled, crumpled and ripped, her palla of amaranth and violet sindon thrown back over the flagstones, she stared at him, her eyes coaxing, her lips quivering.

The Egyptian, for a few moments, seemed to be ruminating something. Something suddenly spurted from his mouth: an enormous jet of spittle, which, falling directed between Messalina's breasts, poured its white foam down into their cleavage.

Then the Augusta, annoyed by that outrage, which she felt must be the only one, cried with mad chagrin: "What I can do? You ask that? There's Filiola, who I also hold in my power, the Christian that you adore, I know. You said yourself, just now that a woman can't possess a man against his will, but a man can violate her and soil her. Well, listen, Filiola, your lover, who's said to be a virgin—and I believe it, since you're a eunuch—I'll deliver to my favorites! The filthiest of my Augustans, Melkior, the old Archon, will take her first, and then all those who want her—Avicius Miso, the ignoble consul, I'm sure.

"After that—that isn't all—she'll still be good for the beasts. And you—you, Sepeos the eunuch, crucified, will watch her from the height of your gibbet, gasping under their claws; you'll see your Filiola torn apart by their teeth, whom a hundred games, expert or brutal, will have soiled beforehand, like a lily over which a hundred snails have paraded their sticky drool. . . ."

BOOK FOUR
The Martyrs

I

Verses of the Lily

1. THE black slaves have come to the prison hollowed out under the Porta Capena. And they have shown the guardian an ivory tessera on which an order is engraved:

2. *Give us Filiola, the young maidservant, in order that we may take her before Messalina, the magnificent divinity, as we have been commanded.*

3. And the back slaves said to the Virgin in the white tunic, whose eyes, in the depths of her subterranean prison, were maladapted to the light: "Our Empress has instructed us to untie your hands and feet, for you are destined for the sweetest embraces."

4. Now, shivering, the Virgin allows herself to be led away. She is carried in a litter to the palace of the Caesars on the Palatine hill.

5. And Messalina has quivered with joy on seeing her fearful and trembling before her, her hands joined and her eyes upraised to Heaven for a supreme imploration.

6. Old men and young men, behind the Augusta, made jokes as they examined the Virgin. The Empress designated Filiola with her right hand. "Is it not," she said, "an imperial gift that I want to make to my faithful followers?"

7. She summoned the Archon and said to the old man, whose concupiscent eyes beneath the wrinkled forehead and shiny cranium, were fulgurant with ignoble desire: "You are the most venerable, Melkios; it's you who will respire her perfume first. Take her. She's for you, to begin with.

8. "Then for all my friends, who are yours. I want them all to have their turn and each to have his share of that virginity."

9. And the Augustans cried: *"Evohé! Vivat Augusta perennis, Diva!"*

10. Then the Archon took the virgin away, unconscious, in his lectica, carried by twenty Nubians with heads turbaned in crimson.

11. That evening there were thirty, three by three, on beds around the table of a magnificent feast. At the back stood an immense bed of repose, draped with extraordinary fabrics.

12. The Archon wanted the little captive—whose fragile grace was visible through the veils of Cos in which she had been dressed, like a woman of pleasure or art, a singer, courtesan or dancer—to come and to hold her against his body during the orgy.

13. He forced the virgin to drink heady wines, having her held in order to be ingurgitated with precious wines, to oblige her to drunkenness. And the men laughed. Divorced patriciennes and two celebrated professionals of joy applauded.

14. Now, Filiola, naked, her white body inanimate, is lying on the cushions in the center of the room, among scattered rose petals.

15. All of them—men and women alike—after the vain efforts of the sadistic old man to be the first to violate, in accordance with the caprice of Messalina, the white flower-woman, have raped her. Unconscious, she remains inert, exhausted to the point of permitting the belief that she is dead.

16. The lips of men and women have burned the icy flesh, the intimate flesh, of Filiola, wounded and stained all night long. Males, brutally, tore her young virginity, each one bruising her more pitilessly

17. Amid laughter and, at intervals, the caresses of women.

18. And when, pale with a pallor of death, the white little maidservant was taken back to the subterrain where she was to await the hour to die, delivered, she was similar, exactly similar, to the cup of a great lily from which stupor was overflowing everywhere.

II

At the Foot of the Cross

THE CROSS, enormous and very high, was erected directly in front of the imperial box, crimson and white with vestals and Augustans. It was made of a great sycamore and the trunk of an oak, which a crude mortar and ropes bound together. At the top of the atrocious and vile instrument of torture, Sepeos, naked, suspended by his arms bound to the cross-piece, his ankles bruised by a cord, dominated the perimeter boxes. His eyes were ardent with dolor and anger, and in spite of his suffering, he raised his head to defy the Caesar and the Augusta, sprawled in the crimson of soft cushions. The Circus, full from the arena to the arches, was quivering with the long murmur of ferocious or pitiless voices. Cries of *"Eheu!"* and *"Ai! Ai!"* mingled cruel or ironic acclamations, like human voices and the cries of birds confused in the swell of the sea.

Buccinas, tubas, cymbals, and the shrill resounding grating of sistra suddenly fell silent. And now the viols, double flutes of wood and flutes of silver sang, in a suave harmony, as if announcing a celestial apparition.

That day, no designator had proclaimed the order of the spectacle, so the crowd, curious and expectant, did not know what new horrors or what frissons, what sanguinary sensualities, had been prepared for them by the solicitude of the candidate for the praetura.

But a bronze door opened and an adolescent girl appeared, alone and naked, with forms at once slender and of a full plenitude of youth ripened by amour. With her abundant golden hair and her extended hands she veiled, awkwardly, her shame in being visible in her entirety.

To those who knew nothing about her, people explained: "She's a maidservant in a popina in Suburra. It appears that she belongs to the new sect. Messalina began by having her deflowered by the Archon Melkios, and after him, all those who wanted her."

"Oh, she's of the sect that worship a fish or a lamb. . . . I don't know . . . well, what does it matter?"

"Undoubtedly, but they're beginning to be the cause of frequent tumults, and they declare that they will only render to Caesar what is Caesar's and to God . . . because they separate them . . . what is God's. Now, the Emperor is God, isn't he? So they're guilty of sacrilege and lèse-majesté in denying the divinity of Claudius and the Augusta."

"Oh, truly?"

"Sepeos, furthermore—the gladiator, you recall, who had made such a good debut but has ended up before us on the cross—obstinately turned his head and closed his mouth at the last games during the salute to Caesar."

"It's his little lover, then, at the foot of the cross?"

"She's young and very nice. By Venus, I believe she'd do me. . . ."

At first, quivering with wounded modesty, Filiola had not seen Sepeos on the great cross. The thousands of gazes that were inspecting her youthful beauty were like as many red hot irons on her flesh. Then she raised her eyes in the direction of Heaven, for a supreme imploration.

Filiola saw Sepeos, in his dolorous nudity, in which the muscles, terribly extended by the ropes, stuck out. She almost fainted, and uttered a loud scream. Her entire body shivered with terror and pity—and also with love, for at that moment, Filiola was no longer thinking of veiling her body, either her flower or her breasts, with her hands and her hair. Great sobs shook her beneath the golden mantle of her hair.

A cry of enthusiastic admiration saluted her:

"*Quantum pulchra!*"—How beautiful she is!

To the foot of the cross, the lover, a violated lily who remained white, had retreated. She was weeping, raising toward her beloved and to Heaven eyes of prayer and adoration. Of the wood of the cross she made a refuge, hoping to veil her body from the eyes of the people panting with desire for blood, amour, suffering, sensuality and carnage. Sepeos, from the height of the cross, launched his fulgurant glare at the infamous Empress and the entire Roman people.

II

An Amorous Bear

MESSALINA, whose implacable smile, in her fixed and painted face, was emphatic and sarcastic, was enjoying her triumph, that dolor at the foot of a calvary, bitterly. At a sign from her, the door of a vomitorium opened, and from the shadow, a heavy gray-white creature appeared: a bear, waddling placidly, licking its chops. It was one of those giants of the Alpine summits, which the most audacious mountain men fear.

The crowd applauded noisily.

The beast raised its enormous muzzle, looked vaguely around, growled dully, then uncovered its jaws, where sharp teeth gleamed in the pink of its gums. It stretched itself and roared, scratching the sand with its long curved claws.

The public judged that the beast was not showing all the ferocity that was hoped of its limbs and its hunger. For, during the two days preceding the games, the beasts fasted, for fear that, too quickly sated, they might refuse the abundant pasture of too many victims, which had happened several times during the reign of Tiberius.

"Whip it! Hoo, hoo, bear!"

"What stupidity! The flagellators!"

Already the valets of the Circus were cracking the thongs armed with iron spikes that were employed against gladiators who lacked courage and retreated. But the bear spotted the young woman breathless with fear and anguish, and walked toward her

214

a little more rapidly, breathing in noisily.

Filiola was still embracing the cross, hiding from the violations of thousands of eyes, but she took two paces back in order to see Sepeos, on his tree of torture, and to smile at him sadly in their common distress. Suddenly, she saw the bear, which was looking at her, stop dead. She fell to her knees, terrified, and the atrocious fear drew a piercing scream from her.

The bear took two steps toward her. With a thrust of its strong paw, without clawing her, with an almost gentle rudeness, it knocked her over. And Filiola lay there inert, having fainted. Her entire white body seemed like a great white calyx in which roses—at her breasts and lips—had let crimson petals fall.

The beast was no longer growling. It rolled strange ecstatic eyes between its horrible red eyelids. What did the bear want, then? Why had it sniffed and scented that flesh without sinking its fangs into it?

"No! It's not possible!" was heard on the steps.

And inconceivable desire of the wild beast was, however, suddenly affirmed. The monstrous muzzle licked that lovely nudity, seemingly dead, between the legs.

An immense burst of laughter, like thunder, swelling as it passed from neighbor to neighbor, spread from the top to the bottom of the colossal circus. The animal shook its massive head disdainfully, now waddling above the frail adolescent. Ridiculously, with the maladroit allure of an ardent and pot-bellied old man, the bear squatted down over Filiola, still unconscious.

What did the shifting of the hairy mass signify?

The public knew the young woman's story by virtue of the gossip of the Palatine and Suburra. And as the Archon stood up in order to get a better view, leaning over the edge of the podium, a hundred voices, which became thousands, saluted the appearance of that shaky head with the nose carmined by tubercles, bright in the snow of his beard. The people howled, joyfully, pointing at the bear:

"It's the Archon!"

"Bravo, old man!"

"Melkios is amorous for the slave!"

"He'll have her!"

"He won't have her!"

"But yes! But yes!"

"Oh! Oh!"

The body of the enraptured beast seemed to quiver with joy. Finally getting up, the bear contemplated the blonde child; then its tongue brushed her breast and licked her face, affectionately.

Finally, it stood aside, its head lower, swinging slowly.

The Emperor leaned toward Messalina, laughing, amused by that unexpected episode, and said to the Magnificent, stuttering:

"N . . . n . . . now, Lili, wouldn't it be b . . . b . . . better to l . . . l . . . loose the dogs?"

IV

Pasture for the Dogs

THE EYES of the Omnipotent became more ardent. From the height of his cross, Sepeos had seen the horrible scene. Messalina fixed her eyes on him and saw his gaze of hatred, which suffering had not extinguished on his dolorously taut features.

She snapped an order.

"The dogs! Loose the Lithuanian dogs on the bear."

The Augustans and the vestals repeated: "The dogs, the mastiffs! Give the slave to the dogs!"

The cry spread, magnified by thousands of ferocious and joyful voices. Again, they abused Alpine bear, which, crouching not far from the young woman, seemed sad.

Twenty dogs, tawny, russet, black and brown, bounded from the bronze door, barking excitedly, as if crazed by liberty and hunger.

Jostling and leaping, they precipitated themselves toward the rosy flesh offered to their appetite, to their cruelty of famished animals that hoped to feed.

First they sniffed the little slave with their savage muzzles. Under the warmth of that breath, Filiola opened her eyes again. Frightened, she tried to get up, to kneel on the saffron-tinted sand and join her hands toward Heaven and toward the cross. The chorus of mastiffs yapped, without attacking.

"Kiss! Kiss!"

"Go on, then!"

"Ho the dogs!"

Finally, one of them, an enormous iron-gray dog bit her shoulder. A carmined shred bled in its maw. Filiola fell back, with a despairing cry.

Another nipped her breast with the tips of its teeth, like a gourmet nibbling a choice morsel. The others charged, jostling one another sullenly as their bodies collided, while, furiously, for fear of being frustrated, they battled one another around their prey.

V

The Gratitude of a Beast

SUDDENLY, the bear, the bestial lover, the presence of which the dogs seemed disdainful, hurled itself into the midst of the pack, growling.

Applause saluted that sudden intrusion. The monster wanted his share of the prey. The crowd stamped its feet in joy because of the fine animal combat they were about to enjoy. But the bear sniffed the blood of Fililola's wounds and licked the wounds with its rough tongue, pitifully. The hounds growled terribly, resentful of the enormous beast that was driving them back with its clawed feet and menacing muzzle, ripping away at each blow a compound of flesh, hair and skin.

The dogs launched themselves furiously at Filiola. One bit her thigh; teeth scored her breasts and white torso with bright carmine. Tatters of ripped skin hung down from slavering maws, between terrifying and frantic fangs. The pretty martyr's body was clad in crimson; horrible wounds gaped over all that devastated flesh. Boldly, the bear stood up to the mastiffs. All of them, furious at seeing their victim disputed, hurled themselves at the bear, which, in driving them back over the saffron arena, pushed away the poor human rag, no longer showing any sign of life, that Filiola seemed to be.

The dogs strove to drive the bear back against the perimeter of the circus, but the wild beast, in the middle of the baying cluster, fought terribly, and every one of the blows delivered by its claws and teeth tore an adversary, which fell, twitching, and the pack trampled. Sometimes, the enormous beast disappeared under the flood of assailants, whose backs heaved in a mass patched with white, gray, black and brown, from which the gray, undulating back of the bear sometimes emerged

Howling with anger and pain, the dogs, decimated, gripped with their jaws but, shaken off, disemboweled and killed, there were soon no more than six valid, which fled toward the bronze door, fearfully, howling mortally.

The Roman people cheered the Bear frantically.

The beast, whose fur was patched with blood here and there, returned placidly, swinging its head lower than its shoulders, to the poor little body of the martyr. It caressed her with the end of its muzzle and then, calmly, paying no further heed to the fleeing dogs, lay down beside her.

Now, a clamor of admiring pity departed from all the steps, as if the crowd were weary of being ferocious. People cried for mercy. They all turned toward the imperial box. The Roman people, touched by the devotion of a beast, whose amorous recognition was better than human, demanded grace for Filiola.

Messalina still had an enigmatic smile on her painted face; motionless, the fascinating gleam of her eyes remained. She seemed impassive, thinking about the completion of her atrocious work. Around Caesar and the Omnipotent, the Augustans and the vestals waited anxiously for the sign that would permit them to decide, in accordance with the imperial will, death or life.

Sepeos, from the height of his cross, could see everything, and his heart, at that moment, was torn by an anguish worse than all those he had yet suffered.

The clamor grew, louder and more imperious, rumbling.

Already, Messalina was raising her arm nonchalantly. To condemn or grant mercy? The host of heads inclined more boldly toward the imperial box. Thousands of hands, with their thumbs raised, demanded mercy.

The military tribune Severo came into the box and murmured a few words before the divinities.

"Be merciful, Omnipotent; the plebs are growling like a she-wolf, and I can't guarantee that a sedition . . ."

"What of your soldiers, then, Severo, and your courage?"

"Divine, I've just seen an old centurion of the praetorians weeping!"

Messalina smiled with disdainful pity. "The she-wolf will be content," she murmured, with a sinister menace implicit in her muffled voice.

Her thumb raised, Messalina decreed the pardon.

The crowd applauded, acclaiming the Empress and Claudius Ahenobarbus, who was ruminating, bewildered, between his wife and Silius.

Animal-handlers came to fetch the bear to take it back to the vivarium, where it would wait to serve further agonies.

Crows—valets whose black helmets affected a resemblance with that bird of prey, who were charged with finishing off the dying or taking away the dead and the wounded who had been granted mercy—arrived, lifted up the bloody naked body of Filiola, and carried it away into the vomitoria.

On his cross, Sepeos quivered with mental and physical pain, while—before other combats, during which strident fanfares sounded—a rain of rose-petals fell, in a dew of nard and cinnamon.

VI

The Miracle

THE LIVES OF THE SAINTS,[1] in the pages devoted to Saint Macris, recounts the miracle that happened during the night that followed the martyrdom of Filiola as follows, and the author of that book was only transcribing the legend related by a pious hagiographer.

Macris had remained in the prison hollowed out beneath the ramparts, near the Porta Capena. The praetorian guards and the valets of the circus had not taken him away at the same time as Sepeos and Filiola. Nor did they take him among the number of captives who were to be delivered to the beasts at the end of the spectacle, either because they had forgotten him in his prison or because the designated number did not require his departure.

All through the previous day, as the unfortunate divined that the hour had come, hearing the comings and goings of soldiers and the nearer roars of ferocious animals that the animal-keepers were bringing from the vomitoria of the beasts into the arena, Macris had catechized the condemned.

He remained alone and disappointed. He even confessed, later, to being tormented. "Why," he asked himself, "has my master spared me? Is it to punish my pride because I believed myself worthy of suffering death for the glory of his name?" But he

---

1 Champsaur's *La Vie des Saints*, which I have translated literally, refers to the French translation of the 17th-century *Acta Sanctorum*, not Alban Butler's English translation. The fictitious Macris does not, of course, figure therein.

repented of his presumption, begged pardon from the Christ, and went to sleep, profoundly, after having prayed.

Suddenly, a voice extracted him from his sleep, calling him by name.

"Macris! Macris! Jesus has sent me to you, to lead you out of this jail, for God has founded great designs on you."

"Lord! Lord, is that you! The lamp is extinct, but I believe I recognize the celestial voice of which Peter and Paul of Tarsus speak, who had the joy of knowing you before your servant."

"Get up," said the messenger of God, "and follow me."

"Lord, the guardians have put chains around my ankles whose ends are sealed in the wall, and my hands are also bound with iron chains. How can I stand up and walk? Who will open the doors?"

"Do you no longer have faith, you who have confessed your belief in the midst of tortures? Get up, I tell you, and follow me."

Macris, unable to see anyone or anything, stood up on his bruised feet and perceived that his ankles were free, and that no chain any longer retained him. At the same time, those binding his hands together fell away. He praised the name of God, which permitted these prodigies, in favor of his people.

He began to distinguish a luminous shadow, human in form, the aureole of which guided him. The door of the dungeon was open. In the guard-room, everyone was sleeping profoundly. Several were missing, who had gone, after the circus, to celebrate the kalends with the denarius of wine and oil and the wheat of the morning distribution.

Macris and the Unknown traversed an empty atrium, and then found the janitor asleep in his lodge. And the last door opened, without Macris knowing how, by what power, the heavy bolts and the lock had been undone.

But he had no doubt that it was a miracle of the Christ.

Outside the darkness was opaque, as if made of cloud. But the Being said to him: "Go back to the house on the Transtevere, and no one will disturb you, for your hour has not yet come. Bless the Christ and tell the brethren how he has saved you from the hands of the executioners and the claws of the ferocious beasts."

VII

The Strength that Faith Gives

IN the house where the apostle occupied a poor room, uniquely inhabited by Christians, all of whom exercised insignificant métiers and were forced to accumulate in hives constructed by the patricians of the populous quarters in order to extract the maximum possible profit from the rents of the poor.

On the stairway he encountered one of his brothers of the same church, who had received the same minor orders, Salvius. Filled with a sudden joy, the latter exclaimed: "How are you free, brother? Who has liberated you?"

And Macris told him the astonishing story of his escape from the Capena prison. Then Salvius went through the house, announcing the prodigy and praising Christos. And everyone there glorified the Son of God.

They hoped, aloud, that further miracles would save those of their faith condemned under various pretexts, who were being kept for the representations in the circus, which would last all week. But the gaiety of the companions was brief. Too much heavy sadness and mourning weighed upon their hearts that day.

Macris incited them to thank God. Then he asked about their brothers and sisters, and the representation in the circus. As the porter Girbal was telling him about the abominable torture of Sepeos, put on the cross since the previous day, Christians inhabiting the house arrived, carrying Filiola on a stretcher, covered with their mantles.

The young woman was laid down in Macris' own room. The salt-merchant Marchius ran to find Mirzan, the slave physician of the lanista Casper, who, without being converted, had a sympathetic curiosity for the new sect, and he came back with the Syrian, whom he had found in his master's house.

Poor Filiola remained prostrate and inert. Sometimes, feverish tremors shook her lacerated body; she let slip cries of pain, and her lips articulated inconsequential phrases, words of horror and exclamation, mingled with the name of Sepeos and pious and suppliant invocations.

Mirzan shook his head, and prescribed cares and remedies, which he promised to bring in the evening.

Macris said to his brethren: "Although he is not yet a Christian that gladiator has approached the mildness dear to our Master, and he has served several of us in various circumstances."

"I have even seen him with Filiola at one of our ceremonies," said one of his listeners. "He will draw nearer to Christos, whom he has commenced to know, for, in spite of his cruel métier, he is not wicked."

"The Lord will aid us," said Macris. Turning to Marchius, he questioned him, eager to find a means of getting to the cross. "You say, my son, that they have left him attached. At least the praetorians have not broken his legs?"

"I don't think so, Macris."

"But how have you been able to recover Filiola? Perhaps, by the same means, we could . . ."

"No," said Salvius, who, being a Roman citizen, knew the usages of the circus. "The Empress granted mercy to the child; by virtue of that fact, she is free, and besides, her former masters scarcely care about a sick slave who might perhaps die."

Marchius the salt-merchant concluded: "As soon as the games had finished, we went to the spoliarium, where the victims of the beasts and the blades are heaped up. We had to wait for hours, otherwise we would have been back long ago."

They deliberated. Finally, it was agreed that Macris would go to find the janitor of the western gate, which gave access to the vomitoria, from which they would be able to penetrate into the arena.

The porter in question was a freedman of the consul Avicius Miso, whose wife, converted by Paul of Tarsus, received Macris and several members of the Roman sect, in secret from her husband. A number of the servants of their *familia* believed in Christos, and the freedman Verax was of that number. They also decided to take two gladiators. They were not Christians, but they were acquaintances of the barber Lucius Viro, who answered for their devotion in return for a sum of money to be agreed on. Viro left to look for them; only one was found, at the caupona of the Nubian Lion in Suburra.

The eleventh hour was nigh. They all knelt down to pray. Macris exhorted them. The task was perilous and not easy to carry out. But had he not been saved himself by a miracle?

Fervently, Macris invoked the saints after Jesus. By the protection of the Son of Man, their faith and audacity would save them. And Sepeos, liberated, would become their brother in Christos. There would be celebration in Heaven then, and in their souls.

They were seven, clad in dark mantles, who followed the apostle Macris: Girbal, the potter Salvius, Marchius the salt-merchant, the barber Viro and two others, humble artisans of the Transtevere, Carbo and Loricus, both young men. The gladiator Vermer marched beside the apostle, in order to prevent any alarm. But it had been necessary to instruct him only to strike on a precise order, and not to provoke anyone on the way. Adroit and very strong; he would help in taking Sepeos down from the cross.

It was pitch dark. Somber clouds covered the stars and the moon had not yet risen. They walked quickly, skirting the walls, two or three abreast, each carrying a horn lantern to light the way in the opaque shadows. They did not speak, except when footsteps approached, in order that they might be taken for citizens belatedly retuning in haste to their lodgings.

They followed the Via Trastevere and then, cutting across the Via Nomentana, reached the deserted Forum. They went as far as the foot of the Celio; there they extinguished their lanterns, on the advice of Girbal, who feared giving the alert to the posts of praetorians spaced out around the palace and the employees of the spoliarium, who, during the night, had the cadavers carried away by the crows, the most infimal of laborers and Roman slaves, in order to be burned in heaps on immense pyres whose red glow, on the bank of the Tiber, mingled with the variety of green, carmine and white lights of the boats moored along the shore.

They prowled around, without knowing quite how they would succeed in evading the vigilance of the sentinels. It was necessary to get to the lodge of Linas, the Christian janitor. Macris and his followers did not know how to do that without falling into the ambushes that surrounded hem. To tell the truth, they were counting greatly on Providence; they had more faith in a miracle than in a vague plan of inconceivable audacity, which left a large margin of uncertainty.

The potter Girbal put an end to the anxiety of the little troop, which, behind the colonnade of a temple dedicated to the Phrygian Venus, held council in low voices.

"Linas won't dare refuse us entry, above all because of Macris, whose arrest he knows about, but not his unexpected liberation."

"Perhaps," said Salvius, "we'd do better to split up and search, separately, for some friend. There are a large number of Christians among the valets and slaves of the bestiarium."

"No," the apostle replied. "Linas will permit entry to all of us, or at least several of us, unless he fears the vengeance of the Gentiles."

They resumed marching through the shadows at a slow pace. They dissolved in the darkness, one by one, some way distant from one another, in order to disappear at every street corner, to become one with the colonnades, to fade away into the opacity of walls. Soldiers went past them who did not see anyone. They heard a troop pass by a few paces away, which halted in front of the eastern gate and broke up. They distinguished the voice of the centurion giving orders, and by the light of a lantern attached to the top of a shield, which served as a beacon, they even distinguished the silhouette of the officer.

"That's Virgilius Licis," said the salt-merchant, in a whisper, to Macris. "It's claimed that he's a neophyte, or, at least, favorable to Christos."

"Yes, but he's a praetorian," riposted Salvius. "His own soldiers will denounce him."

The soldiers drew away in groups, at a rhythmic pace.

The black mass of the amphitheater suddenly surged forth in the night, formidable and somber. On the side of the hill, and isolated, the colossal circus seemed a great monster lying curled up, a huge sleeping wild beast. Murmurs escaped from its flanks; confused voices that seemed to be its respiration. In the entrails of the circus, from the subterranean depths of the bestiarium, roars rose up at intervals, and one might have believed that those growling voices announced the awakening of the enormous beast.

The companions followed the walls, ducking down to pass under projections, disappearing into the frames of doors, becoming one with the stones drowned n darkness, bearing the patina of the years.

In that fashion, they approached with infinite precaution the Northern gate, where they hoped to find the janitor Linas, the Christian freedman—and no one suspected the presence of those beings, which a nocturnal passer-by might have mistaken for shadows playing over the walls, nocturnal mirages.

VIII

Mater Dolorosa

FOR many minutes, which seemed to them to be hours, they marched, with continual halts. Macris stopped and, turning to Salvius whispered to him:

"Can you hear, brother?"

"Yes, there are plaints. Some poor martyrized being that they're keeping in the cells, or else it's a prisoner."

"That voice," said Marchius, "isn't locked up; it's changing its location, and one might think that it was following us."

They had arrived within a few paces of the northern gate. The janitor Linas had emerged from his lodge and, without rudeness, was pushing away an old woman with unkempt white hair protruding from a red and gold turban.

"All day I've been looking for my son, I tell you—and I know that he's in the circus, that they've put him on a cross. Just let me see him."

"At present, I can't open up to anyone without an order from the aediles, the consuls, or Caesar."

"Oh! Oh, he's going to die! And I'm his mother, I tell you. I'm old Geo, the mother of the King of the Iron Ring. He's going to die and I won't be able to close his eyes. Janitor, oh, janitor—you don't know! They told me he was a Christian, my son. They're mad. The soldiers pushed me away. The crowd, today, jostled me and trampled me, for I arrived here just as the atrocious spectacle was ending and everyone was coming out of the games. Let me pass, janitor! I'll ask the fays to heap you with presents. You'll be rich, happy; women will follow your footsteps in the hope of obtaining caresses from you, uniquely, in spite of your not being a young man. Listen! I know how to ward off the worst of maledictions and conjure Destiny. Let me see my son! My son! My son!"

"*Eheu!*" said Linas. "I pity you, woman, but I can't. Go find the aedile. Soon, if you continue to wail and moan like that, the praetorians, when they make their nightly round, will strike you rudely with the flat of their swords. And it won't be my fault!"

"You don't know. I've run all over Rome looking for him. In Suburra, they told me that he was a gladiator, and then that he was a Christian. I didn't want to believe that, of course! But when he left me, after he was set free—for Messalina had her guards beat him—I went to Iberia, thinking that he'd come to join me there. Our brothers were waiting for him to give him the ring. The tarot cards told me that he was in Rome and that he'd been victorious four times. Then I came back."

Linas pushed her away gently. "Go ask the centurion. It's Virgilius Licis; he's good, perhaps he'll permit it. But don't make any more noise. . . .

"Oh no, no! He'll have me beaten again."

"It's his mother, an old nomad," said Macris.

As Linas closed the door, and as if collapsed in her multicolored rags, the old woman was still moaning, interrupting herself to utter bizarre maledictions Girbal and Marchius approached her.

"Shut up woman; you'll bring us misfortune, and you too. Rather pray and hope."

Macris took her hands.

"You're his mother; we're going to free him, God willing. Be quiet. Your wailing will only obtain blows with rods and the flat of swords, and you'll doom those who want to save your son."

Salvius said: "It's necessary that it's not her who knocks on the door. Linas won't open it. It's necessary to let the knocker fall four times, as if it were a signal. He'll fear making a mistake and open up."

At that moment, Macris raised a hand to order silence. Under the conduct of a centurion, uptight and carrying a vine cep in his right hand, soldiers in gilded armor passed by, heading for the Palatine. Their footfalls faded away toward the bottom of the hill.

Macris raised the hammer four times.

The others followed him.

Linas open the door a crack, and, amazed to see Macris, whom he thought to be in prison, perhaps dead, he said: "They haven't killed you, then, Father?"

"Jesus has liberated me. Let me and the men who are following me pass, in the name of Christos, our Master."

"All right!" said the janitor, shivering. "But I'll be put to death if anyone . . ."

"Have confidence! The Lord is guiding us."

Full of respect and fear before Macris, saved from the executioners, Linas, the Christian freedman, let them enter the Circus, trembling with fear.

Geo followed behind with Salvius. Linas wanted to stop her entering, but Macris raised his hand and said: "This woman is with us."

Cautiously, Linas closed the heavy bronze door again on those of his sect.

IX

The Descent from the Cross

LINAS, the worthy janitor, had guided them to the entrance of a long dark corridor that opened near the boxes reserved for the senators and magistrates.

"Go, and go quickly; bring him back this way—but don't linger until the twelfth hour, because the night guard in relieved then and a patrol does a round of the amphitheater."

They set forth, scarcely able to see. On penetrating into the colossal circus Salvius had relit one of the lanterns with horn walls. Geo began to lament again, mingling her plaints with voluble incantations. Rudely, the gladiator closed her mouth with his hand.

"Shut up, witch! If we have to die, at least let it not be because of stupidity. We're going to find your son."

Without another word they went along the corridor behind Salvius' flickering light. The door, a block of iron, slid in its groove soundlessly, because the metallic tracks had been oiled for the day's performances. Then, bent low so as not to surpass the steps and to melt into the stone, the nine moving shadows ran furtively, briskly and silently, behind Macris and Salvius.

They held their breath, stopping at the slightest rustle, because the wing-beats of a night-bird traversed the shadow, or an insect suddenly brushed their faces. From step to step, through the corridors between the boxes, the finally reached the rim of the arena and leapt on to the sand.

And they all assembled around the cross, in the shadows, which barely allowed an enormous silhouette to be divined: the vague shadow of the gibbet, which they felt with their hands.

"Is he there?" asked Geo. "My worn-out eyes can't see in this darkness."

"Shut up, by Jupiter!" replied Girbal. "Do you want us all to die?"

At that moment, the moon tore the backcloth of cloud that formed a ceiling over the gaping Circus. For an instant, the boxes and the circular steps, appeared, arranged like the paths between the shelves of a beehive, or like the interior of a disembowled termitary.

In the center of the arena the Cross surged forth, enormous, projecting a huge shadow on the ground. Suspended from the huge stout branch that formed its arms, Sepeos had allowed his head to fall forward, on to his breast. The human form could be distinguished confusedly, hanging lamentably from the top of the gibbet; the feet, swollen by the weight of the body and the cords binding the ankles, made a bizarre projection strangely exaggerated by the reflection on the sand. But new clouds covered the moon, and the light was killed again by thick shadow, in which the steps of the circus could no longer be seen. The old bohemian woman clasped the wood of the cross passionately, and, on her knees, wept copiously.

"Let's hurry!" said the gladiator. "The twelfth hour is near."

Girbal took the desolate mother by the armpits, murmuring words of consolation and promise, and undid the grip that sealed her to the Cross where her son, prey to the worst dolors, was agonizing. In low voices, they concerted.

The two youngest, Carbo and Loricus, would climb up to the arms. The gladiator would take hold of the detached body from below until Girbal, having joined him, had unfastened the feet, and another, succeeding him, finally brought the victim down to the ground.

Carbo and Loricus had already taken off their mantles. They were about to climb up to untie or cut the cords around the wrists—but suddenly, Salvius whispered: "Lights! It's a patrol."

In the blink of an eye, all of them lay flat on the sand, mingled with the grayness, and vanished, holding their breath. Elephants suddenly trumpeted, to which the roaring of lions and the sinister mewling of tigers responded.

Then the conspirators saw the glimmer of torches moving along the steps, in the amphitheater. Breastplates gleamed in the distant gloom; heavy footfalls and the impacts of metallic soles prowled around the circus.

Finally, everything fell back into darkness; the patrol had passed by without seeing them.

The two young men quickly reached the arms of the gibbet, in order to sit thereon and untie the hands. The gladiator, hoisted up as far as half way up Sepeos' body, received it in the left arm while the while clinging to the trunk with the other. Inert, the body sagged in the fashion of a cadaver set upright.

The old Egyptian woman let a muted groan emerge from her lips.

The feet were finally unfastened—and gently, with infinite precaution, Macris, Salvius and Marchius received Sepeos in their arms. He was laid on the ground. The apostle palpated his flesh. It was still warm.

"Christos," he said, "will render him life."

Geo threw herself down on the motionless Sepeos. She raised his head, lifted the eyelids closed over convulsed irises, and murmured bizarre words in his ear. From the folds of her tunic she took roots and leaves, with which she rubbed his temples. Then she poured a few drops of a mysterious elixir between his lips.

"Hurry up!" said Girbal.

Geo muttered maledictions between her teeth. Her tremulous voice conjured infernal spirits. She included in their number the Christos who was the cause of all her son's misfortunes.

With the aid of Salvius and Macris, the gladiator took the moribund, whose head was slumped on his shoulder, in his arms. Already, Linas had appeared at the entrance to the corridor, holding a candle. They thought they had been discovered, but the janitor made signals as he approached, and said:

"Before my clepsydra is empty the main patrol will make the round."

Behind the porter the cortege set off again between the steps of the amphitheater. Linas had extinguished his light. He marched in front through a maze of corridors that were unfamiliar to them. Once again they heard the formidable roars for a few minutes, to which lions and tigers responded, and the repulsive sobbing of hyenas. Then, again, the colossal circus fell silent. Their footsteps, resonating on the stone of the corridors, frightened them.

Finally, on the threshold of a lower door, Linas murmured: "Thanks be rendered to Christos, his Father and the Spirit. May they be with you, brothers."

The cool night air was now bathing their faces again. The moon, emerging between two clouds, shone palely in the sky, where a few stars were shining in gaps between other clouds. And by way of tortuous and deserted alleyways, they made their way back to the house in the Trastevere, where anxious fraternal eyes were watching out for them through small windows overlooking the street.

X

Christian Dawn

MIRZAN, the physician, hearing the tread of sandals on the stairway leading to Macros' room, where he was watching over Filiola, opened the door slightly. Girbal occupied two fairly large rooms on the same floor, where his wife and two children lived with him. They were awake, waiting anxiously. The potter opened the door and the unconscious Sepeos was laid down on his own bed.

Mirzan, amazed—for he had scarcely believed, until then, in prodigies other than those of science and necromancy—looked at them, hardly able to speak. Finally, he went to Macris and bowed profoundly before the apostle.

"Father," he said, "you have accomplished another miracle. Bless a man who would like to be your son."

"Christos guided us as he guides you, Mirzan. Believe in him and you will be saved."

The physician now examined the crucified man. With minute care, his head and shoulders were lifted, and Mirzan patted his temples with a cloth soaked in an odorous essence, while old Geo, kneeling beside her son, contemplated his face passionately—but she darted suspicious and jealous glances at the other people present. Meanwhile, the clerk Salvius showed the gladiator out, thanking him, having given him a purse containing a few denarii.

Soon, while Amilla, the potter's wife, made the invalid drink a broth of meat and herbs, the physician said to the mother:

"Woman, your son is safe; his life is not in any danger from now on."

Recovering consciousness, Sepeos examined the people around him and the poor décor.

"Where am I?" he murmured. Then he recognized Macris and Mirzan. "Filiola?"

"She's here, close by. You can see her."

"Is she alive?"

"Thanks to Christos, who saved you," replied the apostle.

Mirzan explained, in the musical voice of a man of the Orient, how the young woman had been lacerated by the dogs, without any of her wounds being very deep.

"I want to see her! I want to see Filiola!"

Girbal, Salvius and the other two Christians, led by Macris, went to the apostle's room. Filiola, lying on a litter made of webbing and cushions, appeared before Sepeos, very white in a linen tunic, from which the weary flower of her visage emerged, the eyes burning with fever. The injured girl was set down beside the gladiator, who raised himself up, reanimated.

"You! It's you, my Filiola!"

"Yes, it's me. Christos didn't want us to die."

Making a great effort, they were able to join their pale hands. A sob made the Egyptian turn his head. Geo had retired into the nearest corner, so that she could not be seen.

"Mother! My mother Geo! How are you here?"

"Even before these men, my son, my King, I was searching for you through the city; I met them near the circus, when they were going to take you down from the gibbet. But they frighten me—and it seems to me that you're no longer the same."

"Mother! Don't judge me."

The old woman covered Sepeos' face, eyes and swollen hands with caresses.

"They've saved you, these men, but in order to steal you from your brothers and your beliefs." As she spoke she indicated the sectarians facing them, who had knelt down to pray. Then, indicating Filiola: "This woman you love now isn't of our race either."

"Listen Mother! And all of you, sisters and brothers. A strange light is illuminating me. I have seen it burning in your eyes, Filiola. Now I understand, I hear, I see. Yes, I know now the power of the God of Filiola and Macris. On the Cross, at the spectacle of the death of the Christians, I understood. I believe in Christos. Filiola! How I love! I can see the truth shining, my mother Geo. A strange serenity illuminates me."

Morning was just beginning to taint the distant horizon; a pale light draped the windows overlooking Rome, still drowsy. Tears suddenly formed in the corners of Filiola's eyes, and she said to Macris: "I'm guilty. I love him too . . . but Christos wants to be the only one to possess the hearts of his faithful."

"No, you're committing no sin. It's him, your God, who is sending you human love; it's on you, martyr, that he founded the design of bringing the heart of Sepeos to him, for his is the God of love."

"Father," said the Egyptian, "receive me into the faith of Christos and baptize me. I know enough of your doctrine, enough of your law, to know the immense good I'm asking of you."

Wildly, Geo cried: "You're going to renounce your own people, Sepeos? And me, your mother—and your crown?"

"There's one more beautiful, Mother. And then, I believe in Christ and I love Filiola."

At present, Rome was beginning to emerge from the night. The streets were revealed between the hills, in the soft gray of the morning. Salvius brought a black earthenware ewer full of pure water, and salt on a spatula. Then Macris poured the water on Sepeos' head.

"I baptize you, in the name of the Father, the Son and the Holy Spirit!"

Then he put a little of the symbolic salt on his tongue, and Sepeos, repeating the words that Filiola pronounced, murmured the prayer of the confessors of the new faith:

"Credo in unum Deum . . ."

All the faces of the kneeling sectarians betrayed the immense delight of their souls. Macris took Sepeos' hand and placed it in Filiola's.

"Love one another, then, body and soul, for the greater glory of the Divine Master.

Tears in the eyes of the Egyptian and the little maidservant declared the intense emotion that gripped the fiancés.

To the east, over the Tiber, the brighter lights of dawn invaded the sky, tinted with silver, orange and sinople. The sun had not yet appeared, but, like torches before a patrician's chariot, light clouds seemed to be ablaze, announcing a splendid aurora.

Crouching in a corner of the room, Geo muttered incantations, and her eyes fulminated, uniquely alive in her wrinkled face. But in their joy, transported by mystical love, none of those present paid any heed to her vain conjurations.

Macris indicated the sky, and, having blessed the lovers, whose hands were clasped, he spoke:

"There was night, my brethren, and now the day is rising. There was night over all the earth, before the God made man was born. Now, as light succeeds shadow, Christos and his thought will reign over the world. There was night, a night of thick darkness, in which sinister torches gleamed, in which blood flowed. The gods of the Gentiles wanted hatred, commanded jealousy and violence. They were hungry and thirsty for human dolor. Savage triumphs delighted them. But Christos has raised the sign of his cross over the world. And that cross, which, before him, was the infamous gibbet of slaves, has liberated humans from ancient and heavy servitudes.

"Glorify yourself, Sepeos: he has chosen for your martyrdom the sign of his mercy. It is the dawn in verity, I tell you; it is the aurora in the sky and in hearts. The tortures of the faithful announce the Reign of the Faith, as those gleams announce the sun. And the ignominies that you have suffered, Filiola, and your atrocious crucifixion, Sepeos, are nothing but convulsions of the darkness that the light of God is chasing away. Filiola, little flower, Barbarians have soiled your body, but your soul is pure, and virgin is the immaculate lily that the feet of coarse men have not been able to crush beneath their dusty sandals. Love! The light is in you, as it will shine more intensely, from hour to hour, over the entire earth. An aurora of joy and amour is commencing, which will illuminate the Universe for centuries of centuries."

"Amen! Amen!" replied the Christians.

The silver disk of the sun emerged at that moment between two hills, irradiating the azure. The clouds, rapidly chased away by a morning breeze, had disappeared. The immense blue horizon was strewn with flamboyances and reflections, like luminous flowers.

A new dawn of the eternal Sun rose over Rome; a marvelous dawn of the unknown God rose over the world.

INTERLUDE

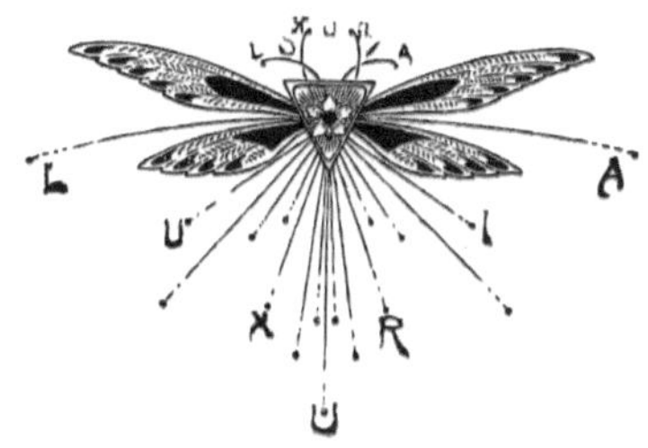

IN the same way that etchings by Félicien Rops have sketches in the margin, and a musical drama has the flutter of a ballet, in this antique poem, before its denouement:

AN INTERLUDE,

Of which the leaps will create around Messalina, at her intimate toilette before an Iberian philosopher, Seneca: a faun and a nymph, an evocation of an old mythology in the process of agonizing in eternal nature; Luxuria, which is to say, Messalina again, the Naked Empress, elevated as a symbol and purified by art—Luxuria, her star with the fires of the clitoris and rubies; then a merchant sailing on the Aegean Sea and a lover awaiting on her terrace a messenger of Aphrodite; and finally, a degenerate Roman of illustrious family, no longer believing in the gods, nor in the sensuality of living, scorning Jupiter and not understanding the unknown God whom slaves, the poor, the humble, partisans of Jesus, a Judean prophet crucified nearly fifty years before,[1] were beginning to proclaim.

---

1 This is an evident miscalculation, the action of the story taking place in 48 A.D., nearly fifty years from Jesus' supposed *birth*, and less than two decades after his crucifixion.

Seneca and Messalina

SENECA, a philosopher with a very fine brain
Was in Messalina's home at the hour of rising
Weary of the brothel. "Master, I want to dream.
Shake with your words my unsatisfied soul."

She directs toward him, a goddess with eyes in fête,
A long seductive gaze intended to captivate.
Seneca, a courtier, like a consummate ape,
Climbs to the summit of his philosophy.

From there, casting all the light of a vivid torch,
He celebrates the gods, then duty, beauty,
The good, the just, and finally dreams in the nude.

An Egyptian slave-girl, in the nest of her amours,
Washed and perfumed the naked Empress,
And Seneca confused the thread of his discourse.

April and Winter

(Diptych)

I

The Echo of the Faun

THE NYMPH:

The beloved is belated again;
My heart is burning with desire.
Days and nights without pleasure,
And solitude are devouring me.

I have dreamed of him straighter than a poplar trunk,
The supple adolescent with the limpid eyes
As profound as the waves. With his avid lips
My youthful lips dream of being joined.

THE FAUN:

Being joined, for days and nights, our lips!
My hands seek, in order to seize
Your body reckless with desire,
My hands in the air, my feverish hands.

I have often seen you on the summit of a rock.
Your golden hair scattered over pale shoulders;
With slow furtive steps in the willows, I have followed
Your youthful grace, without daring to approach you.

THE NYMPH:

Approach me! What strange voice
Repeats words new to my heart?
Is that not you, my sister Echo?
The echo repeats, but does not change.

At last, mysterious lover with honeyed words
Would you like to pick the flowers in bloom
Of the nymph with eyes the color of columbine?
Voice, are you earthly or descended from the sky?

THE FAUN, *appearing, superb in his goatish hair*:

From the sky I come not, O blonde
Who is more dazzling than the day:
Faun of April, sick with amour,
In love with a nymph of the waves,
Of your golden hair I need the harvest!
Not Echo but Eros in quest of a calyx,
Using an artifice before showing myself
From Echo I borrowed that mask of song.

THE NYMPH, *gradually abandoning herself to the Faun's
embrace—and finally entirely*:

Your deceptive song has been able to please
Cypris, in the game in which her Beauty,
Promising three flowers of sensuality
Requires cleverness and mystery.

The artifice was good to deliver you my body,
Goat-foot whose voice troubles me with promises,
And you may now kill with your caresses
The nymph who dreams of a strong-armed embrace.

II

The Frozen Nymph

THE FAUN, *on the edge of a frozen pond, searching with his eyes for the nymph of spring*:

The nymph of spring, in the hollows of the stream,
Who cheered the reeds with a bright babble,
Has been killed by the snow. Where are the birds
Of which the shady valley, yesterday, was still full?

Taking with you the songs of the forest,
Leaving us the north wind, O nymph, have you gone?
Of the flower of Aphrodite couched in your robe,
Will you hide from me now the secret?

Here, no longer hearing your seductive song
The trees seem dead; and not seeing you,
No longer admiring, leaning over your mirror
Your blue eyes reflected in the crystalline wave.

I, the amorous faun who spied on your beauty
Seek your face beneath the implacable ice.
Is that not you asleep? Is that not your image,
Your shadow, perceiving the saddened sylvan?

O Pan, powerful Father of the Eternal Sap
Will you wake her for springs similar
To the vanished spring? As soon as the sun shines again
I will sacrifice two young turtle doves to you.

Under the white wall fixed between your banks,
Listen to my syrinx celebrating our raptures,
O nymph, and cursing the jealous goddesses
Who have imprisoned your body with unbreakable ice.

Mortal Error

*I*N *the atrium of her palace, lying on crimson cushions and clad in an Asiatic robe the color of flame, where chimerical birds flutter between the branches of silver, gold and antimony trees, Luxuria, languorous, her eyes painted with ocher and blue, her head coiffed in a gold tiara, studded with silver gems, her hair sprinkled with lapis powder, is speaking to her favorite slave, Lagella, and giving her instructions.*

LUXURIA:

When Félix comes, Lagella, I'll receive him alone, and I don't want anyone to disturb our conversation. It's him I love, now. Félix has eyes with an ardent caress, and his gaze burns. I want to be consumed by that flame of amour. I haven't yet tasted the joy that his lips distill. I want to burn with amorous fever between the muscular arms of the new lover of whom I'm dreaming.

LAGELLA:

As you command, O voluptuous divinity, Félix, Félix will be brought to you, alone. And everyone, slaves and powerful, will be sent away to leave your caresses free.

(Lagella leaves.)

LUXURIA:

Will he come soon, my beloved? His fine brown hair will tickle my breasts deliciously, where I want to rest his amorous adolescent head, in which the flash of his eyes and the crimson of his mouth shine, for a long time after making love.

LAGELLA, *re-entering*:

I have transmitted your orders, Luxuria. But the commander of the guards asks what reply he ought to give your lover of yesterday, the patrician Honorius, when he arrives at the seventh hour.

LUXURIA:

He bores me. I'm weary of his monotonous embraces. His presence irritates me. . . . Oh well, let his head, still grimacing with the kiss of the blade, be brought to me.

(Lagella leaves.)

LUXURIA, *pensively*:

For the new lover I have perfumed my body with the most odorous essences. The ardent desire of Félix, his unknown tongue, his unknown embrace, are burning me.

Her eyes wide open, lying back on the crimson cushions, Luxuria dreams of the imminent pleasure, almost enjoying, cerebrally, the orgasm that she expects. Lagella, who has just returned, fans her with a flabellum of pink flamingo feathers.

Heavy footfalls sound outside, on the tiles of the patium, and Asiatic guards appear, clad in lacy and gilded coats of mail, armed with spears in the form of scythe-blades, punctuated by the backbones of fish.

The executioner advances between them, and presents to Luxuria a brown-haired adolescent head. The hair is dipping blood and the eyes are staring beneath half-closed lids.

Luxuria, leaning forward, with her hands on her knees, in order to gaze into the fixed eyes, contemplates the face of the decapitated man, toward which she suddenly raises her arms.

With a heart-rending cry:

Stupid man! (*With a furious gesture she threatens the guards motionless in front of her.*) O mortal error! You have killed the kiss for which I was waiting!

Sobbing, she falls back on the crimson cushions, where the golden embroidery of her robes and her face burst forth like a jasmine flower, lost in blood.

Aphrodite's Dove

(Diptych)

I

Phallos

(*T*HE *lover, in a pale green chlamys, at the poop of his ship with brown sails, is holding a dove that he must release while pronouncing the name of Eros*):

Around Cythera and her antique temples.
White pigeons fly over the sea in all directions;
They carry desires and mystical perfumes
For the Victorious with the troubling blue-green eyes.

I have captured one in its hectic course,
A bird of Cypris flying toward Paphos;
A message I have put beneath its wing
And I bid it "Go where Eros takes you!"

(*The dove departs into the blue sky.*)

Keep watch, Smyrnan brunette!
The bird, finding its route,

Will doubtless arrive tomorrow.
Keep watch, from the break of day.

I am going westwards to procure gold,
In Carthage, Sicily and the peninsula,
By selling the iridescent pottery there
That Jewish slaves paint in the ergastule.

And for the betrothal I shall bring back rings;
In Tanagra, I have bought a lot of statuettes.
Of dancing girls cheerful and slender;
For the women, new Athenian make-up.

To decorate her red lips
The florets of her breasts,
To stimulate mischievous kisses
And flex the arc of her loins!

II

Chrysis

(*THE female lover, high on a terrace on the edge of the sea, to the dove perching on her finger, beating its wings*):

Making you desert Amathonte and Cythera
The amorous bird-catcher has trapped you in his hands.
But Cypris is clement and is not angry
So he sends to my mouth a living flower.
I saw it out there over the ocean waves,
Coming from the isles of amour toward Cyprus.
Dove, has he told you the secret of our souls,
He whom the waves are bearing westwards?

Since dawn you have perched
On the roof of the house;
While I listened to the song
Of the morning in the dew.

(*Chrysis has discovered, in the beating of the wings, the little correspon-dence. She reads it*):

"O mistress with blue eyes, the color of the waves.
I retain in my heart a thirst for your delights,
And your vagina is for me the matelot's star
Since I have tasted the chalices of your flesh.
To your beauty I vow an immortal love;
In return, your jewels will prove the richness
Of a lover animated by active tenderness,
Who dreams of ornamenting your body as an altar."

(*Approaching the dove to her lips*):

For his trouble, I kiss the beak
Of the bird, gentle in my hand
Which, this note beneath its wing,
Has discovered the way.

Stupidity and Wisdom

CAIUS GRACCHUS was a noble and good young man,
Descended from tribunes, very rich and knowing much,
Dreaming of bounty, justice and the ideal,
An eccentric, if he was not completely mad.

He was seen once, in a temple in Rome,
Crying to the gods to break an annoying silence
And reply to him. Now, exactly as before,
On their pedestals the gods still slumbered.

Then, full of disgust and devoid of belief
He wanted to stun himself. Squandering his wealth
He sang and feasted, forehead ringed with verbena.

Then, one evening, in the bath, weary of life and the noise
Of the word, he became again, by cutting his veins,
A nameless soul dispersed in the brilliant night.

THE DEATH OF MESSALINA

A Tragic Farce in Ten Tableaux, with a Nuptial Ballet

I

The Sovereign Lovers

*O*N *a bed of golden cloth, which detached and dying rose petals embalm, while incense fumes in cassolettes, the perfumes of which mingle with an odor of amour, Messalina, naked or nearly so, sighs with joy, enraptured, in the arms of Silius.*

MESSALINA, *gradually recovering her senses, stammering while her nervous fingers knead Silius' flesh and her mouth reaches for his*

My love, you're more handsome than Apollo . . . stronger than Hercules. . . . More ! More!

SILIUS, *his expression preoccupied, anxious, stimulated by the cresses, lips andhands of the weary but never sated lover*

You're happy? I too, Messalina, savor the most exquisite happiness with you. . . .

MESSALINA, *pushing away her lover's hands*

No, no more! I don't want any more . . . in a little while! (*She pulls her palla over her slightly and puts her arms around Silius, hiding her face in his neck, which she pecks. Then she raises her eyes, stretches her limbs, and remains propped on her elbow among the scattered petals, looking into Silius' eyes, parting his hair over his forehead with a tender gesture.*) What's the matter, Silius? You seem worried. Are you sad? What are you thinking about? You're happy—didn't you say so, just now?

SILIUS

Yes, Lina, happy, drunk on you. . . . You've drunk me, but it's me that's intoxicated.

MESSALINA

What, then?

SILIUS

But our joy can't last forever. You love me, but one day, you'll cease to love me. Others, one day, will come to supplant me in your heart and in your flesh.

MESSALINA

Tease! You know full well that no one supplants better than you.

SILIUS

Listen, Messalina. Are we, then, free to love one another? Your husband, the divine Emperor Claudius, is the only man in Rome ignorant of our passion. One word from an informer, and we're doomed. Is it necessary for us to wait, we who are beautiful and young, while that imbecile sovereign dies slowly? Are we going to waste the better part of our lives with odious dread eating away at us, fearful that he might discover our love, that exile or death will separate us forever?

MESSALINA, *hesitantly*

He's so stupid, my adored one! Let's make love! Let's make

love, and laugh! If he learns anything at all, he'll only ever believe that which it pleases me to persuade him. Two words, a flattery of the hand, and the Emperor is more docile than a bleating lamb and a dove combined.

SILIUS

You're reckoning without his sudden fits of wrath. You might be absent from the Palatine at he moment when it's necessary to defend us. And then—this thought is as odious to me as to you, my love, you have to caress that filthy old man, that senile idiot, who is your husband.

MESSALINA, *bursting into laughter*

Oh, all my caresses can't make a man of him. You can be tranquil in that regard. He's content with so little. What, are you going? You're getting dressed.

SILIUS

I'm only putting on my tunic. (*As if animated by a sudden decision.*) Even so, it only requires an order to cause our deaths. Each of our kisses, Messalina, is like those sinister moths that flutter on the shores of Erebus and around the infernal gates. (*He rests his head on Messalina's heart, putting his arm around her midriff.*)

MESSALINA, *sadly*

Perhaps. Death stands sentinel on the threshold of Amour. Is not nature at its most beautiful in Autumn, Silius? And it's the dusk of the year, before the night, the death of things, in the winter. . . . What does it matter? Nevertheless . . . (*she kisses Silius' mouth for a long time*) . . . I don't want to die . . . not yet. Oh, no!

SILIUS

Follow my advice, then, Lina. Believe your devoted lover. Our secret has too fragile a veil, which a breath of cold wind will rip apart one day or another. Only audacity can save us from the dangers without number that lie in wait for us everywhere in the shadows.

MESSALINA

What do you mean, my lover? Oh, what a good lover you are!

SILIUS

Marry me, Messalina. Divorce that crowned idiot Claudius Ahenobarbus. For you, I'll break my marriage with Junia Silana. I haven't had children; your son Britannicus will become my son. Your power won't be diminished, and we'll no longer have anything to fear.

MESSALINA, *having become very grave, is no longer caressing Silius. Coldly, she stares into his eyes, as if the fathom his thoughts*

Villain! Yes, you'd reign in his stead. I understand. (*With a disillusioned smile.*) Perhaps also, being unable to rise any higher, you'd cease to love me. You'd reject me like a bruised pear.

SILIUS, *indignantly*

Oh! Can you conceive such a thought? By Pollux! (*In a softer voice.*) Have I not proven my love a thousand times, Messalina? Have I given you the right to doubt it? (*He remains silent for a few moments, and cajoles his imperial mistress.*) We have all the chances in our favor. All those who know what ties bind us, all the accomplices of our adultery, will help us. It won't be Geta, the prefect of the praetura, ready for anything, or any of the officers of the palace, who'll oppose obstacles to us. Their interests are ours, if we dare.

MESSALINA, *shaking her head apprehensively*

No, Silius, I don't want to commit that crime. I've been reproached with enough ignominies. The people are unjust to Messalina.

SILIUS

We'd be united forever, and both omnipotent. Together, we'd be the sovereigns of Rome and the entire world. Before us, amour would illuminate the road of our life with its torch. We'd be the sole masters of sensuality, of happiness! Our own masters!

MESSALINA, *shivering under the special titillations that
Silius is lavishing on her ardently*

Yes, forever! You'd be mine forever, and I'd be yours. No one could prevail over our power. We'd be lovers, spouses, before the law and the priests. But to do that, Silius, it will be necessary to have strong souls. (*She falls silent momentarily; Silus embraces her. Sighs.*)

SILIUS

Do you want that, Lina? Speak.

MESSALINA, *radiant*

Well, yes. It's an enjoyment to have. . . . Claudius is leaving Rome the day after tomorrow. He's going to Ostia for several days, to oversee the disembarkation of grain. He'll celebrate sacrifices there, amuse himself, indulge in orgies with his favorites and courtesans. In the meantime, we'll celebrate our wedding. (*They embrace passionately*.) The Senate is full of your friends. The praetorians will proclaim you emperor and a god, my beloved.

SILIUS

Claudius will abdicate. Power weighs heavily upon his decrepit shoulders.

MESSALINA

He's afraid of his own shadow.

SILIUS, *enthused by gratitude*

What joyful days we'll live together, Messalina! What will I not owe to you, my Beauty!

MESSALINA, *distractedly, returns Silius' kiss, then bursts into laughter that swells her beautiful bosom and agitates her whole body*

No, listen, Silius, it's even funnier. I have an idea! To be an adulteress is too easy. (*Laughing more loudly*.) Poor Claudius! He's so stupid! You know, my adored one, that the great augur Salicius can refuse me nothing. Oh, don't pull that horrible face. That was over a long time ago, and we've agreed not to be jealous of our pleasures . . . or our affairs.

SILIUS

What do you want to do with that haruspex?

MESSALINA

The Emperor loves the science of auguries, on which he's made a report to the Senate.

SILIUS

So what?

MESSALINA

It's a means of leading Claudius to serve our projects. Yes, I want him to consent to our marriage. I want him to divorce me voluntarily and endow me. Do you understand?

SILIUS

But he loves you. He'd never consent.

MESSALINA

Claudius has no affection or hatred that I haven't suggested or prescribed. It's not as difficult as you think. I know how to catch him. . . .

SILIUS

Messalina! I'm jealous.

MESSALINA

. . . by flattering him. The gods will inspire me. (*She laughs. They caress one another, become excited, and recommence.*)

II

The Evil Omen

CLAUDIUS, Messalina; then Silius; Carulles, the praetor

Claudius is sprawling on a golden bed of repose covered with leopard and panther skins on which crimson cushions are scattered. He is wearing a violet tunic that allow the wattles of his neck to be seen. The Emperor seems preoccupied; his face is disturbed by a visible fear. Messalina comes in, and embraces him tenderly, pampering him.

MESSALINA

You summoned me, my august spouse?

CLAUDIUS, *stammering*

Cer . . . certainly. Y . . . y . . . you alone can console me, Mess . . . Messalina (*His stammer grows worse*) in the f . . . f . . . frightful si . . . si . . . situation in which I f . . . f . . . find myself, vis-à-vis the gods.

MESSALINA

You have nothing to fear from the gods. Are you not a god yourself, not only by virtue of the purple you wear by virtue of your intelligence?

CLAUDIUS

You're v . . . v . . . very kind, Messalina.

MESSALINA

Your speech on the accession of superior men of all peoples
to the government of the Empire, on the amity that ought, after
our wars, to unite victors and vanquished, Claudius, has a politics
so profound and an eloquence so great that, even emerging from
the mouth of a freedman, it would merit being inscribed on tablets
of bronze. "All the things that are regarded as the most ancient,
conscript Fathers, were new at one time. Rome initially took its
magistrates from among the patricians, then the plebeians, than
the Latins, and finally from the other nations of Italy. Why stop
there? The foremost hairy citizens of Gaul have the right, in their
turn, to public honors. Let them bring us their gold and resources
instead of keeping them, separated from Rome. . . ." I know it
by heart, grand master, even more eloquent than Cicero—a mere
chickpea by comparison with you. And he didn't conquer Brittany,
as you did!

CLAUDIUS

Un . . . un . . . undoubtedly.

MESSALINA

You're not only a great orator and a great general. You're good.
You decided that the murder of a slave by his master would be
considered as homicide. Was it not also you who had the aque-
duct constructed that brings the water of the *Anio novus* to Rome?
Your benefits have gone as far as augmenting the alphabet with
three new letters.

CLAUDIUS

One c . . . c . . . can express oneself m . . . m . . . more easily.
But it's not a matter of that. . . .

MESSALINA

What is it, then, my adored one?

CLAUDIUS

A presage.

Messalina sits down beside him, on the bed of repose, and cajoles
him like a fearful child whom it is necessary to reassure.

CLAUDIUS

Th . . . th . . . there was an owl on the Palatine yesterday. A
dirty b . . . b . . . east of an owl that sang by night . . . all night. . . .
I hope by now it's dead, quite dead. . . . I gave orders for it to be
caught and killed.

MESSALINA

A presage of death! Castor and Pollux! It's necessary to con-
sult the great augur, Salicius. He'll tell us immediately, at least after
the sacrifice.

CLAUDIUS

He's just left with Vettius Valens. They sacrificed a white bull.
And do you know what they read in its entrails? It's f . . . f . . .
frightful!

MESSALINA, *shivering*

Heavens! What are you saying? I'm going to die!

CLAUDIUS

No, not you. (*He strikes his breast.*)

MESSALINA

Pallas? Narcissus? Geta, the prefect of the guards?

CLAUDIUS

No, you don't get it. It . . . it . . . it's . . . Messalina's husband! You have no other husband than me, do you? In consequence (*he makes a gesture designating himself*), I'm a dead man.

MESSALINA, *bursting into sobs*

Oh, don't tell me such things. You'll make me perish in a slow fire . . . I want to share your pyre. . . .

CLAUDIUS

That, I forbid you. (*Tenderly.*) My poor Messalina. What will you do, when you're a widow?

MESSALINA, *hiding her head in the Emperor's bosom and sobbing harder*

Claudius!

CLAUDIUS

There is a remedy, however.

MESSALINA, *raising her head*

Speak, quickly, my love.

CLAUDIUS

I can outwit Jupiter.

MESSALINA

How?

CLAUDIUS

The great Haruspex said to me: "There's one means: that's for someone else to pass for your husband for a few days. Someone who will put on a semblance . . ." But I don't know who could play that role. It would need a devoted man, who would do everything necessary to deceive the gods.

MESSALINA, *thoughtfully*

Yes, a serious fellow . . . of a good family. Otherwise, Jupiter wouldn't believe in my new marriage.

CLAUDIUS, *anxiously*

But you know, darling, don't amuse yourself, out of devotion, by delivering yourself to him. It's for the sake of appearances, you understand. And once the presage is avoided, I resume my rights.

MESSALINA, *stroking the old man*

Yes, of course! That goes without saying! Except, my love, its necessary to be very good! (*She sighs.*) Not to love one another, for all that time. . . .

CLAUDIUS, *his mouth drooling*

I'm leaving for Ostia shortly. I'm not taking you this year . . . because of the presage.

MESSALINA, *repressing the sudden joy in her eyes and a smile*

Do you have someone in mind?

CLAUDIUS

What do you mean?

MESSALINA

To marry me.

CLAUDIUS

I'll think about it. . . .

A herald appears and announces the noble Caius Silius.

MESSALINA

He's a well-born patrician. That's what we need.

Claudius makes a sign of assent.

CLAUDIUS

Ah, my dear friend. Come in, Caius; let me clasp you to my bosom.

SILIUS

How good you are, my sovereign.

CLAUDIUS

Sit down beside us. (*He makes room for him on the cushions.*) I was just talking about you, to the Empress.

Messalina and Silius look at one another. Behind Claudius' back, while he embraces the young man, they squeeze one another's fingers.

SILIUS, *to Messalina*

Goddess! I want to offer my homages before . . .

CLAUDIUS, *obliging Silius to sit down again as he gets up to salute the Empress*

Stay there! No ceremonies between us. (*Gravely.*) Silius would you like to render me a great service?

SILIUS

Anything that is within my power, Claudius, to satisfy you.

CLAUDIUS

W . . . w . . . would you consent to marry Messalina?

SILIUS, *feigning astonishment*

Marry Messalina! (*He looks at Claudius, then the Empress, with an amazed and interrogative expression.*)

CLAUDIUS

That astonishes you? Well, my dear friend, you'd be saving my life. Oh, but it's not to give her to you. It's to make Jupiter believe that you're her husband. Oh, Caius, if you do that, and don't die of it . . .

MESSALINA

I know, Silius, that you're devoted to us.

SILIUS

I don't understand. What devotion is there in that?

CLAUDIUS

This is it: if you're Messalina's husband, the presage concerns you.

SILIUS

What presage? I don't understand at all.

MESSALINA, *pointing through the window at the gardens on the hillside*

The owl that sang there a few nights ago, in the gardens of the Palatine, announces, so the great augur says, the imminent death of Messalina's husband.

SILIUS, *warmly*

It's my life, Caesar, that you're asking of me? It belongs to you—take it!

CLAUDIUS, *embracing him*

I expected no less of you. You'll be in the Elysian Fields very soon. I'll give you a sumptuous funeral.

SILIUS

At the expense of the state.

MESSALINA

It's necessary for us to regulate the matter as soon as possible.

SILIUS, *to Messalina*

I'm at your disposal.

MESSALINA

That's fine. It's great, what you're doing, Caius.

CLAUDIUS

And truly worthy of a consular personage. But as you might die of it, I want to endow your spouse. I'll give her a million sesterces from the public treasury. That means that if you only fall ill, if you escape death, you'll be one of the richest men in Rome.

SILIUS

Lord, so much generosity confounds me. (*Aside.*) Get away, you old scoundrel!

MESSALINA

It's necessary to draw up the act right away. With sacred prodigies, one never know, Claudius . . . they arrive when one least expects them.

CLAUDIUS, *nodding his head approvingly*

Silius! Make a semblance of being her husband from now on!

CLAUDIUS, *stammering increasingly*

On, n . . . n . . . no, not like that! That's . . . that's . . . that's too
much!

MESSALINA

It's for Jupiter. Are his eyes not upon us at present?

CLAUDIUS

No! I don't want him to kiss you like that. . . .

MESSALINA

A husband, however . . .

CLAUDIUS

It annoys me, that . . .

SILIUS

Jupiter is watching us. Let's make haste . . . what if you were
to die?

CLAUDIUS

D . . . d . . . d . . . die! Never in th . . . th . . . this life! (*He strikes
a gong. A slave appears.*) Go look for . . . run . . . praetor Carulles.
Tell him to bring his scribe. Hurry.

He's in the atrium now, waiting for Caesar to be kind enough to receive his visit.

CLAUDIUS, *joyfully*

That's lucky! Send him in. Jupiter won't see a thing. Silius, my good Silius, you're a loyal friend.

*Enter Carulles, with two slaves carrying a table, stylets, tablets,
brushes, a roll of virgin parchment and wax. The seal of Rome
is hanging round his neck.*

MESSALINA, *in a low voice, to Silius.*

There you go! A million sesterces. It's a tidy sum.

SILIUS

Thank you, my goddess!

*While Claudius solemnly stammers orders,
they embrace profoundly, their lips coming together.*

CLAUDIUS

It's for the ma . . . ma . . . marriage of my wife, praetor.

III

The Marriage of Messalina and Silius

The Departure of the Groom.

IN front of the house of Caius Silius, half way up the Quirinal, the guests, friends of the consul designate, crowd together. They have come to find the husband.

Bronze and silver trumpets and buccinas sound resonant fanfares. The crowd proclaims its joy as popular senators and magistrates pass by, and howls, as usual when it sees someone appear to whom vexatious measures or excessively vile infamies are attributed. On the threshold garlanded with roses, the husband stands among his intimates, in a saffron tunic, with the crimson toga of Caesar's friends.

He is congratulated. Naked dancing girls, their vaginas enclosed with golden jewelry studded with gems, twirl, carrying symbolic flowers. Silius climbs into a litter. The cortege moves off among hymeneal cries and cheers, to go to the Palatine House, where he is to meet the Empress.

Before and behind the cortege of the much-loved consul, male and female dancers, Greek, Numidians or Asiatic, clad in laméed gauzes and coiffed in gold, silver or antimony miters march, dance and whirl while viols, lyres and flutes vibrate, and the trumpets and buccinas resonate triumphantly from time to time, and sistra and tambourines are agitated by Iberians with black hair and blazing eyes.

And everyone, as Silius passes by, acclaims him: *"Hymen Io! Hymen Io! Hymen . . ."*

✳

The Bride.

On the Palatine, the two corteges of Silius and Messalina, each coming from a different direction, arrived at the same time before the temple of Jupiter, where, at the top of the steps, the vestals were waiting for the spouses. Messalina was carried on the shoulders of twenty Numidian soldiers, on a large platform, florid above the drapes of amphitapus, with all the known corollas of the world: a marvelous platform forming an altar. Sitting in the middle, on a golden throne, she was naked, scarcely veiled by an amethyst tunic whose color symbolized her rank and her divinity. Only an enormous scarab of sculpted gold on her right shoulder, whose eyes, antennae, elytra and deployed wings were made of precious stones, retained the light veil, florid with yellow irises and violets, transparent over her marvelous body, ornamented with a black iris.

Then, while troops of actors and ballerinas danced fervently on the square, Messalina stood up, amid the clamors of the populace, songs and hymeneal cries springing from all direction, let her tunic slide away, and, on her pedestal of men and flowers, appeared a splendid living statue. Her body, its svelte plenitudes and gracious curves, stood out against the roses, like mouths, in delicate pinks, ardent reds and virginal whites, against the mauve of irises and the suave blue of myosotis, reminiscent of minuscule and intense eyes, wide open, at the base of that quivering marble, admiring it. The little bells of fuschias, comparable to swarms of miniature ballerinas in multicolored skirts tinted with bright or pale hues; the arrogant stems of gladioli, golden, red, saffron, pink, or blue constellated with drops of blood; snowy tufts of clematis an violet lilac, columbines and anemones, branches of syringa, and magnolia flowers blooming in cups surrounded Messalina with a perfumed incense.

278

Everything that was not Her fell at her feet; she was completely nude, and a goddess. Thousands of enthusiastic spectators saluted the naked Empress, Flora and Venus combined, and the voices of the crowd clamored:

"*Ave, diva Messalina, Regina florum!*"—Hail, divine Messalina, Queen of Flowers.

Her breasts were more beautiful than the freshest of white and pink poppies. Her mouth was a bright blood-red, so intense as to eclipse the buds of flowering grenadines. Her eyes of gold and amethyst seemed made of the delicate and lucid petals of Indian orchids, bathed in light. Her torso, marmoreal, her harmoniously swelling hips, her long thighs, firm and fleshy, her smooth white knees, her feet and pink hands—all that living magnificence turgid with amorous sap—was suggestive of an Olympian who, escorted by the marvels of nature, had descended to Rome.

Ave, diva! Regina florum!

The Dowry.

When the Flamina of Romulus, Dial—clad in a white laena with long hair, attached at the throat by golden brooch gemmed with a large amethyst and coiffed with a skullcap with a woolen tuft whose pointed apex was in olive wood—had blessed the marriage, the praetor counted out the million sesterces to Silius.

Slaves loaded them, in a coffer, on to the back of a mule, which two freedmen conducted to Silius' house, where the Hearth was.

The Nuptial Orgy.

In the Gardens of Lucullus, lying on triclinia, the guests of the newlyweds are drinking and eating. Entire beasts, roasted, are carved up by slaves. Peacocks and pheasants are brought, ornamented with their plumage. Messalina is amused, very content. A sow, standing in the midst of suckling piglets, dominates the table. And the drunken faces are laughing beneath crowns of flowers. A few young women are already semi-naked. And vaporized perfumes fall from the awning with the petals of stripped roses.

Gladiators, in three couples, are fighting with sword and buckler. Three fall successively, bathing in their blood; and everyone applauds excitedly. Actors proclaim verses. Finally, Greek dancing girls mingled with svelte negresses with small, firm breast—naked, black and white, but beautiful—come in long processions bearing immense odorous garlands. They dance, offering lascivious poses. Men and women, excited with amorous folly, enlace. Here and there, vigorous slaves carry away an abandoned Augustan woman whose bed-companions are too drunk for intercourse.

In the palace, Messalina, at present more lustful than ever, was celebrating the simulation of a vintage in the splendor of autumn. Around the grape-presses, and vats from which the new wine flows, women girdled with animal-skins were fighting, sacrificed, crazed bacchantes. Luxuria herself, her hair scattered, was waving a thyrsus and caressing it, while Silius, crowned with ivy, directed the lascivious chorus with the nodding of his head and the stamping of his feet.

Finally, toward the twelfth hour, the spouses leave for the nuptial house, while the guests still standing brandish torches, shouting among hiccups: *"Hymen! Io! Hymenée!"* But the orgy continues, and soon patriciennes are lamenting, wallowing on cushions in poses offering pleasure, to which their extenuated lovers can no longer reply, crying: *"Advenant asini!"*

At once, the requested donkeys are brought.

Now, in the gardens, into which the orgy in the palace overflowed, Vettius Valens, a young haruspex, distinguished and protected by the Empress, had climbed to the top of a tree, from which he indicated, with erotic gestures, what the newlyweds were doing at that moment. Then, several people asked him, suddenly, what he could see from up there, and the haruspex gaily proclaimed, amid laughter:

"I can see a frightful tempest coming from Ostia."

IV

The Freedmen

*O*N *the Forum, people are discussing public affairs. Around rostra and in front of the temple of Concordia, citizens are crowding in numerous groups. At times, the crimson togas of Augustans stain the general whiteness of the crowd, as do togas only bordered in red.*

Present are: Marchinius, Tullianus, Cormis, Vero, senators; Avicius Turo, sixty years old, a patrician in a toga; Miso, consul; Caesoninus, patrician; Charmis, popular tribune; Carulles, praetor; Narcissus, Pallas, Callistus, affranchised; Carillo, Severninus parasites, Belilia, courtesan; senators, lictors, prowling slaves, courtesans, citizens, etc., etc.

The senators emerge from the temple of Concordia. Some climb into litters; others mingle with the crowd, chatting to one another, ostentatiously affable.

CARILLO, *saluting Avicius Turo*

Noble lord, I listened to your speech on mores with the attention that is owed to genius.

AVICIUS TURO

That means that you're hungry?

CARILLO

Thanks to the liberalities of Caesar, no citizen is reduced to the extremities of evil days. However, if you were so generous . . .

TURO

I invite you to dinner. (He draws away precipitately and mingles with the group formed by Marchinius, Tullianus, Cormis and the consul Miso.)

CORMIS, *from the height of a rostrum*

. . . For it's necessary that we can all live; that's the law: all and everyone. You have been promised, citizens. Augustus Claudius is seeing to that elsewhere, and is disembarking at Ostia for Rome, the wheat, oil and Saracen corn due to the people.

CARULLES, *accosting Miso*

Be careful, consul; you were at the orgy. If Claudius finds out, before Silius . . .

AVICIUS, *not far away, in a group*

Malediction! The Emperor is betrayed; the people don't know what to make of it. Silius . . . (*He shakes his head*) . . . is better than Claudius. Why is he going to sleep in debauches? At least I, personally, am outside all intrigues. I merely deplore the excesses of this ignoble epoch . . . the gods will intervene.

MARCHINIUS

I fear the gods less than the living Emperor and his fits of anger. Silius hasn't come out of the Palatine House for three days. The Empire is full of rumors of their indecent feasts.

CORMIS, *sarcastically*

You were, however, in the Gardens of Lucullus, Marchinius Salvator.

MARCHINIUS

We've been deceived, but we were in good faith, I swear!

VERO

The entire Senate is compromised if the Emperor doesn't recognize that union and renounces the divorce.

TULLIANUS

To warn Caesar would be dangerous.

CARULLES

Silius has friends. Geta, the prefect of the praetura, is his intimate.

TURO

It's necessary to know what the soldiers think of it. At present, the armed force prevails over the toga, alas!

BELILIA, *stroking Turo*

If you have chagrins or cares, come home with me. It's better to respire the perfume of my flesh than to weigh and compare gold and swords, as you're all doing.

MARCHINIUS

Which of the two princes do you think is better, little pleasure-girl?

BELILIA

The Emperor is god, so be it. But he's old, like all divinities. Silius is young, and he's a man.

Two military tribunes, preceded by their lictors, traverse the Forum

TULLIANUS, *anxiously*

They're going to the camp.

MARCHINIUS

That's also the road to Ostia.

MISO, *trembling*

Silius isn't with them. Are they for or against Messalina's new husband?

Narcissus, out of breath, emerges from the Via Palatine.
He is assailed by questions. He smiles.

TURO

Do you have news of Caesar?

NARCISSUS

I'm awaiting some. You, Marchinius, are one of the Augusta's friends. What say you?

MARCHINIUS

Does one know destiny?

NARCISSUS, *sarcastically*

You're not a man for conspiracies, of course.

*Pallas runs out from between the columns of a temple.
Narcissus joins him with Callistus, another of the Emperor's
freedmen, who emerges from a group of knights. All three
hold council in low voices at the corner of the temple of Concordia.*

PALLAS

They're paralyzed by fear, these nobles.

NARCISSUS

The senate dare not vote any law or issue any edict. No one is
leading these broken-winded legislators. It's a bad team with no
coachman.

CALLISTUS

What should be done, then, in your opinion, Narcissus?

PALLAS

Siluis is nothing but a sensualist. He forgets everything in
Messalina's arms. Presents, promises and a firm decision would
have rendered him possible.

CALLISTUS

But in sum, what solution seems wise to you?

NARCISSUS

To be faithful to the power we serve, and will serve to the end.

CALLISTUS

So be it! Messalina hasn't thought at all. Let's think for her, and for Claudius. He'd be furious, if he knew.

PALLAS

Let's enlighten his justice. But what if he doesn't want to believe us? What if he gets angry?

CALLISTUS

It's necessary to make him afraid.

NARCISSUS

And show him his strength. He has the stick; we'll direct it. But let's hurry.

PALLAS, pointing at the Palatine

She'll persuade him of whatever she pleases. Between two kisses in Messalina's bosom, Claudius is like a drunken man.

NARCISSUS

I'll break the concha! Farewell—and not a word.

286

V

Claudius at Ostia

*C*LAUDIUS, *drunk, is sprawling among cushions; a crown of roses circles his head; at his feet, Calpurnia and Flavia are singing erotic ballads softly. Caesonia, Merysta, Cleopatra and Axia are trying a reawaken his numbed senses. Yet other courtesans, by order of the freedman Narcissus, Claudius' friend, are harassing him with their ironic remarks.*

AXIA

You can't suffer any longer the scandal that is dishonoring your reign. . . .

CLAUDIUS, *dropping the cup that he was raising to his lips*

What scandal?

CALPURNIA

What, you don't know? You're the only one in Rome, Caesar Augustus!

CLAUDIUS

You're annoying me; I don't want to know anything.

FLAVIA, *interrupting her singing*

Messalina is amusing herself.

CLAUDIUS

So am I.

FLAVIA

No, you're only putting on a semblance. And then, even if you were, you're the master, while she owes you submission and obedience.

CLAUDIUS

In sum, of what is she guilty?

MERYSTA

You won't be angry?

CLAUDIUS

No, I'm too tired.

CALPURNIA

This evening, but what about tomorrow? When your anger reveals itself, it's terrible.

CLAUDIUS

You've said too much not to go on to the end. I've never punished courtesans; we have no one but them to relieve our reign.

CAESONIA

Listen, then. They're making mock of you.

CALPURNIA

Messalina is playing an unworthy comedy, my dear, and you've been cut from the script.

CLAUDIUS

I've been cut? Me?

MERYSTA

Do you know what the Augusta has dared to do?

CALPURNIA, volubly

When food and wine mixed with spices have exasperated her senses, she takes off all her clothes, and, while slave women blow into silver trumpets, she delivers herself to Silius.

CAESONIA

And Silius delivers her to his friends.

CALPURNIA

Yes, in order to begin again thereafter. But Silius can't satisfy them all; they demand Priapus with loud cries. The triclinium resounds with their lascivious and multiple gaieties.

AXIA

Truly, we haven't done as much.

289

CAESONIA

That's not all. Yesterday, Messalina's lovers were disguised as monkeys to please her.

CALPURNIA

That wasn't enough; she demanded a donkey.

CLAUDIUS, *drooling and stammering*

C . . . c . . . come on—y . . . y . . . you're exaggerating! A donkey?

MERYSTA

You doubtless think that a goat would have been sufficient?

CLAUDIUS, *completely drunk*

Ha ha ha! I'd like to have seen that!

CALPURNIA

It's a spectacle you could offer all your subjects. And then, if you doubt our word, ask Narcissus to inform you. People are mocking you, today, yesterday, always. . . .

CAESONIA

Listen again: Messalina, with other women, has gone to insult the goddess of Modesty and foul her pedestal—you can imagine how—with an orgy more complicated than the others. Afterwards, they lay down stark naked and embraced one another frantically, to attract the passers-by.

CLAUDIUS

That's not true!

CALPURNIA

Not true? Would you like more details? Interrogate Narcissus, who is your true friend. He's ready to beg your pardon for having hidden Messalina's adultery with Rufus, Calpurnianus, Mnester, Caesoninus, Virgilianus and many others. But from today, if you let it happen, you're no longer the master of the Empire. Messalina has repudiated you, Caesar; her marriage with Silius had for witnesses the people, the Senate and the army; if you don't act promptly, Rome belongs to her new husband.

CLAUDIUS

That's not possible. But just in case, I'll have all those who are suspected of having had Messalina killed.

CALPURNIA

Stop there, Caesar Augustus—you'll depopulate Rome!

VI

The Road to Ostia

*M*EANWHILE, *Messalina, warned by public rumor and counseled by the high priestess Vibidia, has quit Rome is order to try to recapture Claudius and disculpate herself in his eyes. She traversed the city on foot, accompanied by only three people, so great was the solicitude formed around her, in an instant, by the tempest. Everywhere, there is a sudden horror of her shameful actions, without any mercy. Eventually, she seduced the driver of a dung-cart and, perched on the filth, she is going to meet the Emperor on the road to Ostia. But Narcissus, Pallas and Callistus, the three freedmen, are alert to the salvation of the State. And while Messalina, on accosting the august cortege, laments and takes the gods as witness to the purity of her conduct, they occupy the attention of the indecisive master.*

MESSALINA, *raising her arms to the heavens*

I'm the mother of Octavia and Britannicus, I'm your Messalina! Oh, Claudius, cast a favorable glance upon me. Are our children not beside you? I ordered them, however, to come to throw themselves into their father's arms. . . .

NARCISSUS, *to the emperor*

Your stomach is upset by the orgies in Ostia; this evening, we will make sow's udders and flavorsome breast of grouse . . . and during dinner, an extraordinary aretalogus will make you laugh.

CLAUDIUS

I'd like a roast peacock stuffed with pink sea-urchins.

MESSALINA, *weeping*

I'm the one you have oppressed in your arms so tenderly, the only one who can reanimate your tottering desires. . . .

CALLISTUS, *replying to a question from Claudius*

No, no shellfish in fish sauce—you know that you nearly died of indigestion last time they were put on the table.

MESSALINA

What somber projects is that spy taking about? Don't listen to him—he'll make your misfortune and mine. Oh, Narcissus, Callistus and Pallas, those three collaborators are damned souls! They'll turn you away from me. Claudius, Claudius! I'll give you the kisses you desire! I'll pour the wine of Caecuba and the Falernian you like so much into your cup! We'll intoxicate one another, as in the past!

CLAUDIUS

Wha . . . wha . . . what is that woman s . . . s . . . saying?

NARCISSUS

She wants to make you drink poisoned wine.

CLAUDIUS

But it's Messalina, I believe! My d . . . d . . . dear . . .

NARCISSUS

Yes, it's the guilty wife, the degraded creature who has soiled your bed. Don't listen to her, or you're doomed.

CLAUDIUS, *still stammering*

I ha . . . ha . . . have a headache! Why are Largus Caecina and Vitellius hiding the s . . . s . . . sight of the Empress from me? In spite of her sins, she's agreeable to c . . . c . . . contemplate. Then again, no, you're right; the courtesans in Ostia have tired me out. A nice fat sow's udder in Libyan honey will be better for me.

The imperial litter continues on its way in the middle of soldiers who raise their pikes, making Suburran jokes, against Messalina's cart. The cortege enters the city, and Claudius is pleasantly drowsy when the priestess Vibidia utters a long ululation near the gardens of Lucius and Calus.

VITELLIUS, *militarily*

Good, here's the old screech-owl now. We'll never get to the end!

CLAUDIUS, *waking up with a start*

Woe betide me! It's the vengeful owl that sang all night on the Palatine last week. (*He hides his head beneath his crimson mantle.*)

VIBIDIA

Father without entrails! You have sent away your children, Britannicus and Octavia! Husband without a heart! You have not listened to their mother, the good Messalina! You will, at least, hear the counsels of the sacred Vestal, who has no fear of braving the jeers of the crowd to cry: Danger! Where are you going? Where are you going?[1]

------

1 It is probable that this is a deliberate ironic echo of the title of Sienkiewicz's *Quo Vadis?* (1895), which cites the question ostensibly asked by Peter of an ap-

VITELLIUS

Back, old sandal! Worn-out sock! We've had enough! The Emperor is no longer in swaddling-clothes; he knows what he's doing. Go back to your spirit-lamp, and may the sacred fire reanimate other fires in you than those of revolt!

VIBIDIA

Woe! Woe betide those who misjudge my divine functions. . . .

CLAUDIUS, *frightened*

Perhaps we're wrong, all the same. . . .

NARCISSUS

Can't you see that that woman is a man who has put on the sacred vestments?

CLAUDIUS

A man! Are you sure?

NARCISSUS, *to the praetorians*

Get rid of the indecent fellow so that we can go along the Triumphal Way to Silius' house.

CLAUDIUS

So, you're saying that it's a man dressed as a woman?

---

parition of Jesus encountered while fleeing Rome. Jesus' answer is "I'm going to Rome to be crucified again."

Yes, who wants to save the Augusta . . . one of her recent lovers.

With that, Narcissus and Pallas, more correct, assure the Empress, still on her dung-cart, that the Emperor will give her an opportunity to disculpate herself, and tell the Great Vestal that she must return to her sacred functions in the meantime—and the cortege proceeds.

VII

The House of Silius

OW, Claudius is in front of Silus' dwelling. The door has been broken down with blows of an ax. The Emperor, still dazed, with a vague headache, contemplates, as soon as he crosses the threshold, the spoils of the Caesars. First he has seen, in the vestibule, a statue of Silius' father, images of whom had been proscribed by an edict of the Senate; he discovers precious items of furniture, valuable works of art, vanished from the palace of the Caesars and given to the handsome patrician by the Empress, in recompense for his kisses and his felony.

CLAUDIUS

That's the porphyry basin in which Augustus and Tiberius took their hip-baths, seasoned with nard and Chios wine to give them tone, before fierce combats. . . .

NARCISSUS

There's the golden bowl from which you drank the liqueur of Tasos, mingled with cantharides, when you wanted to give the Empire an heir. (*To Vitellius, who is observing all these events silently.*) Say something, censor. You look as if you don't know anything!

VITELLIUS, *mechanically*

O crime! O sin!

CLAUDIUS

That memory makes me emotional. (*He weeps.*) It was thus that Britannicus was born.

NARCISSUS, *drawing him into the atrium and the thalamus*

On the contrary, it ought to make you bound with rage. What! The sweetest and most cherished of your treasures are here, in your rival's house . . . all these familiar riches!

CLAUDIUS

My word, that's true. It's necessary to punish. No more p . . . p . . . pity!

NARCISSUS

I'm glad to see you in these virile dispositions. Yes, no more pity for the adulterous wife! No more shameful complaisance for those who scorn your rank and your power. You've come, you've seen . . . it remains for you to conquer, Caesar! We shall conquer! (*To Vitellius.*) Speak, then, stupid!

VITELLIUS, *pulling himself together*

O facinus! O scelus! (O crime! O sin!)

VIII

The Praetorian Camp

*C*LAUDIUS, *inflamed with anger, has come to the praetorian camp. Emissaries have announced his arrival and the ten thousand soldiers who are camped in leather tents have taken up arms.*

CLAUDIUS, *very emotional*

My friends . . . my g . . . g . . . good friends . . . I always r . . . r . . . remember that I owe you my elevation to the throne in the t . . . t . . . troubles that followed the death of Caligula.

A SOLDIER

It's me who discovered you, hiding in the palace behind a tapestry, and was the first to salute you as emperor. I brought you to this camp.

CLAUDIUS

I promised you, and later gave each of you fifteen thousand sesterces. Isn't that t . . . t . . . true, my brave fellows?

THE PRAETORIANS

That's true, Caesar. Well, what do you want of us now?

CLAUDIUS

C . . . c . . . comrades, they are making mock of your Emperor,
w . . . who . . . out of weakness or generosity of soul, has let it
happen, until now. B . . . but . . . (*all in a rush*) the moment for
reprisals has come. Seditious individuals have usurped power; is it
your opinion that they should be put to death?

THE PRAETORIANS

Yes! Yes! To death! To death!

CLAUDIUS

It's a matter of high-ranking persons.

THE PRAETORIANS

So much the better! To death! To death!

NARCISSUS

Go fetch Silius and drag him, with his accomplices, to the foot
of our tribunal.

> *While numerous contingents of cavaliers spread out in the streets of
> Rome, the executioner prepares the block.*

CLAUDIUS, *to the executioner*

You seem p . . . p . . . paltry for your estate.

THE EXECUTIONER

Oh, strength proves nothing; skill is everything. I can behead
a man like no one else! There's a trick to it, Divinity.

CLAUDIUS

You can also cause s . . . s . . . suffering?

THE EXECUTIONER

Certainly, but it doesn't amuse me; they all make the same grimace. It's amazing, how little imagination people have in dying.

CLAUDIUS

This time, go slowly, and . . .

NARCISSUS

Not at all; the important thing is to decapitate them as quickly as possible. It's not a matter of distraction today. Don't you have slaves for the habitual games? Look, here's Pompeius Urbicus and Saufellus Trogus. One executioner won't be enough.

At a sign from Claudius, soldiers take possession of the two guilty parties and decapitate them. After them come Titius Proculus, the bodyguard— which was certainly not a sinecure —given by Silius to Messalina; Decius Calpurnianus, the prefect of the watch; Sulpicius Rufus, the steward of the games; Vettius Valens and the great Haruspex. The heads of all these suspect individuals roll at the feet of the Emperor, who contemplates the executions with an atonal gaze. It was the turn of Caesoninus, a charming and handsome fellow; at this point twenty superb praetorian intervene, and his vices save him. Claudius is slightly sickened by the sight and odor of the blood, when the executioner has the famous actor Mnester brought forward, who tears his garments and almost disculpates himself, lamenting with some eloquence. Claudius, shaken, inclines toward clemency.

NARCISSUS

Don't you see, Divinity, that he's still playing the comedy?

Mnester is executed, in spite of his discourteous howls, which extend his torture. Now there is Traulus Montanus, a young Roman cavalier of very regular morals but an attractive body. Messalina had summoned him and sent him away the same night, finding him too stupid, and, in any case, having passed rapidly from desire to disgust. Juneus Virgilianus is dragged to Caesar's feet, imploring his mercy; and, seeing all the headless cadavers that are about to be piled up, his teeth chatter with terror, to such an extent that he can hardly pronounce a word:
"Cae . . . Cae . . . Cae . . . Cae . . . Caesar! Pi . . . pi . . . pi . . . pity!"
Narcissus, indulgent for some reason, opines in favor of the head.

CLAUDIUS

No! He ann . . . nn . . . nnoys me. I don't like anyone st . . . st . . . stammering more than me. (*The senator loses his head.*) And Silius?

NARCISSUS

He's just been arrested in the Forum—here he comes.

SILIUS, *arrogantly*

For what am I reproached?

CLAUDIUS

F . . . f . . . for what are you reproached? Truly a singular question! You've stolen my father's statue, the relics of Augustus and Tiberius! You've robbed me! You've sat in my throne and l . . . l . . . lain in my bed! You've taken my Empire and my wife. You've w . . . w . . . wallowed in my purple!

SILIUS

All right, I'm ready.

CLAUDIUS, *choking with rage*

Blackguard! Bandit! Dog! Pig!

SILIUS

Cuckold! (*With a gesture, he orders the executioner, in vain, to wipe the block, which is, indeed, red with the blood and clots of his predecessors, whose separated heads and bodies are lying all around. Overcoming a slight disgust, he kneels down gracefully.*) I die handsome!

CLAUDIUS

Cuckold! You too, Silius! I'm well c . . . c . . . content; I have the last word.

Blood spurts; the marrow of Silius' brain splashes the feet of the Emperor, who makes a libertine comparison, mentally.

IX

Dust of Desire

*I*N *order to recover from so much emotion, Claudius has returned to his palace and had himself served delicate and comforting things—but the vehement pâtés, the venison seasoned with basil and ginger, the pepper sauces, the sugared hot wines charged with canella and musk have inflamed his senses, and he is suddenly ardent for the unworthy Messalina. He tells himself that his seething meninges are worth as much as those of Silius, and that the Empress, for once, will have nothing to regret.*

CLAUDIUS, *his eyes shining, his fingers agitated by a slight tremor*

F . . . f . . . fetch me Messalina!

NARCISSUS

What! You want . . . ?

CLAUDIUS

Why not? Fifteen or sixteen men, for having suborned her, have had their heads cut off; she's sufficiently expiated her temporary deviations thus. I want "poor Messalina" to come to justify herself. I feel energetic this evening. And then, possessing a weeping woman has a particular spice.

304

NARCISSUS

Weeping? You don't know Messalina! She would have violated your centurions while they were decapitating her lovers. . . .

CLAUDIUS

They're with Pluto; it's a settled account; let's not mention it again. Messalina is ardent and expert. I'm truly only at my best with her! A finger of that old Falernian will get me completely in form!

NARCISSUS, *taking away the cup he is about to raise to his lips*

You've drunk enough, Divinity, and your eyes are fluttering.

CLAUDIUS

I want a w . . . w . . . woman, Narcissus.

NARCISSUS

There's no lack of them in the palace.

CLAUDIUS

No, I want mine. She has a way . . . (*He strikes the table violently.*)

NARCISSUS, *pretending to give in*

Well then, I'll go look for her. Go on, drink in the meantime, Supreme Divinity! (*He puts within reach of the Emperor wines of Tasos, Cecuba and Chios. In the hope that he will get heavily drunk, and give no further thought to his amorous caprice.*)

X

The Last Spasm

MESSALINA has taken refuge in the arbor where her nuptial feast was held. She is weeping and howling, wringing her hands and striking her forehead against the ground; blood stains her long, loose hair. Her mother, Domitia Lepida, puts her arms around her and tries to console her.

MESSALINA

It's necessary to die! *Eheu! Eheu!*

LEPIDA

Your career is over, but don't give the people the spectacle of a fear unworthy of you. For the sake of the name of Messala, which you have valiantly borne as far as amour and crime, go to death with dignity. Women who die young are beloved by the gods.

MESSALINA

I prefer being loved by men.

LEPIDA

You're blaspheming, my daughter.

MESSALINA

Oh, kisses on red lips!

LEPIDA

One wearies of them, like everything else. And then, it's always the same.

MESSALINA

It's not the same when one has imagination. The sensuality is in us, not the others.

LEPIDA

With age, one no longer feels anything. Come on, courage, here's a stiletto—don't wait for the executioner.

MESSALINA takes the weapon, weeping,
and tries to stab herself with it

I can't! Kill myself for that clown! If only I could see him, he wouldn't be able to resist my seductions. Come on—through the little door, I'll slip all the way to the triclinium, put my hands over Claudius' eyes and say "Cuckoo!"

LEPIDA

I fear that it won't work any longer.

MESSALINA

You'll see, Mother

She drags Lepida away, and is about to disappear with her into the secret passage, but centurions run from all directions and capture the two women, who fall to their knees.

THE TRIBUNE *charged with the execution*

Messalina, Claudius has ordered us to put an end to your days.

MESSALINA, *looking at the tribune with eyes charged with fear, dolor and passion*

You won't do that, handsome tribune!

THE TRIBUNE

Alas!

MESSALINA

I'll caress you so nicely! (*Embracing him.*) Here! Taste my kiss!

THE TRIBUNE

It's ambrosia!

MESSALINA

And my tongue?

THE TRIBUNE

A divine spice!

MESSALINA

In this arbor—no one will see us, and we'll escape through the gate. . . .

NARCISSUS, *arriving*

What, again? I was right to say that she'd violate the centurions and the tribune!

MESSALINA

Mercy! For you, too, I'll have caresses!

NARCISSUS.

Oh, for myself, I prefer the handsome lads of the imperial
militia.

MESSALINA

Fie!

NARCISSUS

You can't know what it is! So let's not talk about it any more.
Tribune, give her your sword. It's necessary to finish it.

THE TRIBUNE

Let me take her away. We'll do it a little further away. . . .

NARCISSUS

No, she'd come back. I order you to strike her in the heart; if
not, I'll kill her myself.

THE TRIBUNE, *moved*

Here's my weapon, adorable Messalina, I'd rather have shown
you another, as rigid but more courteous. . . .

MESSALINA, *kneeling and applying her breast to the weapon*

Let the will of the gods be accomplished.

*But she does not move. Then, Narcissus, from behind, sets his knee
against Messalina's rump and his hand on her shoulder, and with an
abrupt thrust shoves her on to the blade, which sinks into her, and makes a
sheath—vagina, in Latin—of her for the last time.*

NARCISSUS

Bah! The prick is a little longer, that's all!

A scream. It is over.

XI

Apparition on the Threshold: Nero

*C*LAUDIUS, *drunk on Chios, Cecuba and Falernian, is waiting for Messalina in the triclinium. He has his crown of roses on backwards and, with a magnificent diatreta—a cup of carved crystal, with the ornamentation in relief preciously perforated and fitted with rubies—in front of him, he opens a flap of his tunic.*

CLAUDIUS

The one evening I feel energetic, they keep me waiting! Messalina! Messalina! My darling little Empress! Come and give me the t . . . t . . . tickles you know in the c . . . c . . . cuckoo! I won't go to bed without having honored Venus, I swear by the sacred ph . . . ph . . . phallus of Tiberius, which that swine Silius stole from me!

NARCISSUS, *coming in*

What! He isn't dead drunk!

CLAUDIUS

Narcissus, bring me Messalina!

NARCISSUS, *striking a great blow*

Messalina has been killed in the Gardens of Lucullus

CLAUDIUS

That's a pity—I would have been quite remarkable.

NARCISSUS

You will be, with another.

CLAUDIUS

No, she alone could lift my weakened c . . . c . . . courage.

CALLISTUS

We have what you need, and we guarantee success.

CLAUDIUS

We'll see! Brunette, blonde . . . ?

PALLAS

A flower of youth, blooming on the illustrious stem of Caesars.

NARCISSUS

Brunette, supple, elegant . . . but look, here she is . . . I told her to come, just in case.

Julia Agrippina, the daughter of Germanicus and, in consequence, Claudius' niece, the mother of Nero by a first marriage to Caius Domitius Ahenobarbus, grand-daughter of Octavia and the great Emperor Augustus, has approached the sovereign with a feigned emotion. She cajoles him ardently, embraces him, kisses him on the lips; then, kneeling down, she lifts the saffron tunic bordered in crimson.

CLAUDIUS

What are you doing?

AGRIPPINA

I know all the caresses, and don't want you to regret anything.

CLAUDIUS, *relaxing, and then panting*

That's as good as Messalina . . . ! Ah!

And while Claudius abandons himself, enraptured, a child lifts the curtain closing the trinclinium. Standing on the threshold, he watches the Emperor momentarily, and his mother, in the process of winning him the Empire.
It is Nero.

Tristitiis mutatis, as Tacitus said: one only exchanges sadnesses: the sequence of the Latin Orgy in the history of the Caesars of the decadence, Nero, Otho, Vitellius, etc., Augustas and Augustules.

APPENDIX

Lust In Life, Letters
And The Arts

IN spite of the twenty centuries that separate us from the epoch that it retraces, this book is current; it will be tomorrow still, and forever, for humans do not change much in spite of the diverse appearances of times and mores, because our virtues, vices, agitations and grimaces resemble the virtues, vices, agitations and grimaces of vanished ancestors. Thus, in thousands of years to come, those who are alive will be neither better nor worse, only slightly differentiated by progress and the inventions of science, with souls neither more elevated nor uglier.

To convince oneself of the accuracy of this affirmation it is sufficient to cast a glance at the life of Europe this year. Does not the drama that is reddening the walls of the Konak in Belgrade recall the tragedies caused by the passage of the imperial crown from one head to another in Rome?[1] Is not Colonel Maschin, with a band of Serbian officers, in 1903, slaughtering King Alexander and Queen Draga, a woman and a degenerate, the tribune Chereas killing Caligula in 41, in a corridor in his Palatine palace? Rightly or wrongly, Queen Draga was nicknamed Messalina. The masks of Claudius, the omnipotent Caesar, and Alexander of Serbia, in death and in history, have the same faint, slightly idiotic smiles, dominated by sensuality. From the triclinium of Claudius, the

---

1 On 10 June 1903 the King and Queen of Serbia were assassinated in Belgrade at the behest of army officers, including Colonel Maschin, the brother of Queen Draga's first husband.

Roman Emperor, and the banal bed of a petty king, Messalina and Draga similarly governed. Precise facts complete the illusion of that analogy. The officers who took part in the nocturnal butchery in Belgrade, a Serbian newspaper asserts, received three hundred thousand francs, which they shared, as the wages of assassins. In the same way, the murderers of Caligula received from Claudius, his successor, fifteen thousand sesterces—about three thousand seven hundred and fifty francs per head. The identical procedure is found, with its special shame, cruelties and treasons.

But it is not only the faces of sovereigns and their wives that are resuscitated, there is also the grave and clear faces of pontiffs. When this novel, *The Latin Orgy*, commences, Peter the Fisherman had been in Rome for six years, 42 being the date that marks the installation of apostolic authority in the capital of the pagan world, become the Holy City. Two hundred and sixty-some popes have succeeded, through events and cataclysms, and now, from the latest conclave, a child of the people emerges, his forehead magnified by a tiara: Sarto, son and brother of poor folk of Venetia.[1] A humble individual, who seems to merit his quasi-divine destiny, Pius X, a Pope in accordance with the spirit of the earliest times of the Church, renewing the Christian tradition too often interrupted, ascended the Roman throne for his solemn coronation on 9 August 1903, simultaneously heir to the emperor Caesar and the fisherman Peter, the humble individual with whom a long and glorious series of pontiffs commenced. In a time of priests, bishops and cardinals—self-seekers, for the most part, as the reportage of the conclave has proven by picturesque anecdotes—there was yesterday, in a momentary return to the point of departure, as in the beginning, a triumph of simplicity, faith and bounty.

Another current aspect of this book: the courage and the scorn for death that is found, with the same intensity, among the gladiators of the first centuries of our era and the bold jousters of the twentieth. In May 1903, men clad in animal skins, on

---

1 Giuseppe Sarto, Pope Pius X, was one of the ten children of a village postman.

monsters of quivering iron and steel, launched themselves forth of the road from Paris to Madrid for a frantic and terrible race. So forceful was the energy saturating the drivers in that contest for the victory of the emblem of one automobile manufacturer or another, so ferocious the primitive and brutal instincts awakened in them, that the words spoken during the obligatory halts at various checkpoints along a road strewn in places with the dead and the wounded, evoked in their tranquil cruelty, noted by sporting journalists, the dialogues of gladiators in the wings of the two Roman circuses under Tiberius, Caligula, Claudius, Neo, Galba, Otho, Vitellius and, later, in the amphitheater of Vespasian inaugurated by Titus in 80, the Coliseum. But then, compared to another circus, the one that Nero loved, which stood between the Janicule and the Vatican, close to where the Basilica of St. Peter stands today, the Circus Maximus, the most considerable of all time in Rome, created under the kings, enlarged and furnished with stone steps by Caesar and embellished by successive emperors—the Circus Maximus the greatest, superlative circus, filling the valley between the Aventine and the Palatine with its powerful and primitive architecture, in which a hundred and fifty thousand spectators could revel in barbaric festivals, was certainly already, for the populace, the colossus, the Coliseum.

The Circus, for the Romans as for foreigners, was a place of incomparable delights: the Circus, with its yellow sand, and, here and there, pools of fuming human blood; the Circus where, in spite of the immense awning, the ardent fire of the sun ignited fevers; the Circus, with its variegated crowd in delirium; the Circus, the brothel of human stallions chosen by amorous and impatient female spectators; the Circus, where the nimble retiarius, plying his net with the supple graces of the mime and the acrobat fought the giant red-haired Gaul with a long drooping and quivering moustache and white skin, the small, lustrous brown, wiry and sturdy Greek, or so many other superb males of all lands. It is Amour and Death confounded in a reek of lust, dolor and pleasure, anguish and sensuality; on the pallid lips of women and incomparable emotion of desire and danger, which, during the spectacle, will drive them crazy with lust.

Expedited from all the provinces of the Roman Empire, the condemned, sometimes for trivial misdemeanors, provisioned the Circus, serving for the amusement of the sovereign people, who affirm themselves there, in their durance and their strength, becoming impassioned by the mortal duels of gladiators; the sovereign and criminal people who distract themselves further in the refined contemplation of the nudity of virgins and the palpitations of flesh beneath the teeth of wild beasts, of a pretty girl, in the crowd of victims, hiding her breasts or her flower with a chaste gesture, in terror. Rome, the former lair of bandits, nurslings of a she-wolf obliged to steal women from neighbors, at present cosmopolitan, enriched by eight hundred years of conquests, the spoils of all the known world, enjoys in the Circus unprecedented plastic forms, ferocious perversities, violent and original images; that public, which does not know pity, intoxicates its eyes and senses, watching torture as connoisseur and artist.

The colossal mass of the Circus Maximus, vanished today, dominates the actors and the events of this book; it covers them with its revenant shadow, its gigantic phantom. It is itself the principal character, alongside which the others seem diminished. But that monstrous arena, the terminus of centuries of struggles and wars, is also, under the Emperor Claudius, a departure. A number of those condemned—for various, often minimal causes, in more than one case, it is necessary to repeat, other than their faith—were the first sectarians of a doctrine of gentleness and love. Humanity found, in those hecatombs, at least for the old world, liberation, the end of slavery; woman took the first steps therein of her elevation and emancipation. Thus was manifest, for humanity, in the blood spilled, a chimerical Supreme Being; to the immense pantheistic life, the respiration of nature in a population of gods, the Olympian feudalism that reigned over the earth, succeeded the moral unknown that many still designate by the name of God.

There were gods; then there was one God.

Rome, enraptured in victory and debauchery, was the capital of the pagan world, *Urbs*, the city *par excellence*. The long and frightful baptism of the Circus made it the capital of the Christian world; and the Latin genius, resuscitated since the Renaissance, agonized for a long time in the first centuries of the new faith, in the mystical and forbidding shadow of churches. Rome, the conqueror of the world, the exemplar of valor, the spirit of pursuit, strength and joy, preached henceforth the renunciation of worldly goods, to the profit of a clergy murderous of energy. There was, in the night of the Middle Ages, a destruction by priests, monks and lords—bandits with crenellated towers, ignorant and intoxicated by their faith—of pagan temples, palaces, manuscripts, marbles and masterpieces.

All that remains to us today are wrecks forgotten in that rising darkness of barbarity and obscurantism. That frightful night lasted until the sixteenth century, when, finally, the great, bellicose but intelligent, erotic and refined Popes, Julius II and Leo X (Jean de Medici), followed closely by a great libertine king, François I, were the instigators of the Renaissance in letters and arts, in Italy and then in France. (Ariosto, Machiavelli, Bembo, Michelangelo, Raphael, Leonardo da Vinci, Benvenuto Cellini, Primaticcio, Marot, Ronsard, Delorme, Cousin, Jean Goujon, Rabelais, for the most part immoral, or at least amoral.) In accordance with what law are epochs of elegant lust—as, later, the eighteenth century, with its licentious geniuses, Voltaire, Diderot and Mirabeau—the precise historic moments of the most spectacular or the most formidable evolutions of ideas?

At a crossroads of history—when the civilization of the old world is shaken and a new Society is born of the human purple bathed by the sun—*The Latin Orgy*, as will be seen, is not only a dramatic novel unfurling its action through agonies and sensualities; it is also an educator, which depicts, in a sincere fresco, the life of a people, the color of an epoch, and, in order to personify it, reanimates an extraordinary woman, as much legend as woman: Messalina, the ardent and insatiable, the Empress Luxuria, wife of Claudius and mistress of the Roman people; Messalina, avid for the unknown, for frantic caprices, a seeker of sensations, by the grace of the lascivious goat, of unsated intercourse;

Messalina, worthy of incarnating an epoch, for Messalina is not only a woman but a crowd—that of our ancestors.

She is a crowd, yes, because she had, when alive, the entire Roman people at her feet, in a contemplation compounded of hatred and desire: the Roman people, with its consuls, its augurs, its tribunes, its patricians, its gladiators, its soldiers, its street-porters and its prostitutes; the Roman people whose blood flows in our veins. Yes, that crowd, noble visages and sinister silhouettes, agitated by virtues and vices that we have inherited. The horrible spectacles in the Circus Maximus and the Flavian amphitheater still exist in Spain, transformed and softened—as in the south of Frances, at Nimes, Arles and Béziers, in the ancient Roman arenas—with combats of man against the bulls of the Camargue and Andalusia. The lust of Imperial Rome, its ardors its heroisms, its strengths and its weaknesses before its decadence, the invasion and renewal by barbarians, is rediscovered in sensuality, tastes, revolutions or wars, energies and depressions—in sum, in the temperament—of the Latin nations.

Roman Law, for example, an immense heap of debris, a formidable mass of ruins, a necropolis of laws that calm evil instincts, brake passions, and ultimately protect the State, the city, the streets and the hearth, which has become since the National Assembly of 1789 and above all since Bonaparte, the modern Caesar, a construction-yard, has furnished almost all the materials of the present French Code, its essential stones. *Italia, Galliae magna parens*: Italy, mother and nurse of France.

Rome—on whose strong central administration ours is modeled—has impregnated our minds; we have the seeds of its thoughts, its liberties, its sentiments, its sensations, its bravery, its audacity, its sensuality, and its final corruption, which flow in our blood; and, at an interval of eighteen centuries, Caesar and Bonaparte, Augustus and Napoléon, the two great Latin heroes, have held for a fleeting moment of the duration of the earth, the scepter of the world, is a similar imperial apotheosis.

✳

This is in order to make it clear that in this book there is not only a study of Roman lust. Certain people resemble, undoubtedly, those pigs that are taken into oak-woods, in beautiful locations, in order to unearth truffles. The animals dig in the ground with their snouts, without seeing the beauty or what surrounds or overhangs them: the flowers, the movement of the branches, the incessant frisson of the leaves, the birds, the insects, the charming life of a forest, and above all, the immense blue sky radiant with sunlight. Those people, in this evocation of a past of glory, faith, amour, energy and also lust—for that is eternal, being life itself—will only see in this book, *The Latin Orgy*, an opportunity to prowl in the intimacy of the warm streets of Suburra, in its taverns of gladiators and whores, its brothels, and to caress, in dream, the naked Empress, perhaps still unsated in the mysterious afterlife.

The imbeciles or Tartuffes who threw ink at the group of Carpeaux's dancers at the Opéra were negators, unconscious, I would like to believe, of Life itself.[1] Sensuality is neither a vice nor a sin; it is the goal toward which all our aspiration, dreams and efforts converge, and it is therefrom, throughout the universe, that the perpetuation of species and races emerges.

Truly, since the most illustrious masters have represented naked men and women in every century, since, in the Louvre museum, to name but one, one admires images of Dionysus and Heracles with phalluses wrapped in fleeces, allowing their muscles to bulge harmoniously; the Discobole, in its marvelous equilibrium of grace and force, an entire gallery of bronzes and antique marvels as scantily clad; since all the painters and sculptors (Tintoretto, *Suzanne in the Bath*; Jan Massys, *David and Bathsheba*; Rembrandt, *Woman in the Bath*; Titian, nudes, giving the illusion

---

1 *La Danse*, by the sculptor Jean-Baptiste Carpeaux, including several nude figures, was commissioned to decorate the façade of the Opéra Garnier; controversially installed in July 1869, an unidentified vandal threw black ink over it in August. The sculpture was moved to the Louvre in 1964.

of verity; Correggio, Rubens—rivers of flesh, in Baudelaire's expression—Jordaëns, Michelangelo, *The Slave*; Jean Goujon, *Diana*; Jean de Boulogne, *Mercury*—and the smiling cortege of mischievous petty masters of the eighteenth century, Fragonard, Boucher, Lavreince, with the licentious engravings: *The Garter, The Two Cages, The Enema*; closer to us, Canova, Clodion, Ingres, Henner, Gérôme, Rodin and so many other whose listing would require several catalogues), since all Italian, French, Spanish, and Flemish artists had been constantly concerned with nudity, for which so many pagan or religious anecdotes are merely a pretext, with the nudity that remains the acme of plastic works; since even postcards make known to the entire world the prettiest women of the art and amour over every country, seized by the objective lens of the camera in suggestive poses accentuating their semi-clad, or sometimes simply naked forms; since albums are published in book form of reproductions of photographs of nude models; since, in annual salons of painting and sculpture, the public of young men and women, mature gentlemen, old soldiers and mothers, circulates around completely naked marbles and statues, chatting and flirting—why should nudity, permitted to other artists, seem to be forbidden by hypocrites to literature?

And since, speaking of literature, it can depict avarice, not to mention all the sins of the mind that great writers have been able to observe and characterize in their masterpieces; since, in the tragedies of the Greek masters, Aeschylus, Sophocles and Euripides, al the horrors of human passions, incests, poisonings and murders are mingled continually; since religions, moralists, arts and literatures, lyric and epic poets. Military and civic eloquence in abundance have not ceased, since Cain and Abel to glorify war, which is to say, mass murder, carnage and large-scale theft, pillage with random rape—Death, in sum—why forbid the celebration of Amour, beyond its preludes, even its apogee and its natural goal, sexual intercourse? Why always draw over two conjoined individuals, like a banal curtain, several lines of dots? War, whose official praise-singers are esteemed and recompensed with honor in all lands, is Death; and lust, I repeat, is Life.

"One night in Paris will replace all that," said Napoléon I on an evening of victory, on a battlefield covered with thousands of cadavers. Then why is the study of lust, more useful than war, nobler than avarice, less criminal than the thefts, poisonings and murders that are the adventures of so many dramas and books, and clutter the histories of all peoples; why should a study, among other endeavors, of lust be forbidden to the modern novelist—artistic, of course? He is certainly not occupied in writing books for little girls; he ought to write for men who think and women who feel, for adults who have loved, who do love and will love, for liberated and emancipated eyes capable of reading anything, for minds matured and fecundated by joyous or sad contact with universal life.

Every hero of a novel or drama being, in principle, an exceptional being, Messalina, certainly, ought to be chosen to incarnate Lust: Messalina, as insatiable for stupor as for poetry, furious, lubricious, curious about everything and everyone, never sated any more by eroticism than the ideal. In her, the Empress Luxuria, all of Latin sensuality—before and after Messalina—is summarized and magnified.

It is necessary not to celebrate or denigrate in her—and the intelligent, lustful sensuality that causes money to circulate in society like the blood in our bodies, perhaps as admirable, if not more so, than solitary and sterile chastity—only the apogee, the flowering in an extraordinary and immortal orchid, a blossoming of pagan debauchery.

No.

This book, steeped in verity, goes back to the sources of the Catholic, Apostolic and Roman religion, to show among the slaves, the poor and the simple, the infiltration into minds and hearts of the ideas of a sect that has become one of the most powerful religions on Earth. Unfortunately, that sect had installed hypocrisy in the world, whereas, before Jesus, all religions and all civilizations, Latin, Greek and Oriental, had glorified the phallus, the priapic member, the lingam, procreation and fecundity—in sum, the act of life.

Christianity hid, like a shame, the organs of generation, disdained concern with the body for the sole exaltation of the soul, to such an extent that in the Middle Ages and later, under the triumphant establishment of Catholic domination, hygiene was scorned. For centuries, people were dirty, kings and queens, burgers, serfs and manual laborers. Even today, in small provincial towns, there are no bath-houses, and if there is one, it is not much used. Last winter, in a prefecture in Brittany, a traveler went to the only establishment of that kind, and was asked: "Would you like to wait until tomorrow? Two baths have been ordered for an engaged couple who are marrying the day after, and you can take advantage of their hot water?" In the majority of rural areas, to consent to take a bath it is necessary to be ill and to have a doctor's prescription. The secret ablutions of women are considered a depravity, and those women who devote themselves to the cult of water are more easily accused of loose morals, and, for a glimpse of a bidet, calumniated by the gossip of the region. All of that comes from the indecency of being naked, although, in antiquity, young women wrestled unclad on the Agora, without thinking about the gazes that might scan their voluptuous forms or pause on the brown nipples of their breasts.

Under the Roman Emperors, the beaches of Ostia, Baia and Neapolis were famous, attracting the Caesars, the patricians and the rich. Since the death of paganism, however, the sea-baths have been abandoned, like those of fresh water. The innumerable hot springs of the ancients have disappeared. Catholicism has glorified the dirtiness of Saint Hilarion, in the fourth century. Saint Anthony resisted temptation wallowing in filth with his pig. Saint Mary the Egyptian, who was a courtesan, once converted and retired to the desert, neglected all carnal cares in the sole anxiety for her eternal salvation. Simon Stylites perched and prayed in his excrement. Let us distance ourselves from those odors of sanctity. (Have you noticed that scatological jokes are familiar to monks, priests and devotees?) And again, in 1859, Catholicism beatified Saint Labre, who lived and died in dirt, out of disdain for his carnal rags. The essential thing, for that doctrine, it to save one's soul; the rest is of scant importance. A bizarre coincidence: it was a Neapolitan princess, having the Latin blood and tastes of her ancestors within her—married to the Duc de Berry, in 1816—who began and made fashionable in France the exodus toward the beaches.[1] She adored holidays by the seaside, and thus the nobility returned, by imitation, to the pagan habit, timid as yet, of sea-bathing.

Christian wives, in 1903, certainly think it only good for common prostitutes to be constrained to frequent intimate washing, and to dip their breasts in water to make them firmer, judging that those practices summon Satan and are indecent. Considering that their bodies ought not to be seen, in their entirety, by any man, not even their husband, Catholic wives, having not abandoned all shame, have long had special chemises with a small slit for the connections of conjugal duty. Imagine what cloacas the impure sexual organs must be.

I knew in my childhood a worthy individual, an aged old-style magistrate, President Pécou, very pious and a churchwarden, who always, before unbuttoning himself to "make water," took care to pick up a piece of paper, in order not to soil his hand by touching "the filthy member"—with good reason since he abstained from washing it. For myself, I remember at the age of twelve, on the morning of my first communion, in the dormitory of the seminary, unintentionally perceiving the prick of my comrade, Pépin des Grillons, and, not at all tranquil, fearing no longer being in a state of grace in order to receive the sacrament, hastened to confess my sin to the venerable director, Abbé Cougourdon, who smiled as he gave me absolution.

---

1 The reference is to Marie-Caroline de Bourbon-Sicilie, Duchesse de Berry (1798-1870); her husband, assassinated in 1820, was the son of the future King Charles X, and their son was regarded by Bourbonists as the legitimate king of France during and after the reign of Louis-Philippe.

And that is the fault of Catholicism.

Jesus is not responsible. The apostle of Galilee had for his body the cares that were and still are in the customs, and even the religious rituals, of Orientals. Having the great Aryan generosity for all beings, he did not scorn amorous women, several of whom, according to the gospels, followed him and assisted him with their wealth; one of them, Mary Magdalene, the sister of Martha, anointed Jesus with perfumes and, after the habitual ablutions, wiped his feet with her long blonde hair. Jesus, clean and neat throughout his body, is naked on the cross, for the adoration of his eternal amorous female followers. I no longer know which Church father claimed that he wasn't handsome, but one pretty woman remarked: "Then he wasn't God." The disciples of the Jewish master have, as is evident, deformed his doctrine, being the parasites that take possession of every fecund theory and envy generous life in order to obtain benefit from it, and often turn it to travesty.

It is necessary to react, to proclaim our corporeal rehabilitation, in an ardent pagan faith, to celebrate recklessly the splendor of the flesh, to rebel against the devout conception that forbids and troubles with an idea of sin the observation and the worship of human beauty.

Oh well, stopping here the development of a necessary idea to get back to Messalina, a type-specimen of the Latin genius in her era, *and since*: look, in spite of the contestable purification of Christianity, look, on the same Latin peninsula, at the long new blossoming of art, crime, magnificence and pleasure: the Medicis in Florence; the Borgias—remove the initial, the capital flourish, and what remains is *orgia*—with an incestuous Pope, Alexander VI, who died poisoned in 1503; his son Cesare Borgia, a cardinal immortalized by his crimes and by Raphael; Lucrezia Borgia, the Pope's daughter and lover, also immortalized by her beauty, her dissolution, and by Hugo.[1] Italy remains the land of amour, the land of adventures, with artistic and priapic pontiffs, gallant lords, and the great ladies of petty courts, kingdoms and duchies, of Ferrara, Tuscany, Naples, Sicily, with the lustful and luxurious merchants of the Republic of Venice. All have caused to flourish, in other forms, the same sensuality and debauchery.

Messalina was not, therefore, a creature unique in lust; she incarnates, as is evident, an entire race. And recently, during after-dinner chat in Rome, an erudite and venerated cardinal replied, smiling, to an illustrious cantatrice who had asked him a question, leaning over in a circle of black suits, prelates and exquisite women toward his beautiful white head and red robe: "*Peccato di carne non è un peccato*"—a sin of the flesh is not a sin.

The prince of the Church, inheritor of the Roman purple, was not addressing a banal compliment to the French artiste, southern, brunette and beautiful, who appeared shortly afterwards, in one of the fêtes of the magical principality, at the Palace of Monaco, and at a costume ball at the home of a queen of the art in Paris, as Messalina; he was simply translating the intimate character of a race, and betraying in himself the Latin sensuality of three nations.

Money and Woman are the two great motives of the effort of men, and they frequently only want to have the former in order to conquer the latter. A pretty woman: that is fundamentally, the unique joy; her heart and her beauty are the forgetfulness and the recompense of bitter battles for lucre; she is the smile of life, in the temporary earthly abode where, passing through, all condemned to death, tomorrow's dust, we agitate frantically. A beautiful woman, a marvelous inspirer of art, is a masterpiece herself, as powerful as any masterpiece of poetry, sculpture or painting. It is sufficient to list a few names:

1 Victor Hugo's play *Lucrezia Borgia* (1833) was also the basis of an opera by Donizetti.

Helen, Greek princess, daughter if Jupiter metamorphosed into a swan and Leda, abducted at the age of twelve from the temple of Diana, where she dances, the subject of the Trojan War, so beautiful that the old Trojans, sitting on the ramparts, around which the battle had raged for ten years, on seeing her pass by, got up to salute her, forgiving in favor of her beauty all the harm she had caused;

Campaspe, illustrious courtesan, mistress of Alexander the Great and painted by Apelles, who became so infatuated with his model that the King, out of admiration for the Artist, renounced his love and permitted him to marry her;[1]

Phryne, courtesan, Praxiteles' model for his statue of Aphrodite, who, when accused of impiety, showed herself, at the end of Hyperides speech, completely naked to the heliastes, who acquitted her in order not to deprive Greek artists of that image of the goddess, so rich through her beauty that she offered to re-build Thebes at her own expense, only asking that an inscription should publish that the city destroyed by Alexander the Great had been rebuilt by Phryne;

Aspasia of Miletus, Athenian courtesan, friend of Socrates, Pericles and Alcibiades, who provoked the wars of Samos, Megara and the Peloponnese;

Cleopatra, Queen of Egypt, inconstant seductress of Caesar, others, and then the triumvir Antony and for whom, on the eve-ning of Actium, in the crimson light of the indifferent sun, on the blood-stained blue waves, Roman galleys clashed;

Messalina;

Theodora, daughter of a keeper of ferocious beasts for the circus games, actress, dancer, courtesan, Empress of the East;

Diane de Poitiers, Montespan, Ninon de Lenclos, Wanda de Boncza, slender, dark and pretty, whose morbid and troubling eyes still shine in the memory of those who knew her.[2]

---

1 Campaspe is an invention of Pliny the Elder, whose legend inevitably became as popular as many other mythological accounts of unusual sexual magnetism. The other anecdotes cited in the list are equally dubious.

2 The Polish-born actress Wanda de Boncza (1872-1902), a star of the Comédie Française, had recently died when Champsaur—who presumably knew her—

That is what imaginations engender of visions of nacreous flesh, of nudities beneath transparent veils; those voluptuous women remain prodigiously moving, even dead, since they have thousands of times, and will have, at college, the first desires and first saps of many twenty-year-old hearts.

In brief, on the world's stage, where mortals are like marionettes that make three little turns and then exit, where people agitate and jostle while waiting to leave, as late as possible, Woman is the portal of our existence, and its goal.

It is necessary to neglect lust, eunuchs and moralists affirm, because it is distinctly secondary in the world's concerns. In fact, if a mere streetwalker is murdered, all the newspapers, which keep quiet about a fine book, dedicate articles to her every day for weeks on end; and the disappearance of that trough, at which rich hogs gorged themselves on lust, makes more racket than the death of a great philosopher, a thinker, an artist or an inventor.

Men toil afar, over the seas, under the burning skies of the tropics, in order to amass the gold that will permit them to come to Paris, to reward themselves with the beautiful woman, celebrated by the newspapers, whose image troubles their sleep. And that beautiful woman, whose success and ostentation corrupt far more than a book, is honored and respected, her fortune made; she receives, in her salon, ministers, academicians or people who desire that status. However little she belongs to the theater—the theater whose stage is sometimes a more elevated sidewalk, the Japanese peddler's tray of the flower-houses of Yoshiwara—when she dies, leaving a million or two and several hundred thousand francs' worth of jewels, the Republican minister who refused to award a strip of red ribbon the day before, at the hospital, to a poverty-stricken poet on his deathbed will lead the funeral cortege of the official *theatreuse*. And in the evening he will go to the home of an old prostitute enriched beneath the entire Second Empire, appointed by him an Officer of Public Education, to dine in the company of men of the elite.

---

decided to include her in this list of mostly-more-celebrated beauties.

And that is only just, and has been much the same in all times, in Babylon, Alexandria, Athens, Corinth, Syracuse, Rome, London, Vienna, Paris and Berlin, which appear, in the past or in the present, as great simultaneous rendezvous of all human energies, letters, arts and sensualities.

Yes, the more brilliant is the civilization of an epoch, the more women rejoice on the evenings of battles, truces and armistices renewing—when they do not kill—energies.

So what? *Sat prata biberunt*, as Virgil says: the meadows have drunk enough; and it is time to beg pardon for the author's sins. Messalina is here.

Félicien Champsaur.
Paris, 19 October 1903